Nichole Severn writes explosive romantic suspense with strong heroines, heroes who dare challenge them and a hell of a lot of guns. She resides with her very supportive and patient husband, as well as her demon spawn, in Utah. When she's not writing, she's constantly injuring herself running, rock climbing, practising yoga and snowboarding. She loves hearing from readers through her website, nicholesevern.com, and on Facebook.

Juno Rushdan is a veteran US Air Force intelligence officer and an award-winning author. Her books are action-packed and fast-paced. Critics from *Kirkus Reviews* and *Library Journal* have called her work 'heart-pounding James Bond–ian adventure' that 'will captivate lovers of romantic thrillers.' For a free book, visit her website: junorushdan.com

Also by Nichole Severn

Red Rock Murders
Manhunt in the Narrows
Disappearance at Angel's Landing
Murder at Lava Point

New Mexico Guard Dogs
K-9 Detection
K-9 Shield
K-9 Guardians
K-9 Confidential
K-9 Justice

Also by Juno Rushdan

Ironside Protection Services
Big Sky Slayer
Big Sky Safe House
Big Sky Showdown

Cowboy State Lawmen: Duty and Honor
Wyoming Ranch Justice
Wyoming Undercover Escape
Wyoming Christmas Conspiracy
Wyoming Double Jeopardy
Corralled in Cutthroat Creek

Discover more at millsandboon.co.uk

A DROWNING IN EMERALD POOL

NICHOLE SEVERN

BIG SKY MANHUNT

JUNO RUSHDAN

MILLS & BOON

All rights reserved including the right of reproduction in whole or in part in any form. This edition is published by arrangement with Harlequin Enterprises ULC.

This is a work of fiction. Names, characters, places, locations and incidents are purely fictional and bear no relationship to any real life individuals, living or dead, or to any actual places, business establishments, locations, events or incidents. Any resemblance is entirely coincidental.

Without limiting the exclusive rights of any author, contributor or the publisher of this publication, any unauthorised use of this publication to train generative artificial intelligence (AI) technologies is expressly prohibited. HarperCollins also exercise their rights under Article 4(3) of the Digital Single Market Directive 2019/790 and expressly reserve this publication from the text and data mining exception.

® and ™ are trademarks owned and used by the trademark owner and/or its licensee. Trademarks marked with ® are registered with the United Kingdom Patent Office and/or the Office for Harmonisation in the Internal Market and in other countries.

First Published in Great Britain 2026
by Mills & Boon, an imprint of HarperCollins*Publishers* Ltd
1 London Bridge Street, London, SE1 9GF

www.harpercollins.co.uk

HarperCollins*Publishers*
Macken House, 39/40 Mayor Street Upper,
Dublin 1, D01 C9W8, Ireland

A Drowning in Emerald Pool © 2026 Natascha Jaffa
Big Sky Manhunt © 2026 Juno Rushdan

ISBN: 978-0-263-42028-9

0426

Printed and Bound in the UK using 100% Renewable Electricity at
CPI Group (UK) Ltd, Croydon, CR0 4YY

A DROWNING IN EMERALD POOL

NICHOLE SEVERN

To the readers who love grumpy heroes.

This one's for you.

Chapter One

Two pink lines.

Over ten days late.

Assistant medical examiner Drennan Hawes stared at the stick until those lines blurred into one. If she stared long enough, maybe she could convince herself it wasn't true. She wasn't pregnant. But then another round of nausea forced her to her knees, and she lost everything she'd eaten at breakfast.

Okay. She was pregnant.

Oh, hell. What was she going to tell her mother? Drennan pressed a hand to her forehead as she flushed the toilet and pressed her back against the wall. She could already hear the criticism clawing its way into her brain. All that education and she'd gone and gotten knocked up like an impulsive teenager.

She should've stayed in Ohio like her mother had wanted. None of this would've happened if she'd just listened for once. It didn't matter that taking this job with the medical examiner's office in Hurricane, Utah, had been the escape she'd needed or that staying in the same place that'd broken her over and over would've eventually turned her into a bitter, toxic thing like her mother. Athena Hawes knew best.

A sick sensation that had nothing to do with morning sickness flooded through her. Her skin turned clammy.

Worse. What would she tell the father? *How* would she tell him? They'd parted that night without exchanging names or contact information. For all she knew, he'd only been passing through, visiting the park on a weekend with friends. Though she guessed being in that bar could've made him a local. It certainly had been off the beaten path and not as popular as some of the other bars in town. Blood drained from her face and neck until it felt like it was pooling in her feet. She couldn't move, couldn't think. Their one night together wasn't supposed to be anything more than a bit of selfish fun. Now they were having a baby? After years of following the plan that'd been strategically put in place for her since kindergarten, she'd buckled under the endless pressure to succeed, achieve, do more. She'd quit her job at the hospital, stopped answering her friends' calls and messages and quietly disappeared from the life she'd spent decades building for herself.

A mental breakdown, her therapist had said. Utterly disappointing, her mother had said. Couldn't even stand to look at her. What good was a trauma physician who couldn't keep her patients alive?

And Drennan had realized it then. That no amount of overachieving or money would earn her mother's love. That possibility had died a long time ago. All she could do was run. Escape. Her search for a new job—a new life—had come in the form of an assistant medical examiner position in the middle of nowhere Utah. A job where she couldn't call the wrong shots, her patients were already dead and no one knew the dumpster fire that her life had become. Her mom's angry voicemails and demands laced with cutting threats had dwindled in the four months since she'd bought out her apartment lease, packed up her car with everything she owned apart from furniture and headed straight toward the sunset. But not entirely.

It'd been one of those voicemails—it'd taken weeks of practice to silence her mother's calls—that had driven her to the hole-in-the-wall bar in Springdale, the tiny tourist town right outside Zion National Park. That night with a handsome stranger who couldn't seem to take his eyes off her had helped in forgetting what a screwup she'd become. For once, she'd chosen herself rather than some out of reach level of approval.

Drennan's hand shook as she checked the test for the two hundredth time. She tapped her head back against the wall. "And here is your reward."

She was going to have a baby.

Her phone rang from the nightstand in her bedroom, and Drennan forced herself to her feet. Acid coated the inside of her mouth, but whoever was calling wouldn't notice, and she rounded into her small bedroom. She'd done a lot of work in making it feel homey without being able to paint. Lots of hanging green plants, dark bedding and macramé accents. She'd set up a reading chair where she spent most nights trying not to doom scroll, but being on call 24-7 kept her tied to her phone more than she wanted. Still, it was worth it, the peace she'd found here surrounded by red rock, rolling desertscapes and mountains that seemed to pierce the sky. The opposite of Ohio in every way. Drennan slid her thumb across the screen as the office's phone number scrolled. "Dr. Hawes."

"We've got a body." Iain Yarrow didn't bother with pleasantries. In fact, she was pretty sure the older medical examiner who'd hired her had a phobia of small talk, but it was one of the reasons she loved working for him. Straight to the point, direct without any manipulation or lies and always calm. Another opposite of Ohio. "National park rangers called it in about five minutes ago. A drowning from what they can tell."

There went her plan to cry over her stupidity in forgetting to stay on top of her birth control with all the changes she'd undergone in the past few months. She checked her smartwatch, one of those new ones she decided to splurge on with her massive severance from the hospital. Only to realize she probably should've saved that money. Because now she'd need to buy supplies—for a baby. A crib, for one thing.

Drennan scanned her bedroom. The one-bedroom apartment wasn't big enough. Where was she supposed to put it? No. She couldn't think about that right now. She had a job she very much wanted to keep. "Okay. I can be at the office in about ten minutes."

Though she couldn't really call the basement of Metland Mortuary an office. Desert far outweighed population in Southern Utah. With a hundred different small pockets of people peppered throughout the lower half of the state, there was no real need for each town to have its own medical examiner or coroner, an oversize hospital complete with a morgue or an entire building dedicated to the medical examiner's office. Their office in Hurricane—pronounced Hur-i-can, as she'd learned the hard way—served their local population, the tourist town of Springdale and Zion National Park with just one medical examiner and now an assistant. She and Dr. Yarrow were the only staff, acting as rulers of their too-small kingdom covering an exam room lined with cabinets, a single stainless steel exam table and a wall of narrow, horizontal refrigerators to house their patients. The funeral home director also had access considering it was his building, much to the detriment of Drennan being able to do her job in a timely manner most of the time.

"You won't be assisting me this time." Static or movement—she couldn't tell—filtered through Dr. Yarrow's end of the line. "I'm in the middle of a priority autopsy. I need you at the scene to take custody of the remains."

The scene? Nerves and another dose of nausea shot through her. "I've never visited a scene."

"There's not much to it. Mostly preliminary stuff." The medical examiner's voice echoed through the line. She could clearly picture him standing over their exam table with his tape recorder—old-school and inefficient—picking up every word of their current conversation. "Photograph the body and the surrounding scene, make sure no one has moved or touched anything, get information from whoever found the body and load it up to bring it back to the office. Ask the rangers on the scene for help."

Sounded easy enough, but Drennan's nerves wouldn't settle. Despite the months since becoming a Utahn, she had yet to set foot inside Zion National Park. There just hadn't been an opportunity. From the photos that'd come up on her search for a new life, the park was nothing short of heaven, with a river cutting straight through, mile-high red rock views and winding scenic drives through acres of wilderness. She'd always planned to visit. Guess today was as good a time as any. "All right. I'll call you if there are any issues."

Grabbing her gear at the door, Drennan jogged down the stairs from her second-story apartment and collapsed behind the wheel of her SUV. She hit the park's toll entrance within thirty minutes after switching her SUV for the ME van, lining up behind a rush of visitor vehicles, and her stomach flipped. "You cannot throw up in the car."

She wasn't sure if she was talking to herself or the tiny bundle of cells dividing in her uterus at an alarming rate.

The promise of fall nipped at her exposed skin as she hit the window power button and showed her credentials to the ranger behind the dark booth glass. "I'm responding to a call one of your rangers made to the ME's office."

The ranger directed her to park at the visitor's center, board the shuttle and make her way to the Grotto, the trailhead that would take her to the Emerald Pools trail where the body had been discovered. Hikers, families and selfie-obsessed visitors geared with backpacks, hats and sunscreen bumped and tossed her in the herd as they departed the shuttle. It took a few breaths of exhaust-tainted air for her to get her bearings. The Grotto acted as a nerve center for hikers to access several trails from one location, with Emerald Pools located across the asphalted one-lane road and over a man-made slat bridge. Impossibly tall trees added a bit of shade and brought her temperature down a couple degrees, but it wouldn't last long with the sun angling into the vast canyon that made up the park. It seemed she couldn't stop sweating as her body adjusted to the rush of pregnancy hormones, and she was little more than eight weeks along from her calculations. Things were about to get so much worse.

The trail entrance had been roped off. Clearly the rangers had enough sense to limit access to the scene where the body had been discovered. Another flash of her ME credentials got her through the barrier, and she started up the winding—sometimes too narrow—switchbacks leading to the lower, mid and upper pools, gear in hand. Her breath sawed in and out of her chest, her heart rate too high. Damn, she felt as though she'd run a marathon. Part of that was the pregnancy—yay for unending, bone-grinding exhaustion—and the other part was the altitude. Her body wasn't used to thriving on less oxygen yet.

After what felt like more than an hour—honestly, how

much farther did she have to climb?—Drennan reached the lower pool. Well, more of a dying stream. Beautiful, as expected, with moss-lined water cutting across the rocks before diving over the ledge into the green pool below. Evidence of a rockslide broke up the smooth lines of natural architecture, but she couldn't linger to study why. The middle pool, located farther up the trail, was much deeper, though smaller and less impressive than she'd expected. Dead branches and mud caked the edges draining down the mountain.

It was the upper pool, which required every ounce of energy and some ankle-rolling, winding maneuvers to reach, that took her breath away. A sheer cliff protected the sprawling emerald-color water in layers of jagged red rock, black stains and a flowing waterfall that sprayed against her face with every gust of wind. Drennan stood stunned at the beauty, forgetting entirely why she'd had to haul herself up this mountain in the first place.

"I take it you're here for the body." The deep, very male voice resonated through her a split second before familiar glacial-blue eyes registered. Instant recognition flared across the ranger's bearded, handsome face as she turned to face him. His entire body stiffened as though he expected a fight. "You."

Drennan took in his uniform, complete with the National Park Ranger badge sewed across his broad chest—none of which he'd been wearing the night they'd met eight weeks ago—and her throat went dry. He was exactly as she'd remembered. Towering, muscular but honed in a lethal way rather than bulky with guarded dark eyes. Her nerves got the best of her this time. "I'm pregnant."

Chapter Two

He couldn't have heard her right.

National Park Ranger Harvey Knight forced himself a step back as though he could rewind time. He'd spent his morning pulling a body from the upper pool, but those two little words threatened to unleash a mountain of emotion he'd locked away for good reason. None of this made sense. What was she even doing here? Uneven ground around the natural pond caught at the edge of his heel, throwing off his balance. But it was his head he couldn't get straight. "I'm sorry. What are you even doing here? How did you get through the rangers at the trail entrance?"

Distinct lines deepened between perfectly shaped brows that matched the dark blond of her hair. Hell, she was just as beautiful as he remembered, with those wide green eyes framed by the darkest lashes he'd ever seen. Even dressed in a plain sweatshirt and jeans with tennis shoes she somehow wiped his memory of any other woman he'd been with. He could still feel the press of her mouth against his from that night two months ago, remember what it felt like to have her in his hands. The sounds she'd made beneath his sheets as they worked to forget reality. For one night, he'd been able to ignore the rage that'd driven him to that bar in the first place. Because of her. They'd parted without so much as exchanging first names, and Harvey had resigned himself to never feeling that kind of intensity with another human being again. There hadn't been use for words, empty promises or plans. That night had simply become two people who'd found each other in a moment of need. A once in a lifetime encounter he hadn't been able to stop thinking about since he'd walked her to her car and watched her drive away.

She grabbed for the lanyard around her neck, showcasing a washed-out photo of herself, though he couldn't focus enough to catch any of the information stamped into the reflective surface. "I got a call about a body. I'm here from the medical examiner's office."

"*You're* the medical examiner." His shock put a disbelieving twist on his tone he hadn't meant to sound as offensive as it did. Damn it. He had to get ahold of himself, but, if he was being honest, this woman was the last person he expected to show up at this scene.

"Assistant medical examiner." A hardness that didn't belong overtook her expression as she transferred a duffel bag—presumably full of gear—from one hand to the other. At nearly a whole head shorter than his six-three, she leveled him with a look that could strip paint. "Drennan Hawes. Did you hear what I said a minute ago?"

I'm pregnant. The news rushed back and nearly plowed him over. Gravity intensified until he was sure he'd become nothing more than a pile of blood and tissue if it went on long enough. Scraping a hand down his face, Harvey swiped at the thin layer of water coming off the falls to his left. "How?"

"What?" She cut that brilliant gaze matching the color of the pool to him.

"How are you pregnant?" This wasn't happening. They'd

had the discussion beforehand. They both tested clean during their last physicals and took precautions. He hadn't gone to that bar with the intention of sharing his bed that night, but he wasn't reckless, either. They'd been careful. "You told me you were on birth control."

Drennan—her name was Drennan, because of course everything he'd learned about her fit just as perfectly—lowered her voice, as though suddenly aware they weren't the only officials on a death scene. "I was. I *am*."

"Knight, we've got to get a move on." The head ranger of law enforcement division, a man who resembled a WWE wrestler more than an outdoorsman, wound one finger in a circle to hurry him up. Ranger Murray Simpson wasn't big on patience.

"This isn't the time." Slipping his hand between her rib cage and elbow, he gripped her arm, dragging her away from prying ears. And, damn it all to hell, that was a mistake. Hints of her perfume—the same scent that'd clung to his pillows and sheets in the days after their encounter—caught at the back of his throat. It'd faded after a while, but his body had somehow become accustomed to the light citrus scent. He hadn't been able to sleep for weeks, going as far as to try to hunt down that particular perfume just so he could get some damn sleep. Only now he realized it was all her. Natural and unobtainable. "I have a body on one of our most popular trails, and the superintendent is breathing down our necks to get Emerald Pools reopened as soon as possible. We'll talk about this later."

He added the much-needed distance between them, careful not to throw off her balance as he released his hold, and headed for the small grouping of rangers hovering over the body he'd found face down in the pond a little more than two hours ago.

"Are you the ranger who called it in?" Drennan's voice cut through the buzz of panic, more distant than a moment ago, as she raced to catch up to him.

He'd offended her. Hell. His fantasies of coming into contact with her again had gone out the window the second she'd opened her mouth. Harvey slowed his escape but fought the urge to take her gear to ease her effort. Pregnant. Son of a bitch. He didn't know how to act around a pregnant woman. He'd been an only child of miserable parents and practically raised himself. No cousins or nieces or nephews to help with. Kids, having a family, a wife, had never been in the stars after the way he'd witnessed his mother take insult after insult. Not to mention the bruises that'd followed. His path had led him straight into the military. As far from home as possible. "Guess neither of us were interested in exchanging names. Harvey Knight."

Harvey shut down the urge to extend his hand. Considering how they'd spent their first meeting, they were well past formal introductions. "I found the body a little after seven this morning on my patrol route. The park is open 24-7, so it's hard to tell how long she's been up here. My guess is between sunset last night and early this morning. The last shuttle coming down from Temple of Sinawava heads back to the visitor's center at 7:15 p.m. Most hikers make sure they're back at the trailhead before then."

He pulled to a stop outside the duo of rangers guarding and studying the remains as if they knew a damn thing about what to do. They parted at his approach, revealing the woman he'd pulled from the pool. Positioned on her back, the drowning victim stared back with nothing but emptiness in her expression. "She was face down when I found her. Fully clothed and geared up."

Drennan—he wanted to roll her name over in his mind

a thousand times—dropped her gear then crouched beside it. Pulling what looked like a dark blue windbreaker from inside, she threaded her legs into a full-length bodysuit. Bright yellow letters announced her as a representative of the ME's office as she zipped up the front of the bodysuit and snapped into a pair of latex gloves. Next came a camera she wound around her neck with a thick strap meant to handle a good amount of weight. She snapped an initial photo of the body then checked the viewfinder. "How deep is the water?"

A gust of wind whipped another layer of water at their small grouping and splattered it across the face of their victim.

"A few feet at its deepest." Harvey set his hands on his hips, not really sure where to go from here. The law enforcement rangers retained jurisdiction in cases like this, but Simpson had wanted him here to answer questions for the medical examiner. "We warn hikers not to go in because of the algae and moss that can make the rocks under the surface unstable, but sometimes they're more interested in getting the perfect selfie than paying attention to their safety."

A never-ending endeavor to keep people alive from their own ignorance.

If their victim had slipped, her phone or camera could be lost to the pool. It'd take time the superintendent wasn't really willing to give them to fish it out. The victim's skin had taken on a waxy pallor, pale and smooth, with some bloating compromising her once thin features. No bruises as far as he could tell, but Harvey knew better than most that some people were capable of violence that couldn't be seen to the human eye. He didn't even know what he was doing here. He was a regular trail ranger who worked his shifts five days a week and went home, and right now, this body was keeping him from doing just that. He was just the unlucky bastard who'd found the poor woman.

"Who all has touched the body?" Drennan shifted to a new angle and took another photo of the remains, once again checking the viewfinder as though she didn't trust herself with the results. Then again, what did he really know about her other than a single night of sex and a claim she was carrying his baby?

The muscles in his jaw ached under the pressure of his back teeth. She seemed to go out of her way not to look at him, to treat him like any other ranger, keeping her tone neutral and distant. She obviously wasn't happy with the way their conversation had gone, but what had she expected him to say at hearing the news they were having a kid? Harvey dug his fingertips into his sides as that familiar anger tried to bust through his control. "Nobody. Just me."

"How did you pull her from the water? Where did you touch her?" Toeing the thin line between the end of her tennis shoes and the victim's body, Drennan shoved her hands into the victim's jacket, coming up empty, then moved on to the next pocket.

"By her jacket." As much as he hated the third degree, she was doing her job. He had to remember that. "I wasn't really keen on touching her anywhere else."

Pulling the woman's backpack free of both arms, the assistant medical examiner who'd barged into his life not once but twice in the past two months handed off the bag to him. "Let's see if we can find an ID. My office can take care of next of kin notifications if you need."

"I'll take care of it." Harvey didn't know Ranger Simpson well, but from what he'd heard, the man took every case of his personally. It wasn't any surprise he'd volunteered to make the call. Simpson searched every section of the bag, setting out a water bottle, a handful of snacks and sunscreen. "No ID or phone. It's possible they're at the bottom of the pool."

"In most cases of drowning I've come across, we can get an ID from dental or DNA. Fingerprints will take a couple days of dehydrating the skin on her fingers, but I'll keep in touch with any updates our office has for you. I'll need help getting her to my van at the visitor's center." Letting her camera drop to her stomach by the strap around her neck, Drennan shoved herself to a standing position, then tipped to one side. Her hand shot out, meeting nothing but air.

Harvey rushed forward before she hit the ground. He caught her around the middle as both other rangers moved in for support. All too aware of how perfectly she fit against him. "Are you okay?"

"Fine. Thanks." Her exhale tickled along his jaw and reinvigorated his senses with that hint of perfume. Righting herself, Drennan shook her head. "Guess I'm just not used to the elevation out here yet."

She pulled a folded black bag from her duffel bag of tricks. Throwing out one end, she laid it parallel to the body, zipper side up. "I have what I need from the remains for now. I'll get her back to Hurricane to assist Dr. Yarrow with the autopsy in the next couple of days and send any findings to your law enforcement division."

"Don't you need to clear that with her family first?" A restlessness flooded through him at the idea of her walking out of here after without another word. Some small part of him wasn't willing to leave them in this distant, emotionless, professional emptiness they'd found. Though Harvey knew that was exactly what he should do.

"Not when a death is considered suspicious. You see this thin layer of foam around the victim's mouth?" Drennan crouched beside the body, pointing to a collection of froth he'd assumed had come from buildup at the waterfall's base. "It's called hemorrhagic edema fluid. Mucus in the body mixes with the water in her lungs. She was alive when she went into that water. Considering the lack of blunt force trauma to her head, the depth of the water and the weight of her pack, she should've been able to stand on her own two feet to get out. But these bruises on the back of her neck?" She shifted the victim's hair out of the way, displaying a clear outline of a handprint spanning the waxy skin. "They tell me she was murdered."

Chapter Three

She couldn't stop her hands from shaking.

Drennan slammed the door to the van closed, sealing the young woman from the emerald pool inside. It'd taken all four of them to get her remains down the trail and a whole lot of maneuvering on the narrower edges of the switchbacks, but they'd done it in less than an hour. She'd had to record the temperature of the water the victim had been found in, weather conditions and the rangers' statements before leaving with the body. There was no way she'd be able to manage getting back up there a second time. The tiny life form growing in her uterus was already demanding a second breakfast and a nap and wanted her to throw up all at the same time.

Clutching the van's door handle, she tried to breathe through her nose. Crisp fall air helped with the permanent acid lodged in her throat but did little to ease the shock assaulting her every few thoughts. She could only imagine what her baby would think of all the embalming fluid and bodily fluids that made up her day when she got the body back to the office. Drennan swallowed a rush of nausea, slapping her hand against her mouth.

A baby. She was going to have a baby. There was no denying the symptoms anymore. No trying to blame the flu or some other kind of illness.

"You okay?" The deep rumble of his voice soothed her stomach.

She'd recounted that voice so many times in the past two months. Imagined how it would sound whispering all the words she craved to hear. Not just from that night, but if they'd ever come into contact again. Drennan forced herself to face him.

Harvey. The name fit him. Rough around the edges, kind of like him, with a shadowed side and a fierce expression. His thick beard worked to hide his expression, but the deep tan he'd gained on the trails and the lines between his brows told her he much preferred to be outside than be cornered and forced to make conversation. He'd swiped his styled hair back away from his face. Not a hint of gray despite her guess putting him closer to forty than thirty. Then again, what did she really know about him other than the feel of his body pressed against hers, how it felt to have his mouth at her neck, his heightened breathing etched into her memory. He was even more handsome than she remembered. A mountain of muscle stretched against his ranger uniform. One wrong move would split the seams, and a flush of heat washed over Drennan at the random thought she'd pay good money to see that.

He'd said something. Right? Oh, hell. He was staring at her with nothing but expectation and disappointment—a look she'd come to know all too well—as if she'd grown two heads. Wait. Did she technically have two heads right now? No. It took more than eight weeks for the baby's head to develop. "What?"

"You look like you're going to throw up." Harvey offered a metallic water bottle. The black exterior was dented and scratched up. Used. His. "It doesn't take long for dehydration to set in, even in these cooler temperatures. It's all about exertion."

It wasn't until that moment that she realized how thirsty she really was. She took the offering, slugging back three huge mouthfuls of ice water. Streams escaped from the corners of her mouth. She swiped at her face with the back of her hand as embarrassment charged. Her mother's voice instantly scolded her to clean herself up. To stop acting like a child who couldn't control herself. Drennan practically shoved the water bottle into Harvey's chest as embarrassment overheated into shame. "Thanks. Do you usually offer your personal water bottle to anyone who feels like they might die out here?"

"Only the ones who've been in my bed." One corner of his mouth turned up, though it would've been impossible to catch with the amount of facial hair if she hadn't been looking right at him.

"Right. Listen. I'm sorry about before. Ambushing you like that. I'm sure the last person you expected to see today was one of the women you took home from a bar two months ago." Oh, no. Why did that make her sound so needy? He'd probably taken a half dozen women home since the night they'd shared. He probably didn't even recognize her. She wasn't anything special. To anybody. The ground went unstable under her feet. Only this time she couldn't contribute it to the pregnancy. She just wanted nothing more than to get in her too-hot van and shut herself inside the office with no plans to ever leave. Drennan took a deep breath and spun for the van's driver's side door. "You know what? It's been a long day, and you said you wanted to talk about this later. Now that you know who I am, you can call the Metland Mortuary and ask for me when you're ready to talk."

Her hand was on the door handle. She was almost free of one of the most embarrassing moments of her life.

"The only woman." He didn't have to raise his voice for her to hear him over the traffic coming in and out of the visitor's center, as though her senses were intently tuned to him.

The breath rushed from her lungs as Drennan angled away from the van. He'd closed the distance between them, settling his hand against the driver's side window beside her head. Caging her. Not in intimidation or dominance but like he couldn't stand for a mere inch between them. "What?"

"You said one of the women I took home from the bar." His gaze locked with hers. Unwavering and confident. Just as strong as the night he'd caught her attention across a dark, crowded pub when she'd needed it most. "I don't make a habit of bringing women back to my place. You're the only one."

Okay. Why did that make her heart rate do a little dance in her chest? Drennan pressed her shoulders into the van for some added support, but it didn't do a damn bit of good. Because she'd learned real fast when this man infiltrated her personal space, physics no longer had a say. "Oh. Why?"

Instant regret hollowed through her. And then reflected in Harvey's expression. He added a couple of inches between them, removing his hand from beside her head. The cage was open, but she found herself missing it. Just as she'd missed it since backing out of his driveway two months ago without even knowing his name. She could've gone back. She remembered the exact location of his cookie-cutter house in the middle of a cookie-cutter neighborhood in Springdale, but that night... It'd been special. A once in a lifetime experience she didn't believe could be replicated or should be replaced with new memories. But if she hadn't sounded needy before, she certainly did now. "I mean, why me? Not that you couldn't or shouldn't take home whoever you want. From bars or the grocery store or work. You're handsome and attractive, and I bet you can get any woman you want if you put your mind to it."

Wide blue eyes narrowed on her, and the random thoughts in her head disappeared. "Take a breath, Drennan."

Her name on his lips shot something electric and addictive straight to her low belly, which she was sure was not his intention in the least. Her body seemed to obey his command all the same, and she drank in a full inhale, letting it out with an exaggerated sigh. What on earth had he seen in her that night he'd taken her home? She was a mess. And things were about to get much worse.

"Are you sure you're pregnant?" Harvey sounded so calm, her nerves automatically settled, which didn't make sense. This situation they were in was anything but calm. "You said you were on birth control."

The ego it'd taken to be one of the best emergency room physicians in the country wanted to take offense at that, but it was a valid question. She couldn't blame him for wanting confirmation. "The six tests I took seem convinced I am. Not to mention all the fun stuff coming out of my body."

"All right." He scanned her face from forehead to chin. Looking for the lie? Unfortunately for him, he wouldn't find one. "And you're positive the baby is mine?"

"You're the only..." She cleared her throat, focusing on the impossibly tall cliffs that seemed to blend right in with the clouds. Every second that body waited in the back of the van to be transported to Dr. Yarrow was another second the evidence could be compromised, but this... This felt more important. Like she was standing on the edge of one of those cliffs, and Harvey was the only one who could save her. She could fall alone, or he could pull her back.

She had no idea what to do with a baby. She'd only taken a semester of obstetrics, and most of her work with pregnant mothers in the ER was referred to the maternity ward. She understood the basics of pregnancy and childbirth, of course. But what would happen after she took her baby home from the hospital?

Real fear simmered under her skin. How was she supposed to work and care for the baby at the same time? Where was the baby supposed to sleep in her one-bedroom apartment? What all did a baby need to survive? Would she and Harvey share custody or would he expect her to move in with him after she delivered? Question after question with no end in sight.

Sweat that had nothing to do with the midday temperature slicked the back of her neck. She…she couldn't do this on her own. "There isn't anyone else it could be."

Harvey slid both hands into his uniform slacks and broke his gaze off from hers. A hardness that hadn't been there a moment ago edged into his jaw. "Then what is it you want from me? Money?"

Her lips parted with an answer, but she didn't have one. Was that what he thought of her? That she'd told him for a payout? A sinking feeling crushed the last bit of nausea, intensifying the heaviness in her limbs, and she felt as though she really was standing on the edge of that cliff. Reaching for him and meeting nothing but air. And a small part of her that'd hoped for a different reaction—the part she'd clung to since seeing those two pink lines—died.

Her job as an assistant medical examiner didn't pay much—no government job did—but she'd been smart with her salary in her former life. She didn't need to work for a few years, but starting fresh here had meant using her skills and ridiculously expensive education for something new.

Continuing to help people, providing answers and closure to the families she worked with. Drennan shook her head. "No. I just...thought you deserved to know. It's your baby, too. I think you should have a say in how he or she is raised."

Harvey scrubbed a hand down his face. "So you're keeping it?"

The thought of not seeing this pregnancy through hadn't even crossed her mind. From the moment she'd read that first pregnancy test—and the five after—she'd known her decision. There wasn't anything more important to Drennan than the family she'd had once upon a time—before everything had changed—and if there was even an ounce of the love she'd felt as a kid she could give to this child, she would do everything in her power to make it happen. A surge of defensiveness arced through her. "Yes."

"All right. I'll help. Clothes, college, braces, even your doctor appointments, I'll support him or her. If you want me to pay child support and have a lawyer draft up an agreement, I'll sign it, but I think I need to make something clear, Drennan. I'm not interested in being a father." Harvey stepped into her, close enough to touch, and lowered his voice before maneuvering around her to the front of the van and toward the visitor's center. "When it comes to raising this baby, you're on your own."

Chapter Four

He wanted to kick his own ass.

Harvey set sights on his SUV parked across the lot of the visitor's center and headed toward. His shift had ended nearly two hours ago, and he was working off less than a handful of hours of sleep. The estate lawyer just wouldn't give up. Calls, messages, voicemails, letters. He didn't want any of it.

He didn't want a damn thing from his father.

Every decision he'd made over the past twenty years had been in exact opposition to the son of a bitch who'd claimed to raise him, but even in death, his father was going out of his way to make Harvey's life hell. The military had given him an out, but twenty years hadn't provided nearly enough distance between them. Then the bastard had to go and die from a stroke and leave him everything. Life insurance policy, checking and savings accounts, the house… What had been going through his father's head when he'd signed his will and trust, Harvey didn't know. They hadn't talked in decades. Just how Harvey had liked it after everything that man had put him and his mom through. The abuse had killed her in the end. Not all at once, but a slow draining Harvey had never been able to put a stop to, and he wouldn't accept a penny or sign a single document admitting he was his father's son. No matter how many times the estate lawyer tried to convince him otherwise. Everything he'd done had been to ensure he never ended up like that man. Miserable. Angry. Strung out and blaming his problems on anyone but himself. Harvey wasn't going to be that person.

Except he'd just offered to financially support his and Drennan's kid. And while his biweekly National Park Service paycheck covered rent, food and transportation, it wouldn't stretch as far with a baby in the picture.

Hell. He could've handled her news better. Should've taken the time she'd offered for him to get his head straight. To explain. A baby. He was going to be a father whether he was involved or not, and the shot of terror he couldn't swallow since she'd given him the news doubled.

Harvey added more weight to his opposite leg, but there was nothing that would relieve that pain until he got off his feet, popped a few ibuprofen and iced his knee until his next shift tomorrow morning. Switching his water bottle from one hand to the other, he attempted to balance his weight, but it wouldn't do any good. Never did. The army had spit him out without an option to re-up thanks to the piece of shrapnel lodged under his kneecap, and he'd decided the best choice to prove them wrong was hiking up and down these cliffs all damn day. Seemed he had a knack for making stupid decisions.

Screeching tires peeled through the parking lot. He caught sight of the plain white van he'd helped load a body into skidding to a halt. The driver's side door shot open, and Harvey abandoned his escape.

Drennan scrambled from the driver's seat and doubled over, hands pressed against the van's panels as she heaved.

Harvey was already moving across the parking lot toward her, a knot of something he didn't recognize squeezing his chest. Pain flooded from his knee into his upper thigh as he picked up the pace, holding him back from an all-out sprint to get to her. "Drennan?"

She flung a hand out. "I'm fine. Just stay back. You don't... You don't want to see this."

Her hair fell over her shoulder as she heaved again. The water she'd gulped after their descent from Emerald Pools splashed across his boots. Harvey gathered her hair back out of the way and set his free hand along her spine. His stomach convulsed at the thought of her so miserable in this heat. "Believe me, I've seen worse."

Her shallow exhales caused her back to arch against his hand, and he started soothing circles into her skin. Nothing but a distraction she needed to breathe through the nausea. It helped sometimes. He'd seen enough soldiers lose their breakfasts, lunches and dinners from the crap they'd had to face overseas on the front lines in Afghanistan. Bodily fluids hardly scared him.

Drennan swiped at her mouth but didn't move to straighten. Waiting for the next wave? "You're right. Pulling a body from the pond this morning is worse. You win."

"I wasn't even thinking about that." He couldn't stop the laugh escaping his chest. Even in the face of one of the most uncomfortable situations, she managed to shift his mood. But hadn't that been why he'd approached her in that bar in the first place? She'd smiled at him from her single table with a beer in hand, and all that rage and betrayal he'd held on to since the funeral disappeared. Instant magic. It hadn't taken much to convince himself to chase that feeling straight into his bed, and hell, she'd done an amazing job in helping him pretend the world could stop turning.

"You've seen worse than a dead body?" Drennan shifted away from the fluid inching into the cracks of the broken asphalt.

"I was military. Infantry. You see a lot of stuff you never thought you'd be able to stomach on the front lines." But he didn't want to think about any of that. "Are you sick, or is this…"

"Morning sickness?" She faced him then, tugging her hair free of his hand, a little paler than when he'd told her he wouldn't help her raise this baby a few minutes ago. Despite the circumstances, she couldn't even bother to look anything short of beautiful with all those sharp features, an inner glow and a few shards of hazel in her green eyes. Otherworldly and powerful as she'd been the night they'd met. She closed her eyes, her shoulders rising on a deep inhale. "Sure. You could say that. Except it's almost lunchtime, and the body I have stashed in the back of the van is starting to smell of algae and decomposition in this heat."

His cringe filtered into his expression. He didn't know a whole lot about pregnancy short of what his mother had told him of his birth story and the cravings she experienced while she was pregnant. Everything else in that arena he'd picked up in health class or by experimenting with girlfriends. His dad certainly hadn't given him any of those talks other than threats if Harvey had ever got a girl knocked up. Funny how the old man's death had led to just that. "Anything help?"

"Not that I've found." Swiping at her face with her sleeve, Drennan motioned to him. "Thanks for the assistance. My hair appreciates you keeping it vomit free."

"Anytime." The word had slipped out naturally, and Harvey instantly regretted the offer. He'd made it clear he'd support their child financially. Getting involved any further opened him up to a world of mistakes he wasn't looking to repeat. Ever.

Silence cut between them as Drennan seemed to weigh

the slip. A good man who'd gotten a woman pregnant would want to know every symptom, every change she was going through to ensure her and the baby's health. He'd go out of his way to make things easier for her and go the extra mile to meet those midnight cravings. But Harvey wasn't a good man. He'd been corrupted the moment his dad's fist had first met his face, and he'd do whatever it took to protect Drennan and this baby from that future.

A horn blared from behind him. A car had rolled up a few feet short of the van, waiting for them to get out of the way.

Drennan practically jumped out of her skin, and reality rushed to meet them all over again. She hiked a thumb over her shoulder, stepping backward toward the driver's side door, and that sick feeling charged through him. "I better get going. Heat tends to speed up decomposition. Could alter the time of death readings and compromise any evidence."

He needed to let her go. To go home and ice his damn knee and recover enough for him to hike those trails all over again tomorrow. Except he was stepping into her all over again. "Give me your phone."

"What?" Those already wide eyes of hers grew impossibly brighter.

"Come on!" The car horn blasted a second time.

Harvey turned, holding up a single finger for them to wait. "Your phone."

Slipping the device free of her back pocket, she handed it off with shaky fingers. "I think they want my parking spot."

"I don't really give a damn what they want. You're more important than a parking spot." He made quick work of tapping the phones together. "Now you have my number. Message me when you get the bills from the doctor's office or if there's an emergency."

"Okay." She took her phone back—still shaking—and

made it one more step toward the driver's seat. "How about now?"

His instincts fired in warning. Harvey countered her retreat. "Drennan?"

"I don't feel so good." She reached for him. Just before her eyes rolled back. She swayed on her feet as she had at the edge of the upper emerald pool.

Harvey caught her a split second before she hit the side of the van. Pain flared up his leg from her added weight. He couldn't stop the strength from giving out. His knee slammed into the asphalt, and they fell together. "Drennan."

"I'm okay." Her voice had gone breathy, barely audible over the grumble of the waiting car's engine, but she'd yet to open her eyes. "Just dizzy. I think... I think I need to lie down."

A car door slammed. Movement registered in his peripheral vision. The driver waiting for the damn parking spot. "Hey, man. Is she okay?"

"Help me get her in the passenger seat." Harvey did his best to get to his feet, but his knee had reached its limit. It took everything he had to trust the driver with the woman in his arms. A ridiculous notion considering he and Drennan weren't anything more than acquaintances, but possessiveness strangled him all the same. Together, he and the driver maneuvered Drennan into the van, but the vice around his rib cage refused to release until he'd climbed behind the wheel and tore out of the visitor's center parking lot.

Screw the body in the back. Something was wrong. Pregnant women didn't just pass out for no reason. He might not want to be part of this baby's life, but he'd sure as hell step up when it came to its well-being. He owed Drennan that much.

Pulling in front of the small Springdale emergency clinic,

Harvey left the van running with air-conditioning to counter the heat collecting around the body in the back and rounded the hood to Drennan's side. His knee threatened to give out a second time, but he bit through the shredding discomfort, lifting her against his chest with an unfamiliar panic building behind his sternum. "Almost there."

The glass doors parted as he pushed himself to his limits. Two nurses caught sight of him and rushed to meet him halfway with a stretcher. Harvey laid her out, every sense he owned screaming to get her back in his arms. "She passed out about ten minutes ago after throwing up. She's pregnant, about eight weeks."

"We'll get her checked out as soon as we can." The nurse strapped a blood pressure cuff around Drennan's arm and pressed a stethoscope to her chest as the stretcher headed for the back rooms. Then cut her attention to Harvey. "Sir, you have to let go of her hand. Unless you're family, you're not permitted back here. Are you the father of the child?"

He hadn't realized he'd intertwined his hand with Drennan's and released his hold. Instant cold flooded through him at the loss of her warm skin pressed against his, but Harvey had survived this loss two months ago when he'd let her drive away. He'd do it again. For Drennan and the baby. "No. I'm not the father."

Chapter Five

Ugh. She hated that sound.

Drennan could feel the tug of the IV in the back of her hand. The slight cold burn of fluids eased through her veins before warming up in her forearm. Every sense she owned felt intensified, from the overly loud pulse of the heart rate monitor to her left and the shuffling and voices outside the curtain surrounding her bed to the air-conditioning blowing straight down on her.

A hospital. The unconscious haze cleared with deeper inhales. Familiar calls on the muted PA and scuffed tennis shoes hit that aching place inside of her that missed her former life. An ER—even on slow shifts—had never been boring.

The stained cream-colored curtain ripped to one side on metallic shower hooks, putting a thin dark-haired woman with a clipboard clutched to her chest swallowed by her white coat in Drennan's personal space. Rich brown eyes locked on her with a hardness that had no business on the doctor's face. "You don't call. You don't write. The first I hear about you taking that job with the ME is by your ass landing in my ER."

Drennan attempted to sit up, only to be humbled by the overwhelming sting in her hand from the IV line. Hospital.

Throwing up. Passing out. Her heart rate double-timing as panic took hold. "The baby—"

"Perfectly healthy. No issues that we could see." Dr. Cassidy Duffy navigated around to the side of Drennan's bed, checking her IV bag and the stats the machines picked up every few seconds. The woman exemplified the girl next door, with long brown hair, a soft smile that reached her eyes and an openness that calmed patients under her care into a coma. Her accent—straight from the streets of Boston—could do wonders in a crisis. "Seems you got a touch of dehydration, and by a touch, I mean you could've died out there. You're smarter than this, D. What the hell were you thinking?"

Okay. Scolding and that accent didn't go well together. In her former life, Drennan had been the one armed with criticism in her Ohio ER. Cassidy had been the one to follow. She sank deeper into the clumpy pillows that'd seen far more than she wanted to think about. Acid coated the inside of her mouth, and she reached for the glass of water positioned on the small bedside table. "I can't keep anything down, especially fluids."

"Ah." Lowering onto the rolling stool beside the bed, Cassidy lost the clipboard and leveraged both hands on her blue scrubs. Once one of Drennan's subordinates, she'd gotten out of Ohio to take the lead in her own ER, as small as it was. Cassidy had never explained the sudden move, but Drennan could probably relate more than most for the need to make drastic changes. "You see an ob-gyn yet?"

Drennan sipped at the water, not looking for a repeat performance of what'd happened in that parking lot. Definitely not her finest moment. "Just found out this morning. The constant throwing up was a good indicator. Well, that, and the missed periods. Got a recommendation?"

"Dr. Santori. She's on staff here at the clinic. I'll tell her to expect your call and you need an appointment, especially after what happened today. But for the next hour, we've got you hooked to electrolytes and fluids." Cassidy scanned her from head to toe then back, shaking her head. "So I take it the irritatingly handsome bulldozer demanding answers from my front desk staff is the father?"

Harvey? Fractures of memory filtered through the embarrassment doing its best to drown her in the middle of this mattress. Oh, hell. She'd never be able to face him after this. Passing out from simple dehydration? Her mother's voice was right there, incessant and needling. *What kind of doctor are you? Eight years of medical school didn't teach you you have to drink water to survive? How are you going to help other people when you can't even take care of yourself? Forget about—*

"Stop that." Cassidy's voice went from friendly to firm in a split second, and Drennan couldn't help but let appreciation chase back the darkness that'd started moving in. This was why Cassidy Duffy had made an excellent assistant emergency physician. Her ability to read people, to know exactly what her patient needed in the moment, had saved too many lives to count. "I know that look. She's not here, Drennan. You left her behind in Ohio for a reason."

Tears burned in her eyes. So stupid. She could blame the hormones, but she'd had this reaction every time she thought about the relationship she was supposed to have with her mother. How close they could've been. Only now it was worse. Because there were things she needed from her mother. Questions she needed answered from the one person who was supposed to be here for her during this time, who'd gone through all of this once before. Baby showers and registries, breastfeeding or formula advice, visits from

Ohio and hugs when it got to be too much—she wouldn't get any of it.

Not from her mother. And not from the father of her baby.

Her stomach convulsed, but there was nothing left to throw up.

It wasn't supposed to happen this way.

She hadn't given a whole lot of thought into Harvey's role in this pregnancy, but she hadn't expected him to not want to be involved at all. Sure, he'd offered financial support, but she'd already told him she didn't need his money. So, what? She had to do this completely alone? No discussion? She knew the research. Children raised in single-parent homes could thrive as well as dual-parent homes. It wasn't the structure of the family. It was the quality time and love that determined the success of a child.

But she'd wanted more for her child. She'd wanted him to be excited and to maybe give her a hug to calm the sheer panic that'd followed her around all day. But, apparently, she'd have to settle for him paying for this emergency room visit.

"Your mother doesn't get to live in your head for free." Cassidy's plain, long fingers swept Drennan's hair out of her face and twisted the ends into curls on the pillow. "Make her pay rent. Understand? You set the rules. You decide how much influence she and everybody else has in this new life you're starting."

Drennan didn't know what to say to that. As much as she appreciated Cassidy's attempt to bolster the boundaries she'd been working to construct since leaving home, some things just couldn't be fixed so easily. A chasm wasn't made in a single day. It eroded little by little—forgotten birthdays, criticism about her weight, spewed regret for having a daughter like her. Years of covert toxicity with sprinkles of genuine affection had trained her to be grateful for whatever affection she could get, and she just needed some of that warmth to help her through this. From anyone.

"Now tell me what's going on with you." Cassidy grabbed for the clipboard and ran an observing eye down the page. "You called me up for a recommendation letter for a job you're too qualified for, then you show up pregnant and unconscious in the middle of nowhere Utah three months later."

Drennan didn't have the energy to get into it, but Cassidy could quite possibly be the only friendly face she had in this new life. Dr. Yarrow hadn't batted an eye at her work history, and he was pleasant enough when things were going his way, but he was her boss. Nothing more. And Harvey… She didn't know where they stood. He'd gotten her to the emergency room in Springdale, but that had probably been more out of obligation to their child rather than genuine concern. The heaviness he carried in his expression hadn't been there the night they'd met. She didn't know anything about how it'd gotten there. Didn't know him other than he worked as a national park ranger and had once been in the military through his own admission, and while she couldn't even think about regretting this baby, she hadn't planned for this, either. They weren't friends. They were barely more than acquaintances, pulled in together on a case of drowning in the park. "It's a long story."

"All right. Another time then." The head of the ER leaned back on her stool before shoving to stand. Hints of soap and disinfectant tickled Drennan's nose as Cassidy leaned across the bed to detach the IV. "Well, you've had your required fluids and electrolytes. You know the drill. Little sips of water throughout the day. Eat calorie dense foods to get as much energy as possible. I can prescribe the anti-nausea meds if you think that will help with the vomiting, but Dr. Santori will want to follow up with you in the next day or two. That bulldozer out there going to take you home?"

"I'll call a rideshare." Oh, crap. Defeat drained the last of her reserves as she hovered on the edge of the bed. The van. She'd been on her way to the funeral home when her stomach had lost its ability to put up with the smell coming from the back cargo area. Drennan checked her smartwatch. Three hours. She'd been here for three hours. The heat would've severely altered the body's decomposition rate and any evidence that might've been left behind. She'd compromised a homicide investigation. "I have to go."

"Don't let me catch you in here again, D." Cassidy hugged her clipboard to her chest. "You take such good care of everyone else. I'll box your ears if you're not taking care of yourself."

"I don't know what that means, but I'll be careful." Her feet didn't feel like her own as she shuffled free of the curtain and headed for the front of the clinic. The bandage on the back of her hand itched like crazy, and she felt like a rhino was sitting on her bladder, but that was nothing compared to the shock of seeing Harvey pace back and forth across the waiting room. Her stomach dropped out, her throat going dry. A swell of heat had her grabbing for the nurses' station desk.

He'd waited for her.

That intense gaze that'd dragged her in like a strong pull of gravity that night at the bar settled on her. Harvey closed the distance between them. "You good?"

"I'm fine. To be fair, you warned me about dehydration out in the park. I guess with the death scene and the news, it slipped my mind more than usual." Was she fine, though? A strange twist of warmth knotted in her lower belly, and

Drennan tightened her hold on the cold surface of the desk to keep herself from leaning into him to get more of it. She sucked in a sharp breath to contain herself. She pointed to the front doors. "You didn't have to wait. I planned on calling a rideshare."

"I wasn't just going to leave you here to deal with everything alone. They wouldn't let me in, though, since I'm not a relative." His hand shifted as though he might reach for her. Right where their baby was growing, but he pulled back, thinking better of the contact. Clearing his throat, Harvey straightened impossibly taller. "The baby?"

She...didn't know how to do this. The hot and cold back-and-forth. One minute he wanted nothing more than to keep his distance in every regard but financially, the next he'd admitted to his concern for her. Or was it just societal pressure and customs to make sure the woman you knocked up after a one-night stand was physically okay? Drennan couldn't read him as well as she could that night, and she hated it. The constant need to be on guard for the next threat to her mental health, the fact he felt the need to protect himself from her in the first place. "No problems."

"Good." He grabbed for her hand, rough calluses and another dose of that comforting heat scraping into her palm. "Then I'm taking you home."

Chapter Six

What the hell was wrong with him?

Harvey maneuvered his SUV into the driveway as carefully as possible, all too aware of the woman passed out against the window in the passenger seat. She'd fallen asleep almost the minute she'd settled in the vehicle. Exhausted and still recovering from this morning. He'd offered to drive her home, considering Dr. Yarrow had made a special trip out to collect the van with the body still strapped into the back, but the second he'd left the clinic parking lot, he'd dreaded waking her to ask for her address and headed straight to his house.

Drennan had been through a lot in the past few hours. Not only passing out from dehydration but having to make the climb and descent down the Emerald Pools trail while pregnant. Most hikers struggled with the incline on a good day, and she'd tackled it like a pro. Well, a pro who'd shown up strictly to do her job and hadn't considered she'd need a few hours' worth of water and calories.

He shoved the vehicle into Park, unable to help himself from studying the soft lines of her face in sleep. His brain had conjured a whole catalog of false situations and imaginations when it came to this woman. Not a single one of them had help up against the real thing. Drennan Hawes wasn't like anything he'd fantasized about. He didn't know a single person who would've kept as calm in her situation as she had. Most of the women he'd dated over the years had gone to the extremes to get his attention, to demand his concern, and yet Drennan had been more than ready to get herself home after being released from the clinic. Then again, she was a medical professional. He didn't know much about what it took or the education it required to become a medical examiner, but she was obviously levelheaded under pressure.

Where he'd nearly driven the nurses at the clinic to call security to remove him over his worry for her, she'd managed to bring him out of that spiral the second she'd walked into the lobby on her own two feet. How was that possible?

He was former military. Two decades of training had forced him to think logically instead of overreacting to any threat, but when Drennan had collapsed in that parking lot, every ounce of logic had died. He couldn't explain the sudden protectiveness that'd reared its ugly head. Just as he couldn't explain why he'd brought her back to his house. He and Drennan weren't a couple. They were barely acquaintances. Hell, he'd only learned her name a handful of hours ago, thrown together on an investigation he never wanted part of in the first place. But the tension in his chest wouldn't relent.

Shoving free of the SUV, he rounded to the passenger side, keys in hand. He popped her door and reached across her middle for her seat belt. His forearm brushed her low belly, right where their child was growing. Harvey froze, air crushing from his lungs, gaze locked on the soft rise and fall of her shoulders. No. Not theirs. Hers. Her child. He had no claim on the baby, and he didn't want it. He compressed the release for her seat belt, then threaded his arms behind her shoulders and at the backs of her knees.

His knee barked louder than ever before. One of the nurses had recognized him from a previous visit, noting the exaggerated limp as he carved a deep back-and-forth gorge through the lobby while the physician was tending to Drennan. In minutes, she'd arranged a cortisone shot to ease the inflammation, but the effect wouldn't take hold for a couple more hours. He'd survived worse injuries in his years growing up in his childhood home, and after everything she'd been through today, he wasn't going to ask Drennan to give anything more before she was ready.

A moan escaped her throat as he shifted her against his chest, her eyes fluttering against the sun's western assault. Her mouth parted on an exhale and reminded him of the few short hours she'd been tangled around him the night they'd met. How he'd played that exact sound over and over in his head, how she'd trusted him of all the people she could've gone home with in that bar. How she'd given him a gift of reprieve he'd have to work the rest of his life to repay. Starting now.

"Shhh." Harvey intensified his hold on her, that dark hole of all the things he'd imagined going wrong with her and the pregnancy calming as her body heat filtered through his uniform. She was here. She was alive. She and the baby were healthy despite what'd happened in the park. He hauled her up the three stairs leading to the front door and tapped in the key code for the smart lock, then kicked the door open. "I've got you."

She turned her face into his chest, as though seeking him out as they crossed the threshold. "Harvey."

An electrified shock shot straight from his head to his toes at the sound of his name coming from her lips. He'd been more than happy to go along with their silent agreement to leave everything they were out of his bedroom that first night he'd brought her home, to just be in the moment. But now, regret from not hearing her say his name on repeat as she'd shattered beneath his touch struck hard.

Using his heel to close the door behind him, Harvey headed straight for the back bedroom, bypassing his sad living room, the too-small galley kitchen and bare walls. Still carrying her in his arms. Where she belonged.

The thought brought him up short of crossing that second threshold. He stared at the crisp black comforter and sheets begging for her scent as much as his senses craved that dose of her in the weeks after she'd gone. Her lithe weight barely registered as an internal battle waged, though his knee had a bit more to say. Part of him recognized how easy it would be to settle her back in his bed. To allow her to claim it all over again, even just for a few hours of rest. Drennan would be comfortable and be able to sleep off the physical lethargy of the pregnancy, as she deserved. But that other part of him, the one that refused to drag her and the baby into the pain and suffering he couldn't stop carrying had him retreating back into the living room.

The couch wasn't new, the navy fabric stretching in some places and stained in others. A hand-me-down that served its purpose as a place to ice his knee and catch the next hockey game on his days off, but for the first time, he wanted to drive straight to the furniture store and buy something worthy of the woman in his arms. Something new with deep cushions, lots of space to relax or take a nap on and without stains. Maybe in her favorite color.

This whole house had come furnished apart from his mattress to serve as a low-rent option for rangers assigned to work Zion National Park. The one-bedroom, one-bathroom layout provided privacy without the need for a roommate and an escape when his people skills had run dry, which was more often than he wanted to admit. His lease kept him from painting the beige walls with a color from this century or from tearing up the peeling linoleum in the kitchen and the shag-like carpet through the rest of the place, but he'd managed to add some personal touches here and there. Though the stark realization of how little his child would enjoy a place so empty and bland shocked him straight to the core.

Damn it. Not his. He hadn't brought Drennan back here to play house. He wasn't going to have weekends with his kid or first steps in this room. The baby wasn't going to have a decorated room of their own or birthday parties at the kitchen table. This was nothing more than him ensuring the woman he'd gotten pregnant didn't pass out while behind the wheel on her way home. As soon as she was out of here, he'd go back to his pathetic life, his job that got him out of his head and keeping his distance from her.

Easing Drennan across the longest side of the L-shaped sectional, he untangled her fist from his uniform shirt and arranged a pillow behind her head. Dark eyelashes fanned across the tops of her cheeks, and he couldn't help but hold on to her hand a little longer as he realized how at ease she'd become despite barely knowing him. She needed to be more careful. Harvey smoothed a couple strands of hair away from her face, a jolt of want squeezing the air from his chest.

For quiet moments like this as they wound down from their jobs at the end of the day, for home-cooked meals spent right on this couch in front of the TV together. Probably burned if he was in charge of dinner. For breaking in this couch, the dining table, the kitchen counter, the hallway wall with their lovemaking, and filling this empty house with Drennan's gasps. For mornings when he could feel the baby kicking before she woke up and late night runs to the grocery store to fulfill her weird cravings.

His body moved without much conscious thought on his part. In this moment, Harvey could see it so clearly. Wanted it more than he'd wanted anything else in his life. He took a seat at the edge of the couch, careful not to rouse her, but Drennan turned into him, once again seeking him out.

But none of those wants were real. And they wouldn't ever be real. He was too corrupted by the evil that'd raised him to have anything so pure and beautiful to himself. Hadn't his father always warned him of that? That no matter how hard Harvey tried, he would always end up hurting the people he loved. He couldn't outrun it. That vicious streak for cruelty ran in his blood. Had become part of him from a young age. The betrayal, the rage. The military had helped him shape it into something useful, but now that he was a civilian, Harvey could feel it building up under his skin. Just waiting for the perfect opportunity to lash out. He would always crave to release the inner burn of anger in the most violent way possible, but he could do better than the men in his family had. He could make the choice not to let it ever touch Drennan or his baby.

The demon that resided inside of him—inside his father—would only be put off for so long. Mere days seemed to be the longest his dad could go without coming home from work wound too tight and ready to spring. On those nights, Harvey had managed to find someplace to hide for the most part, but he'd been too weak to protect his mother from taking the brunt of his father's anger. The bills they couldn't meet, too few work hours, his lack of promotion, spending money Mom didn't have permission to spend—it all combined into a hell Harvey hadn't been able to escape until he was eighteen. And in that hell an angel had suffered.

His mother's smiles had shone less as weeks and months and years under her husband's fists passed. The circles beneath her eyes had gotten darker. She'd gotten thinner. The most beautiful and kind woman he'd known had wilted to almost nothing by the time Harvey had been ten years old. It was why he'd never spent more than one night with a woman over the years, why he'd kept to himself in junior high and high school and throughout college and isolated himself from friends. No close relationships, even in the military, and he hadn't wanted them.

Until Drennan.

Harvey dropped his hand away from her face, forcing himself to stand and back away from the temptation sprawled across his couch. The hollowness that'd made him one of the army's finest infantrymen seemed to hiss at the loss of her skin pressed against his, but emotional—physical—distance was for the best.

He'd let her get some sleep, make sure she was eating enough for the benefit of the baby, then take her back to her place.

Stick with the plan, see it through.

It was the only way to protect her.

Chapter Seven

Her stomach groaned loud enough to wake her.

This was not her house.

Oh, crap. Had she passed out again?

Drennan shoved her upper body up, her elbows sinking into a sectional that'd seen much better days. Flickers of memory tried taking hold as she studied the simple living room. The layout looked familiar. A stinging in the back of her hand reminded her of the IV. Then Cassidy. And Harvey. He'd offered to drive her home, and then... She'd fallen asleep.

Collapsing back onto the mountain of pillows behind her, she stared at the swirling design in the popcorn ceiling. Harvey had brought her home. He'd carried her inside, set her up on the couch and covered her with what she could only imagine as the softest blanket she'd ever touched. Why? Why not take her straight home? Why go through all this effort for someone you had no intention of sticking around for?

Because he didn't know where she lived.

Right. Embarrassment at the slightest thought he'd gone out of his way for her out of affection flared.

You're nothing more than an obligation. You know that, right? He doesn't want you. It's that baby that's got him sticking around. Though I can't imagine why. Kids are nothing but a burden. Just like you.

Her teeth ached as she snapped her jaw shut. Her mother always seemed to have perfect timing when it came to reminding Drennan of who she was. Not the one people missed or the one someone worked to keep around. A passing thought, maybe. The one who took on the responsibility to check in with friends and go out of her way to ensure they had the support they needed. Never the one who was checked on. The only reason Harvey had brought her here was because she'd fallen asleep on the drive, and he hadn't wanted to wake her up.

Bits and pieces of the house's layout filtered into her memory from the one and only night she'd been here before. The hallway to her left housed a laundry closet. The doors had nearly buckled as Harvey had hauled her into them, his mouth insistent and desperate at her throat. Across from that, a small bathroom with a single vanity sink, toilet and shower stall where he'd disappeared to clean up then returned with a warm washcloth to help her do the same. Then the bedroom at the end of the hall. Where she'd lost herself in a man who'd looked at her as though she was the only woman in the world for him. Where she'd felt wanted and sexy and free for the first time in her life. No expectations. No promises. No disappointments.

She'd known her first one-night stand would change her life. She just hadn't expected it to change so much. She hadn't gotten the chance to tour the rest of the house, but she imagined the kitchen waited on the other side of the arch separating the living room from the rest of the house. All so different in the daylight.

Her stomach growled again. Somehow louder than before. Sitting upright, Drennan took a deep breath against the hunger pains threatening to eat her from the inside out. She slid her hand across her low abdomen, where she imagined the baby was having the time of its life with the concert her body was performing. "This is your fault. You won't let me keep anything down."

She scrubbed both hands down her face. She'd only found out she was pregnant this morning, and she was already talking to the ball of cells like they'd known each other for years. She needed to get out of here. The front door was right there. She could just leave. She could pretend she hadn't come face-to-face with the father of her baby at a crime scene and focus on the job she was meant to do. Though, she wasn't sure where her purse had ended up. Or her phone and keys. Oh, and the van with the dead body in the back. For crying out loud.

She grabbed for the blanket draped over her. It was worn, softer than expected for being knitted or crocheted—she didn't know the difference—and obviously well loved for years. Little bubbles of yarn caught between her fingers, laid out in boxlike patterns while the rest of the design seemed to frame each one in braids. The yarn itself had frayed in certain areas, especially at the edges, but there was something comforting about the muted gray color. Soft and warm and heavy. The afghan was like a giant security blanket specifically purposed to put her at ease. She hadn't noticed it the night Harvey had brought her home, but it was obvious from the scent of his body wash—something bright and earthy—he used it often.

"It was my mother's." His voice did something no amount of romance novels had accomplished, squeezing her insides until she was sure she'd snap from the tension. Harvey took position under the squared arch between the living room and where she imagined the dining room and kitchen waited.

"Took her years to finish it, but once she did, she curled up with that thing with a book and tea in hand every day waiting for me to come home from school."

"It's beautiful." *Was his mother's. Did that mean she'd passed?* Her heart immediately jumped, wanting to find out as much as she could about the man who'd waited for her in the clinic lobby, but that little voice in the back of her head warned her off. Whatever this was between them, it wasn't more than responsibility. She had to remember that, but she didn't have to stick around to dig the knife deeper. Drennan couldn't help but give the blanket one more caress before she shoved to stand, straightening the imaginary wrinkles in her sweatshirt and jeans. Where were her shoes? "Well, thank you for allowing me to confiscate your couch, but I should get going. Dr. Yarrow has probably tried to get ahold of me a dozen times since this morning. I'm sure he's losing his mind wondering where that body is."

Oh, hell. The body. She could only imagine the damage done to the evidence in this heat. Hours of sped up decomposition could make or break this case, and she'd wasted nearly an entire day unconscious. Tears stung her eyes, but she wasn't going to let them get the best of her. At least not here where Harvey could hold it against her. She caught sight of her shoes and her purse near the door and made a point to focus on escape rather than the tendril of fear that grabbed hold at the thought of losing this job. It wouldn't be the end of the world with what she had in savings, but she genuinely needed this to work.

"I think he was more worried about you than the body." Harvey moved into the living room. And offered her a cup of pale-colored tea. Taking a sip from his own mug, he exuded calm when her entire nervous system threatened to throw her off the tracks. "I had some tea stashed in the cabinet from the last rangers who lived here. It's peppermint. I'm not sure if it's still good, but I read the caffeine in coffee increases the risks for miscarriage, leads to low birth weight and causes cognitive issues for the baby. And the peppermint is supposed to help with the nausea."

Her breath rushed out of her. Drennan wasn't sure if she was more caught off guard by the fact he'd spoken to Dr. Yarrow or that he'd read about the effects of caffeine on pregnancy. She took the mug, not entirely sure what to do next. Again, her stupid heart wanted to read more into his actions, but she shut that traitor up with a gulp of warm tea. The peppermint soothed the emptiness in her stomach, but she'd have to attempt to eat something soon to keep from passing out again. "You talked to my boss?"

Harvey stared at her over the top of his mug as he took another sip. He'd changed out of his uniform and into what she'd always thought of as lumberjack chic. The red-and-black-plaid button-down highlighted the thickness of his facial hair and intensified the blue in his eyes. His dark jeans carved out a very clear picture of how well he took care of himself as the muscles in his legs flexed with every shift in his weight while his boots held on to lines of crusted mud. Much like the night they'd met. He was a man who could lose himself in a national park, sit at ease in a crowded bar or hunt his own dinner. "Figured you'd need time to recover from what happened. Considering you've been passed out on my couch for the better part of three hours, I think it's safe to say I was right. I called him from the clinic. Told him to come pick up your van with the drowning victim in the back."

Holy hell. Her insides twisted in a way that had nothing to do with hurling her guts up. Drennan nearly choked on her next mouthful of tea. "Did you...did you tell him I'm pregnant?"

"No." Those dark, intense eyes held her prisoner as Harvey leaned against the archway guarding the rest of the house. "Wasn't sure if you were telling anyone."

She wasn't. At least, not until she'd wrapped her head around it first. Or maybe she was putting off telling anyone at all. Sooner or later, Dr. Yarrow would notice changes in her physical appearance. There wouldn't be any chance of hiding the pregnancy, but a piece of her wanted to keep the news to herself for a while. To have something that was solely hers, that no one could criticize her for. A ravenous flood of warmth assaulted her from head to toe that Harvey had made that same call she would've made on her behalf. "Thank you. For reaching out to him. You didn't have to do that."

She'd spent the better part of her life learning how to be alone despite having a living parent right there in front of her. But she wasn't alone anymore. And she wouldn't be for the rest of her life.

"Couldn't have you passing out on the way back to Hurricane and getting in an accident. Not sure your medical examiner could handle the influx in autopsies." His mouth twitched underneath all that beard. "I cooked up chicken and avocado quesadillas if you're hungry. From the sounds your stomach has been making, I'm guessing I'm not too far off the mark with that one, either."

Drennan waited for that all too familiar internal criticism laced with resentment, a lifetime of disappointment and failed dreams to cut through her. And waited. Her heart thudded hard in her throat. Seconds turned into a full minute, but the voice had gone quiet, and while the tension eased from her shoulders, confusion was making a comeback. "Why?"

His brows pinched together. "What do you mean?"

"A few hours ago, you made it clear you don't want anything to do with me or this baby other than paying child support." She fought against the urge to cross her arms over her chest, a surefire way to reveal the vulnerability she'd stopped letting people see a long time ago. "I mean why did you bring me back to your house? Why did you read up on caffeine and pregnancy, and why would you cook for me?"

Harvey didn't answer.

Maybe he didn't even know the answer, but Drennan had enough sense to recognize a one-sided effort when it was staring back at her. Yeah, it'd taken three decades to escape the one she'd left back in Ohio, but she was a much faster learner now. And a lot more self-aware of her part in letting people get away with disregarding her. She and Harvey were having a baby together, but the family she'd always wanted with the three kids and the house and the dog and the sickly-sweet passionate can't-keep-your-hands-off-each-other romance that should've come with it—those weren't realistic. Not for her, anyway.

"Why did you choose me that night?" It was the question that had rolled through her head every night when she stared up at her ceiling wishing for life to be different. For someone to want her as desperately as her dad had wanted her mom. And her heart hurt at the idea she'd never have it. Even with the father of her baby.

Harvey slid his hands into his pockets, every ounce the former soldier she imagined him to be. Brooding. Secretive. Heavy. "Because you were in as much pain as I was."

Chapter Eight

He could see it in her eyes.

The effort it took not to dart for the exit.

She didn't belong here in a crap-hole bar in the middle of nowhere. Harvey knew it. She knew it. The bartender throwing glances her way knew it. The sheer anxiety coming off her in waves pulsed every so often, a siren call he couldn't ignore. He was already two beers in, but he was clear-headed enough to take in everything about her, from the long fingers she curled around her own bottle to the slight bounce of her right leg on the stool. Long hair worked to escape the haphazard ponytail she'd attempted. Most likely in a rush. No hint of makeup, other than maybe around her eyes, or a whole lot of effort put into her outfit. Not meeting someone then. At least, not romantically.

He couldn't argue the jeans fit her like a glove, but the plain sweatshirt and tennis shoes did nothing to exaggerate her small frame. Like she'd gone out of her way to avoid garnering attention. Didn't help. He'd honed in on her the moment she'd stepped through the door. He hadn't noticed her in here before. So why in the world was a woman like her coming to a place like this?

Harvey wanted to find out. No. He needed to find out.

Her name, where she was from, where she'd gone to

school, if she was in town long—all of it. An invisible hook had snagged in his chest and refused to let up, itching and clawing and aggravating. Dragging his bottle across the soft, dented and scratched wood of the two-person table, Harvey navigated around a couple of regulars, barely dodging a collision with one of the waitresses who'd made it all too clear she got off around ten. He wasn't interested.

Heading straight for the bar, he clocked the patrons, their drinks, their moods and the exits. Couldn't stop himself. There were just some habits that refused to die after leaving the military. He hated that the training had been so ingrained it'd practically become part of him, eroding the man he'd been before he'd enlisted. Someone his mom might've been proud of. Couldn't say she'd be happy with him now, though. And maybe that was why he'd driven here straight after the funeral.

It wasn't often he felt the need to forget there was an entire world outside of these four alcohol and sweat-soaked walls, but he didn't want to remember today. Ever.

The woman's gaze—the greenest he'd ever seen—centered on him before he even had the chance to get close. As though she'd sensed him as much as he'd sensed her. Every move, every dart of her tongue across her bottom lip, every shaky inhale as she watched him approach. But more than anxiety resided in those eyes. Pain. A pain that called to his, matched his, maybe even outdid his. It blistered one second and healed over the next as though it'd never existed, but Harvey had more than enough experience to know it would never really die. Whatever had driven her to this bar wouldn't surface just once but a thousand times over. And some internal instinct told him she needed help outrunning it for the night. Anticipation widened her eyes, and he could've sworn she clutched her untouched beer a bit tighter.

Movement registered from his right and cut into his path. Broad shoulders blocked his view of her and pulled Harvey up short.

The man towered over her seat on the stool, leaning in. Hell, Harvey could smell the whiskey on him from three feet away. He'd been here a while, throwing them back with the two friends looking on from their table. College kids based on their baseball hats and hoodies, from over in St. George. "I've been watching you from over there. You all alone? You should join us."

Yep, that was the way to go. Intimidate the living crap out of her. Harvey couldn't stop the cringe from taking hold, and he tightened his hand on his beer much the same as she had a moment ago. He took up residence a couple stools down. Close enough to overhear, far enough away to pretend he wasn't interested in every word out of her mouth.

She swiveled in her chair, legs crossed, spine straight. Twisting the bottom of her bottle into the bar, she flicked her gaze to Harvey then to the man between them. Her shoulders deflated on a smooth exhale. "That depends. Are you the kind of guy that expects to me to laugh at your terrible jokes, pretend you're not thinking about getting in my pants the entire night and then let you send dirty pictures to your friends in the morning? Because I should warn you. I was raised to take care of my partner. Wash his clothes, clean the house, wear gloves, get rid of the body and act very sad at the funeral."

Harvey couldn't hold in the laugh caught in his throat but saved it with a cough. Or six. He tried taking another drink, catching the kid's attention from over one shoulder, and waved the bartender off.

"Forget you." The kid shoved off the bar, taking two wobbly steps backward, providing Harvey with another uninterrupted view of his current obsession. "You're like my mom's age, anyway."

She raised her beer in mock salute and took a drink. "I'm sure that sock by your bed will be happy to hear it."

The flash of despair was back, though she made sure to cut her attention back to the bar. But Harvey had seen it. He couldn't seem to look away. Holding his breath for the next moment that darkness reached out to him.

He turned to face her, never more patient in his life for her to look at him. And when she raised that green gaze to his, the confusion and rage circling in his head vanished. As though it'd never existed. He closed the distance between them, his beer forgotten on the bar. Not a single word spoken between them as he offered her his hand and nodded toward the door. It wasn't needed. Because whatever connection that'd drawn him in gripped her, too. Understanding on a cellular level he couldn't explain.

With a smile, she slid her hand into his.

"I DON'T KNOW what pain you're talking about." Drennan cast her gaze around his bland house, anywhere but on him.

It was that same sense of anxiety he picked up on in the bar. As though her skin crawled with a thousand shards of glass. He understood that feeling, the need to escape. He shouldn't have approached her that night and saved her from his proximity altogether, but once she'd so creatively turned down that college kid's offer, he'd been snared. "You're good at hiding it. I'll give you that. One moment it's there in your eyes, then gone the next. Like your brain is recalling whatever happened over and over to keep you safe, and you're trying to live your life separate from it."

Her mouth parted, and Harvey had the distinct feeling he'd hit a nerve. He'd surprised her. Good. It was only fair considering the news she'd given him in the middle of a crime scene this morning. "You never actually drank your beer that night. In the bar. You kept picking at the label like you hoped someone would come along and take it away and tell you to get out. You didn't actually want to be there. I don't think you were hoping anything would happen. You just had nowhere else to go."

"You were watching me." She leveled her chin parallel to the floor in a show of confidence, but he couldn't help but watch the hint of pink slip up her neck and into her face.

"Kind of hard not to with the way your leg was bouncing off that stool." When had he stepped close enough to catch that addictive scent of hers? His entire nervous system latched on to the barest hint and settled a split second later. "The entire building was threatening to come down if I didn't distract you."

"Is that what you were doing when you came over?" Her voice turned breathy, as though just now recognizing the mere inches between them. "Trying to distract me?"

He angled his head to one side, heart rate climbing every second he stood his ground. "I'll admit I wasn't expecting the death threat you delivered to that kid, but I can't say I wasn't a little curious if you had one saved up for me that night."

"I might have." The humor drained from her expression, and the darker shift was back in her eyes. "But judging by the two bottles you had on your sad little table in the back corner, you were there to pretend reality didn't exist for as long as possible as much as I was."

He…hadn't expected that. Cold doused him from the inside out, and Harvey added that much needed space between them. Threading his hands through his hair, he let a low-key laugh escape his chest. Hell, she'd hooked him all over again. Dragging him in little by little with that gravitational pull that had caught him in the bar. And look where it'd led them. "Everyone needs a break from reality once in a while."

"You said you felt I was in as much pain as you were." Her accusation didn't come with pity. Just a simple request to understand what had brought them to this moment. They'd gone all night without saying more than a few requisite words to each other, using one another to escape hard truths and shattered expectations, and while he didn't owe her anything—they didn't owe each other anything—he could give her this. He could give her some insight into the man she'd tied herself to for the next nineteen years.

"The day we met, I'd just come from my father's funeral." He hadn't told anyone but his supervisor, and that had only been to get the day to drive north and back once the service ended. He'd been the only one to show at the small local church that'd hosted, and hell, wasn't that saying everything about his and his dad's relationship. There'd been nothing between them for the past twenty years, but Harvey just couldn't seem to let go.

Her expression shifted into sympathy. "I'm sorry."

"Don't be." He shook his head, adding another step between them as though his mere proximity would corrupt her. "He wasn't anyone to lose sleep over. Certainly not a man who deserves your sympathies. He was an abusive bastard who ruined lives, and I'm glad he's not able to hurt anyone else."

Drennan nodded in understanding, that intense green gaze fully locked on him as it had been that night he'd brought her home. Not a single ounce of judgment or criticism aimed in his direction. "But you went to his funeral."

"I needed to see him in the ground. I needed to make sure he got what he deserved." He'd never said the words out loud before, and that all too familiar growl of anger resonated through his chest. Nearing out of control. "I enlisted the second I turned eighteen. It was my way out, but that meant leaving my mom behind. I think she understood. She wanted me to get out, but six months into my first tour, I got the news she died. Scans showed evidence of chronic traumatic encephalopathy."

"Permanent brain damage from too many concussions." Drennan latched on to his forearm, squeezing it to provide comfort. She was a medical professional. It was in her nature, but all it did was remind him of the times his mom had tried to reach his dad in those late-night fits of yelling matches. And ended up paying the price. "Harvey, I'm so sorry. I'm sure your dad's funeral was hard no matter what your relationship with him entailed, but what happened to your mom is not your fault."

He wanted to believe her. Wanted to take her words and use them to drown the guilt and grief and rage until it couldn't get hold of him again. If anyone could help him forget the mess in his head, it was her. That invisible hook that'd snared him the night they'd met pulled taught, urging him to see the good she saw in him. But the demon in his blood wouldn't let him.

"I don't blame myself for my mother's death, but you need to understand something, Drennan." He stared at her hand, every cell in his body on fire, and backed out of her reach. Her face fell, stabbing the ache in his chest deeper. "My grandfather was an abuser. My father was an abuser, and I can feel it in me, too. This pent-up darkness just waiting to get out. It's what made me such a good soldier. Their legacy is in my blood."

She took a step back. Good. She should be scared of him.

"So you need to go home. You and the baby need to stay away as far from me as possible. I'll keep my word. I'll pay child support or whatever you need to raise him or her." It took everything he had not to promise he would be better than the men in his family. That she was safe with him. Harvey shook his head, keeping himself in the moment. Here, with her. "But as long as I'm in your or this baby's lives, I'm a danger to you."

Chapter Nine

She'd learned to walk on eggshells.

She'd learned to recognize certain footsteps, tones. How to tell if her mother was in a bad mood and when to avoid her. Drennan had learned to study people at a young age and could read almost everyone like a book before they spoke.

It was a trauma response.

Medical school had taught her that much. Hyper-focusing on what people said or thought was how she'd stayed safe in her unpredictable environment. At least, according to the psychology professors who'd required each and every student to participate in therapy sessions during the term focused on the mental health of future patients. Every shift in mood or behavior hit her upside the head because she was the one who would face the consequences of those shifts. She'd become habituated to the high levels of stress since her father's death. The result? She'd been a "good" girl. Praised for not having big feelings, not making messes, not making noise.

Until the pressure of being that good girl had torn her apart from the inside. Drennan forced herself to take a slow breath. Observation was still hard. Being watched. Noticed. It'd become a precursor to punishment once upon a time, but the way Harvey had looked at her that night… It was the same way he was looking at her now. As though he'd been broken into a thousand shards of himself, begging for someone to come along and put him back together. He was right before when he'd said her pain had called to his. The same thing had happened in her chest. Latched on to him and refused to let go. In that moment, she'd wanted to be that person for him. To be the one to piece him back together. Just as she'd treated and mended so many others.

Drennan took a step into him. Invading his personal space. His shoulders tensed, his body preparing for the threat his brain was trying to convince him existed. A feral animal backed into a corner. One wrong move and he'd lash out, but she wasn't scared of him or of anything he'd told her about his family history. It was true a correlation existed between living through abuse and becoming an abuser. An entire third of children continued the cycle and patterns of neglect and abuse brought down on them through their childhoods, but Harvey wasn't ever going to hurt her. Not like that.

Because that same part of her that recognized the shared pain he'd talked about also recognized his pure need. He probably didn't even realize how he'd held her a bit tighter that night, how he'd sought her out in the dark as though he couldn't stand to be parted from her, how he'd trusted her and himself to get close. And she was going to prove he wasn't anything like the parent that had taken the last shreds of his worth. "Do you want to hurt me, Harvey?"

Surprise relaxed the muscles around his mouth and eyes, and he seemed to draw his own deep breath. Clarifying. Cleansing. His gaze snapped to hers. "No."

She took another step, her chest brushing against the hard planes of muscle beneath his shirt. Her pulse thudded hard at the base of her throat to the point she thought he might actually be able to hear it. How could he not? According to him, she was putting herself at risk just being near him, but Harvey had gone out of his way to take care of her—to take care of this baby—since the moment he'd learned her name. "How about now? Do you want to hurt me now?"

The struggle to back off and put as much distance between them as he could manage flared in the flexed tendons of his neck and forearms. If she wasn't a medical professional, she might think the tension hurt as it tried to break free of his skin. His chest rose on a strong inhale, and he closed his eyes. Still fighting. "No."

"Do you see me as a threat, Harvey?" She wasn't a psychologist or a social worker. She had no business testing his limits without putting protections in place for herself, but whether Harvey trusted himself around her and the baby or not, she wasn't going anywhere.

He shook his head, as though not about to trust himself to speak, but still refused to look at her.

Drennan reached out, watching her fingers slowly slide up his forearm. Feeling the tendons beneath his skin. Dark hair parted under her touch, followed by a row of raised goose bumps. She ran her hand farther up his arm, across his shoulder, framed the side of his neck. Not a single inch of space separated them now, his shallow breaths skimming her jaw. A deep jolt of heat speared through her nervous system as she caught another dose of that earthy scent she'd associated with him since the night they'd met. "Do you know why men like your father feel the need to overpower those weaker than them?"

Harvey didn't move, didn't even seem to breathe now.

"They manipulate, control, dominate and destroy anything and anyone that makes them feel because they're not emotionally mature enough to cope with the people in their lives and their surroundings. Their emotions and opinions weren't welcome or important growing up, and so they found a way to make themselves important. Heard, even. They suppress everything until all that's left to break through is anger, outrage and stress. They let themselves be overrun by it minute to minute and end up taking out that immaturity on the people they're supposed to love." Her voice threatened to lodge in her throat on that last word. Tears sprang in her eyes as her attempt to get through to Harvey hit too close to home. Always the mediator, always the one who needed to fix things so she wouldn't be punished. So she would be seen by the one parent she had left. It didn't do any good. It never changed a damn thing, but she could help him. Right here in the middle of his living room, she could make him see the truth. Drennan leaned in, her mouth brushing at the corner of his. His beard pricked at her skin, sending a shock of sensation through the rest of her. She set her free hand beneath his opposite wrist and tugged his fingers to her hip, then did the same with his other hand. "I trust you not to hurt me."

Harvey's eyes snapped opened, brilliantly blue and as compelling as she remembered. He took an initial step back, but Drennan only tightened her hold on his hands at her hips. "You shouldn't."

Gravel coated those two simple words, and her heart broke a little more for him. For what he must've been through as a child, for the darkness he surely carried having to leave his mother behind to escape, for the pure self-loathing that simmered beneath every word out of his mouth.

"I trust you because you offered me your hand that night at the bar." She pressed a kiss to the side of his mouth, instantly lost to the feel of a warm-blooded man who'd wanted her. Who didn't see her as anything like a tool to be used or someone to exert power over. "You gave me a choice."

She swept her bottom lip across his, countering his step to escape, and kissed the opposite side of his mouth. He opened to her slightly, his breath mingling with hers until she wasn't sure where she began and he ended. "You brought me to a place you feel safe. You touched me with nothing but respect and followed my every cue. You let me take control of the situation as though you were simply grateful I was there. So no matter what you might think of yourself, I know you're not like him or your grandfather or anyone else who has used their power to diminish someone else's."

One second. Two. She'd made her point, and despite the unfiltered desire heating her blood, Drennan moved to step back. To give him the space he obviously needed. Once again, he'd swooped in to save her, to take care of her, but this was the kind of man who would never see himself as any kind of hero. And she would leave if that was what he required.

But his hands tightened on her hips, holding her hostage.

Her adrenaline spiked for a moment, and she forcibly had to remind herself of everything she'd just tried to prove to him. She wasn't scared of him. If anything, she wanted more, and that scared her more than anything. Her desperation for him to want her, to choose her when no one else had.

"Who hurt you?" The gravel hadn't left his voice, and with the descent of the sun coming through the front window, she couldn't be sure of his expression.

This wasn't about her, and that ingrained urge to downplay everything she'd been through—because there were people out there, like him, who'd been through so much worse—reared its ugly little head. But she'd left Ohio for a reason. She'd seen the signs and sworn never to justify them again. Never to overlook the hurt and disregard, the neglect—any of it again. Drennan pressed her fingertips into the backs of his knuckles, steadying herself. But that didn't mean she had to expose that leaking wound. She'd moved on. She'd started a new life with a new job, a new apartment and a new outlook on life. And she wouldn't ever put herself in a position to be that victim again. Not even for him. She shook her head with a tight smile pulling at her mouth.

Harvey used both hands on her hips to back her against the arch separating the living room from the kitchen and dining room beyond. The corners dug between her shoulder blades with the weight of his body pressed against hers. Not to control or intimidate but something just as dangerous if she wasn't careful. Angling his head to one side, he skimmed his nose along her jaw, near the sensitive spot beneath her ear and down the side of her throat. Hovering over her pulse. "Do you know what I did in the military? What made me such a good soldier?"

She couldn't even shake her head, too lost in the full dose of heat sinking through their clothing. It was the same illogical reaction that had convinced her to go home with a practical stranger, bypassing every warning she'd been taught in school. Her fingers fisted in his shirt, to add much-needed space between them or draw him closer, she wasn't sure.

"I was an interrogator." His mouth slid to all the places his nose had visited, eliciting an eruption of desire in her low belly. "I could read people better than most. Tell when they're lying."

The muscles down her spine tightened one by one. A defense he'd definitely noticed given the hitch of his mouth into a smile against her skin. "And did you have to get this close to them to be able to tell they were lying?"

"No." Harvey slid his thumbs from her hips, to the hem

of her sweatshirt then up. Calluses scraped against the bare skin of her stomach in small circles, working to ease the panic closing in around her throat. "Being this close to you when all I've thought about for the past two months is tracking you down and re-creating that night is just an added benefit. Who hurt you, Drennan?"

He'd wanted to find her? Drennan couldn't get her head around that. She shook her head, trying to convince herself more than anyone else. "It doesn't matter." It didn't. She wasn't a victim anymore. She didn't have to—

"You should know I have other ways of getting to the truth." A growl reverberated through his chest and straight into hers. He pulled back slightly, and the cold rushed in. His gaze dipped to her mouth then back. "And I'm very good at my job."

Harvey crushed his mouth to hers.

Chapter Ten

He hadn't meant to kiss her.

But Harvey pulled her toward him, dropped his head and lost himself in that near-constant craving he'd had for her since the night they'd met. Deeper, harder, more ferociously. His mouth smoothed over Drennan's as she met him stroke for stroke, like a dance they'd rehearsed a thousand times. In a matter of seconds, his entire body felt as though he'd been stunned with a Taser. His heart thudded hard enough from behind his rib cage, he was sure Drennan could feel it trying to escape.

His senses rocketed into overwhelming territory. Every sweep of his tongue against hers. He couldn't fight the urge to savor everything he'd convinced himself hadn't been real all over again. The slight gasp as he let up, the way her fingernails dug into his shoulders. How she pressed against him as though unconsciously seeking him out. His hands and legs prickled with sensation. Heavy as he folded her against him.

This. This was what he'd been missing the past eight weeks. Her touch, her scent, the way her hair slid between his fingers. Sex had always been nothing more than a biological necessity he was happy to get through, but with

Drennan… How had his brain minimized this connection between them?

Harvey slid his hands down, over her back end, down to her thighs and lifted her off the floor, securing her legs around his waist. Turning, he pressed her back into the archway. To get closer. To neutralize this need for her he thought might not ever be satiated. Years of numbness and avoidance broke under the small moan escaping up her throat. And Harvey wanted to hear it again. He wanted to hear it every morning and every night. Every time he touched her. It belonged to him, that sweet little sound. She'd never make it for any other man. She was his. Right here, right now. Whatever this was between them just made sense. The ache in his chest—where a hole had been for years—matched the one building through the rest of his body as he pressed into her. Only she could soothe it. Just as she had that night.

The night she'd gotten pregnant.

Blood drained from his upper body, too many sensations assaulting him all at once. His baby. She was having his baby. He was going to be a dad. And that…that couldn't happen. Right?

Pressing his forehead to hers, Harvey broke the kiss, breathing heavy. Her, too. He'd done that to her. Brought out that woman who'd shot down a college kid trying to get lucky, the one who'd taken his hand without a moment's hesitation and somehow shattered everything he'd ever known about himself in a single night. He wrapped her in both arms, holding on to her with everything he had. He wanted her. More than he'd ever allowed himself to admit to wanting something before.

She squeezed her thighs around him as his thumb traced the waistline of her jeans. Trying to drag him out of his head and back to her. Drennan arched her back to close the distance between them once more. "Harvey."

That breathy sigh nearly did him in. She skimmed her fingers over his jaw, turning his gaze to her. "Hey. Are you okay?"

It would be easy to haul her back into his bed, to chase that high she was solely responsible for addicting him to, but he'd always want more. Do whatever it took for the next hit, maybe even override her desires. And that... He wasn't that man. He wouldn't let himself be that man. Harvey loosened his hold around her rib cage, all too aware of how little pressure it would take to keep her for himself. "I can't. I can't do this."

She unlocked her ankles, sliding down the front of his body with both hands on his shoulders for balance. Lips swollen with the evidence of their kiss, Drennan ran a hand through her hair, still so close he could feel the gallop of her heart rate. "You realize we've done this before, right?"

He fought the laugh charging up his throat. Harvey pressed his hand into the archway at her back and shoved off. "Yeah. I'm aware, but this isn't happening. Not again."

"*You* kissed *me*." Her expression fell along with the volume of her voice. Almost as though she'd severed some innate part of herself from her emotions. From feeling anything at all. But Drennan was too alive for that, too beautiful for that.

And he hated it more than anything. He hated that she felt the need to protect herself from him, like he was a threat. But that was what he'd warned her about. That a switch he couldn't see inside could be flipped at any moment. That he could lose control and she would be the one to pay the price. He'd witnessed that same reaction from his mother too many times to count, that desperation to emotionally—

sometimes physically—protect herself from his father. To detach. Which only added to his belief someone had hurt Drennan. No matter how much he wanted to push for answers—to have a name to put to the pain he caught in her gaze every once in a while—he wouldn't force her hand. He wouldn't add to her misery. Harvey backed up a few steps. "I made a mistake."

"You're not him, Harvey." She gripped the ends of her sweatshirt in both palms, seemingly unsure what to do with her hands, but not out of nervousness. "And I'm not a mistake. I'm a choice standing right in front of you. One you can make without the influence of the person who hurt you. I understand that sounds easier said than done, but it can be done. I'm proof of that. We're going to have a baby together. Isn't that worth something?"

He couldn't stop the flinch tensing his entire body. No. She wasn't a mistake. She was everything he'd ever dreamed about. And he couldn't have her. Not without breaking her as thoroughly as his mother had been broken. She deserved better than that.

"That's the thing." Heat that had nothing to do with the remnants of her taste on his tongue seared through his chest as he backed up another step. Wrong. This entire conversation on his end felt wrong, but he couldn't stop. For her. For the baby. He had to see this through. "You don't know me. I'm just some guy you met in a bar. You have no idea what I'm capable of."

"I thought I did, but you're right. How much do we really know about each other?" Her throat worked on a deep swallow, and Drennan darted her gaze to her things by the door before heading for them. He thought he'd seen a hint of silver lining her eyes, but it was gone before she turned back to face him. She grabbed for her purse, checking her phone briefly before shoving it into her bag. "It's been a long day, and I'm tired. Thank you for getting me to the clinic and letting me recover here. I'm going to call a rideshare and go home."

A hit of surprise nearly knocked him off his feet. She was leaving? Of course, she was leaving. He'd given her every reason to walk right out that door with the intention of letting her. He wouldn't stop her, but that deranged part of him that had been searching for her the past eight weeks wasn't ready to let go. "I can give you a ride."

Drennan slung her bag to one shoulder, and a wave of exhaustion played across not just her face but down her entire body. "Why, Harvey? Because you feel obligated to make sure the woman you got pregnant makes it home or because you want to give me a ride?"

He didn't have an answer for that. At least, not one that would convince her he wasn't completely out of his mind.

"You asked me who hurt me." She gripped the strap of her purse hard enough for the whites of her knuckles to show through the delicate skin on the backs of her hands. "There are people in this world who pride themselves on never putting their hands on someone who doesn't deserve it while tearing their victims down any way they can. Sometimes it's by making promises they never intend to follow through with or building up hope while intentionally planning on how to use their victim's weaknesses against them. They belittle, they lie, they exaggerate and turn your words back on you. Over and over until you're convinced you're the bad guy and they're the victim, but the worse part? You still want a relationship with that person. Because, in your mind, one glimpse at the good instantly outweighs all the bad. You want those moments where you matter to be true more than anything in the world."

Every muscle down his spine tightened under battle-ready tension. And he instinctually knew Drennan was speaking from experience, that someone had strategically torn her apart piece by piece. Preyed on her affections and used her vulnerabilities against her. It was an invisible kind of abuse that no one noticed—psychological warfare—and he'd... Oh, hell. He'd gotten her hopes up with that kiss.

"You said you didn't want anything to do with this baby. You don't think you're fit enough to be a father, and I will believe you if that's what you want. I will support your decision, and I will never hold it against you." Drennan shifted her bag farther up her shoulder.

The sincerity in that simple statement nearly crushed him. His choices had never mattered. Not as a kid and sure as hell not in the military. There was always someone overriding his free will and making decisions for him. From what he ate, to how long he slept, to where he was allowed to go and when. The only real freedom he'd experienced in the past few years was in the middle of nowhere trying to keep hikers from doing dumb things. Like get themselves killed. But Drennan... She'd just accepted him as if his decision mattered. Like he mattered. How? How was it possible that of all the people he'd been with over the years, this woman had the one thing he'd craved for years but was the one person he couldn't let himself have?

"What I won't do is let you play with my emotions or use me to test the limits you've set for yourself." Her shoulders rose on a strong inhale as she reached for the front door. "I've just stopped being an easy target for someone else. I won't be one for you."

Harvey didn't know what to say to that, what to think. He wanted to know who. Who had dared to convince Drennan she was anything less than the capable, optimistic, indispensable woman standing in front of him? A former boyfriend? A husband? "Drennan."

He wasn't sure if he was trying to stop her from leaving or if he just needed to say her name, to have it etched deeper in order to hold on to her a bit longer. Because she was going to walk out that door, and once she did, every ounce of training he had told him she wasn't coming back. That while he'd drawn the line between them, she would uphold it better than he ever could.

Swinging the front door open, she kept her hand on the knob, barely angling her chin over her shoulder, as if she couldn't even stand to look at him. And he deserved that. Hell, he deserved worse, and he would take anything she threw at him. "I don't need your financial support for the baby, Harvey. I was just hoping for you."

She stepped out into the night, closing the door behind her.

Chapter Eleven

Something oily took up residence in her veins.

Vulnerability felt like that. Thick and uncomfortable. Crap. She'd basically told Harvey that she'd wanted to be a couple before she'd escaped his house last night. To try to make this work between them.

Drennan was furious with herself for letting that buried little secret slip. She knew better. How many times had she voiced her wants and had them thrown back in her face or used against her over the years? She'd promised herself she wouldn't do this again, and she couldn't breathe through the tightness in her chest because of it. Embarrassment didn't cover it. This was outright fear. Conditioned into her over years of being told nobody in their right mind would choose her. That she was—

"No." Her voice echoed through the basement exam room, harsher than she'd expected. That voice didn't get to live rent-free. Like Cassidy had said. Drennan closed her eyes, setting her hands against the cold stainless steel of the exam table.

But that kiss... It'd held the kind of passion she'd always wanted. The desperate, hot kind that made her feel wanted and important. And while more than one night together hadn't been the agreement, she and Harvey really hadn't planned for a baby. That changed things, didn't it?

"Did you say something?" Dr. Yarrow entered their dark little exam room as she imagined someone might enter a formal event, all smooth lines, pressed seams and straight posture. Even his forehead didn't dare wrinkle despite his age being somewhere in the mid-sixties. The lab coat protecting his slacks and button-down hung off his shoulders with a little extra give down the sides. The man had single-handedly led the Office of the Medical Examiner here in Hurricane for over thirty years. With more natural deaths than homicides between the locals, Zion National Park and Springdale, there'd been plenty of time to take care of his physical health, but the stress around his eyes was starting to show.

"No. Sorry." Drennan got back to arranging the tools the ME would need to start the autopsy of the drowned victim from the park, everything from the bone saw to specimen tubes to collect bodily fluid samples as they progressed through their established routine. Thankfully, it seemed Harvey had acted quickly enough to call Dr. Yarrow to collect the body from the clinic parking lot that not a whole lot of damage had been inflicted on the remains by the extreme heat. She wasn't going to lose her job. Yet. "Just talking to myself."

"Must've been a hell of a conversation for me to hear it down the hall." Dr. Yarrow rounded the exam table and folded down the thin sheet providing a small modicum of privacy to their patient.

The victim had been stripped of her personal items, including her hiking gear, the beanie she'd been found in, her jacket, shirt, underwear, boots and socks. Impeccably arched eyebrows framed almond-shaped eyes, the deepest shade of brown Drennan had ever come across. Full lips, a blade of a nose, clear skin and healthy mid-back-length dark hair spoke of someone who took the time to take care of herself. Her body was soft, revealing the victim's preference for cardio rather than strength training. The blisters on the bottoms of her feet and the lack of wear on the hiking boots said this woman hadn't been much of an outdoorswoman or she'd started a new interest.

There hadn't been reports of any missing women as far as Drennan had been able to find when she'd contacted Springdale PD and Zion's law enforcement division head she'd met at the scene, but that didn't mean someone out there wasn't missing her or simply hadn't known where she'd gone. Drennan made a mental note to check in with the surrounding police departments. The victim was potentially young enough to fit in with the college crowd from St. George. Maybe someone had inquired after her there. Still, they had very little to go off of when it came to uncovering her identity. No driver's license or other form of ID had been discovered on the remains or in her backpack. It would take DNA, fingerprints or dentals to solve that puzzle unless the rangers could recover her missing personal items.

Dr. Yarrow tipped the victim's head back, unlocking her jaw to peer inside the woman's mouth before stepping back and donning his protective eyewear, gloves and mask from the secondary table she'd arranged while trapped inside her own head. "Are you feeling better today?"

Drennan nearly dropped the syringe she'd been in the process of handing off to collect fluid from behind the victim's cornea. Vitreous humor. It was just one of many samples they'd preserve for toxicology and reexamination down the line. She managed to hand off the syringe without losing the rest of her dignity. "Um, yes. Thank you."

"That park ranger—what's his name, Knight?—said you'd collapsed from dehydration." Strapping the magnifying glasses over his head, the medical examiner positioned the tip of the needle to the side of the victim's eye and pushed forward, pulling on the plunger at the same time. A filmy white fluid filled the syringe.

Drennan tried not to roll his name around in her brain for too long, but the unsolicited reaction started in her toes and tightened the skin on her scalp. Images of that kiss, of the way he'd held her weight against that archway as though she weighed nothing, attacked before she could assemble her defenses. Her mouth dried.

"It shouldn't have happened. I'll be more careful in the park next time." Her skin heated with another dose of that thick oily feeling in her veins. It wasn't a lie, but she wasn't ready to explain what else had led to her throwing up all the fluids she'd drunk yesterday. Not until she had to.

Setting aside the now full syringe on the metal rolling cart to collect various samples, Dr. Yarrow went back to the victim's mouth to collect DNA with an oversize Q-tip. "Well, pregnancy is certainly hard no matter where your health starts. Just let me know if I need to adjust your duties or your hours."

That... She hadn't expected that.

"What?" Drennan shook her head, no longer seeing the woman's face but a blur of white lab coat and darkening at the edges of her vision. She was holding her breath. Forcing herself to breathe through the surprise, she focused on capping the Q-tip Dr. Yarrow had swabbed and adding it to the sample cart. She'd just taken a pregnancy test yesterday morning and gotten her own confirmation. Her boss couldn't have known before her. Right? "How did you..."

"You've been more tired lately." The medical examiner didn't miss a step in their routine, inspecting the inside of the victim's mouth for wounds, missing teeth, crowns that might identify her or disease. The light coming from his magnifying glasses turned the woman's skin a waxy white. "Eating a lot more, too. I noticed you've been favoring more fresh fruit and vegetables."

"You concluded that I'm pregnant from all that?" Was that even possible? A new workout routine could end with those results.

Dr. Yarrow notched his head up to put her in his direct line of sight. The brightness of the light on his glasses skewered her vision. "Well, I might work with the dead, but I'm still around the living plenty. And I remember when my wife was pregnant. You wouldn't believe her cravings. Who voluntarily eats cottage cheese with watermelon?"

She didn't know what to say to that. She hadn't planned on telling him for a few more weeks and only because she'd need to take some time off after the baby came. Their work here wasn't strenuous, but she'd wanted to give him plenty of time to hire and train a new assistant if that was what he needed.

"Did you photograph these bruises on the back of her neck?" The medical examiner tilted the victim's head to one side, exposing the purple and blue marbling at her nape.

Drennan took as much of a cleansing breath as she could in a too-small exam room with a decomposing body that'd been out of the freezer for nearing two hours. "Yes. I already uploaded the photos to your laptop."

"These look like a handprint. Like someone held her down and squeezed." Dr. Yarrow straightened with all that grace she'd never been able to achieve, even as a little ballerina, and tore his gloves free. He scratched at his nose with one thumb, his attention locked on the body. "Considering how long she was in the water, I can't imagine we'll get clean fingerprints off her skin, but the size of the handprint is a start. You said you couldn't find her ID?"

"No, and there are no missing person reports at this time. I was going to expand to other departments in the state, maybe even into Mesquite and Arizona to see if any of them filed a report matching her description later today."

"Something might come up on the X-rays. It's possible she's had surgery in the past and has a pin or plate with a serial number we can use. This is the fourth homicide I've seen in as few months coming out of that park." The medical examiner's eyes narrowed on their victim, and he removed his magnifying glasses. "It'll take a few more hours to finish the autopsy and at least three weeks for the crime lab to return the toxicology on the samples we've collected. I don't want to wait that long. Go back to the scene. See if you can find anything that tells us who she is. Make sure you take enough water this time and the waterproof gear. It's in the corner."

Back to the scene? Up the near three miles of incline and into water that looked like an algae breakout? And possibly run into the man she'd admitted to wanting more from? Oh, hell. Dread settled in the pit of her stomach, and a rush of acid charged into her throat. She swallowed it back, but like the thick oily feeling in her blood, it clung. This was her job. Her only source of income unless she wanted to burn through her savings. There were no other options from this point. She'd given them all up when she'd resigned from her position in the ER. No one would hire her back after what'd happened.

Drennan peeled her gloves free and tossed them into the biohazards wastebasket. Her breath shook on a long exhale. "I can do that."

She could. She'd done it once before. This time, she would be more prepared.

It took about twenty minutes to reach Zion National Park's front entrance and even less to park and catch the shuttle to the Grotto, where the Emerald Pool Trail began. Her legs burned from overuse on ascent, especially given the weight of the waterproof gear. Was Harvey assigned to patrol this trail today?

Her breath sawed in and out of her lungs with a burning at the back of her throat as she attacked the steplike boulders leading into the upper pools. Wasn't it rare for this area to be so empty of hikers? She'd bypassed a few on the ascent, but they'd been coming down from the pools. She'd expected a few hikers on the shore angling cameras up toward the hundred-foot waterfall blowing every which way from gusts as she donned the waterproof one-piece and boots. But this was good, too. There wasn't anyone to get in her way as she dredged the few-foot-deep pool.

"Ugh." Yeah. She was going to have to get in that water. For hours. Not how she intended her day to go. Drennan took her first step, surprised by the silt that gave way under her weight. She extended both arms for balance, then carefully tipped forward to get a better look into the murky water. Maybe she should've given Harvey or the other rangers a heads-up she'd come out to search the scene. They could've at least ensured she wasn't attacked by a pond monster, but the idea of seeing Harvey so soon after their last conversation… She needed time.

Piercing the surface with her net, she dragged the apparatus along the bottom of the pool. Coming up empty. There had to be something here. A phone, a wallet, the victim's ID very clearly identifying her remains. "Come on."

A shadow crossed the surface of the water to her left.

Drennan turned to warn the hiker not to get closer.

Lightning exploded across her vision. Along with the pain.

And then she was lost to the Emerald Pools.

Chapter Twelve

He hadn't been this nervous since reporting for basic training.

Harvey memorized the property through the windshield of his SUV. The Office of the Medical Examiner wasn't in a hospital or attached to the police station as other towns might've set it up. Nope. This one was in a freaking funeral home.

The bright white exterior was almost enough to convince him there weren't horrors waiting inside. Greek-like columns upheld the second story over an open walkway lining the entire structure with rows and beds full of pastel flowers and thick green shrubs. The property as a whole had obviously been well taken care of and designed to create a sense of peace in the visitors who walked through those elaborate double doors at the front.

Having the ME's office inside a funeral parlor made sense in a town with less than twenty-five thousand residents. Sort of. Both the ME and the funeral director handled remains. They both needed access to exam rooms, used refrigerators to stop decomposition and had all the tools that came with preparing a body for burial, but he couldn't shake the prickling dread at the back of his neck at the thought of walking in there. Not even for any big reason but a thousand little ones.

Most recently having to visit another funeral home on behalf of a man he honestly should've left to the state to bury.

But he wasn't here for that. He was here for Drennan. To apologize. To give her the respect she deserved. Because she was right. What he'd done—kissing her to convince her to give him what he wanted—was inexcusable, and he wasn't that man. Truly. Every cell in his body hated the idea she felt as though he'd turned her into a challenge to be conquered instead of the beautiful, caring, compelling woman she was. And she'd called him out on it, refused to get caught in self-imposed rules or used as a tool in some greater design. And, damn if that wasn't one of the sexiest things he'd ever seen, her putting him in his place.

I was just hoping for you.

He hadn't been able to stop repeating that single statement since the moment the words had left her mouth. Drennan didn't want his financial support. She'd wanted something more. And while he admired her ability to speak her mind and ask for what she wanted, it wasn't possible. He couldn't give her that. Not ever. She knew that, and yet… He couldn't stop thinking about the potential, either.

She wasn't just having *a* baby.

She was having *his* baby.

Maybe a boy who looked just like him with dark hair and wild blue eyes and got into all kinds of trouble wearing his mama down. Or a girl whose knowing green gaze that resembled a spring morning widened every time he walked through the door at the end of his day walking the trails. Laughter would fill his bare house as he scooped up his kid and spun them around until they were both dizzy. Drennan would be there with that wide smile she seemed to reserve just for him, and he'd finally feel that tension in his chest release from being away from them when he dragged her mouth to his in greeting.

He could see it. Right there in front of him. All he had to do was reach out and grab that reality. Make it his. Drennan wanted that. Had admitted to wanting them to try.

But the image bled away to sharp reds and swallowing blacks, leaving nothing but the fitful nightmares of his childhood behind. To the bruises his mother had always caked in makeup to try to hide, to the scrapes and scabs on the backs of his dad's hands and the sickening smile on the old man's face when Harvey went out of his way to avoid getting anywhere near him. He could still feel the tightness in his arms and legs every once in a while, the automatic bracing at loud noises, to the point he thought his tendons might snap. A lot of those same bruises had found a way to him, his mother's begging and pleas going unheard as his father punished Harvey for some imagined slight. Low grades, not coming home from school fast enough, walking in front of the TV, not cleaning up his plate at the end of a meal. And while Harvey had found little ways to rebel against his dad, years of survival and pain had ingrained itself in his cells. It was part of him.

But he wouldn't let it touch her.

His fingers curled around the steering wheel, knuckles working to escape the backs of his hands. Harvey killed the ignition and forced himself from the SUV and through those doors. The too-sweet and stale floral scent filled the lobby in a cloying, invisible mist he'd have to work at to get rid of. Just like the last time he set foot in a funeral home, gleaming wood coffins angled and glinted across the sales floor, ranging in an array of colors and prices right down to a plain pine box. He'd chosen the cheapest option for his father because that was what the bastard deserved. Actually, he'd deserved less. Unfortunately, due to zoning laws burying the son of a bitch under the animal shelter to spend the rest of eternity getting crapped on wasn't possible. Though deserved.

But it wasn't until now Harvey realized he didn't know what his mother had been buried in, what his father had chosen to lay his wife of twenty-two years to rest in. Had there been a service? Flowers? Had anyone showed with their favorite casseroles to pay their respects to the woman who'd sacrificed her body and mental health to protect her son? He hadn't gotten more than a text message from his father letting him know she'd died and already been laid to rest. Taking that last ounce of hope she'd save herself.

His throat dried. A sign for the Office of the Medical Examiner at the front directed him to a set of stairs off to his right, leading down into the basement. The temperature dropped a few degrees with every step until he faced a set of wide steel doors. Shoving through, he pulled up short as a pair of terrifying oversize bug eyes locked on him. "What the hell?"

His skin tightened down his arms as he realized the magnifying glasses were worn by a light-haired man with a scalpel in one hand and a pair of tweezers in another. Other details started registering, too. Like the blood staining the front of the man's once white lab coat. And the female body stretched open on the table in front of him.

"Well, you're not supposed to be down here, Ranger Knight." Dr. Yarrow set aside his tools on a small rolling cart and peeled off his gloves before going for the lit magnifying glasses on his head. They'd met in the clinic parking lot to pass off the woman Harvey had recovered from the trail yesterday morning, but seeing the medical examiner in this light came with a whole new set of nightmare material he didn't need. "I assume you're here about our drowning victim?"

He wouldn't look at the remains on the table. He wouldn't look—

He looked. And, hell, he wished he hadn't. Wished he hadn't seen the victim's chest splayed open and pinned back like one of those butterflies he'd once seen spread out and framed in his boss's office. Harvey cleared his throat, feeling the blood drain from his face. "Sorry. I'm looking for Drennan. She working today?"

Dr. Yarrow came around the table, maneuvering in front of what Harvey could see of the victim and her insides. "She's out on an errand. If you're here about the autopsy of the victim recovered from the park, I won't have a final report for another few days. I still have multiple samples to be taken and organs to be weighed. Based on the bruises at the back of the victim's neck, I believe the manner of death is homicide by drowning. She was held under the water for several minutes, but we don't have an identity. That's why I sent Drennan back to the trail about an hour ago. We should have something for you soon."

"To the trail?" Warning signals exploded through him, and Harvey took one step farther into the exam room that smelled of fruity decay. Well, he certainly wished for the cloyingly thick scent of flowers now. "You sent her alone?"

"Ms. Hawes is more than capable of dredging the pond for the victim's personal effects on her own as well as determining if there is any evidence we need to consider for this investigation." The medical examiner grabbed for a new set of gloves. "Besides, I expect nothing less from a former trauma physician to be able to pick up the slack so I can make it home for dinner on time for once. My wife tends to get sensitive if I am not where I am expected to be when I am expected to be."

Dr. Yarrow's smile crested and fell in equal time as he donned the new set of latex. "Is there anything else, Ranger Knight?"

"Have you heard from her?" He couldn't explain this simmering in his chest.

The medical examiner checked his watch, the lines between his brows deepening. "She should've checked in by now."

Harvey backed toward the door, a deep, resonating urgency taking hold in his blood. He had no doubt Drennan was far more qualified to collect any evidence at the scene than the rangers on staff, but knowing she was in the park alone—where a killer had recently murdered a lone hiker—didn't sit well. Of course, there was no evidence the killer would target an assistant medical examiner, but he couldn't get the warning bells in his head to quiet down. "Thanks."

He shoved through the double steel swinging doors meant to keep temperatures balanced on both sides and hauled himself up the stairs, rushing by the time he got to the top. He had no reason to think Drennan might be in danger, but some instinctual drive inside of him had Harvey jogging out of the building and to his truck and tearing out of the funeral home's parking lot. He'd given her his number to call in case of emergency with the pregnancy, but he hadn't saved hers. Navigating back to the highway, he headed straight for Zion, calling the visitor's center on the way.

The ranger on the other end hadn't seen or heard from the medical examiner's office, but the upper pool was still closed at Ranger Simpson's direction due to the investigation. Drennan must've bypassed the visitor's center and set out on the trail herself. Damn it. He should've reached out to her before now, but he'd wanted to give her space after their argument last night.

No. That wasn't it. His gut churned as the truth surfaced. He'd assumed she wouldn't want to talk to him, and her rejection… He didn't want that.

He put in a call to the head of the law enforcement division next for no other reason than to assure himself someone knew she was on that trail alone. The call connected.

"Simpson." The ranger's no-BS greeting didn't faze him one bit.

"It's Knight. That medical examiner we met yesterday at Emerald Pools. She reach out to you?" Harvey pressed down on the accelerator, his blood heating and humming in his veins. "Her boss sent her back to the trail to dredge the pond a little more than an hour ago. He hasn't heard from her since."

"Cell coverage is spotty up there, but no. I haven't seen her. I've got a ranger in the area. Give me a second. I'll have her check in." The silence on the other side of the line ratcheted Harvey's heart rate into dangerous territory. Two minutes. Three. Five? He lost sense of time, desert and sharp mountains ripping by as he navigated around slower vehicles down the highway toward Springdale.

"Knight, you're not going to like this." Simpson interrupted the chaos working to unravel him from the inside.

Harvey's entire body braced from a threat he couldn't even see coming, as automatic and painful as those nights his dad's footsteps were just a little bit louder than normal outside his bedroom door. He swallowed through it. "What happened?"

"Her gear is all there, man." The law enforcement ranger swore low enough Harvey didn't catch it. "But your medical examiner is not."

Chapter Thirteen

Her waterproof gear was no longer...waterproof.

And heavy. Or maybe gravity had doubled in the time since she'd died. Ugh. Drennan blinked against the onslaught of sunlight overhead. Sheer cliffs rose up on either side of her, trees peppering her vision every few feet. Water spit into her face with a strong gust of wind. Her skin prickled with the sudden change in temperature. Twisting her head to one side, she cringed against the tender spot at the back of her head. The one pulsing with every beat of her heart. Water had infiltrated her gear. Her clothing clung to her frame, holding her down, hair plastered to her face and neck.

Fluffy white clouds skimmed across the sky overhead.

This wasn't the Emerald Pools trail.

Where the hell was she?

Wind kicked up a second time, spitting another few drops into her face. The short waterfall was nothing like the one that'd towered over her at the upper emerald pool. Drennan tried shoving to stand, though she didn't trust herself to make it far. Head injuries weren't like those in the mindless action movies and TV shows she liked to binge. There was no getting straight back up and walking off this trail like nothing had happened. Headaches, sensory issues such as vision and hearing, unconsciousness. Comas. She'd seen enough of them in the ER. Car accidents, assaults, domestic disputes.

Wait. Was that why she couldn't remember how she got here? No. She remembered...something. Pain speared through her head the harder she tried to recall the seconds leading up to waking here, but there was nothing more than a shadow. Had she passed out again? She sucked in a sharp breath. Was the baby okay?

Her wrists burned, the tendons in her shoulders pulling taut. She wrestled with whatever had pinned her hands. Then stilled. Drennan understood then. Why she couldn't push herself to sit up. Why her arms hurt and she couldn't remember how she'd gotten here.

Someone had hit her.

Someone had attacked her.

She'd gone to Emerald Pools to dredge the bottom of the pond for the victim's personal items, and... The shadow. It'd come up from behind. She hadn't gotten a chance to turn around before her attacker knocked her unconscious. Drennan struggled against the rope digging into her skin. It was dry compared to the rest of her. There wasn't any swelling to the strands, but it wouldn't budge. She wasn't strong enough to—

"I wouldn't do that if I were you." The voice sounded close and yet too far away at the same time. Like it'd set out to play a trick on her. Disembodied. No owner in sight. "You'll tear your wrists up real good that way."

Her breath guttered in her chest then pressurized until she was forced to release it. Scanning her surroundings, she studied every tree, every rock, every shift to pinpoint the source of the voice. "Who—"

"That's not the question you should be asking, Dr.

Hawes." The crunch of dirt and rock registered from behind. Footsteps.

The hair on the back of her neck stood on end. Unfiltered warning exploded through her. Drennan twisted—too fast—aggravating the thudding pain in her head. The moan escaped without her permission, and she closed her eyes against the sudden brightness that lit up the back of her brain. One breath. Two. The pain receded slowly but surely. She forced her eyes open to keep her attacker in her line of sight, but it was too soon. Searing agony rippled across her head, and she had to close her eyes again, tripping the panic she could barely keep under control. She didn't like this. Being in a position of helplessness, of not knowing where the threat was coming from. Or from whom. There'd been too many times when her mother had doted on her, gone out of her way to include her and said all the things a mother should say to her daughter. It was disarming and promising. Only to have that hope ripped right out from under her.

His laugh worked to soothe the rough edges of her building anxiety against her will. Low and rolling, light considering the circumstances. She wasn't supposed to like it, but it reminded her of Harvey's. Deep and warm when he let go of thinking he was a monster.

"That had to hurt." That unexplainable sixth sense every human on the planet owned told her he'd taken up position in front of her. The small drop in temperature, too. He'd blocked the sun from beating down on her. "I was hoping to avoid this, but you have something that belongs to me. I would've gotten out of this hellhole free and clear if that ranger hadn't interrupted me."

Relief spread quick and fast as she attempted another glance at the man who'd hauled her off the Emerald Pools trail. He was tall. Taller than most of the men she'd known in her life, including her father and Dr. Yarrow. Thick beard growth and eyebrows matching dark hair—at least what she could see of it with the sun haloed around his frame—masked a large part his facial features. It didn't add to his attractiveness. It just made him look more weathered. Worn. He filled out his T-shirt well enough, though not nearly as well as most outdoorsmen. Pressed slacks that were stained with what she assumed were water spots and red dust from the trail had kept their crease as he crouched in front of her. Who in their right mind wore slacks out here? Well, other than park rangers. The sun was back in her eyes, and Drennan was forced to turn away, but she'd seen enough of his face she could identify him to police and the law enforcement rangers. If she got out of this in one piece.

Then his words registered. Her stomach flipped. Harvey. He was talking about Harvey. About discovering the body face down in the upper pool yesterday morning. Which meant... "You killed her. That woman who drowned."

"I warned her what would happen if she kept pushing." The weariness in what she now noted in his gray eyes aged him at least a decade right in front of her. "I didn't want to kill her, but she just wouldn't listen to reason. I had no other choice."

It took everything Drennan had left not to flinch against the familiar victimization of the predator in front of her. And even then, she failed. How many times had her mother played that part so well? Blamed Drennan for something that hadn't been her fault in the first place? Her mom's moods, her bad days, her grief, her life. How many times had Drennan internalized it? Tried to make things better? Apologized for things she never should've apologized for just to avoid losing another piece of herself?

The man in front of her might have a different face, but

Drennan identified the abuser beneath the mask. Knew that no matter what she said, he would never see himself as anything other than a reasonable man. Because in his head, he'd done no wrong. Her attacker caught the reaction, a slow smile spreading underneath all that beard growth a split second before he reached out for her.

She leaned back but was only able to go so far. His fingertips grazed her cheek, all the way down to her jaw, cold and alien. Her insides revolted at the touch. He was making her uncomfortable on purpose, trying to get a rise out of her when she'd spent so many years shutting down her emotions so they wouldn't be preyed upon. The rope seemed to tighten around her wrists, cutting off the blood flow to her fingers and digging into her low back.

"You remind me of her, you know." Wayward hair fell into his eyes as the wind kicked up, but he didn't bother to remove it. Almost like he didn't even realize it impaired his vision in the first place. So focused on her with a look she couldn't place. "She fought me, too. About everything. Where we would eat, which movie to watch, our future. It was one of the things I like about her the most."

A hint of grief charged into those steel gray eyes that seemed to contain several hundred years of thunderstorms, but it only lasted a minute.

"I don't..." She shook her head. "I don't know you. I don't have anything of yours."

"Sure you do." He shoved to stand, towering over her all over again. Every muscle in her body tightened at the prospect of all that power—that strength—turning against her. "You have her body."

Her... What? Air crushed from her chest.

"And if I can't get it from you, I'll get it from your colleague. Dr. Yarrow, right? I'm sure he wouldn't put up much of a fight." Her attacker slid his hands into his slacks pockets as though he'd done it a thousand times before, looking more comfortable in a boardroom or behind a desk rather than the middle of a national park, and it showed. The styling product in his hair had given up its fight, sweat darkening the collar of his shirt. An undershirt, she realized then. It didn't really go with pressed slacks, which meant he'd probably taken another shirt off somewhere. "Or that ranger you seem to like so much. Now, he seems like the kind of man who'd fight back, so I have no doubt whatever happened would get messy, but I've never shied away from getting my hands dirty, as you well know."

The blood drained from her face and neck. No. Acid surged up her throat. Not Dr. Yarrow. Not Harvey. While she'd learned to distance herself from others out of a sense of survival, she wasn't as heartless as former colleagues and friends had accused her of being. Dr. Yarrow had given her an opportunity to start over. He'd been nothing but supportive in the adjustment it'd taken for her moving to a new town and into a new position. He recognized her pregnancy symptoms and offered to be flexible in her work hours with understanding and compassion. She wouldn't let him get dragged into this. He had a family. A wife and grown kids that came around for Sunday dinners every week. A grandkid on the way.

And Harvey...

Her skin heated with blistering intensity. Harvey had gifted her something she'd never be able to repay. For one night, he'd chosen her. Made her feel wanted and beautiful. He'd looked at her as someone worthy and loved, not even having known her name at the time. Because that was the kind of man he was. Yes, he was brooding and unforgiving, but he'd been there when she'd needed him the most. Despite his internal hatred for the blood he carried in his veins and his fears of unleashing it on her and this baby, he'd been there without question. Took care of her as though she was the most important person in his life. He was brave. Braver than most. His father wouldn't have made that choice, and no one had done that for her since… Since her dad died. No one had willingly chosen her. But Harvey had, whether he accepted that fact or not. Just for a little while.

It was enough. For her to risk fighting back. For her to protect them from the predator closing in. He wouldn't get to them. Not ever. Whatever his plan, it wouldn't work.

Another dose of pain nearly dragged her under. The headache was getting worse, urging her to give in. Had she sustained a concussion? "Who are you?"

"A desperate man, Dr. Hawes." Her attacker wrapped a hand around her upper arm and hauled Drennan to her feet. Unforgiving muscle flexed under her palm as she worked to add distance between them, but it was no use. He was strong. Stronger than her. And he knew it. "Desperate men will do whatever it takes to get what they want. Remember that before you try to escape from me."

"But I thought you liked it when women fight back." Drennan put everything she had into the strike. Shoving her knee so far between his legs, she could've sworn she heard something burst. The impact threw her off balance, but she wouldn't let it stop her.

She ran.

Chapter Fourteen

His blood had reached a boiling point.

Harvey hauled himself up the last few step-like rocks leading up in the natural bowl carved out from the surrounding cliffs and up into the upper emerald pool. Ranger Simpson—Zion's head law enforcement division ranger—was already there with another Harvey didn't recognize. The rangers both faced him, their expressions hard as stone. He couldn't remember closing the distance between them. All he could focus on was the sheer panic eclipsing everything else in his body. He'd spent years under duress at home and in the military, and yet every single wall he'd built to keep himself in check crumbled in an instant. Harvey fisted both hands into Simpson's uniform, knocking the six-foot giant back. "Where is she?"

The words were more animalistic growl than human. The demon he'd been working on exorcising for as long as he could remember licked beneath the surface of his skin. He was too hot, too raw. Out of control.

The second ranger—he didn't get a look at her name tag—blew a bright pink bubble from the safety of a couple feet away. It popped, triggering his nerves to flinch. Her bleached blond hair threatened to get tangled in the gum she openly chewed. Other details bled into focus. A hot-pink kerchief around her throat, a matching manicure and the fact she'd switched out her standard issue laces for bright fuchsia. "You might not want to do that. Murray is capable of ripping each one of your fingers off and sticking them up your nose."

What? Harvey barely had the sense to think past the red haze turning him feral.

Strong hands gripped his wrists and clamped down. Steely eyes pinned Harvey in place, but the threat of danger was nothing compared to the tumult swirling in his gut. "I know what you're feeling right now, Ranger Knight. I've lived through that crushing feeling of guilt and concern, to the point you have trouble taking your next breath, but if you don't remove your hands, I will do exactly what Ranger Jordan has suggested. Or something as equally creative. She's very good at coming up with death threats, and I've always wanted to test one."

"It's true. I'm trying to come up with the perfect one for him to try. Right now, we're thinking about touching someone's face with a shovel. Really hard." Too-white teeth flashed across the woman's face, and Harvey realized this was the one other rangers had called Ranger Barbie for so long. He hadn't worked with her directly before she'd joined the law enforcement rangers, and he sure as hell wasn't interested in working with this too bright, chaotic rainbow of a woman. "You want to try one? It might help with all that—" she motioned to his face "—tension."

"I don't care." It took everything in Harvey to release his hold. Violence had been ingrained in his blood, in every muscle he owned from a young age. Beaten into him since his first memory. It was how things got done, and he'd so easily slipped back into that place he wanted to forget. Into the man he didn't want to be. But he would. He'd give up everything for Drennan and the baby, to give them a chance to be free of him. Oxygen seemed to thin with every controlled inhale, but it wasn't enough. "Where is Dr. Hawes?"

"Not here." Ranger Simpson smoothed down the collar of his shirt, erasing the lines Harvey had pressed into it with his grip. "We've got her gear left unattended. We found a duffel bag and a net in the pool, but no medical examiner. Ranger Jordan just returned from searching the lower pools as well as the trail that continues up and around the waterfall."

"And?" His entire body hung on an answer he wasn't sure he wanted.

"No sign of her." Ranger Jordan had lost that too bright quality with the change in subject, becoming the law enforcement ranger this park—that he—needed, though her high pigtails sat in opposition to every word out of her mouth. "But I made out a set of footprints. Large. Most likely male. One set heading toward the pool, a deeper, identical set going back the way they came from through those trees."

She nodded to the expanse of wilderness behind him. There was no official trail there. Nothing but miles and miles of open terrain. "We believe the treads are deeper due to the fact he was carrying something heavier than when he entered this area."

"Drennan." Harvey closed his eyes against the very real possibility of losing something he'd never even had. Something he'd fought against from the very beginning. "Who the hell would want to take an assistant medical examiner?"

Ranger Simpson shook his head, crossing his arms over a too large chest more than capable of following through on whatever death threat Ranger Jordan came up with. "The trail has been closed off since you discovered the body yesterday. Whoever it was didn't stick to the public access. They had to have come from backcountry, which means—"

"They were waiting for her." Harvey set sights on the gear Drennan had left behind. The duffel bag, the net. Dr. Yarrow had sent her to collect any evidence that might supply them with the victim's name. "Or someone from the medical examiner's office."

"I have rangers gearing up to search the wilderness, but it'll take time." Simpson shifted on his feet, obviously as eager to get out there as fast as possible, but there were procedures. Protocols and clearances they had to follow. Not to mention, they had no idea what kind of threat they might be facing out there. "Time your ME might not have."

The law enforcement ranger was right. Every second Drennan was out there—alone, potentially injured or worse—was another opportunity her abductor had to ensure Harvey never saw her again. And that…wouldn't happen.

"She's not mine." He'd told Drennan the same thing, hadn't he? That nothing could happen between them. It was too dangerous. A future full of nothing but misery and pain, and yet the thought of watching her move on with someone else… Because she would. She'd meet someone new, someone who didn't come with a whole bunch of red flags enough to stock a carnival. Who wanted to be with her and would have no problem raising another man's child. Because she was worth it. Because her smile—the genuine one she didn't show often—didn't just light up a whole damn room. It lit up pieces of himself Harvey was convinced had been brutalized out of him a long time ago. Who in their right mind wouldn't fall for a woman like that? In the few short hours Drennan had spent with him, she'd believed him to be a better man than he was. Told him he wasn't his father without knowing a single thing about him. Trusted him to take care of her, to take care of their baby, to reveal parts of herself he doubted many knew about.

"Whatever you say, Knight." Simpson eyed him as though he'd backed a feral animal into a corner and was worried for the coming fight.

And, hell. Harvey was feeling more than a little feral at the moment, but he wouldn't let it get to him. Not while she was out here alone. How? How was it possible she'd become central and indispensable in his life in such a short amount of time? He wasn't a backcountry ranger, but his military training supplied enough experience to prepare him for anything. Including the worst-case scenario. "I need a survival pack. Any one of yours will do."

He caught the trepidation in Ranger Simpson's expression. Right before the ranger motioned for his companion to give them some space. "As the head of the law enforcement division, I'm supposed to say it would be better if you waited for the search team."

"I'm not waiting." He didn't give a damn about rank or orders or anything else that might keep him from bringing Drennan and the baby back safely.

"You didn't let me finish." Simpson stepped in close, lowering his voice. "I said I'm *supposed* to say it would be better for you to wait for Search and Rescue and follow protocol. Except I know that look and the thoughts racing through your head. Knowing she's out there, that she needs you, is going to drive you into near madness. Use it. You're the best chance she has of surviving whatever that bastard has planned for her."

Harvey didn't know what to say to that. What to think. The division head of the law enforcement rangers was voluntarily overriding protocols put into place to keep rangers and hikers alike alive. Why? "You sound like you're speaking from experience."

Ranger Simpson glanced over Harvey's head, as though expecting a whole new threat to come crashing through the trees on the other side of the trail. The unfocused blur in his gaze disappeared so fast Harvey wasn't sure if he'd imagined it. "I am."

Ranger Jordan returned, two black backpacks in hand. She tossed one to him, which he caught against his chest, keeping the second pack for herself. "Try to keep up. We've got a lot of ground to cover and not a lot of time to do it in." She cut her attention to her supervisor. "You ready for the hell that's coming your way?"

"I'll cover for you." Simpson uncrossed his arms, facing off with Ranger Jordan, not in the least bit intimidating despite his size. Well, at least not toward the woman less than half his size. "Branch won't know you're going off the reservation, but don't make me explain how you ended up dead. None of us will survive that. Check in every hour with your location. I'll hold him off as long as possible. Channel four."

She gave an exaggerated salute and headed for the trees. "Good luck."

Harvey extended one hand in a peace offering meant to make up for the aggression still rolling through him. "Thank you."

"It's nothing." Simpson took his hand. "I wouldn't wish that madness on my worst enemy, but I wasn't lying when I said it will give you the best chance of recovering Dr. Hawes. She's obviously important to you. Use it."

Harvey didn't feel like explaining to the law enforcement ranger he'd spent the better part of his life doing just that. Using the poison in his blood to survive, to fight back and to carry out his orders had made it easier to call on it each time. Until he wasn't sure he'd ever be rid of that demon he hated so much. And with Drennan... Damn it, Simpson was right. She'd become important, but Harvey never wanted her or the baby to see that part of him. Ever.

He followed in Ranger Jordan's footsteps, nearly in a jog as they met up with the treads she'd identified earlier. Tree branches scratched at his face, neck and forearms as they ran deeper into the backcountry. No landscaped trails. No packed dirt to make the hike easier. Out here, every tree, rock and stream could kill them without warning. The sky remained a crystal clear blue and didn't promise heavy rains that would wash the evidence of Drennan's abduction out. They'd be able to use the tracks to hunt down the man who'd taken Drennan as far as they could. Maybe straight to her.

His blood hummed as they picked up the trail. He clung to the pack's straps to keep it from bouncing, increasing his speed despite nature's determination to slow him down. Drennan had been taken, but he'd get her back. Her and the baby. There was no other option.

His father had taken away everything. Choice, freedom, his sense of worthiness, hope. But the son of a bitch couldn't take the one bright light in his life or the memories that came with it. He couldn't take Drennan.

All Harvey had to do—when, not if, they brought her back—was reach out and claim her for himself. Claim their future. If he was brave enough to take the risk.

Chapter Fifteen

Fatigue was a real bitch.

Every muscle she'd forgotten she owned—all of which she'd memorized during years of medical school—screamed in protest with each step forward. Drennan had lost sight of any hint of a trail an hour ago, heading through miles and miles of tall trees, jagged rocks and the biggest mountains she'd ever seen. More than an hour? Time had no meaning out here in the middle of nowhere. She wasn't sure which direction she'd run, how far or how long. At the time, all she'd been thinking about was escape.

Well, she'd done a hell of a job at that.

She was so turned around, not even a killer could find her out here.

But she didn't dare stop. No matter how hard her stomach twisted with hunger, how blistered her feet or burned her scalp and face. How could she have been so blind? She was lost. In the middle of a national park with no food, no water, no supplies of any kind. She'd never been allowed to join the Girl Scouts or go camping with the other girls in her local church. She didn't know the first thing about wilderness survival, except apparently what not to do.

Sweat had stopped beading at her hairline and the back of her neck and had now gotten trapped in her clothing and gear. Fall brought lower temperatures in most areas of the country. In Ohio this time of year, it'd be on the low end of forties, but Zion itself was so far south, it felt like she'd descended straight into hell.

Tendrils of scrub brush scraped against her waterproof bodysuit, slowing her down. Her gear was weighing her down, draining her of the last remnants of energy. And, thanks to the baby, she didn't have that much to begin with. Not like she'd had any real choice. Running had been the only option. Otherwise, her body might've been the next Harvey found on the trail.

Drennan forced herself to take the next step. And the one after that. But her shoe slipped off the smooth surface of the rock underfoot and jutted to one side. Her whole ankle angled outward, taking her body weight, and she went down. The ground rushed up to meet her, and she threw her bound hands out, doing what she could to avoid face-planting. The impact jarred through her right side. Gravel and dirt embedded in her palms, and pain lightninged into her right hip. She'd managed to absorb most of the fall onto one side instead of her middle, but the agony refused to relent. Insects quieted at the sound of her gasp, throwing her into bone-chilling silence.

If the killer had been following her, he'd most likely heard it.

Peeling herself from the ground, Drennan spit the dirt that'd forced its way into her mouth. Her weight shifted enough to reignite the pain in her side. One of the jagged rocks she'd been trying to avoid had cut through her waterproof suit. No signs of blood. That was good. The chances of infection out here—without a first aid kit—were higher than she wanted to think about, but the injury would slow her down nonetheless.

Hell. She didn't even know where she was going. Which direction she'd started running. She remembered one of the psychologists back in Ohio checking a patient for cognitive issues who'd taken a tumble down Mount Airy—the only real mountain hiking around Cincinnati—telling nurses about the brain's tendency to walk in circles in open spaces. Even with use of all five senses and determination to walk a straight line, humans had a tendency to veer right or left, bringing them in circles. Was that what was happening now? Drennan didn't think so, but it was impossible to tell which rocks she'd already passed, if that was the same tree she'd passed before or if she was putting herself back in range of a man determined to use her to get to his first victim.

She wished Harvey was here.

Dryness coated the back of her throat. The sinking sensation that came with that thought pulsed in time with the beat in her right hip. He'd know what to do. He'd have supplies to help. Because it was literally his job. He'd keep her focused, help her get back to civilization. He'd make her feel safe, as he had that night in the bar. She hadn't told him, but she'd known he would've stepped in if she'd needed help warning off the guy who'd approached her. That was just the kind of man he was. Aware of others. Ready to take action if needed. He was a good man, even if he didn't believe it himself. She didn't know any abusers who would've taken her home to give her time to recover from passing out, and the ones she did would've ensured that a small price was paid later down the line, hanging that favor over her head for eternity. But that wasn't Harvey. He hadn't asked for anything from her in return or gone out of his way to remind her of what he'd done for her benefit, and she...wasn't used to that. Being taken care of by someone else was new, but she liked it. She liked him.

Testing her weight on her ankle, Drennan nearly buckled a second time, catching herself against a tree. Rough bark cut into her palms along with the gravel and dirt already doing their job.

She'd screwed this up so bad. Dr. Yarrow had sent her on a simple assignment. Collect any personal items or evidence their victim might've left behind at the scene to help identify the remains. Instead, she'd gotten herself abducted and now couldn't hike her way out of a wet paper bag. If she didn't come across a ranger or another hiker—something, anything—soon, she would die out here. There was no question. She pressed one hand over the cut in her suit, aggravating the sensitive tissue underneath. Most likely a bone bruise. Not lethal but intense enough to steal her breath. She would live. For a little while longer, anyway.

"It's okay. It's going to be okay. We're going to get out of here." Her hand automatically smoothed across her midsection. Directly above that little bundle of cells with the power to change her life. Had changed her life. Whether that change was for worse or better, she didn't know yet. But she wanted to find out. She wanted the opportunity, to have something that was just hers. A chance to love something unconditionally without the threat of it being taken away or used against her. She wanted a family again.

So she had to stop, to think about this. Continuing on through Zion's backcountry without any supplies or food would only kill her faster. Adrenaline had long worn off. She hadn't registered any hints of the killer for the past hour, though she was sure it wasn't hard for even a novice hunter to follow her tracks at this point. Maybe he'd given up. Decided she wasn't worth it. But that only meant he'd turn his deadly intentions onto Dr. Yarrow. Or Harvey.

Drennan sank back against the tree. Sharp edges dug into

her spine as she slid onto her rear. The sun angled into the canyon, built by two impossibly tall walls of sheer red rock, from her left. Okay. That meant the sun was arching into the west, right? So it was past noon, and she was facing... north. Though there wasn't much to see from her current position. She'd been running east with the sun at her back, she didn't know how long, but it had to have been three hours—maybe four—at least. She'd parked at the visitor's center around ten in the morning and gotten to the upper emerald pool around eleven. She tried recalling the layout of the park from the few times she'd picked up a map and thought about getting out into nature as part of this whole new life thing she had going, but that'd been months ago. It was no use.

Someone had to realize she was missing, right?

Dread pooled at the base of her spine. Dr. Yarrow would clock out precisely at five and most likely assume she'd done the same after collecting whatever evidence she could find from the trail. Or presume she'd needed more recovery time from yesterday due to the pregnancy he was very much aware of. No one had been at the base of the trail or at the scene when she'd arrived. Only signs had designated the Emerald Pools trail closed to the public until the ME's office and the law enforcement rangers had what they needed for the investigation into the victim's death. And Harvey... She hadn't heard from him since she'd walked out his front door last night. She'd wanted to give him time to think about this whole them-having-a-baby-thing, but what she'd really done was run away from potential rejection like the coward her mother had always accused her of being.

Nobody knew she was out here.

Nobody would know she was missing.

And the voicemail her only remaining parent—a woman

who was supposed to love her—had left on her phone the night she'd been driven to the bar replayed in her head. *You're going to die alone. Nobody will care that you're gone. You think you get to be happy by leaving me here all alone? Your father believed in fairy tales, too. Look what happened to him.*

Well, her mom was finally right about something, wasn't she?

She closed her eyes against the vile words stuck in her head, setting her head back against the tree bark. Her mother hadn't always been so bitter. She'd been happy once, in love. Whole. There'd been weekend road trips to the lakes and the movies, big birthday parties and Christmases, family dinners every night and help with homework when she needed it. Smiles and laughter, inside jokes and flirtatious teasing. Drennan had always feigned gagging when her parents had kissed, but deep down, she'd wanted that too someday. Her own family and all the joy that came with it.

But grief did terrible things to the heart and soul.

It corrupted all those happy memories into someone Drennan didn't recognize anymore. Someone who'd turned on her own daughter because the pain had become too much to handle alone.

A twig snapped nearby.

Drennan forced her eyes open despite her body being more than happy to give in to the tug of sleep, and a surge of awareness gave her new energy. Every sense she owned strained for the hint of something tangible to grab onto, but the trees were still. The insects had gone quiet again. Nothing moved. She wanted to trust her senses, but her brain was telling her to get up. To run.

Pressure built in her chest the longer she dared to hold her breath. Putting weight into her left leg, she bit against the flare of discomfort and slid herself back up the tree. The ache was deeper now, swelling through her entire hip, but she couldn't think about that right now.

The hairs on the back of her neck stood on end.

Drennan backed away from the tree she'd collapsed against, blindly navigating into the open. It might not be the smartest move, but she'd have a much better chance of running without having to maneuver through packed trees or going too far off course.

Keeping her gaze on the surrounding wilderness, she let the tension bleed out of her shoulders. There wasn't anyone there. Just a falling branch or—

"Hello, Dr. Hawes." Muscled arms pulled her against a wall of human granite. Her scream cut off with a slap of her attacker's hand over her mouth. "I've been looking for you."

Chapter Sixteen

They'd lost the tracks.

Harvey's legs threatened to give out from under him, the muscles along the backs screaming for relief, but he only pushed himself harder. Forced himself to take that next step and the one after it. It was all he could focus on to keep himself from spiraling down into raw desperation. Drennan was out here. She'd been abducted—his baby had been abducted—and he and Ranger Jordan were her only hope of bringing her back. The boot treads they'd followed ended at a stream crossing that branched off the upper emerald pool. Harvey had searched every inch of that riverbed, but the tracks had simply disappeared.

His blood thundered—too hot—in his veins. "They couldn't have just vanished."

"I've searched at least a hundred feet downstream and back on both sides. The treads don't reappear." Ranger Jordan hauled her pack higher up her back by the straps. "We're assuming these tracks belong to Drennan's kidnapper, and if that's the case, I think we're dealing with someone knowledgeable of wilderness survival and hunting."

Understanding hit as Harvey studied the stream. It wasn't any deeper than a few inches with smooth stones staring up through clear moving water. Unhurried and pristine this deep into the park. It wasn't until the stream reached the Emerald Pools that algae and a whole lot of other organisms latched on. But here, it was perfect with the whisper of the wind off the cliffs, the birds and insects trilling nearby and sun glinting off the surface of the water. He shook his head. "He moved into the stream to make sure we couldn't gauge which direction he'd gone."

"Chances are he hasn't double backed toward the pools, but that still leaves us with two separate directions to search along the stream." Ranger Jordan twisted her head to one side, as though looking for the right answer, and her hot pink kerchief dipped down her neck, revealing the thick, jagged scar beneath. "If our guy still has Dr. Hawes, he'll be moving more slowly, maybe even stop somewhere out of the way to camp depending on his ability to make her comply. Search and Rescue will have arrived on the scene by now. They'll have more manpower and search capacity than us running up and down this riverbed blind. We should wait."

Harvey wanted to ask about the scar, wanted to know who'd done something so horrific to her and if they'd suffered, but now wasn't the time. As much as he didn't know about Drennan and her outdoor experience, the pregnancy and this heat would take more out of her than she could spare to fight back. Her attacker would use the exhaustion against her and get the upper hand, and Harvey was betting she hadn't brought supplies other than those the law enforcement rangers had recovered at the upper pool. He checked his watch. They'd already been out here for close to an hour and a half with no additional signs of where she'd been taken.

She could be anywhere. In any kind of condition.

He swiped sweat from his brow, his clothes sticking to him with layers of sweat and salt. Harvey shook his head.

He'd had plenty of water. Anything he had left would be reserved for Drennan when he found her. "She doesn't have that kind of time. We can't search this entire river one direction at a time. We need to split up. You head east. I'll head west. Stick to the streambed, call in anything you find on the radio."

Every cell in his body honed in on that one purpose. To find Drennan. Now. It latched on to every thought and drove the lactic acid buildup in his muscles to a dull sting. He'd already failed her enough to haunt him for the rest of his life. He couldn't leave her out here to fight alone.

Ranger Jordan stepped in, dragging her water bottle from her pack and sucking down a strong mouthful before returning it to the compartment at the side of her bag. "Trail rangers aren't trained to confront a suspect. I am, and I'm armed. We don't know who's behind Dr. Hawes's abduction or if he's carrying a weapon. It's enough we have one missing person. We can't have you disappear on top of that."

"You're right. Trail rangers aren't trained to confront suspects, but soldiers are." That training was already taking hold. Sinking deep into his nervous system. Calming his heart rate and spreading a numbness he hadn't let himself feel in a long time. It was the same kind of numbness his father sank into right before the son of a bitch exploded. The calm before the storm, but Harvey was willing to do whatever—to become whatever—he needed to find Drennan. To bring her back alive. "Don't worry about me. If splitting up comes back on you, tell Simpson it was my idea, and you tried to stop me."

He turned west, keeping to the riverbed as Drennan's abductor would. No longer looking to escape the predator hiding under his skin. He wanted it right at the surface. Whoever'd taken Drennan had a few tricks up his sleeves.

Water lapped around his boots, quiet and unchallenged, as he followed the stream. He didn't want to give away his presence too soon, not knowing how a scared animal would react to surprise. He couldn't risk the kidnapper deciding Drennan wasn't worth the effort and doing something rash. That familiar heat he'd run from most of his life built with every yard gained, his senses tapped out. The birds had quieted with his passing, as though sensing an apex predator had neared. Harvey didn't have any weapons. He didn't need them, but that didn't mean whoever had abducted Drennan had the same beliefs. And if she was hurt… He stopped the growl rumbling through his chest. He couldn't think about that right now.

He'd consciously made decisions in exact opposition to his father over and over. Anger management, self-help books, therapy, keeping his emotions under control in even the most dire situations, strict routines, isolating himself to protect others. The women he'd been with over the years had been nothing more than passing interests. Purely physical. They'd known there wouldn't be anything more once they parted ways. No dates or vacations. No meeting the parents or talk of the future. He'd done whatever he had to in order to keep himself from becoming the man he hated most, the man who'd ultimately killed Harvey's mother because he'd been too weak to control himself.

And it'd been enough. For a while.

Right up until two months ago when he'd seen her from across the bar and recognized the same haunted look in Drennan's eyes that stared back at him from the mirror every morning. And he'd wanted her. More than he'd wanted anyone or anything in his life. He'd wanted to make the shadows in her pretty green eyes fade, to know who or what had put them there and to make sure they never touched her again. And he had. For a little while at least. And she'd done the same for him. He'd looked in the mirror the next morning and almost hadn't recognized himself. The heaviness that'd aged him in a matter of days after learning about his father's death had lifted. His gaze had been brighter, some color had come back into his face, but more, something inside had shifted. Released to the point he felt as though he could breathe for the first time in years.

Drennan had done that. And he'd gone and thrown that gift back in her face when she'd told him she was pregnant. What would his father have done? Hell, his dad would've made sure that child—and the woman carrying it—suffered. That they both broke under the sick bastard's influence until they were just as miserable as Harvey and his mother.

But he wasn't his father. He didn't get his rocks off at a woman crying at his feet or a child stepping in front of its mother to protect her. He didn't enjoy putting others' lives at risk or seeing how little it took to manipulate people into fearing him. He didn't want any of that, and he sure as hell wouldn't ever lay his hands on an innocent woman or their child.

Harvey wasn't that man, and Drennan... She was everything he'd ever wanted. She was the dream he'd dared to envision all those times he'd let himself think of the future, of escape, of being anywhere but stuck under his father's thumb. She was strong and caring with a smile that could knock him off balance. A woman who enjoyed giving pleasure as much as she enjoyed experiencing it and went out of her way to stand up for herself and the people she cared about. Drennan Hawes was intelligent beyond belief with a sharp tongue that could eviscerate him in a single sentence while putting other people ahead of herself. Dependable and kind and soothing in a way he'd never experienced to the point she risked burning herself out just to make sure everyone else had what they needed.

A woman like that needed someone who would step in and put her first. A protector to make sure she didn't give too much of herself, that she was getting enough to eat and reminding her to go take a bath or a nap when things got to be too heavy for her to carry alone. And, damn, Harvey found himself wanting to be that guy. He needed to be that for her and for the baby to destroy the sins of his father, but he had to find her first.

Pressure wedged between his shoulder blades. Slowing to a stop right there in the middle of the stream, he listened to his surroundings for a series of breaths. His fingers twitched at his side. He hadn't held a gun in a long time, but something about being watched from behind brought back the need for the comfort warm steel provided. Nothing had changed. Birds still flew overhead. The stream hadn't altered course apart from around his boots. He saw nothing to get his defenses raised, but his instincts told him he wasn't alone. Harvey craned his chin over one shoulder. There. Movement in the corner of his vision, behind the copse of trees to his right. "You take her?"

"Gotta say, she didn't make it easy." That dark outline keeping to the trees shifted. "But if I'm being honest, I'm surprised you're here alone. Figured SAR would be all up my ass on this one, but NPS has so much red tape to cut through, it's a wonder anything gets done around here."

SAR. NPS. That was a whole lot of acronyms for a random man kidnapping a medical examiner. Tension bled into Harvey's shoulders. Drennan had fought back, but how much had the son of a bitch made her pay for that choice? He didn't recognize the owner of the voice as he faced the threat head-on. "Where is she?"

"Safe. For now. And you. I know who you are, Ranger Knight." Dress slacks that'd lost their clean lines hung off the man's waist. He was tall, maybe taller than Harvey, but not as developed in other areas. His T-shirt was too tight and darkened with sweat around the collar and under his arms, and Harvey just didn't like the look of his face with all that gray beard growth and slicked-back hair. Like the guy couldn't stop running his hands through it. Drennan's abductor reached behind him, pulling a gun. Taking aim at Harvey as he descended the slight dip toward the stream. In a matter of feet, the gun barrel pressed into Harvey's chest. "Dr. Hawes is going to run a little errand for me. Until I'm done with her, I suggest you turn around and walk back the way you came."

Harvey scanned the trees, searching for something—anything—that could lead him to Drennan. "You know who I am? My background?"

The bastard nodded.

"Then you know you have exactly three seconds to put the gun down and bring me Drennan." Harvey had had plenty of weapons pointed at and used against him. He was prepared for whatever came next. "One. Two."

He didn't wait. Harvey slammed his palm over the barrel of the weapon and ripped the gun free of its owner. Turning it back around, he dropped the magazine and cleared the chamber, tossing the gun a few feet away. "Three."

"I think I'm going to like facing off with you, Ranger Knight." Hands raised, the abductor smiled as he backed up the incline and slightly to the left. The bastard was running. "But it seems today is not that day."

In seconds, the abductor had disappeared over the sharp incline leading into deeper backcountry, leaving Harvey alone.

"Drennan!" He hauled himself up the easy hill and into the trees, his chest tight and pressurized. "Dren—"

Soft curves overrun by navy-blue gear and long hair sticking to bark materialized at the base of a tree. Her arms had been secured behind her, her chin nearly to her chest with her legs splayed in front of her. Alive. She had to be alive.

His heart threatened to break his rib cage as he charged the tree and pulled a blade from his pack. Cutting through the rope binding her wrists around the tree, he caught her upper body from collapsing forward. "Drennan, open your eyes."

Unfocused eyes the color of the water in the Emerald Pools flickered open. Her gaze settled on him, and the invisible monster beneath his skin curled up and lay down for the first time…ever. Her voice broke. "You're not supposed to be here."

She slipped back into unconsciousness.

Chapter Seventeen

The curtain cutting her off from the rest of the ER snapped back.

"I'm getting tired of seeing you in a hospital bed." Cassidy brought her attention up from her clipboard and used her foot to drag the bedside stool behind her. There seemed to be a few more lines around her friend's eyes and mouth as she looked Drennan over, and a similar heaviness responded in Drennan's chest.

She'd been abducted. Could've died if it hadn't been for Harvey. Between learning of the pregnancy, coming to terms with Harvey's self-imposed banishment in hers and the baby's lives and getting knocked unconscious by the man who obviously had no qualms when it came to killing a woman, she could only shove the terror she'd felt—and still felt—down deep where it would never see the light of day again.

"You and me both." Her gear and clothing had been confiscated as evidence by Zion's law enforcement rangers. She'd been offered a set of scrubs by one of the nurses who'd learned she used to be an ER physician, and it'd taken much longer than it should have to change. Every major muscle in her body burned in protest of movement until she'd given up trying to do anything herself and finally asked the nurse to help get some pants on. The seafoam green did nothing to hide the purple and blue blotches around her wrists and along one side of her face. Exhaustion had been trying to pull her under since Harvey had carried her out of the backcountry and down the trail as she'd clung to him like a koala bear, but she wouldn't give in. Not until she knew the baby was okay. "Tell me I don't look like a piece of bruised fruit."

"I'm not comfortable lying to patients." Cassidy took a seat on that rolling stool and got up close and personal with a penlight aimed directly at Drennan's face. "You know the drill."

Pain arched through her face and deep into her brain at the sudden brightness. Drennan followed the penlight as best she could.

Cassidy watched her pupils for the automatic response to light stimulant, but didn't give anything away in her expression. "Headache?"

"Yes." There was no way she could deny it at this point. Every change in sound or light had punctured her brain as thoroughly as an ice pick to the skull. It'd been a miracle the hit she'd taken to the back of the head hadn't killed her. Drennan didn't let herself touch the soft swell pulsing in time to her heartbeat. The stitches were fresh, and, if she was being honest, she wasn't up for another round of searing agony.

"Blurry vision?" Her friend clicked the light off—thank goodness—and made a quick note in the chart with the other end of her pen. Dry, cracked skin told of countless rounds of hand washing, disinfectant and latex gloves while Cassidy's sunken cheeks testified to long hours, late nights and very little sleep. Was that why their conversation felt so forced?

It took more energy than Drennan had to spare not to demand her friend look at her like a person and not just another patient. To see her. "Not at the moment."

"Hallucinations?" Cassidy ticked off another box on the head trauma questionnaire while everything inside of Drennan went cold.

Her exhale sounded overly loud in the small space, considering the ER was currently packed to the brim with patients, darting nurses and overworked techs. "Yes. I thought my friend walked in here, but it turns out she's been replaced by a pod person."

Cassidy raised a perfectly arched brow. Another second passed before the ice melted from her expression and a soft smile curled at one corner of her mouth. This was the woman who'd jumped to help at the first sign Drennan wasn't okay. The one who'd gone out of her way to recommend her for a job without question, to give her that push she needed to escape Ohio and finally take control of her life. "This is serious, Drennan. You were abducted. You...you could've died out there. I know you're used to having to take care of everyone else over yourself, but I need you to put yourself first for once. For the people who care about you."

Thickness coated the sides of Drennan's throat. She didn't want to acknowledge how much those words meant to her—that someone cared about her—because doing so meant acknowledging how much all the other words hurt. The ones that said her own mother had wished Drennan had been the one to die instead of her father in that accident, that having children had been a mistake or that she was responsible for all the misery in her mom's life. "Where is Harvey?"

"Your ranger was about to bring down the entire building pacing the ER, so I sent him to the cafeteria to get you something to eat for when you woke up. I have a feeling holding still isn't in his repertoire." Cassidy set the clipboard, the pen and the concussion questionnaire aside, that serious look back in her eyes. "You were unconscious for about three hours after he brought you in. The blunt force to the back of your head resulted in a concussion. Any harder, and you wouldn't be here."

She'd known that. How close she'd come, but her abductor had wanted her incapacitated to get what he wanted. Not dead. Though she wouldn't be thanking him anytime soon.

"He's not my ranger." Another burst of pain speared through her head. Dragging one hand across her forehead, she dug her thumb into her eye to relieve the pressure.

"Really? Because you were pretty out of it, but it took two of us to pry you off of him." Cassidy's smile widened. "I think you tore his shirt."

"Must've been the trauma." Because she sure as hell wouldn't cling to Harvey Knight for any other reason. He'd made his intentions with her and the baby clear, and she was nothing if not a champion for boundary setting. No matter how much she wanted things to be different between them, she couldn't live in another one-sided relationship. Getting out of the last one had nearly destroyed her. "I take it you've already done a CT scan to discount any brain bleeds, or I wouldn't be recovering in the ER." Her fingers ached as though she'd been clenching something for days rather than the past few minutes of keeping her hands busy with the seams of the sheets. "I'd like an ultrasound to check on the baby."

"Already ordered. The ob-gyn should be down in a few minutes to take a look." The stool gave a high-pitched squeak as Cassidy shoved back. "Do you remember if you suffered any trauma to your torso or belly?"

Drennan smoothed her hands down her front, resting them against her lower half as if she could add some semblance of protection. Which was ridiculous. She'd only just found out she was pregnant yesterday. She shouldn't have this level of…attachment yet, but the small bundle of cells had become her entire world overnight. She'd do anything to keep it. "Uh, no. I'm not sore or bruised that I can tell. I don't think he… I don't think things got that far."

But they could have. Her attempt to protect Dr. Yarrow and Harvey had nearly gotten her killed. It'd been reckless and a choice she would probably make a second time, but she couldn't just think about herself anymore.

A shiver danced across her shoulders as a man-shaped outline materialized at the foot of her bed. Carrying a tray of food. Her breath crushed from her chest at the sight of his wrinkled uniform shirt and slacks. Dark hair had escaped its normal styling, an equally frantic look in his gaze.

"Hi." Her voice barely carried through the small, private section the curtain provided in the bustling ER, but Harvey seemed to straighten at the sound. Images of the last time she'd talked with him flashed in rapid succession—her admission to wanting more between them, him revealing the truth about his father, declining his financial support for the baby. She'd left him standing in the middle of his living room, determined to do this on her own. But she would've died if it hadn't been for him. She knew that now. That her abductor had wanted her for a very specific reason and that when he was finished with her, she most likely would've ended up face down in a pool of water just like his last victim.

"Hey." That single word sounded as though it'd been pulled over hot coals. Lifting the tray of food, he cut his attention to Cassidy and back. "Figured you'd be hungry when you woke up."

"You mean your trip to the cafeteria didn't have anything to do with the fact Cassidy was going to call security on you if you didn't stop pacing like a caged animal?" She had just enough energy to smile, and Harvey seemed to go completely still.

His mouth turned up at the corners, sucking the oxygen from her chest. He had a dimple. To the right of his mouth, barely visible through the layers of beard growth, but it was there. She'd seen it. "That might've had something to do with it."

"Thank you." Drennan tried to sit higher in bed.

"I'll let your ob-gyn know you're awake and check back on you soon." Cassidy made herself scarce by dipping out another opening in the curtain, and the room suddenly felt so much smaller than a moment ago.

Harvey rounded the bed, taking up position on the stool her friend had vacated. "I wasn't sure what you liked, so I got a little bit of everything."

"I'll take chocolate-covered ants at this point, I'm so hungry." She grabbed both edges of the tray and settled it across her lap. He'd brought her a hamburger, some pasta, what looked like a tuna fish sandwich and a big fat slice of cheesecake. Her mouth watered at the sight of all those plump cherries in syrup he'd added. Yeah. She went for the cheesecake, almost willing to forgo manners and shove the entire thing in her mouth.

His laugh rumbled through the small space and notched her heart rate up higher, which registered on the stupid echocardiogram machine to her right. Great. She wasn't just splayed across this damn hospital bed—in one of the most vulnerable positions—but now her body's reactions would be loud enough for all to hear. "The cheesecake was actually for me."

Drennan paused with the fork heavy with that first bite halfway to her mouth. Disappointment lapped at her fragile steady state. A statement like that had once kicked her need for peace and survival into high alert. A past version of herself would've instantly dropped the fork and offered it back, but she'd earned this cheesecake, damn it. And she wanted it more than anything. "Don't you dare take food from a pregnant woman."

"Wouldn't dream of it." He settled back in the stool as easily as though it had a back support, crossing his feet at the ankles and his arms over his impressive chest. Harvey didn't say anything, simply studied her as though taking his eyes off her would hurt, and she…she didn't know what to do with that.

And she didn't want to know what he thought about having to come to her rescue. Didn't want to know if he regretted getting mixed up with her. He hadn't planned on getting involved in her life at all, still didn't want anything to do with her or the baby beyond financial obligation, and right then, she was sure he saw a woman so desperate for affection that she would seek it from someone who didn't even want friendship between them. And he wouldn't be wrong, would he?

"You don't have to be here." That first bite of creamy filling and the tart burst of cherries nearly dragged a moan from her throat, but the flood of sugar wasn't enough to drown out the chaotic self-deprecating thoughts. "I know you have other places you'd rather be."

"Dr. Yarrow called with an update on the victim we pulled from the emerald pool. She was pregnant, a few weeks ahead of you." Drennan flinched as though he'd physically struck her. His voice dipped into dangerous territory, raising the hairs on the back of her neck. "So while I might have other places to be, Drennan, I'm not going anywhere."

Chapter Eighteen

"You didn't have to drive me home." Drennan shoved her key into the dead bolt slot and twisted the doorknob open. She walked straight into a too-small box that smelled of her. Something light and citrus, like a lemon orchard in the spring.

It drove deep into Harvey's lungs and set up residence in the fibers of his cells. Like she had over the course of the past few days. The hospital had given in to his demand to keep her overnight for observation, but there were limits on how long patients could remain in the ER. While he'd stepped out of the curtained section to give Drennan some privacy, the ob-gyn had assured them the baby hadn't suffered any damage from the abduction. Scanning the small box she called an apartment, Harvey memorized the layout. Living room front and center, the galley-style kitchen and dining space directly ahead, one bedroom off to the left. Probably with an attached bathroom. "What part of 'I'm not going anywhere' didn't you understand?"

"The part where you couldn't run fast enough in the other direction when I told you I was pregnant." She set her keys on the scratched black round dining table. The thing looked like it'd been spray-painted at one point, with natural wood scars peeking through. Worn at one edge where she most likely sat to eat every day. In fact, every piece of furniture in the place looked as though it'd been pulled straight from a dumpster or a thrift store, but all of it was clean. Odd. She'd been a trauma surgeon. She must've made good money before taking up a position as an assistant medical examiner. So either she preferred old furniture or she didn't have the funds to buy new. Maybe she didn't care.

He'd always been able to tell a lot by someone's home. What kind of person they were. Sentimental or functional, social or isolated, relationship focused or independent, habits, routines. Some things were harder to discern, and he was having a hell of a time holding himself back from asking the thousand questions on his mind. Like why she'd left a stable career to move into the middle of nowhere Utah to cut up dead people.

Knickknacks and books peppered the bookshelf set up on the other side of the TV, more books than personal trinkets. She was a reader, but Harvey had already known that. She was wicked intelligent with a medical background. A quick glimpse at the titles told him they were mostly crime thrillers and a handful of romances. All with cracks down their spines and flawed covers, to the point he was willing to bet these particular books were comfort reads. He found himself wondering which one would offer her some semblance of peace tonight.

"Yeah, well, things have changed, haven't they?" He couldn't explain the shift as he navigated around the once light sectional, the part of him that'd dreaded the idea of leaving her alone in that hospital bed. The man who'd abducted her had wilderness experience and used acronyms like a law enforcement official. This case... It was coming back on her. They'd both given a description of her abductor, but without the victim's identity, it would be hard to narrow down the man who'd killed her. He didn't like the statistics, but over 80 percent of women were killed by someone they knew. That was where they needed to start. If they were really lucky, the weapon he'd taken off her abductor would lead back to a name, but the State of Utah didn't require gun registration. Hell, if they could find something identifying the remains at the scene, they could get ahead of this, but the superintendent was ordering the Emerald Pools trail reopened despite the fact any evidence of their victim's death might be contaminated by the public. Drennan's gear had been left behind at the scene, but there'd been no sign of any of the victim's personal effects. Had the killer been there to get to them before she did?

But Drennan was right. He'd made his intentions concerning her and the baby clear, but that was before he'd learned someone had targeted her, and through her, his baby. That the son of a bitch had hurt her. "Besides, your doctor said I needed to keep an eye on you due to the hit you took to the back of your head."

"Of course she did." Drennan moved back into the living room, looking as antsy as he felt inside. He wasn't great at standing still. Being busy meant distracting himself from the buzz of thoughts he didn't want to take too close a look at. The military had been good for that. He'd been told when to eat, sleep and take a leak and where to be 24-7, and discharge had been a bigger shock than he'd expected. Folding her arms across her chest, she showed off the scrapes and bruises marring her forearms. "Well, I have a medical license. I think I am more than capable of taking care of myself."

Harvey studied her—really looked at her—recognizing that all-too-familiar pain in her eyes he'd gravitated to the night they'd met, and his heart stuttered at the rawness. "You don't like it when other people try to take care of you, do you?"

Her chin notched a few centimeters higher, her shoulders pulling back ever so slightly. It wasn't a big change in her posture, but one he'd seen all the same. Like every move she made tugged on some invisible connection between them and got him to pay closer attention. She bit her bottom lip, hard enough that blood beaded quickly. "I never said that."

He was moving before he consciously realized he'd started closing the distance between them. "You didn't have to. The second you woke up in my house yesterday, you were trying to leave. Like your being there was some great burden, even though I never gave you that impression. It's more than not liking the attention, though, isn't it?"

He wasn't sure why he was pushing other than maybe her answer might provide insight he'd been looking for his entire life. Why, despite years of no contact and freedom and his father being buried six feet underground, he couldn't seem to let go of the past. The one thing that would free him, and the one thing that would damn him at the same time.

Drennan didn't answer for a series of breaths. She didn't have any reason to trust him, but he felt more than saw the responding exhaustion filter into her expression. Like she simply didn't have the energy to hide. "I don't want to owe them anything, and I especially don't want to be in debt to you."

"What makes you think you owe me anything?" Instinct had him closing those last few feet separating them. "I didn't bring you back to my house or come after you in those woods to collect some kind of debt."

Her laugh surprised him, though it lacked the key ingredient of humor. "No. Just out of obligation, right?"

Harvey pulled up short. "Obligation?"

"Can you really tell me you would've done those things if I wasn't pregnant with your baby?" Her voice had lost some of its steadiness, the question a mere whisper to the emotion breaking her words. "Would you have stuck around the clinic both times if I hadn't told you? Would you be here now, making sure there's no one waiting in the apartment for me?"

He...he didn't know the answer to that. He knew what his father would've done, and hell, Harvey had gone out of his way to make sure he never followed in that bastard's footsteps. "I was attracted to you before you told me you were pregnant."

She pressed her lips together in a thin line. "That's not an answer, and, you know what? You don't owe me any kind of explanation or justification. I understand you can't help but want to protect your baby, really. But you asked why I can't stand the thought of someone else taking care of me? It's because admitting I need help or exposing what's important to me has always been used as a bargaining chip or to hold over my head, and I will never let someone have that kind of power over me again. Even the father of my child."

Harvey locked down the instant urge to argue with her logic, but he couldn't. She was right. He wouldn't have stayed at the clinic for any other woman he'd spent one night with. And he'd leave the search for her abductor to the law enforcement officers or Springdale police. But with Drennan... She brought out a protective streak he couldn't explain. He'd sworn not to put anyone's life in danger by getting close, but the baby connected them in a way he'd never expected to be linked to another human being. In less than forty-eight hours, it'd altered the very cells that made him who he was, had him doubting every decision he'd made up to this point in his life. That thought should've scared the crap out of him, but it didn't. Because in those hours where he'd imagined finding Drennan dead in those woods... Those had been the worst hours of his life. Hard as it was to admit to himself, losing her and the baby would've ripped him apart. "Why are you here, Drennan?"

Her name had never felt more right on his tongue, said like a prayer. Did she feel it? In the span of two days the woman had learned she was pregnant, passed out in the park, held her own against his stubborn ass and survived an abduction. She was strong, stronger than him. Fierce and ready to go toe to toe with anyone who dared talk down to her, but that kind of strength wasn't born. It was earned. "Why go from working as an emergency surgeon to a medical examiner in the middle of nowhere?"

Her throat worked on a swallow. Drennan took a step back, but she didn't make it far, her lower back connecting with one of her dining room chairs. "It's impossible to heal in the place you're being broken over and over."

Every muscle in his body tensed at the hurt in those words, at the fact that someone had taken this beautiful woman and been so careless. He wanted them to hurt just as much, if not more, to destroy them.

"It's hard to see the truth while you're stuck in the cycle." Drennan gazed at something over his shoulder, not really seeing him. "You're attached to people who have been distant with you. You're paying attention to people who ignore you. You make time for people who are too busy for you. You care about people who don't remember that you exist unless they need something. And even when you do whatever is asked of you, it's not enough. It's never enough, and it doesn't change anything. Years of wanting them to just... see you. Acknowledge that you're just as important to them as they are to you. You get your hopes up at the smallest hint of affection one minute, but then it's ripped right out from under you the next. Every time it breaks off something inside of you. Until there's nothing left. I was dying, and I didn't even know it. So I left."

Tears glistened in her eyes, and something simply *broke* inside of him. Because he'd been in that cycle, too, had watched his mother go through it countless times. Beatings one night and flowers the next. Fancy dinners for an anniversary followed up by a trip to the emergency room. Harvey had seen through the ploys to get him to cooperate, but his mom... She'd never had the chance. It was psychological warfare of the cruelest kind. And somehow Drennan had survived.

"That night at the bar, I just wanted to feel important to someone. To be someone's choice." Oh, hell. She hadn't wanted financial support for the baby from him. She'd wanted a real connection. She'd wanted someone to choose her for more than what she could do for them. Or the baby she carried. "And you offered me your hand with that charming smile, and I felt like the world wasn't burning around me anymore."

Harvey couldn't keep his distance anymore. Sliding his hands up her arms, he mapped the bruises and scrapes by touch, then tipped her chin enough to meet her gaze. "You're important to me, Drennan."

Her eyes snapped to his. "You're just saying that because—"

"No. Not because of the baby. You." He shook his head, having his answer right then and there. He would've stayed in that clinic to make sure she was okay. He would've gone into those woods without a second thought to bring her back. "You changed me that night, Drennan. For the first time in years, I didn't want to be numb anymore."

He traced his thumb along her bottom lip, then devoured her mouth with his.

Chapter Nineteen

This kiss felt...different.

And that was a very bad thing.

A dangerous fire threatened to burst from beneath her skin as Harvey's mouth moved in a tantalizing rhythm over hers. She'd walked through some fires in her life, but this... She wasn't sure she could survive this. Right here, right now, nothing that'd happened between them existed. It was as though this was the first time, when all she could think about was that she wouldn't be able to take her next breath unless he touched her. All consuming, intense, insane.

Harvey kissed her like a man starved. Her mouth, down her neck, over her collarbone. His fingers threaded into her hair and pulled, arching her neck back for better access. Her lower back pressed into the dining room chair, but the pain never came. He didn't let it touch her as he slid one hand between her and the hardwood. He moved back to her mouth and kissed her. He kept on kissing her until Drennan feared she'd never recover from the deep, hot licks along the inside of her mouth. Her legs shook as her insides ached. He snaked his arm around her posterior rib cage, and it wasn't until then that she realized just how much bigger he was compared to her. That he could hurt her in a heartbeat.

But Harvey wouldn't ever hurt her.

He wasn't the man he feared becoming. That much was clear in the limited interactions they'd shared.

And she couldn't turn away from this. Drennan dug her fingernails into his back, most assuredly leaving marks, but she needed to get closer. To pull him into her. Because no matter how many times she reminded herself she'd done the right thing in giving herself up to her abductor in place of Dr. Yarrow or Harvey, she couldn't ignore the thick, oily terror that coated her insides. A shadow that pulsed with fear anytime Harvey got too far away. The killer had threatened her boss and the father of her child if he couldn't get what he wanted from her. But, here, in his arms, those threats couldn't dig its claws in as deep. With him, she could forget about the way her abductor had looked at her as though she was nothing more than a means to an end. She could forget that same look on her mother's face and the pure vitriol saved in the form of voicemails on her phone.

Harvey framed one hand against her jaw, smoothing his thumb along the curve and down the front of her throat. His breathing had reached chaotic levels—matching hers—and she liked it. She liked that she'd had this effect on him, that of everything he'd survived, everything he'd been through and done, she had the power to push him to his limits.

"Bedroom."

Drennan could only nod as he pulled her back against his chest, his mouth seeking hers once more. They walked as one, him backing toward her bedroom door, her too out of her mind to warn him to watch out for the corner of the photograph she'd hung only a couple weeks ago.

His shoulder skimmed the frame and sent it rocking then to the floor. Plastic, a generic photograph of flowers and brushed metal warped, taking out a chunk of one of the baseboards on impact. Hands gripped on her waist, Harvey didn't break his hold as he helped her maneuver around the mess. "I can fix that."

"I don't care." She'd gone too long without his mouth on hers. He could destroy every single piece of furniture in this place and she wouldn't bat an eye as long as she could hold on to this feeling. Hold on to him. For however long he gave her. Maybe just tonight. Maybe longer. Because she believed him after she'd told him about the pregnancy. Harvey didn't want to be a father. His past had contorted the meaning into something perverse and threatening, and there was nothing she could say to rewrite that innate belief he held on to. He wouldn't let himself get close to anyone. She didn't question that, she'd seen that fear in his expression. So she would have this. She'd live in the now, stop trying to shape the future and remind herself she wasn't responsible for making other people happy as she'd been taught nearly her whole life. His fingertips dug into the soft curve of her hips, and Drennan arched into him. "Please."

She didn't know what she was begging for. Only that he was the only one who could meet the out-of-control need.

Guiding her over the threshold of her bedroom door, Harvey swung her around, easing her onto the bed. Gaze locked on her. He swept his fingers over her face and set a strand of hair behind her ear. "You're beautiful, you know that? You're strong and patient and you give a damn about other people." His voice lowered to a whisper. "If anyone is having my baby, I'm glad it's you."

Unfiltered heat seared through her veins. She couldn't remember the last time someone had complimented her. It seemed like an easy thing, but Harvey proved his earlier point when he looked at her like this. Like she was important. "You're just saying that to get me back into bed."

His laugh charged through him. The effect lit up something inside of her she hadn't allowed herself to feel in years, something bright and breathtaking and light. Harvey twisted his head to one side, setting his temple against her chin, then shifted his weight into his elbows on either side of her head. "You know me so well, but as much as I'm looking forward to a second time around with you, you should rest."

Threading her fingers into his hair, Drennan knew he was right. She'd survived her initial abduction, but the hit to her head would likely trigger side effects if she overdid it. Not to mention the drain of growing an entire human being. But his weight had settled more of that oily terror trying to bubble its way to the surface, and she wasn't ready to let that go. She skimmed her fingertips over his jaw, through his beard and back, memorizing everything she could about this moment. Where they were just Drennan and Harvey. No homicide, no victim, no jobs or past. Two people who had somehow found a way to each other, where the outside world didn't exist and there were no expectations. "Will you stay with me?"

"I told you I'm not going anywhere." Harvey slid down her front toward the end of the bed. "Get some sleep, Drennan. I'll keep you safe."

She tightened her hold on him, and Harvey seemed to freeze under her touch. "Here. Stay here. With me. Please."

He didn't move, didn't even breathe as far as she could tell. One second. Two. He was going to do the right thing. He was going to tell her sleeping in the same bed wasn't a good idea, and the disappointment would hurt, but she would pretend it didn't. She'd survived worse, right? Harvey slipped one hand along her rib cage. "Yeah. I can stay if that will make you feel better."

It would. More than he'd ever know, but she'd keep that small slice of truth to herself. Navigating farther up the bed,

Drennan sank into the pillows, suddenly more exhausted as desire drained. Her eyes grew heavy, each blink becoming harder to get through. "Thank you."

"You don't have to thank me for that." Strong fingers curved around her ankle as he pulled one of her shoes off and dropped it to the floor, then the other. The act was simple enough but meant the world.

Nobody cooked for her. Nobody cleaned for her. Nobody made her meals or did her laundry. Nobody from her past life had reached out to check in, to make sure she was okay. Nobody catered to her, period, she was always the one others relied on to help them through. Her entire life, she'd stepped up to take care of everyone else, even dedicated her entire adult life to helping others as a trauma surgeon, in hopes just one person—someone, *anyone*—would return the favor. That step had slowly become an expectation, then a demand. But she'd held on to that hope. Days. Months. Years. Until it'd finally been crushed from her very being.

Except now Harvey had set his hand on her hip, rolling her onto her front so he could drag the blankets out from underneath her and settle them over her frame. The bed dipped with his added weight as he maneuvered in behind her, his front pressed against her back, and her entire body stiffened at the prospect of falling asleep with someone else beside her. She'd never done that before. Past boyfriends hadn't minded. They latched on to the casual emotional distance she'd kept between them, because sixty-hour workweeks didn't allow for anything more. But the heat sinking through her bruised skin now—Harvey's body heat—and into the dull aches and sore muscles, felt better than she'd ever expected. Like slipping into a warm bath or getting lost in her favorite comfort read. It felt like being at home. Soft and familiar and safe.

"Is this okay?" Harvey's exhales skimmed over the back of her neck. Shifting, he slipped one hand over her hip, then flat against her belly. Over where their baby grew. His other arm wedged beneath her pillow, caging her against him, but this cage wasn't meant to trap her.

Unable to form a single answer, Drennan nodded. They'd been intimate together. Hell, they'd conceived a baby together, however accidentally, but this...this superseded casual. This was *more*, and that was a very dangerous place to be. Because she wanted more. With him, for them. She wanted the family dinners and the trips into Zion with the baby strapped to his back. She wanted the ice cream weekends and petty arguments about money and where to go on vacation. For the first time in longer than she cared to admit, she *wanted*. Enough that the realization sucked the breath straight out of her lungs. But the shock that really threatened to unease her? She was allowed to want. There wasn't anyone who would stop her. No one to guilt her into giving up that dream that would take her from that neat little nurturer package she'd become over the years. No one to shame her for daring to imagine a different life. She was free to want Harvey, to want a family of her own.

"You okay?" His thumb circled around her belly button. Once. Twice. She lost count of the passes he made, starting small then spreading out wider until he brushed the edge of her waistband beneath her scrubs top. "You should get some sleep."

She wanted to, more than anything after what she'd survived, but her brain refused to stop spiraling. Every pass of his fingers over the sensitive skin of her belly brought her back to what he'd revealed in the ER. "She was pregnant."

Harvey's fingers stilled. Just for a moment. And that hesitation rattled her deep into her bones. "Yeah. She was."

"Do you think that's why he killed her?" Her voice shook without her permission. "That it was some kind of affair gone wrong?"

Seconds ticked by. Then a minute. She wasn't sure Harvey would answer, and she knew why. Neither of them wanted to imagine two lives ended prematurely by something they were currently working through. It was too real. Too...close to reality, considering his fear of becoming the man who'd ultimately killed his mother. His thumb made another pass around her navel, soothing her nerves, and he seemed to relax muscle by muscle.

"I'm not sure, but I need you to know I'm not going to let anything happen to you." The hand braced under the pillow curled around, threading through her hair and pulling it away from her face. His lips pressed into the hyperaware skin below her ear, the combination of his hands and his mouth dragging her into unconsciousness. "I'm not giving you up that easily."

Chapter Twenty

His body felt heavier than ever before. At…peace.

Harvey blinked against the sunlight coming through the window to his right. Cream linen curtains shifted as the vent puffed out cool air. Plants had been hung in the corner nearest him, the aesthetic natural and calming compared to the chaos outside these walls. Not his room. Not his house. This was… He was with Drennan. Her apartment. Hell, he'd fallen asleep. His chest worked against the weight pressing against him, but he didn't dare move.

Drennan had turned into him sometime during the night, her head nestled against his heart, seeking him out even in unconsciousness. Scraped fingers and broken nails rested over his stomach, with one of her legs thrown over his, pinning him in place. Holding on to him as though she couldn't stand the thought of losing him. She fit so perfectly. Harvey lifted her fingers up, rubbing dried blood from her nails. Law enforcement had gathered what they could of her clothing and evidence from under her nails after the abduction—but the sight of so much damage squeezed his heart.

She was innocent. Maybe simply in the wrong place at the wrong time. Had Dr. Yarrow or he been there in her place to collect the victim's personal items from the pond, it's possible she never would've been taken. Because the alternative meant someone had targeted her, would keep coming for her any chance they got, until they succeeded in whatever plan they'd concocted. Her fingers curled into his, grabbing tight. A soft hitch in her breath kicked his heart rate up. Damn, she was beautiful like this. Without the stress of the past, the pressure of survival and the paleness of creating life in sleep, her face had softened, and a similar ease filtered through him.

He hadn't slept as well as he had last night in…ever. Every noise, every change in his surroundings had potentially been a threat, whether at home or in the military. Survival had trained him to sleep light. Even then, no more than a few hours at a time, but with Drennan here, he'd found something he'd never imagined. Peace. It echoed through his limbs, made him feel heavier, grounded and sluggish. Her body heat seeped past his clothing and soothed his frayed nervous system.

Harvey scanned her bedroom, then the living room through the open door. There was only one access into her second-floor apartment, but the security in this building wasn't strong enough to stop someone from getting in if they put their mind to it. The locks on the windows were cheap, the front door only secured by a dead bolt that could be bypassed by taking out the too-small hinges on the other side of the door. One kick and the entire thing would collapse. Which meant Drennan was still possibly in danger. That his—*their*—baby was in danger.

Setting her hand back against his chest, he counted off her breaths, and the manic concern that'd set up residence over the past couple of days died down. In. Out. Slow. Controlled. He couldn't think of a single stimulus that'd unwound years of physical and mental tension the way her breathing did, but Harvey knew it wasn't just that. It was her. For some unknown reason, she felt safe enough to ask him to stay last night, to seek him out. She...trusted him. Him. A man who couldn't even trust himself, who fought an invisible battle each and every day to keep himself level and from falling into a darkness he'd never escape once he got a taste. And given her past, he understood what a gift that trust was.

To be someone's choice.

Her words had gutted him faster than the KA-BAR knife he'd failed to dodge in Afghanistan. Drennan had never felt important to anyone, and he hadn't lied. She'd become important to him. Not just because of the baby. Long before that, when every cell in his body had argued against letting her walk out his door the night they'd met. And, hell, she deserved someone who would do whatever it took to keep her happy and satisfied. Who could bring out that smile without even trying. Someone she trusted not to use her up and spit her out. Who made her feel important day in and day out.

His chest rose on a deep inhale as he stared up at the ceiling. He could be that. He could choose her and wake up to Drennan clinging to him as though she couldn't breathe without him every morning. He could surprise her with her favorite takeout and spend the night with her legs wrapped around his waist. He could taste her skin and draw that breathy little moan from her lips every night after they put the baby down for bed. He could prove she was important, that she was worth a lifetime of dedication and care. They could be something more than two people tied by the small life they'd created.

If he could trust himself.

His temperature spiked, Drennan's body heat suddenly too much to handle despite her thin scrubs and the fact they'd lost the blanket sometime in the middle of the night.

His heart rate notched higher as he fought the urge to dig his fingers into her arm to hold on to that peaceful feeling for a little while longer. But that invisible demon that'd been passed down in his DNA had already opened one eye and started watching him. Daring him to make a move, to shove her off just so he could breathe a little easier. To give him a reason to attack.

And that was how he would spend the rest of his life.

On the defense. Constantly on alert. Waiting for her or the baby to trigger him into overreacting. To the point all the nightmares he'd suffered over the years became reality. Because no matter how well he'd slept last night or how often he reveled in these too-short moments of peace, Drennan wasn't capable of slaying demons. And she shouldn't have to destroy her life trying. Hoping. He…couldn't put her through that. Couldn't put anyone through that.

"Mmm. Sorry. I didn't realize I was using you as a pillow." She turned her face into his chest, breathing him in as she fisted his T-shirt, and Harvey froze. Her smile lit up her whole face as she blinked up at him and rolled onto her back. With her head on his arm—long asleep from her weight now—she pointed her toes in an exaggerated stretch, showing off all the sweet curves. In a couple months, she'd have one more as the baby got bigger, and something primal inside of him wanted to watch every step of the change. To feel the baby kick and move, watch him or her react to the different kinds of foods Drennan ate. He wanted to rub her feet when the swelling started and make those late-night grocery runs for whatever she was craving. He wanted it all. And he couldn't have it. Couldn't have her. Her eyes cleared of sleep as she turned back into him. "You do make a good pillow, though."

His laugh shuddered through him, easy and quick. When

was the last time he'd really laughed like that? He couldn't remember. But with Drennan, it was becoming easier. "You don't. You're all skin and bones."

"Hey. There used to be some curves here." The feigned seriousness in her expression charged another laugh he couldn't stop even if he'd wanted to. Drennan slipped her hand across his chest, seemingly memorizing him as much as he'd memorized her. "Our baby stole them all. It's not my fault it doesn't like anything I put in my mouth."

His smile slipped.

Their baby. Harvey swallowed the knot of dryness in his throat. She still considered the baby to be theirs. Not just hers. And that…that couldn't happen. Tension bled into his shoulders as he extracted himself from the tangle of limbs and bedding that smelled just as he remembered. No. Better. His clothing stuck to his spine.

"Want some breakfast?" She'd rolled onto her side, watching him as he went for his boots, one fist propped along her jaw. The circles under her eyes had lightened, giving her a brighter appearance. "I haven't really been shopping the past couple of weeks, but I think I have a few eggs and some bacon in the fridge."

"No. Thanks." A hum of warning had started under his skin, urging him to get as far from Drennan as possible. He'd let this get too far. One-night stands weren't supposed to be anything more, and he'd broken his own damn rule by agreeing to stay in bed with her last night. He'd known better than to allow himself to want something more, but he was better than his father. He could do the right thing. Harvey shoved his feet into his boots and tied them as quickly as he could. "I need to get going."

Disappointment washed over her face as she sat up, her voice softer than he'd ever heard it before. The bruises on her face—where the son of a bitch who'd taken her dared put his hands on her—had darkened into a mottled black-and-blue Rorschach pattern he'd never be able to unsee. It hadn't been his hands that'd hurt her, but it was all too easy for his brain to conjure images just like this down the line. Not happening. Ever. Because he would leave. He'd put as much distance between them as possible if that was what would keep her and the baby safe, but the portion of his soul that'd found a sliver of calm in this apartment protested leaving her like this.

"What are you doing, Harvey?"

"I have a shift in the park." He didn't, but he needed to check in with Ranger Simpson. See if anything was found at the bottom of the upper emerald pool that could help identify their victim or tell them who might've killed her. He also wanted to know if a name had been attached to that gun. In revealing the victim's pregnancy, Dr. Yarrow had provided them with a possible motive behind her death, but it wasn't enough. Without an ID, they had no suspect unless the samples taken from Drennan came back with DNA evidence. And considering she'd been knocked unconscious and fallen into the pool, he wasn't hanging all of his hopes on forensics.

"Oh. Okay. In that case, I guess I should check in with Dr. Yarrow." Running one hand down her face, she grabbed for her phone on the nightstand. "See if anything more has come through from the autopsy or if he needs me to go back to the scene."

"You're not going anywhere near the scene. You should ask Dr. Yarrow to give you a few days off. He called with an update last night." Harvey searched for his jacket. He didn't remember taking it off in the living room, but it wasn't in here, and Drennan's scent was starting to drive him crazy, urging him to get back into that bed and breathe it in until it became part of him. "Let him take point on the autopsy and the investigation for now. You shouldn't have to do anything but recover."

Her gaze snapped to his, her thumb hovering over the screen of her phone. "Why would you even think to say that?"

Harvey straightened. "Because you were knocked unconscious, nearly drowned, abducted and tied to a tree yesterday. Not to mention you've been throwing up everything you eat and passed out from dehydration the day before. You're not in a position to go back to work."

"And you're not in a position to make those kinds of decisions for me. I can still do my job." A hardness slipped over her face. Drennan became unnaturally still, and for the first time since they'd met, he thought he might be looking at the woman who'd learned to endure years of mental and emotional abuse by shutting herself down. Becoming nothing and no one to survive. "I...need to see this through."

"Not happening." He took a step toward her. "Not when you're barely able to stand and not when the man who abducted you is still out there."

Her phone pinged with an incoming message, tearing her attention from him, and a release swept through his chest. As though he'd been holding his breath, waiting for the woman he knew to come back to him. "The dental records I requested for the woman found in Emerald Pools came back positive." She lifted the phone before tossing it on the bed, that hard layer of emotionless armor still in place. "We have an ID."

Chapter Twenty-One

Ellender Garza.

The dark-haired woman Drennan had collected from the Emerald Pools trail finally had a name. It would take more than that to discern who could've ended her life, but it was a start. The background check the law enforcement rangers had run told her the victim was only in her early thirties. Never married, employed by Springdale's very own mayor as an assistant for the past several years. She didn't have any large debts or a mortgage that might've gotten her in trouble, and a quick review of her social media accounts hadn't pinpointed any kind of boyfriend who might've been the father of her child. Her parents had passed years before, leaving their victim everything, including her childhood home and two vehicles, one of which was recovered in the visitor's center parking lot once they had the license and registration info. The rangers were searching the vehicle and had brought Springdale PD in to search her home, but as far as Drennan could tell, Ellender Garza was very much an average woman who probably hadn't meant to get pregnant.

Like her.

Hot water coasted down her body as she rinsed shampoo from her hair. Stinging needles pricked at her scalp as the soap made contact with the sensitive skin around the stitches. It didn't matter how many times she'd scrubbed herself from head to toe, she could still feel her abductor's grip around her arms, feel him tightening the rope at her wrists. Taste the scummy water of the pond. She'd fought back, but it hadn't been enough. He'd left bruises on more than her skin. They were etched onto her soul now.

But she thought they might not have ached as much when she'd fallen asleep with Harvey's fingers drawing circles around her navel last night and his hand in her hair. Or when she'd woken in his arms this morning. Having him in bed with her—just holding her—had eased the pressure in her chest and fought back the nightmares that usually came. Dreams her brain conjured showing her exactly what she'd never have. Her parents, happy, healthy and alive, doing random, everyday things like getting into arguments about where to eat for dinner or visiting her long-since-passed grandmother. Most people would consider images like that as anything but a nightmare, but every time they came, her heart broke a little more. What else would she call them?

But she remembered her dream from last night. She'd woken up to it this morning. Real and warm and within arm's reach. Literally. Except something had changed. Regret had infiltrated Harvey's voice, his expression and his body language. He hadn't said it in as many words, but it'd been there. In the way he'd extracted himself from her bed, how he'd rushed to leave. He'd made a mistake. That much she could see of the few minutes they'd had together, and she'd known it'd been coming. She just hadn't expected to be so...hollow. But she wouldn't beg. She wouldn't try to convince him to see her worthy of the risk of getting close to someone. She'd spent far too many years asking people to love her, and not a single one had ended in her favor.

She wouldn't put herself through that again, no matter how much she wished Harvey could see himself as she saw him.

As devoted and aware, to the point he understood exactly what was needed in any given moment. As intriguing and discerning of who he allowed into his life, as she'd failed to be so many times in hers. Curious and impressive in every way that counted. Kind, brave, responsible. He'd told her she was strong, that she was important, but didn't he see the same attributes in himself?

Another slap of pain arched across her scalp, and Drennan turned off the water. Her skin had pinkened just under blistering from the temperature of the water and the amount of times she'd scrubbed herself clean, and already she wanted to climb back into the shower. She wouldn't. She didn't care what Harvey thought she should tell Dr. Yarrow. She needed to get to the office to help the ME finish out the autopsy and provide law enforcement as many details about Ellender Garza as possible. She needed to see this investigation through. Drennan grabbed for the towel she'd left on the toilet seat and stepped in front of the fogged mirror while drying.

Her lower belly looked as it always did as she dragged the terry cloth across her midsection. No signs of showing yet, but within the next few of weeks, her pants would fit tighter and she'd have no choice but to shop for maternity clothes. Had Ellender Garza started showing? According to Harvey, she'd been a few weeks ahead of Drennan's pregnancy, but it'd been hard to tell with the amount of bloat given off by the bacteria in her body breaking down upon death.

The on call ob-gyn had been rerouted for an emergency delivery during the ultrasound to check on the baby. Drennan and Harvey had left the hospital with assurances everything was okay with the pregnancy, and she'd been too tired and beaten to let the anxiety win. But what if the doctor had been wrong? What if something had been missed? Now she'd had at least eight hours of sleep, a shower and soon an entire plate of breakfast food. Her head was clear, and the spiraling thoughts were at full force. The friends from her previous life—including Cassidy—had all been career-focused women putting off having families until their practices were established. She didn't have experience with what was normal or abnormal in a pregnancy, and the one person who might be able to help her through wasn't in a position to do anything for anyone but herself. Ellender Garza might've seen an ob-gyn once she found out she was pregnant. Maybe even the same doctor Cassidy had recommended to Drennan. She would've gotten to hear the heartbeat of her baby and see the sonograms of the little gray-and-white outline growing week by week. She would've had questions and gotten answers and wondered if eating sushi really wasn't allowed.

But someone had taken that from her.

Cut her life short, her baby's life short.

And Drennan had come so close to the same end. That was why she had to see this through, why she'd run herself into the ground if it meant getting justice for those two souls. Ellender Garza hadn't deserved her death. So Drennan would make sure her killer paid the price.

"We're going to be okay, right?" Turning to one side, she slipped her hand over the spot where the baby would round out. Harvey was right. She was skin and bones, the impressions of her ribs peeking through her skin. She'd have to move to a high-fat diet full of peanut butter and avocados if she couldn't keep anything down soon.

Securing the towel beneath her arms, she wrenched the bathroom door open. And saw Harvey. She sucked in a lungful of air as he stood on the other side of the bed, his phone in hand. "Oh. I... I didn't think you were still here."

Her skin flushed with the awareness that all that separated them was a bath towel and her queen-size bed. Honestly, she wasn't sure how they'd fit together so well last night with his broad chest and ability to take up an entire room with his intensity. Drennan clutched the towel harder at the memory of his body pressed against hers, his knee wedged between her legs, how he'd held on to her hip and dragged her closer. His agreement to stay with her might not have sounded like much, but it was everything to her.

"What are these?" His cheeks seemed to sink in, carving out deeper shadows running the length of his jaw and under his eyes. "All these messages from an unknown number."

"Wait. Is that my phone?" Fury replaced the tendrils of appreciation and desire. She took a step forward to grab it from him from over the bed, but Harvey easily dodged her attempt. "You had no right to read through my private messages. Give it to me."

She felt like a five-year-old whining for her favorite toy.

His gaze locked on her. Hard and cold and a little bit terrifying. "First of all, you left it unlocked on the bed so I could read the dental results. Our victim's name is Ellender Garza. I sent that information on to the law enforcement rangers so they can start pulling a victim profile together. Second, I didn't mean to read through your messages. A new message came through while I was reading the results that started with the words, 'You've always been a selfish brat.' So yeah, I clicked on it to make sure it was coming from a wrong number, and I didn't have to pay someone a visit."

Her body locked up on her. Her mind went blank. No. No, no, no. This wasn't part of the deal. Reality wasn't supposed to breach the bubble they'd created in this room. In here, they were just two people who cared about each other and happened to be having a baby together. No talk of the past or the future or the threat outside these walls. Drennan closed her eyes against the shame charging through her. Those messages... She'd kept them and all the voicemails as a reminder not to trust the upward arc of the cycle where her mother said what Drennan wanted to hear and pretended to give a damn. To force herself to see the truth. No one was ever supposed to see them, least of all him.

Harvey tossed the phone on the bed, face up. Full of messages just like that one from her mother. He pointed down at the phone. "Except there are countless others just like that one from that specific number, spanning months. Who the hell has been messaging you that vile crap, and where can I find them, Drennan?"

She didn't know what to say, couldn't remember how to breathe.

"Is this the person you won't tell me about?" He was right there, suddenly standing in front of her. She hadn't heard him move, or maybe she'd been too wrapped up in her own thoughts to track him rounding the end of the bed and coming to stand in front of her. His thumb traced the bottom edge of her lip, so light she could've imagined it. "The one who hurt you? Who is it?"

Tears burned in her eyes. She'd tried. She'd tried to hide it, to not blame herself for all the accusations and disappointment thrown her way, but abuse—in any form—liked to be kept a secret. That was where it did the most damage, isolated its victims and crushed all sources of hope. It'd built until she couldn't handle the pressure anymore, and the control she'd convinced herself was enough broke. Her mouth wobbled the harder she attempted to hold it in. "My dad died when I was eight. It was a car accident. The kind most people don't walk away from, but I did."

Harvey pulled back slightly, but not out of reach. "I'm sorry."

"So am I. He was my best friend. No matter how tired he was at the end of a long workday at the hospital or what else needed to be done, he went out of his way to spend time with me every day." A smile tugged at her mouth, but even she could feel it didn't last long as the grief rolled in. Not as strong as it used to but still there. She wasn't sure she'd ever stop feeling it. "We did everything together as a family. Just him, me and my mom. They were the perfect couple. Teasing each other while they made dinner together, laughing at inside jokes, sneaking kisses when they thought I couldn't see, but after he died, my mom changed. It was like a switch had been flipped. There weren't any more trips to the nearest gas station for a treat or sitting down to dinner together. Her smiles were gone, and I couldn't figure out why she would get this look on her face anytime she saw me. Like I was a stranger."

Straightening to his full height, Harvey gave her a glimpse of the soldier she knew him to be. Alert, ready. "Your dad was a doctor?"

Her heart squeezed too hard in her chest. She nodded. "I thought I could make her proud by following in his footsteps, but she didn't see it that way."

"She took her grief out on you, a child who was grieving her father as much as she was grieving her husband." He lost that hardness as he stepped into her, his knuckles grazing her cheek. The touch elicited a whole new sensation in her chest, as though she suddenly had room to feel something more than the armor she'd built against the people in her life. "And she still is, isn't she?"

"No. Because I won't let her. She sends me messages and leaves voicemails, but I never respond back. I don't answer her calls." She'd never spoken about any of this. Cassidy had been witness to her mother's confrontations in the middle of the ER when she felt she wasn't getting enough attention, but right now, Drennan wanted this to last longer. This…unloading. Where she peeled back another layer of the empty, compliant outlet she'd been nearly her whole life and exposed the woman she knew herself to be underneath. She wanted him to be part of that. She wanted to delay the inevitable moment Harvey realized he'd started caring about her more than he set out to, about what happened to her and the baby. That moment was coming, and there was nothing she could do to stop it, but she could push it off a little while longer. With moments like this. "I took away her power over me, and she's desperate to get it back."

The notches between his eyebrows deepened. Did he know he was still touching her as though he needed that connection between them? "So then why keep them?"

"To remind myself I am not the abuse I endured." Another invisible layer peeled back, revealing a spark of something she'd felt the night they'd met. "I'm the hope that refused to surrender."

Chapter Twenty-Two

She wasn't the abuse she endured.

A resounding echo thudded hard in Harvey's chest.

"No more, Drennan." He turned for the bed, collecting her phone from the comforter that had kept them tangled together throughout the night. He handed the device off. The choice was entirely up to her. He couldn't make it for her. "Stop putting yourself in a position to get hurt. You have good intentions in reminding yourself of what she's capable of, but one of these days, a message will come through that won't do that job. It will do what she intends, and you'll be right back to being her metaphorical punching bag."

She sighed. "I know. I've told myself to block and delete her number so many times." Tears glittered in her eyes. She nodded, as though trying to convince herself—of recognizing—that what he said made sense. "I just keep hoping she'll realize her mistake and she'll remember that I'm her daughter. That she's supposed to love me."

He didn't know the specifics of what her mother had put her through, but he couldn't help but admire the woman who'd come out on the other side of it. How Drennan had stood there and braved exposing a piece of herself she'd guarded for so long. Because he knew she had. He knew the lengths she'd gone through to protect her abuser out of shame and potential disbelief from people who were supposed to care about her. He'd done the exact same thing. Lying to his teachers, pushing away his friends, not making eye contact with anyone long enough for them to realize the bruises on his face hadn't come from falling down the stairs the second time in a week. He'd isolated himself just to avoid having to answer questions about his home life and ensuring his father's wrath if the man ever found out about it. It hadn't gotten any easier in the military, but at least he hadn't been—how had Drennan put it?—trying to heal in the same place he'd been broken.

And Drennan was... She was awe-inspiring. Stronger than anyone he'd ever known, including the men and women in his unit, and everything he wasn't. She'd overcome that part of her that relived every injury and harsh word over and over to get her through the day. He wanted that. More than anything he wanted to move past the hollowness in his chest and find something worth reaching out for. But the man he'd become had been built on years of detachment, grief and pain, and letting go felt like forgiving. Something he wasn't sure he could ever bring himself to do.

He stepped into her, drawn by more than the need to offer some semblance of comfort—if he was capable of that at all. He wanted to feel her, breathe her in, make her and the peace she brought part of him. Harvey pressed a soft kiss to her mouth, excited by her gasp, as he shifted her damp hair away from her face. "People like your mother will always need someone to blame. They teach you that love is not unconditional or deserved, that it's given only when certain expectations and whims are met. They need the control and use manipulation to feel powerful, and when you don't give them what they want or you fight back, you become the villain. But, Drennan, I would much rather see you as the villain in her story than as a victim."

She swiped at her face. "I don't want to be a victim. I want to be the mother this baby needs."

Hell, that threatened to gut him on the spot. She was one of the few, the ones who recognized the cycle and refused to pass it along to the next generation. If his father had been brave enough to make that choice… Harvey didn't know where he would be. "You already are."

Her laugh punctured through the hard layer of ice he'd set in his chest. Clear and full of a brightness he hadn't let himself recognize in a long time. "You don't have to say that. I'm sure all of this is too much to handle, even for you."

"I can handle you." He kissed her again, this one more than an offer of comfort. The sweep of his tongue was driven by the need to reward her for all the hard days, the lonely nights and the tears she'd shed for a woman who didn't deserve a single one of them.

"You should get dressed." Harvey skimmed his knuckles along her throat, reveling in the strong beat of her pulse. Warmth radiated into his hand at the contact, and he wanted to drown in it. To drag her back into that bed and help them both forget the atrocities they'd survived. That was what they were. That was what the pain in her eyes that'd called to him the night they'd met spoke of. Survival. It was something they shared, something that bonded them, but every cell in his body told him even without that, he'd still feel this unexplainable connection to get close to her. He fanned his fingers over her jaw, framing one side of her face. "I want to drop by the clinic to get you that ultrasound before I head into the park to follow up with the law enforcement rangers. Make sure everything is okay with the baby."

"I'll just need a few minutes." Nodding, Drennan clutched

at the towel with a wisp of a smile as she backed toward the bathroom door. "Thank you."

A swell of something foreign climbed his throat, but he wouldn't let it out. Nothing he said in response would be worthy of the woman having his baby, so Harvey sat back on the edge of the mattress to wait. No one had ever thanked him for his advice, but then again, he'd never felt comfortable giving it. While he might've gone through his own personal hell, he'd kept that part of his life locked up tight. But it'd felt good to talk Drennan through those contradictory feelings of wanting to destroy the threat to your well-being while trying to make it love you at the same time. Felt freeing. Healing. True to her word, mere minutes passed before she stepped back into the bedroom clothed in black slacks and a T-shirt and tennis shoes and they were on their way to the clinic.

Harvey maneuvered into the parking lot he was becoming all too familiar with and rounded the front of the SUV to help Drennan out. Based on her hesitation and automatic reaching for the door, he was betting no one had done that for her, either. Or she hadn't let them, needing to prove she could make it through this life without help. He understood that. Didn't mean he was going to let her.

The nurses at the front desk welcomed Drennan with a smile while side-eyeing him at the same time. Couldn't blame them. The last two times he'd been here, he'd nearly brought the entire building down with his demands for them to prioritize Drennan. It'd been selfish considering all the people—young, old and somewhere in the middle—waiting their turn, but he didn't regret a single moment. He hadn't lied to her before. She was important. Maybe the most important person in his life.

Another shard of ice cracked from inside his chest, breaking off into nothingness as though it'd never existed. That... that wasn't supposed to happen. She wasn't supposed to be important. He wasn't supposed to want more of her in his life. Harvey stilled as a nurse led Drennan back into the corridor with private rooms branching off each side.

She turned toward him with a smile. "They're ready for us."

"You go on. You don't want me in there." His voice remained steady despite the storm building inside. Harvey flexed both hands at his sides, trying to get the feeling back into them. "I'll wait."

"I thought you wanted to make sure the baby was okay." The divots between her brows deepened as she studied him. He did, and he wanted nothing more than her to have this. The experience of hearing the baby's heartbeat after everything she'd been through in those woods. Of seeing their child on the ultrasound screen, healthy and unharmed. It wouldn't relieve all the anxiety and stress she held on to, but it would go a long way to ensuring she had a healthy pregnancy, and Drennan deserved his support. She closed the distance between them, lowering her voice. "I know this probably isn't how you imagined our situation going, but I'm not sure I can do this on my own. Please."

Oh, hell. Blood drained from his face. She was scared of getting bad news. Of being alone when it happened. And he'd... Damn it. He was being a selfish bastard. Harvey nodded. More to himself than her. "Yeah. Of course."

He kept to her side as they followed on the nurse's heels. Drennan stepped on a scale outside of another nurses' station and was led into one of the private rooms where the nurse took her blood pressure and monitored her oxygen levels. "Is this all normal?"

"Yep. We just want to make sure Mom is taking care of

herself before we check on baby." The nurse rolled around on her stool, peeling the blood pressure cuff from Drennan's arm before leading her to the exam table. "It's all routine. Nothing to worry about, Daddy."

Daddy. He was going to be a dad in seven months, whether he wanted this or not. A tingling set up in his fingers as he clutched on to the chair arms.

"Go ahead and lay back, Mom. Pull up your shirt and unbutton your pants." The nurse grabbed a condiment bottle with a long nozzle from the cart holding the ultrasound equipment. "Don't want to get any of the jelly on your clothes. It's gonna be a little cold at first."

Drennan followed instructions as though she'd done this a thousand times before. As a physician, he imagined she'd seen it done many times, but living it and observing it were two different things. Her fingers shook as she tried to unbutton her slacks. She was still nervous, and Harvey's instincts kicked in.

"I got it." Shooting to his feet, he set his hand over both of hers and made quick work of the button and zipper before interlacing one hand into hers. The act itself didn't even come close to what they'd shared in making this baby, but the floor threatened to sweep out from under him, anyway.

"All right. Let's see how baby is doing." The nurse took up her rolling stool and detached a wand-looking device from the cart. She pressed it larger side down onto Drennan's stomach, then smoothed it over the jelly.

A rapid *thud thud thud* filled the room. Fast and almost out of control. Drennan's hand squeezed around his and refused to let go.

"There's baby's heartbeat." The nurse shifted the device around. "Nice and strong."

"That's good." Tangible relief drained from Drennan's

shoulders as she stared at the monitor. She collapsed back against the exam table, her free hand pressed to her forehead. The tears she'd held in earlier escaped down the sides of her face, and he couldn't help but try to catch them before they made it to her hair.

"Strong heartbeat." He didn't know what else to say that might keep her concern at bay.

"Yeah." She swiped at her face and sat up again. "I'm so glad."

He couldn't make anything out but a bunch of gray and white clouds across the black background, but then… There it was. The thud matched up with a flutter on the screen, and Harvey's chest nearly exploded from holding his breath. An outline materialized with another shift of the ultrasound wand. Baby-shaped and very real.

Their baby.

His baby.

"I've spent so long dreaming of this moment." A smile broke across Drennan's face as she stared at the monitor then turned her attention to him. "Thank you."

The tingling flared from his fingers into his arms and then his chest. It woke that monster living in his blood like a predator latching on to the scent of its prey, and Harvey felt his body temperature drop. He hadn't heard her right. "What did you just say?"

"Harvey?" Drennan's voice failed to bring the peace it usually did as he dropped her hand. As though she'd burned him. Or trapped him. "Are you okay?"

The tingling contorted into something dark and heavy. Full of rage and unpredictability. The trauma she'd suffered, the grief, the neglect, the outright hatred from her one surviving parent. The loss of her father and how she clung to those memories of their happy little family… Understanding struck. Her leveled reaction to getting pregnant, her asking him to be involved, her lack of any real relationships other than with her doctor friend and her boss. She'd…she'd played him from the beginning. His voice didn't sound like his own as he spoke and his heart rate catapulted into dangerous levels. "You got pregnant on purpose."

Chapter Twenty-Three

She'd expected this moment

She just hadn't expected it to hurt so much.

The nurse sat the ultrasound wand on the cart for cleaning and hit a couple buttons on the screen. Grabbing for a warm towel, she wiped it across Drennan's stomach to clean away the conductive jelly. "I'm going to print off a couple sonographs for you and give you two a few minutes of privacy."

Drennan couldn't feel her body apart from the cold sensation tightening the skin across her stomach. She registered the nurse leaving a strip of thin paper showing their baby on the counter and the door closing behind her, but nothing else would stay in focus. Her tongue felt too big for her mouth, a thousand different emotions clogging her throat. The first of which was a strong dose of disbelief. Followed closely by unfiltered anger.

Seconds passed in silence. Maybe a minute. She tried to breathe through the tears that came with extreme emotions but failed as she finally let herself look at him. Damn hormones.

"Tell me the truth." Muscle and tendon flexed in his forearms as he stared at her. That tightness traveled up the length of his arms and into his neck, hollowing his cheeks and the muscle ticking in his jaw. Harvey cut his gaze to the window—like he couldn't even bring himself to look at her—then back. "The night we slept together, you said you were on birth control. Were you lying?"

Her saliva felt more like a paste. "No."

It was all she could manage as her lungs threatened to burst. Those days leading up to their one night together had been a jumble of emotion and stress and adapting to this new life. She'd never meant for any of this. It'd just...happened, but she wouldn't apologize for it. She wouldn't apologize for the life growing inside of her. And she wouldn't regret it. Ever.

"So you admitting you've been waiting to get pregnant was just, what?" His gaze seemed to burn straight through her. Searching for a reason—any reason—to turn on her. "A colloquialism?"

Pain lanced through her chest. Not the kind anyone could see but just as damaging. The past three days played out in shards of memory—him bringing her back to his house to rest, making her food so she wouldn't pass out again, ensuring she made it home safely, staying the night in her bed. The words he'd said.

You're important to me.
I'm not going anywhere.
I'm not giving you up that easily.

Had it all been a lie? Why? Why go through that kind of effort if he'd been looking for a way out of their situation this entire time? She'd known his reasons for not wanting to be a father, but this wasn't past trauma talking. Accusing her of getting pregnant on purpose felt personal and cruel and... final. He didn't want her. He didn't want this baby, and he was ensuring he burned the bridge that'd been built over the past few days between them to ashes. Along with her heart. Drennan swallowed against the dryness in her throat, suddenly aware her lower half was still exposed by her lifted shirt and unbuttoned slacks. Where she could still feel the imprint of the backs of his knuckles when he'd helped her. She moved to fix her clothing and sat up on the exam table, the scream and crackle of hygienic paper beneath her too loud in her ears. Every sense she owned seemed to be on fire, too much. "Do you really think so little of me?"

"I think that maybe you aren't above using the same manipulation tactics that were used against you most of your life." He diverted his attention again, fueling that knot of uncertainty in her stomach. "Who better to wield them than a woman who has a literal encyclopedia of examples on her phone?"

She sucked in a sharp breath, the sting of which tore through the last few layers of her patience. And it was breaking her heart. She hadn't given a whole lot of thought to what a future between them might look like, but she'd wanted it. For them. For this baby. She'd wanted what she'd lost all those years ago. A family. Despite the red flags, his claims to not wanting to be a father, Harvey had shown her time and again that he cared. That there was something beneath the hard exterior that could make a different choice. And convinced her she was worth the effort. But she'd been wrong, and now she was pissed.

"Are you serious?" Drennan slid off the exam table. This was what he wanted. For her to get angry, to be the one to make the choice for him and give him a reason to leave, but she wouldn't do that. He had to be the one to say the words. No matter how much it might hurt hearing them, she'd let him. She'd let him walk away and never look back. Because anyone willing to throw her past in her face wasn't someone she wanted to be with. "After learning the reason why I don't tell people about what I've been through—that I'm afraid of people holding it over my head—you use it against me?"

He shifted his weight to ease the tension building with every word out of his mouth, but she wasn't the one who'd get hurt when it exploded. "You expect me to believe—"

Her laugh didn't sound remotely light or natural, and he had the audacity to flinch as though *she'd* struck *him*. But he'd started this. She would make damn sure he put the final nail in the coffin of their future together. That cold numbness she'd learned to don over the years descended. "Expect you to believe? I didn't have any expectations of you, Harvey. I have never asked anything of you. I didn't ask for you to drive me to the clinic after I passed out or for your offer to financially support this baby. I didn't ask you to come after me in those woods when I was abducted. You made your position about this baby clear, and I respected that. You made those choices. Not me. You. And I am grateful for them, really, I am, but not enough to let you treat me like this."

Harvey seemed to come back to himself right then. "Drennan, I—"

"No." She maneuvered around him, grabbing for her bag before heading for the door separating them from what was most likely an entire hall of eavesdropping nurses. "You more than anyone should know I could never manipulate another human being like I was manipulated, and the fact you're throwing that in my face only tells me one thing. You're a coward. You had the opportunity to move on from what's happened to you, but you're comfortable choosing a familiar misery. And I don't want any part of that near me or my child."

She grabbed for the door handle as the last dregs of anger drained out of sheer exhaustion. "I didn't get pregnant on purpose, Harvey, but there is not a single bone in my body that regrets this baby. I'm just sorry you do."

Wrenching the door open with a little more force than she expected, Drennan cringed against the solid wood colliding into the wall behind it. But she kept moving. Because if she stopped, she might never be able to put the distance between them she desperately needed right now. She didn't see the nurses who were most assuredly staring at her as she navigated down the corridor and through the lobby, and she didn't know where she was going as she hit the parking lot.

Damn it. Harvey had driven her to the clinic. Her car was… She didn't actually know. Back at her apartment? At the funeral home? She'd collected Ellender Garza's remains in the ME-sanctioned van before passing out in the park, so yes. She'd left her car in the funeral home parking lot. She could only imagine the amount of parking citations collecting under the windshield wipers after three days, but she'd have to worry about that later. Grabbing for her phone, Drennan headed south for two blocks. She wasn't going to wait in the clinic parking lot for Harvey to catch up to her. If she was being honest, she never wanted to see him again.

She didn't need his money. She didn't need his support or for him to have an interest in their baby's life. Not for birthdays or graduations or weddings. Not for weekend custody exchanges or family vacations. Her heart rate ticked up a notch. All she'd wanted was for him to choose *her*, but maybe her mother had been right. She wasn't worth the effort.

Wait. No. She knew better than to let that voice win. What had Cassidy said? The bitch didn't get to live rent free in her head? Ugh. She was crying again. Swiping at her face, Drennan used her rideshare app to order a car to pick her up at the corner and climbed into the back seat when it arrived. No sign of Harvey, thankfully. "Metland Mortuary in Hurricane, please."

She didn't remember the drive. The chaos of thoughts—of what Harvey had accused her of, of her response, of the pain clawing deeper into her heart, the grief of a future she'd never have—it'd all blurred. Until she was climbing out of the car and heading for the front door of the funeral home. It was after hours. The director would be long gone by now, and Dr. Yarrow would've left around five. She'd lost track of the entire day between waking up to Harvey in her bed and the anticipation of seeing the baby on the ultrasound. Drennan pulled up short. "Oh, crap."

She'd left the sonogram photos at the clinic.

Well, they were gone now. Because she wasn't going back, and she wasn't going to ask Harvey if he'd picked them up. He'd most likely left them behind, and that just made her sad all over again. No. She wasn't going to think about that right now. Maybe when she got home and into a gallon-sized roll of egg-free cookie dough later. Then she'd let all this pressure out of her chest. Her key slid into the dead bolt and granted her access inside. The dim lighting overhead told her there wasn't anyone here tonight. While she probably should just collect the parking tickets, get in her car and go home, she couldn't ignore the need to check in on the Ellender Garza autopsy.

Dr. Yarrow would've finished the actual procedure within a few hours of starting, but there was a chance some of the toxicology results had come back. She just…she just needed to do something to help. Following the stairs down in the basement, she keyed in the six-digit number on the keypad securing the morgue before and after hours. There weren't too many times she'd had to use it, but Drennan had a feeling that wouldn't be the case for the next couple of weeks as the tension that'd crested back at the clinic refused to release. The green light lit up, and the thick steel doors unlocked.

She pushed through.

"Hello again, Dr. Hawes." Body heat pressed into her from behind. His mouth was beside her ear as he clamped a hand over her mouth. "I was hoping I would get to see you again."

Chapter Twenty-Four

He couldn't force himself to move.

Couldn't get a full breath.

The things he'd said to Drennan. The accusations he'd made…

Hell. Harvey closed his eyes mere seconds after she'd slammed the door into the wall. Shame unlike anything he'd experienced before burned beneath his skin. That familiar numbness had infiltrated his chest and refused to get out. It was a heavy feeling and he didn't have any desire to speak or move. All he wanted to do was close his eyes and sleep, because the process of breaking was exhausting. He'd tried to make the past few minutes justifiable, but no matter how hard he'd tried, he couldn't connect to that part of him he'd created to survive the worst.

Drennan had eviscerated it in a matter of days.

And that…scared the hell out of him.

The detachment wouldn't come as easily as it had in years past, and a sense of panic swirled up in its place. It was suffocating and dark and gut-clenching all at once. It closed in on him until he couldn't remember to breathe. Harvey fisted his hands at his sides, reaching for some tendril of control, but all he could think of was the utter devastation on her beautiful face.

Devastation he'd put there.

Because she was right. He was a coward.

He'd spent years not wanting a damn thing except to get through the day and the one after that, relying on his pain to drive his choices, counting on someone—anyone—to tell him what to do from one minute to the next. It was easier to live as a shell and isolate himself than to face the fact he might make a wrong choice. That he could put someone he cared about in danger just by being around him.

But Drennan had seen past that. She'd made him feel. She'd made him want. She was…everything. And he couldn't reach for that numbness because she'd made him feel everything for the first time in years. He couldn't go back. He felt her loss, an aching hollow sensation that threatened to bring him to his knees.

Then more.

The grief he hadn't let himself acknowledge when he got the news his mom had passed, a thing of its own that was heavy and full of rage. All the disappointment and heartache every time his father put his hands on him in anger, colder than he expected. The stab in his chest at the words he'd thrown in Drennan's face, burning and twisting.

He'd made this choice.

He'd made every choice that had brought him to this room, just as Drennan had said—not being able to distance himself, dreaming of a life that included her and the baby, hoping—and it was all going to destroy him from the inside out. She'd had every right to walk out on him, but Drennan would never hate him as much as he hated himself right then. But what was worse? The way he'd thrown her past in her face. Because she was right about that, too. She'd trusted him with one of her deepest fears, and he'd used it against her. He'd become his father in the worst way. Using someone's—a person he cared about—weakness against them to get what he wanted. To push Drennan away so thoroughly that there would be no going back, and it made him feel sick. No matter how many times he managed to apologize for that—if she let him get close enough to try—it would never be enough.

And he would have to live with that for the rest of his life.

He did this. He'd broken them and any kind of future he'd imagined between them, tried to break her. This caring, dedicated, strong woman who'd shown him the real meaning of healing. Harvey scrubbed his hands down his face. He needed to find her. Not for a second chance but to take back everything he'd said about her.

Because he knew she hadn't gotten pregnant on purpose. He knew she'd never use her experience with emotional abuse on anyone else for fear of them hurting themselves or others. And he knew he'd never deserved her. Never deserved a family of his own, to be happy. Hadn't his dad warned him a thousand times? That he was nothing and would always amount to nothing without his old man there to take care of their family.

Well, his dad had been right about that. At the first chance of making a different choice, Harvey had clung to that familiar misery because he could anticipate what happened next. He knew how his story would play out, but with Drennan? There had been too many variables and unknowns he couldn't see, even when he'd known it had to be better than his self-imposed suffering. Because she would've gladly been there.

If he'd just given her the chance.

But she didn't want him anywhere near her or their baby, and he'd never hold that choice against her. He'd do what he could to support her from afar, whether she knew that support came from him or not. Send checks in the mail, drop off diapers and wipes and formula if she needed, ask his fellow rangers to help out so she could take a shower or a nap. Hell, he'd willingly learn how to knit or crochet a baby blanket if that was what she required.

Because Drennan deserved better. She deserved the world for how hard she'd fought to get the family she wanted.

Harvey peeled his eyes open, and the storm cycloning through him stilled. And took the air from his chest. The photos left on the counter pierced through the thick wall of shame and guilt crushing him in time to his racing pulse. He took one step closer, then another, his feet heavy as lead. Or maybe gravity had decided to kick his ass for what he'd done, too. He didn't care.

The gray and white patches on the dark background didn't mean a whole lot to him on the screen, but now, there were words on the photos marking exactly where the baby was growing. Their baby. Spindly limbs shot straight out from the middle of the gray-and-white outline, with another set coming out from the narrower end. Despite the mere eight weeks it'd been since that night in the bar, the baby's head had developed significantly, much larger than he'd expected. Echoes of that flutter—too fast and so loud—sounded in his head as he studied where he thought the heart might be.

It was a baby. His baby.

The rage he held on to for himself slowly lost its hold as he memorized the first photo. Harvey was careful as he peeled the line of photos off the cart. The paper was thinner than he expected—fragile—and he didn't want to do anything that might tear or damage it. Drennan would want them. Considering their conversation and the way he'd treated her, he imagined she'd left them behind by accident.

Logically, he'd known Drennan had been telling the truth

about the pregnancy, but this… This made it real. He was going to be a father. His breath rushed out of him, eyes burning just for a second before he got himself under control. How the hell had he convinced himself he didn't want to be a part of this?

An ache set up in his shoulders. He wasn't sure how long he'd stood there or if the nurses in the corridor had called security to escort him out of the clinic. Hell, he wasn't even sure how long it'd been since Drennan had walked out, but he couldn't stay here. He'd driven Drennan to the clinic, and leaving her in the parking lot wasn't an option.

Folding the thin paper in thirds, each photo stacking on top of the other, he slipped the sonogram into his back pocket and headed for the cracked doorway. The nurses at the station outside the room eyed him with expressions of sadness and disbelief. All of which he'd earned. "Did you see where Dr. Hawes went?"

None of them answered, getting back to whatever clipboards and charts that needed to be filled out. Their collective anger pulsed against him, and he would take it. There was no doubt they'd heard every word—every accusation—he'd slung at Drennan, but he didn't have the energy to give it much thought. His father would've lashed out, embarrassed by the negative attention, but he was not his father.

A flood of something swept through him.

He was not his father.

Drennan had told him that, but he'd never really believed it. Until now. Every single decision he'd made to this point had been based on the opposite of what his dad would've done, but Harvey had never given himself that much credit. If his mother had dared to defend herself as Drennan had, his father would've ensured she wouldn't have been able to talk for a week. But he'd never let himself put his hands on the mother of his child. On anyone unless it was self-defense. And that... Recognizing that shed a weight from his shoulders he hadn't realized he'd been carrying for so long. Made him hope there was a chance to fix this. He wasn't his father. He never would be. Not with Drennan. Not with this baby.

"The woman who was in that room with me." Harvey clenched the edges of the upper level of the desk. He'd been an idiot to let her walk out of the exam room without him. She'd been abducted by an unknown suspect twenty-four hours ago. Hell, he'd given her his word he'd watch out for her, and only hours later, he'd broken that promise. "Do you know where she went?"

"She's not here." One of the nurses filed a folder in one of the cabinets. "She walked out the front doors after..." She cleared her throat. "I haven't seen her since."

"Where did she go?" Why did it suddenly feel like he couldn't take a full breath? "Which direction?"

Shaking her head, the nurse went back to her filing. "I'm sorry. I don't know."

Drennan was smart. She knew there was still a chance the man who'd abducted her wasn't finished with whatever plan he wanted to use her for. She'd go to someone she knew. Her doctor friend. What was her name? "Is Cassidy here? She's a doctor in the ER."

"Dr. Duffy?" Another nurse rounded into the station. "No. She's not on call today."

Hell. Then where would Drennan have gone? His skin prickled with unease. He'd driven her to the clinic. Without a ride, she would've requested a rideshare. But not home. Drennan was an expert in locking down her emotions and feelings to the point they might as well not exist. It was how she'd survived so many years under her mother's thumb, and as a former trauma physician, she would want to distract herself from sinking into that void. Which meant she'd most likely gone back to work. Alone.

Damn it. There was no guarantee she hadn't gone home to get as much distance from him as possible. He extracted his phone, scrolling through his received calls list as he headed for the front of the clinic. There was a chance he could catch up to her. That he could fix this. Harvey tapped Dr. Yarrow's information. It was after five. The medical examiner was most likely already home, but this couldn't wait. The line connected.

"Ranger Knight." Annoyance bled through the line. "I hope this is important."

Harvey didn't have time for small talk. "Have you heard from Drennan?"

Silence took a beat. "No. I assumed she was with you."

"She was." He shoved through the clinic's front doors and out into the parking lot. She wasn't here. "The autopsy for Ellender Garza. Have you issued your report?"

"I'm still waiting for the toxicology results." Dr. Yarrow didn't give him a chance to respond. "What is this about? Where is Drennan?"

Harvey scrubbed a hand down his face as failure ruptured from his insides. The same kind of failure he'd barely recovered from after hearing about his mother's death. He hadn't been able to protect her, but he couldn't fail Drennan. Or the baby. Desperation had him scanning the sidewalks and parked cars. Coming up empty. "I lost her."

Chapter Twenty-Five

Rough hands shoved her through the doors.

Drennan barely caught her balance as she was thrust into the exam room. Temperatures dropped on the other side of the doors, sinking through her slacks and T-shirt. All at once, she was aware of the presence at her back, the gun aimed at her head and the fact he'd blocked her from the only exit from the medical examiner's office. "You."

Her throat struggled with that single word.

"You're a hard one to pin down, Dr. Hawes." He moved into her line of vision, all too familiar and overbearing despite him being around the same height as Harvey. Except the man who'd knocked her unconscious and followed her into the backcountry had aged in a matter of days. The lines around his eyes and mouth had deepened, his cheekbones somehow more sunken. He'd shifted away from the doors, but there was no doubt he would catch her if she made a move he didn't want. "But I knew you wouldn't be able to stay away."

"What do you want?" Cold worked down into her lungs. While she'd become accustomed to working in the basement, this was different. Like a warning that forced tremors into her hands.

"I told you before." Only half of his mouth lifted into a

smile. "I need your help. Which one of these refrigerators is holding Ellender Garza?"

"I don't... I don't know." And she didn't. Dr. Yarrow had been the one to store her remains after the autopsy while she recovered from the abduction. Now that they had a positive ID for the victim, Dr. Yarrow would've ensured her family had been notified of her death. Once the autopsy was complete, they could take custody of the remains. She didn't even know if Ellender Garza was still here, but Drennan had a feeling his wanting to get to the body wasn't solely to say goodbye. "I would have to look at the paperwork, but why—"

"She has something I need." Her abductor collected a scalpel from a selection of tools laid out on one of the rolling carts Drennan spent her time as an assistant sterilizing and organizing for the ME. He seemed to study his reflection in the stainless steel.

Drennan's fingers ached for something—anything—she might be able to use as a weapon, but he'd positioned her between himself and Dr. Yarrow's desk. A stapler probably wouldn't come in handy right now. "We've done X-rays and collected her personal items. There isn't—"

Dread pooled at the base of her spine. There was something Ellender Garza's killer might want after her death, but the possibility was too much to consider.

His laugh punctured through the haze threatening to disconnect her from her body. He'd moved closer without her realizing, and Drennan took a step back. "You understand now, don't you?"

"The baby." Her mouth dried, and it took everything she had not to lift her hand to her own budding baby bump to assure her of the life she and Harvey had created. That nothing could hurt their baby. Giving away that kind of information—exposing her vulnerability—could put her more at risk than the scalpel in his hand. "You want her baby."

"Well, aren't you clever?" Pointing the scalpel in her direction, the killer took another step forward. "That baby is the last link between me and Ellender, and I will do whatever it takes to make sure it can't lead back to me."

"You're..." A monster. Emotion clogged her throat. It wasn't enough he'd taken Ellender Garza's life and the life of her child, he wanted to strip her of what could've been the victim's brightest hope. A wall of protectiveness slammed into place, drawing her shoulders back. He wasn't getting to that body or the baby Ellender had carried. She didn't know how she would stop him, but it felt important. Someone had to stand for the victim. Who better than someone who understood what it felt like not to háve that support? Drennan's heart threatened to beat straight out of her chest as a single pained word escaped her control. "Why?"

He took another step, forcing Drennan back into the edge of Dr. Yarrow's desk. The overhead fluorescent lights glinted off something else on his hand, and her heart stopped beating for a breath. A wedding band. A full smile spread across his face. "Isn't it obvious? I love my wife."

Drennan clutched on to the edge of the desk with one hand, the other searching for something solid enough to protect herself with if necessary. She wanted to believe her abductor would let her go if she aided him in getting what he wanted, but that was a stupid, hopeful part of her that didn't match reality. She'd seen his face. Twice. And while neither the law enforcement rangers nor Springdale PD had been able to match his description to an identity over the past two days, that wasn't a loose end he could afford not to tie. "Your wife." Her chest tightened. "Ellender Garza wasn't your wife."

"No. She was not. She was a mistake, one my wife, the mayor, will never know about." He cocked his head to one side, seemingly trying to predict his prey's next move. Her being the prey. "So you can imagine how much I have at risk if that information got out, or if a federal database connects a murder victim back to me."

Drennan's hand connected with something heavy and smooth. The paperweight Dr. Yarrow's wife had gifted him on their anniversary this year holding a perfectly preserved black rose in the center. She covered it with her hand.

"Unfortunately, it's not as simple as losing my marriage." He maneuvered to her right, and she countered, losing the protection of the desk at her back. "My wife and I… It's been over for a long time. At least, on my end, but the National Park Service doesn't like to believe its rangers are capable of making base human choices like adultery. It's not good for public image. I'll lose my job, my connections and the very comfortable lifestyle I've built riding my wife's wealthy coattails, and you see, I just can't have that."

A shiver quaked down Drennan's spine. "You're a ranger?"

"No, Dr. Hawes. I'm *the* ranger, and I'm losing my patience, which is not great for you, as Ellender can attest." The superintendent. The man who ran the entirety of Zion National Park. Harvey's boss. "I recognized him, you know. That day in the backcountry. Ranger Knight lived up to his reputation. That is why I hired him after all, but his interest in you has interrupted my plans more than once, and well, I need this whole thing done with." His tone sharpened. "Now show me where Ellender Garza is being stored."

Clutching the paperweight behind her back, she glanced at the wall of refrigerators. This was a small town. There weren't a whole lot of remains coming through that needed a medical examiner's review. "I don't know—"

He moved so fast, she barely had a chance to register it. The edge of steel pressed into the front of her throat as the wall at her back kept her from retreating. Her scream cut short as the killer clamped a hand over her mouth. "Then we're going to have to do this one by one, aren't we?"

Hot flares of fear and helplessness consumed her from the inside. Drennan squeezed her hand around the paperweight he had yet to notice as her survival instincts kicked in. She'd been in this position too many times to count. A victim, used, her well-being put at risk, and she hated it. She hated it with every fiber of her being as each cutting word from her mother's mouth or sent in a message dug deeper. Slicing her soul into even tinier pieces. And putting others first, making sure everyone else was taken care of in hope the smallest consideration was returned had only made it worse. Because here she was, once again putting herself between someone she believed needed to be protected and the threat. Ready to do what? Give up her life? Her baby's life?

No. Drennan wasn't okay with that.

She didn't want to teach her son or daughter that their needs should remain at the bottom of a priority list. She'd lived that life… It only ended in loneliness and resentment and rage that dictated every choice she'd ever made, and her baby deserved better. She deserved better.

Except once.

She'd made a choice of her own free will that night in the bar. She'd chosen Harvey. For herself, to feel something other than all those crushing feelings of guilt from leaving her mother behind, grief from realizing she'd never have the relationship she'd always wanted with her last parent and fear from ending up alone.

And he'd been everything she'd needed that night.

Dominant but respectful, just enough to make her feel

safe and taking the pressure off her of having to lead. Attentive and passionate, more so than any other boyfriend she'd been with. Understanding and committed, without any confusion about what they'd both sought that night. They hadn't spoken more than a handful of words in the hours they'd lost themselves to one another, but she'd never felt so connected to another person as she had him. She'd used him as thoroughly and completely as he'd used her, and for the first time since her entire world had been turned upside down, she'd felt…free.

Harvey had gifted her something no one else had. For just a night, she'd felt what it would be like to drop the responsibility she'd carried for everyone else's happiness but her own. Because adding hers to the mix had been too heavy and selfish. But he'd shown her how to put herself first, and she loved him for it.

Was *in* love with him for it.

Not just a culmination of one night or a baby, but because of all of it. The way he'd taken care of her after she'd passed out in the park, how he'd gone out of his way to ensure she ate and drank enough, urged her to get her rest. When he seemed more agitated with more distance between them and how he'd battled through his own demons to ensure her needs were met. But more, she loved the genuine care he put into making sure she and the baby were safe in the apartment…and from him. Abusers didn't do that. Neither did cowards.

Because, holy hell, she'd been wrong about him back in that office. Everything he'd done had been for her. At the risk of his job, his trauma and his future. Harvey cared about her, whether he realized it or not, and she'd let her own fears get in the way of seeing it. Until now.

"Move." Her abductor pressed the scalpel deeper, and a

bead of blood slipped down her neck. "Toward the refrigerators."

The bite of pain dumped a dose of adrenaline into her blood, and Drennan had no choice but to do as she was ordered. For the sake of herself and the baby. "A lack of planning on your part does not constitute an emergency on mine."

His free hand bit into her arm as he jerked her to his side, pinning her hand with the paperweight against him as he maneuvered them to the other side of the exam room. Right before he shoved her ahead of him and into the wall of refrigerators. "Find her. Now."

Drennan seized the small bud of courage blooming in the center of her chest. Securing her hand around the paperweight, she gauged the distance between them. He could move fast. He'd already proven that, but he didn't know how far she would go for her child. "No."

She didn't give him a chance to recover, swinging the paperweight as hard as she could at his head.

The superintendent caught her wrist and squeezed the tendons there. Hard. The weight fell without her permission, shattering on the linoleum floor. "That was not a good choice, Dr. Hawes."

He lunged at her with the scalpel.

Chapter Twenty-Six

His fist nearly brought down the door.

"Drennan, it's me." Every cell in his body strained to pick up some kind of evidence that she'd come home after the doctor's office. Her car wasn't in the parking lot, and he'd already tested the doorknob and checked the windows to make sure they'd been locked. "Please. We need to talk."

She had every reason not to answer the door, but this wasn't about what'd happened between them. He just needed to know that she was safe. To settle the panic rolling through him in unending waves of acid and tightness.

Harvey knocked again. No answer. "I know you're upset, and you have every right to be. Just let me know you're okay."

But what if she wasn't? What if she couldn't come to the door because she'd passed out again or she was throwing up from the morning sickness? What if her abductor had intercepted her? Hell. She hadn't answered any of his calls or texts, and every second that passed without hearing from her was being etched into his palms by his fingernails. Dr. Yarrow hadn't seen or heard from her, and there was no way to tell if she'd gone back to the office, but the pathologist had hung up to reach out to the funeral director to check the security system.

"Damn it, Drennan. I'm sorry. For everything. For not supporting you when you told me you were pregnant and all that crap I said at the clinic. It wasn't true. I know that." His voice quaked as he recalled every vile accusation he'd used to put distance between them. He couldn't just stand here letting his head get the best of him. He had to get control of himself, keep himself level. For Drennan and the baby. Except that place of numbness he'd retreated to as threats arose over the years didn't exist anymore. "I just need you to open the door. Please."

Silence greeted him from the other side of the door.

"Screw this." Determination had him looking for a spare key she might've left in case she'd lost her keys or some other kind of emergency. He tossed her doormat and checked the fake plant up against the wall. He burned himself checking the top of the exterior light and got a splinter running his hand over the edge of her doorframe. No key. Frustration and pride battled to win his attention. He needed to get in. There was only one other option. In the name of concern. "I'm going to pay for this."

Harvey craned his head to one side and thrust his elbow through her front window. Glass sliced across the skin of his forearm and up his biceps, but he barely felt the pain as he reached through the pane for the lock on the window. It snapped to one side with his help, and he shoved the frame upward. In seconds, he'd gained access to the apartment. Which, he quickly realized, was in complete darkness. "Drennan?"

Could she be asleep? He doubted it considering the noise breaking the window had made. In fact, he wouldn't be surprised if one of her neighbors called the police. But he'd seen the exhaustion in her face and body language the past couple of days. The pregnancy was taking a toll on her, siphoning everything she had. He scanned the living room, everything exactly where he remembered, before heading into the bedroom.

Pushing the door open, Harvey went for the overhead light. He caught hints of her body wash, that light citrus scent that'd haunted him for weeks after she'd left his bed two months ago. She wasn't here, and a quick glance around told him she hadn't been for hours.

Tendrils of dread shot up his spine.

He'd started his search in the wrong location.

Backtracking through the apartment, he swept through the living room and went straight into the kitchen. His first instinct had been right. She'd most likely gone into work to lose herself in the case. What had she said? That she had to see this through. She had to finish the investigation into Ellender Garza's death. Hell. He'd wasted too much time coming here, but he'd needed to take the risk. He had no reason to believe she was in danger, just as when Dr. Yarrow had asked her to search for the victim's personal items at the scene, but that same sense of knowing—of urgency—took hold.

Harvey grabbed what he needed from beneath the kitchen sink and beelined for the window he'd broken. He wouldn't make it easier for anyone else to get to her. Duct taping the opening, he secured the broken window as best he could, a little concerned the police hadn't already rolled up in response to someone breaking in, but he'd worry about that later.

Walking out the front door, he gave her apartment one last glance. Praying with every nonreligious bone in his body that it wasn't the last time he saw it.

Tearing out of the parking lot, he navigated to the freeway and put the accelerator to the floor. The car accessory system lit up with an incoming call just as he hit the open road. Ranger Simpson. Harvey answered. "Yeah?"

"Wanted to let you know we got a hit on the gun you took off the kidnapper." The law enforcement ranger didn't wait for Harvey's response. "I've cross-checked the serial number with multiple federal databases and reached out to a friend in the Salt Lake Police Department, but nothing came back."

That didn't make sense. "You said you got a hit."

"I followed a gut instinct. The weapon you pulled off Drennan Hawes's kidnapper matches the make and model my law enforcement rangers are issued."

Every muscle down Harvey's back pulled tight. His fingers ached from the hold he had on the steering wheel. The oncoming headlights through the windshield filmed over with a red tint as anger overtook him. "You're telling me one of your rangers came after her?"

He filtered through the faces and names he'd collected over the years working side by side with the law enforcement division, but Harvey hadn't recognized Drennan's abductor when they'd come face-to-face.

"No. Every weapon I've issued to my rangers has been accounted for, but there is one that was issued outside of my division." Keyboard taps echoed through the line. "For the superintendent of the park."

"Pierce Shelton?" Confusion threatened to throw him into a spiral he might not ever come out of. "What the hell does a national park superintendent need with a federally-issued gun?"

"That's above my pay grade and long before I took over as head of this division." The key taps ended, and Simpson's voice lowered as though he needed to be careful of who overheard. "What I'm telling you is the serial number of the weapon you handed me matches the one issued to Superintendent Shelton."

Air escaped his chest. The red haze cleared—for now—

but that part of him he'd always hated rushed to the surface, took control as a new outlet for all the hurt and pain and loss and isolation he'd suffered over the years was exposed. "Drennan was right, wasn't she? Ellender Garza wasn't married, but she'd gotten pregnant. By her killer. He killed her to cover it up."

Simpson shifted something around through the line. "But why go after Drennan? Does she know the victim or the superintendent? Did she see something she wasn't supposed to?"

The pieces were starting to fall into place, rocketing Harvey's desperation into dangerous levels. He couldn't push the SUV any faster without endangering his and other lives on the road, but his blood pulsed with need to get to her. Now. She was at the office. He had to believe that. Because if she wasn't—

"Because she's an assistant to the medical examiner. She has access to the remains." Harvey caught sight of the exit for Hurricane and took it as fast as he dared. "The Office of the Medical Examiner is a state agency with high-end security and data protection. The killer must need something from Ellender Garza's body. I'm guessing evidence that proves he's the father of the victim's baby. He had to have been waiting to see who would come back to the scene for evidence, and Drennan walked right into his ambush."

He'd come so damn close to losing her. Closer than he'd realized.

"You faced off with her abductor, took his weapon from him, and you didn't realize it was your boss who'd kidnapped her?" Simpson was moving now. Harvey wasn't sure why or where, but there was a chance he'd have the law enforcement division at his back. "Remind me not to look at your application to my division down the line."

Harvey slammed his palm against the steering wheel as he rolled through the empty freeway exit. "When was the last time you saw the superintendent in the park? And he wasn't the one who hired me. That was Risner—before he got fired for sexual harassment. Hell, I'd never met the man before."

But he would.

And it wouldn't end how he'd originally imagined meeting his boss.

Because there was no doubt in Harvey's mind the man who'd pointed a gun at him in the backcountry—who'd tied the mother of his child to a tree with intentions to hurt her—wouldn't walk away from this in one piece.

"What is your plan, here, Harvey?" The law enforcement ranger kept Harvey's head in the present. "If you go after the superintendent and we're wrong, you'll lose your job."

"We're not wrong." He didn't know how to explain his confidence, but the evidence was lining up. Whoever had taken Drennan had experience with wilderness survival and strategy, and the gun had been issued to the superintendent in the past. What were the chances a random abductor had gotten hold of it? Then again, what kind of criminal knowingly used a weapon that could be tied back to them? "I've got to go. I'm almost at the ME's office." The SUV's headlights coasted over the funeral home as he pulled into the parking lot. His nerves were tight. If he didn't get sights on Drennan in the next minute, he wasn't going to be able to breathe. "Drennan's not at home, and she's not answering her phone. I can't get ahold of her, and I'm worried something has happened."

"You're just telling me this now?" Simpson was breathing hard now as though he'd started sprinting. "I'll have Jordan take a run at the superintendent. See if she can track him down. I'm on my way."

The call ended before Harvey cut the engine. He wasn't law enforcement. He hadn't been issued an official weapon, but that didn't mean he was going in unarmed. Popping the glove compartment in the SUV, he extracted his personal weapon. Because there wasn't anything he wasn't willing to do to keep Drennan safe.

She was a healer, and Harvey was possibly the most broken person she'd ever met, but she'd somehow put him back together. Piece by piece, she'd helped him see the good he'd carried over the years instead of the bad. Good that had only come out for her, but it was there. He'd just had to look a little closer, to have a reason for it to come through. Drennan and the baby were that reason. She'd seen past the darkness he wielded as a shield. She lit him up, and he loved her for that. Wanted more of her in his life. Wanted to prove he wasn't his father, every day if she would just give him the chance. That he could be there for her, be there for the baby. He wanted to prove that he could make her happy if she forgave him. That he could love her the way she deserved.

Harvey checked the magazine in his weapon and slid it into the back of his waistband.

Ready to let go of the past. And claim his future.

Chapter Twenty-Seven

Pieces of Dr. Yarrow's shattered paperweight skidded across the floor as her abductor spun her around. Pain flared through her face as the superintendent who'd killed Ellender Garza pressed her into the wall of refrigerators from behind.

His body heated against hers, fitting them together in the worst way possible, and a surge of acid clogged her throat.

"I warned you what would happen if you didn't help me, Dr. Hawes." The scalpel he held nicked another patch of sensitive skin against her throat, and Drennan closed her eyes. She wouldn't cry. She wouldn't break. Not for him. "Open it."

She pressed her hands into the refrigerator door, bucking against him to add some semblance of distance between his front and her back. In vain. The killer only fought to hold her in place. "Get off me."

The words sounded strangled, even to her own ears. This wasn't how Harvey held her throughout the night. How his body heat had seeped into her muscles and soothed all the rough edges she'd picked up over the years. This was something dominating and manipulative and gut-nauseating. It felt as though thousands of spiders tiptoed across her skin, raising a rush of disgust.

The pressure at her back disappeared. Just for a moment. "Open it."

Drennan didn't have any other choice. She'd lost her only weapon. She didn't have the skills to fight back against a man almost double her size, and she wasn't about to risk the baby in an effort to escape. She was trapped. Her breath shuddered through her at the thought. Forcing her hands to peel away from the cold refrigerator door, she reached for the handle to her left. The door swung open, releasing a pillowy haze of mist. The morgue refrigerators leaned more toward freezers to slow decomposition of the remains they stored, and a chill tensed the muscles across her shoulders.

"It's empty. The next one." His command tightened around her rib cage. Sooner or later, they'd come across Ellender Garza. And then what? The scalpel was back at her throat, reminding her of how very little power she actually held in this room.

Drennan shifted over one row, grabbing for the refrigerator door. If she could get him close enough, there was a chance she could slam it in his face. Stun him long enough to make a run for the exit, but her abductor was being smart, keeping an arm's length between them. He'd see any move she made, and he'd punish her. He'd make it hurt.

She opened the next refrigerator, and the one after that.

Coming to the last in the row. She'd done what she could to stall, to think of a plan better than trying her luck at confronting the superintendent head-on, and now she was out of time. Her hands shook as she reached for the last door handle.

And swung it open.

A dark head of hair spread out across the sliding table stored inside the six-foot-deep refrigerator. The remains stored in the morgue no longer wore toe tags to identify them, but Drennan recognized the woman covered by a thin sheet inside.

"Pull her out." Her abductor moved in behind her. The scalpel sliced across her skin, and Drennan couldn't stop the gasp at the sting of pain.

She grabbed for her neck to gauge how deep he'd sliced, coming away with a slippery layer of blood. Nonlethal. He hadn't cut anything vital or she would've already been dead, but he'd gotten close. She was bleeding, and she'd continue to do so unless she added pressure.

"Now!" Pinching the back of her neck in one hand, he shoved her into the opening of the refrigerator.

Her entire body flinched from the violence in his voice. Stainless steel bit into her chest as she slapped her hands on the table to stop her momentum. The injury at her neck screamed as blood slipped beneath her blouse and across her collarbone. Drennan blinked against the sudden wave of dizziness. Whether it came from the drop in temperature, her pregnancy, the impact against the storage box or the laceration along the side of her neck, she didn't know. But she didn't have much time. "Okay." That single word sounded as though it'd come from a stranger. "Okay."

His body heat retreated for just a moment as he stepped out of her way.

Drennan tugged the tracked exam table toward her, her heart rate ticking too loud in her head. This...this wasn't how it was supposed to happen. It wasn't supposed to end like this. She was going to have a baby. She was going to be a mom with a family of her very own and turn everything she'd survived in her mother's house into something good. She didn't want to die. Not before she had the chance to see her son or daughter grow up. To take their first breath and their first steps. She wanted the ridiculous kindergarten graduations and themed birthday parties and the constant "mamas" once her child learned how to talk. She wanted the scraped knees and the kisses that fixed them and the floods from the bathtub.

She could see it all. Right in front of her.

And Harvey... She could see him, too. Throwing his arms open for their toddler to run into at the end of a long workday, spinning around until they both got dizzy and sick. She saw him helping her with dinner and kissing the side of her neck where her abductor had sliced through the skin there. She could feel his hands on her hips and his calluses prickling goose bumps up her arms as if he was right here in the room with her.

It was so real...and so heartbreaking. Because Harvey couldn't love her until he learned how to accept and love himself, and she couldn't force him. She couldn't heal for him. But she could fight for them, for their family. However long it took, through whatever hardships that came. Whatever the risk or pain that most assuredly waited on the other side was worth it, wasn't it? He had to see that.

The exam table hit the end of the track, jarring the woman on the table. Drennan tried to back away. She'd given the killer what he wanted, led him straight to Ellender Garza. Her gaze flitted to the double steel doors. Could she make it before he lashed out?

The superintendent ripped back the sheet hiding the stitched Y-cut from both of the victim's shoulders, down over her sternum and into her belly. "Open her up."

Blood that hadn't seeped from her wound drained from her face. "What?"

"I told you what I came here for, Dr. Hawes." He extended the scalpel toward her, blade first. "And I'm not leaving without it. Open her up."

Her stomach pitched with a renewed flood of nausea. She shook her head. She'd cut into a thousand bodies over the course of her education and career, even as an assistant medical examiner, but she couldn't do this. "You can't be serious."

"What about me gives the impression that I'm joking?" He rounded the end of the cold exam table, closing the distance between them until she caught hints of his aftershave. Something gut-wrenching and cloying. "You're a doctor. You know what you're looking for. Get me my baby, and you walk away from this unscathed."

She tasted the lie as it seeped from his mouth. He'd let her see his face. There was no way in hell he'd let her leave this room alive. If she had to guess, he'd leave her body in one of the refrigerators to buy himself some time to escape. Drennan backed up another step. "Please. You don't have to do this. I can delete the DNA from the database. She can be buried or cremated. There are easier ways to get what you want. Don't make me do this."

His gaze narrowed on hers. "Now, why would a doctor beg me not…" Understanding smoothed the lines around his eyes, and his gaze dropped to her midsection. "Ah. So that's why Ranger Knight is so protective of you. You're carrying his baby. I had to wonder why a decorated soldier like that bothered to look twice at a boring as hell assistant ME in the middle of nowhere Utah."

The bite of pain that had nothing to do with the slice to her neck cut through her at his words. Boring. Unnecessary. Selfish. Disappointment. She'd heard the words a thousand times over, and they stung just as much coming from this complete stranger as they had from her mother.

Except Drennan had removed that particular tumor from her life. And she'd do it again. She'd do it as many times as it took. Because Harvey was right when he'd said she was strong. That she was important and that she deserved to be happy. And this son of a bitch was not making her very happy.

"I didn't say that." Drennan shifted her weight between her feet, ready to run as hard as her legs allowed. Would she make it far? Probably not. But she could go for one of the shards of paperweight on the floor.

A disjointed smile curled at one side of his mouth, as though he'd seen it on other people's faces and tried to replicate it himself in the mirror a thousand times, but it never made the full impact. Instead it curdled something in her stomach. "You didn't have to." He took another step, coming to her side of the table, no longer allowing anything to act as a barrier between them. "All right, Dr. Hawes. I'll make this easy for you."

Why did she have the impression he had no interest in making things easy for her? Her hands went clammy with him this close as every possibility played out in her mind.

Twisting the scalpel in one hand, he took that final step that put them toe to toe. "Either you get me what I want, or I take *your* baby."

Oxygen stalled in her chest. He wouldn't. Would he? Her chin wobbled as she forced herself to keep eye contact with the man threatening her child. Her future. No one would hurt this baby. She could do this. "I need a scalpel."

"Here." That smile was back, still a little off. "Take mine, but if you try to use it on me, I will do what I promised and leave you to bleed out on the floor."

Drennan took what he offered, the steel familiar and warm in her hand. "That's not going to work for me."

She struck, stabbing the blade of the scalpel into the soft tissue at the side of his neck, but adrenaline had thrown off her aim. She somehow managed to avoid hitting his carotid artery. The superintendent grabbed for his neck with one hand and backhanded her across the face with the other.

Drennan hit the line of refrigerators face-first. Lightning exploded behind her eyes just before she collapsed. She couldn't breathe, couldn't think.

"I warned you what would happen if you fought me, Dr. Hawes." Her clothing bunched around her neck as he fisted her collar and dragged her around the end of the exam table. He dropped her in front of another row of refrigerators, grabbing for the door. The table slid out next, and everything in her body went tight. No. No, no, no. He swayed above her, keeping pressure on his wound as he hauled her onto the exam table. "I always follow through on my promises."

Cold broke through the sweat along her spine. Drennan's sense of survival kicked in too late as he shoved the table back into the refrigerator. With her on it. She reached overhead for the door. Too late. "No!"

The lights cut out.

Chapter Twenty-Eight

Harvey kicked through the heavy double doors.

A mess of features contorted as Superintendent Pierce Shelton whipped his attention in Harvey's direction. He'd never met the man—hadn't seen anything more than his smiling photo in the monthly ranger newsletter—but every cell in Harvey's body told him this was the son of a bitch who'd attacked Drennan in the park. Who'd wanted to use her to get to the woman currently cut open on the table. Straightening, the superintendent seemed to gauge the distance between him and the door and conclude his chances weren't great. Now unmasked and exposed by the sharp fluorescent lighting overhead, Pierce Shelton's appearance exceeded his midlife age. More gray, more shadows to his face, more wear around his eyes. Not from exhaustion. *Desperation.* His hand shook as he pulled away from the victim on the table.

"Ranger Knight, what a pleasant surprise. I don't expect you're here for an update on the Ellender Garza case? Because I can confidently tell you the case is closed, and your services are no longer needed."

Harvey scanned the office, with its wall of freezers, Dr. Yarrow's desk shoved to one side, and the body Shelton stood over. Ice flooded his veins. *Drennan.* Where was

Drennan? The rumble in his chest barely maintained a human effort as he took a step deeper into the morgue. "Where is she?"

A brittle smile spread across Shelton's face. "You'll have to be more specific."

"Drennan Hawes. The medical examiner you abducted." Her name grounded him in ways he'd never experienced before. No amount of meditation, centering or yoga had come close to the warmth her mere existence produced in his chest. Harvey took that next step.

"Doesn't ring a bell. Then again, I'm not familiar with the people in this office. I have rangers for that." Shelton shrugged, his mouth pinching with the effort. Every word out of this bastard's mouth wasted another precious second Drennan might not have. He was going to drag this out. Wanted Harvey to take whatever bait he spewed to buy himself time.

Which meant...

Harvey's gaze flickered to the rivulet of liquid spreading down the superintendent's uniform shirt. A metallic odor drove into Harvey's lungs. Blood. Shelton's? Or Drennan's? His knuckles screamed for relief as he fisted both hands. "Is that why you're bleeding all over the victim on the table? The woman you got pregnant then killed to cover the affair?"

There was a shift in the air between them. A different kind of unmasking. Charged with intention and an unleashed rawness. Shelton angled the scalpel in his hand down as he rounded the table. "Well, I guess there's no point in pretending any longer, is there? You know, I was hoping you were smart enough to walk away, but that's no longer an option. You'll just have to go in the freezer with her."

The freezer. Harvey's attention cut to the wall of horizontal freezers meant to preserve remains. Drennan... She was in there. She was dying. His lungs emptied of oxygen.

The distraction cost him.

Shelton charged, the lights glinting off the scalpel in one hand.

Harvey shot his fist straight into the superintendent's face. Pain ricocheted through the back of his hand and up his forearm, but he didn't stop. Couldn't stop. A groan bounced off the empty cream-colored walls as Shelton hit the linoleum. And still, Harvey didn't relent. One strike. Two. Three. Blood pumped a hard beat at the base of his throat. Hot and pounding. The scalpel was lost in the onslaught. The superintendent brought his forearms up to block the attack. A boot connected with Harvey's chest, and he lost the upper hand.

"And here I thought you had a future with NPS, Ranger Knight." Shelton shot to his feet. He swiped the blood dripping from his nose and mouth with the back of one hand. His left eye had started swelling under the spread of red inflammation, but the killer stood as though Harvey hadn't made a single dent. "Unfortunately, we're going to have to let you go."

Generations of rage and violence and lack of control flooded down Harvey's arms. *This.* This was what he'd tried to hide from Drennan. To protect her from. This was why he'd never wanted to be a father and had done so well in the military. In a matter of seconds, the fire he'd buried under years of denial and shame had been released in the face of losing the one person he'd never wanted to burn. It was like a physical presence embodied him—his father, his grandfather—as Harvey rocketed his fist toward Shelton's face. He would never allow this evil inside him to touch Drennan or their baby, but he'd let it out to save them. No matter the cost. He missed, swinging wide. He took another shot. Shelton ducked out of the way.

His third attempt landed home. His growl filled the morgue as the superintendent fell back into the medical examiner's desk. Office supplies and paperwork shot from the desk and over the floor.

He had to get to the freezer. Had to get Drennan out. Harvey lunged for the first hip-level door and nearly wrenched it off its hinges. Empty. He moved to the second. There weren't many options to choose from. Shelton would've had to have lifted her into the freezer with a seeping wound. One Drennan had most likely given him. "Hang on, baby. I'm coming. For both of you."

Again, empty.

"Where are you?" Cotton filled his head, undercut by a slow, steady pulse. As though he could hear her heartbeat through the metal, which wasn't possible, but every minute he wasted trying to take down Shelton slowed that pulse. She was running out of time.

Movement registered behind him.

Harvey lunged out of the way as the superintendent embedded the tip of a bone saw into the stainless steel freezer door. The bastard positioned himself between Harvey and the wall of freezers. Keeping him from Drennan. Shelton's shoulders rose and fell with exaggerated gasps, his blood pooling on the floor. "Did you really think it would be that easy, Knight? That you just get to live your happily-ever-after while I lose everything?"

That pulse in his head was getting slower. Softer. He was losing her. Her and the baby. Gauging the bladed teeth of the saw, Harvey closed the distance between them. Locking his hand around the superintendent's wrist, he vaulted

Shelton's hand and the bone saw overhead and curled the blade back into the man's torso.

The saw cut straight through. Lodged in Superintendent Pierce Shelton's gut. One second. Two. That imaginary pulse had stopped. Harvey released his hold on the killer, and Shelton hit the floor. Alive. For now. Stepping over the bastard's prone body, he jerked the next freezer open. Then the fourth.

Air lodged in his throat as a head of beautiful hair escaped the confines of the freezer. He dragged the rolling table free and framed her too-cold face. Her eyes were closed, crystals clinging to her eyelashes as though her tears had frozen in place. Pressing his fingers to her throat, he almost collapsed in relief as her pulse kicked against his touch. Harvey pressed his forehead to hers. "I've got you, Drennan. I've always got you."

Chapter Twenty-Nine

His knuckles were already swelling.

Harvey shut down the pain in his hand as Dr. Cassidy Duffy took up position on one side of Drennan lying across the hospital bed. He hadn't known who else to call. Somehow it'd taken less than fifteen minutes for the doc to reach them in Hurricane, and he was never more grateful to see a physician than he was right then.

He'd almost been too late.

Harvey closed his eyes as he fisted the top blanket on Drennan's bed. The pressure had released some, but he could still see her, that lifeless thing he'd found in the freezer. Unmoving. Unresponsive. Drennan's skin had taken on a blue tint, her lips darker and her skin ice-cold. A section of her hair had broken straight off. He wasn't sure how long she'd been trapped, but the drop in temperature had obviously taken a toll. But she'd survived. He didn't know how. Anyone else would've given up, but she'd always been a fighter.

He locked down that sense of loss creeping into the edges of his mind as the pain in his knee flared to life. He'd pushed himself harder than he had in months, maybe years, these past couple of days, but he'd never regret a single moment. The monitor off to the side of her bed picked up every change in Drennan's heart rate. Strong and consistent compared to the first few minutes she'd been admitted to the clinic's emergency department. He soothed his thumb over the top of her foot, over and over until she'd realized where she'd been taken and that she was safe. Now she couldn't seem to detach herself, her foot following his retreat when he thought she might need space. Like she couldn't stand the thought of not touching him.

He felt the same, and he was prepared to stand by her all night if that was what she needed.

"Vitals are looking good. Your body temperature is almost back to normal." Dr. Duffy shone a penlight over Drennan's face, maneuvering it back and forth. "You'll live. Any pain?"

"Just on my neck." Drennan's voice sounded as though it'd been scraped over glass. A row of stitches lined a laceration along the side of her throat, black against her still too-pale skin. The son of a bitch who'd attacked her had taken a scalpel to her neck.

But she'd gotten him in the end. Well, her and the bone saw.

Superintendent Shelton had been aimlessly cutting into the dark-haired woman Harvey had pulled from the Emerald Pools when he'd arrived. Trying to take her baby, the only proof that'd he gotten Ellender Garza pregnant.

Both Ranger Simpson and Dr. Yarrow had chosen that exact moment to make their appearances and stop the superintendent from dying. The bastard was currently under arrest three cots down with a few new liters of blood and two law enforcement babysitters. Murder in the first degree and the attempted murder of a state official. As for Ellender Garza and her baby, Shelton had been cutting into her lower intestine rather than her uterus according to Dr. Yarrow. Police and law enforcement rangers had all the evidence they needed to connect the superintendent to Ellender Garza's death through DNA and motive.

Drennan's foot pressed into his hand, and Harvey snapped his gaze back to her. Intense green eyes locked on him as Dr. Duffy rolled back on her stool. He squeezed her foot, digging his thumb into the bottom to let her know he was still here. He wasn't going anywhere. She'd been through hell in more ways than one. Had to fight for her life alone against a man twice her size armed with a blade. She was lucky she hadn't sustained more serious injuries, and Harvey would thank a God he didn't believe in every day for that.

"I'm going to have her kept for observation overnight, and I want to get another ultrasound for the baby, considering the last twenty-four hours." Dr. Duffy turned her attention to him. "She needs rest and another round of fluids, but I think she'll be all right as long as she takes it easy. Can I assume you're staying with her?"

Harvey cleared his throat, not entirely sure if Drennan wanted him after their last conversation, but he nodded. "Yeah. I'm staying."

"Okay." The doctor shoved to stand. "I'll be back around to check on her in the morning."

"Thanks, Doc." He didn't just mean tonight. "For sticking with her all this time. Looking out for her."

A small smile transformed the overworked trauma physician as she patted Drennan's leg. "That's what friends are for. Call me if you need me."

Despite the chaos around the emergency room, silence pressed in on him as Drennan leveled that beautiful gaze on him. And, hell, he'd come so close to losing her. As much as he hated seeing her in this bed—again—he'd take this over never seeing her again. "You need water or something to eat? The cafeteria is just downstairs."

"No. Thank you." She clasped a hand on the stitches in her neck as she worked herself higher in the bed. "You don't have to stay. I'm sure there is literally anywhere else you want to be rather than here."

"I'm exactly where I want to be, Drennan." He moved to the head of the bed to help her with the pillow at her back. "And that's with you."

She didn't have an answer for that, but he could feel the hesitation to believe him in the silence that followed. She had no reason to believe him, and he didn't blame her. The things he'd said... "I lied to you."

"About wanting to stay?" Her eyebrows furrowed in the middle, right at the bridge of her nose, and it was so damn adorable the way she looked at him. Would their baby have the same look in a couple years? His chest tightened at the thought, but...he wanted to find out. "You can—"

"No. In the doctor's office. After your ultrasound." Harvey reached into his back pocket, pulling the roll of sonograms free. He smoothed the creases from all three pictures, trying to make up for the added damage they'd suffered during his fight with Superintendent Shelton. "I know you. I think you've let me see the real you more than you've ever let anyone before, and I took that trust and killed it."

She sucked in a sharp breath as she studied the sonograms in his hand, as though she didn't dare to move, wanting to see what he did next. Walking on eggshells. And, hell, he'd spent his entire life doing just that, and to see her have to react the same way... Harvey closed his eyes. He never wanted her to fear him.

"All those things I said about you getting pregnant on purpose and using your mother's manipulation to get what you want, they were lies, Drennan." He handed her the sonogram images, a part of him hopeful there would be more that he could keep for himself, but for now, he had to let them go. "I don't believe for a second you would ever treat another human being the way you were treated since your dad died, and I'm sorry. You were right. I was being a coward. The way I acted? It was what my father used to do to my mother, and I never wanted to be that man. Ever."

She took the sonograms, running her fingers over the outline of their baby. "Then why did you say them?"

"Because I was scared." His pulse thudded hard in his throat. He grabbed for a corner of her pillow, strangling it beneath his hand as vulnerability stripped him bare. "I've spent a good part of my life detached and numb, but the second I set eyes on you in that bar, I knew you were going to mess up my life plan to die alone."

She looked at him then, and the entire world threatened to rip out from underneath his feet. She didn't look at him with anger or the same detachment he'd spoken of. He knew she was the kind of woman who could turn off her emotions and keep them off and that would be it. She'd already proven that by leaving her abuser behind and floundering for a new punching bag. Instead, Drennan looked at him with an openness he didn't deserve.

"Since meeting you, I've felt things I haven't in a long time. I've wanted things I've never wanted for myself before. A future. And seeing the baby on the ultrasound... I realized I was more broken than I wanted to admit, and just because you understood my pain doesn't mean my behavior was acceptable." His voice became gravelly as he tried to hold back. "But you saw all those pieces and somehow found a way to bring them back together. You didn't see the scars I've been using to keep people away. You just saw me.

You made me feel seen, and for the first time in my life, I felt good enough for a brilliant, beautiful woman like you. Someone who I could spend the rest of my life with."

Tears glimmered in her eyes. Drennan swiped at her face. "Harvey—"

"I want you to keep messing up that life plan, Drennan." Harvey slid his free hand across her middle, right where their baby was growing. "You and this baby. I love you. I'm ridiculously in love with you. Please forgive me. Please give me another chance to prove I can be there for you." He cleared his throat. "That I can be a good father."

That brilliant smile that'd always made his heart stop flashed wide. Drennan slid her hand over his, over her nonexistent baby bump. "Does that mean you're going to be there for all my future ob-gyn appointments?"

"Every appointment. Every time you have to throw up. Late-night grocery store runs for food cravings. Massaging your feet when they get swollen and sore." Harvey leaned down, his mouth hovering over hers. "Babyproofing the entire house. Lamaze classes. Learning about breastfeeding. I want to be there for the birthday parties and the Christmases and Thanksgivings. I want the graduations and weddings and proms. I want it all."

Her breath shuddered through her, and the monitor tracking her heart rate ticked higher. Drennan dropped her gaze to his mouth and back, and a searing heat lightninged through him. "And if I wanted you to be more than a supportive father?"

Hell. This woman was going to break him in an all new way, and Harvey had the sense he'd enjoy every second of it. "More?"

"More." She nodded, her bottom lip brushing against his. "Because I'm in love with you, too. I think I fell in love with you the night we met. But I've spent my whole life dreaming of family that loves me, Harvey, and I'm not willing to settle for scraps anymore. Can you give me that?"

"For the rest of my life." Nothing could've stopped him from kissing her then. Harvey crushed his mouth to hers, careful of her injuries and the fact she'd been through so much in the past few days. Her mouth parted at his insistence, and he drank her in. "I told you before, Dr. Hawes. You're mine. Forever."

She smiled against his mouth, slipping an arm around his neck to pull him onto the bed with her. "Forever, Ranger Knight."

* * * * *

BIG SKY MANHUNT

JUNO RUSHDAN

To my readers. Thank you.

Chapter One

Somewhere in Broadwater County, Montana
Thursday, April 12, 1:15 a.m.

One misstep and I'm dead.
The certainty of it sent a shiver through Christina Ortiz.

She trailed behind Hector Ibarra, a lieutenant of the Estrada cartel, farther into the dark railroad tunnel. No moonlight reached this deep inside the old passageway. A frigid breeze sliced through her down jacket. Winters in Montana lasted from October to May. Up ahead, a set of bright headlights beamed, pointed in the opposite direction, the sole source of illumination. She caught a whiff of exhaust fumes in the dank air. A rectangular shape came into view, the back of an idling van parked on the train tracks.

Everything about the situation was off. Wrong. That was saying a lot, considering she'd been a deep-cover asset embedded in the cartel for the past six years. She'd encountered her fair share of precarious circumstances but followed strict rules—or what her handler called Alice in the Underworld commandments. In total, there were ten.

Right now, number two came to mind—listen to her gut. And her gut was screaming. *Get out!*

Despite every instinct warning her to do so, she couldn't

turn and run. Getting shot in the back was worse than the unknown lurking in the eerie tunnel.

Better to see it coming.

"What are we doing here, Hector?"

Silence was his only response.

Not surprising. Hector had never liked her, or the quick way she'd ascended through their ranks. He had a nasty habit of leering at her with a disturbing mix of lust and hate that made her skin crawl. Not her first choice of Estrada members to follow into an abandoned tunnel.

There were two ways in and out, but she'd only seen one. Neither was good, since both would leave her exposed to gunfire. She needed an exit strategy. Fast.

She stepped on a rotted railroad tie, the lumber breaking, and almost lost her footing. Thankfully, she had on her tactical midboots.

Rule number three, wear footwear she could run in. Even to a black-tie event, which required a little creativity. Some women dressed for fashion. She dressed for survival.

"We drove over an hour to get here." Christina trod carefully, literally and figuratively. "Is this is going to take long? I've got to get up early."

"*Paciencia, abejita,*" Hector said, calling her "little bee," a moniker only he used. "You're always buzzing, buzzing, buzzing."

Christina gritted her teeth. Any time a man called her a weird nickname, regardless of the language it was in, it was creepy. Coming from Hector made it doubly so.

She put a hand on her purse, which was large enough to hold a small arsenal and easily concealed her Beretta M9, along with a few other necessities.

Hector had shown up at her apartment in Bozeman close to midnight, hours after her personal bodyguard had left, and insisted she follow him. Not a word about where they were going or why.

It was an order.

She'd taken many from Hector. Orders were always followed, no matter how odd or dangerous. No explanation necessary. Refusal could mean a bullet to the head.

That was the way of the cartel.

But as soon as they'd pulled up to the derelict railroad tunnel in the boondocks, she decided to wear her purse cross-body, unzipped it and switched off the safety on her gun.

Hector glanced at her over his shoulder, but she couldn't see his eyes in the dim light from the van that wasn't too far away. "All will be revealed." The cold grittiness in his voice did nothing to melt the block of ice in the pit of her stomach.

Since she'd agreed to become an FBI asset, fear had been her constant companion. Shaping her words. Guiding her actions. Dictating how much to risk sharing with her handler, Kirk Kehoe, regardless of how hard he pushed for information.

Kirk always wanted more, even though every tip-off put her in jeopardy. What did he care about her future? To him, she was just an asset. A means to an end.

Funny, the special agent who had trapped her in this situation, using her as a tool for his professional ambition, hadn't been the one to keep her alive for the past six years. It had been fear, and a monster she didn't want to name.

Many called him *La Parca*—the Grim Reaper.

A monster who protected her, but that protection had cost her dearly.

Staying about a foot behind Hector, she passed the black cargo van. Music played low in the vehicle, but she made out the sound of something, or someone, rustling around inside.

They rounded the front of the van.

Standing in the light was a guy from Hector's crew, gun holstered on his hip. He was smoking. Two stamped-out cigarette butts were at his feet. He'd been there waiting for a while. "Finally," the guy said.

"Go get him." Hector gestured to the van with his head.

The guy tossed his cigarette down, stepped on it, drew his gun and strode to the side of the vehicle.

She glanced at Hector. He looked older than his forty-five years. Decades of excessive drinking had aged his face, turning his skin closer to dull gray than tan, and his large brown eyes were sunken in. But the harsh light from the van made him appear like a ghoulish toad.

The van door slid open. More rustling as someone tried to speak, voice muffled, like he was wearing a gag. A man was hauled out into the light. Hands restrained behind his back. Hector's thug shoved the man to his knees.

It was Javier. Her bodyguard.

Christina stiffened as her nerves pinged. "What's going on?" she asked, straining to keep her voice calm and her expression deadpan.

"He's a traitor," Hector said.

On his knees, Javier shook his head, his words garbled by the rag tied around his mouth, his face bruised, like he'd been beaten.

"This is a mistake," she said. "Javier would never betray the cartel."

"Give me your gun." Hector held out his gloved palm.

She reeled back. "What?"

"He's your bodyguard. Either I use your gun to put him down or you kill him." Hector's palm remained extended while he placed his other hand on the hilt of the .45 in his shoulder holster. As he stared at her, Christina considered lying, saying she hadn't brought a weapon. "I know you're packing. I don't believe for a second you left your apartment alone to come with me in the middle of the night without your gun."

Kudos to him. He wasn't wrong.

"Why do you think Javier is a traitor?" she asked, desperate to redirect him.

But Hector stepped toward her, bringing his face so close to hers she smelled the stench of booze and cigarettes on his breath. "Buzz. Buzz. Buzz." He narrowed his eyes, his expression growing more venomous. "Give me your gun."

She weighed her options, but there weren't many, and the ones that existed weren't good. Hector could draw on her in seconds, and his guy already had a gun at Javier's head.

Sometimes the cartel threw them into the proverbial fire as a test. Not because they knew anything concrete. It was designed to expose any weak link, or a mole. Someone like her.

Christina had to roll the dice and hope this dreadful scene was a test.

She handed Hector her Beretta. "This is a mistake." No hint of the fear surging through her showed in her voice. "He's a loyal soldier." They didn't come more loyal to the cartel than Javier. A fact that made passing information to her handler not only difficult but also high-risk. Many times, she'd sacrificed face-to-face conversations for dead drops and brush passes. "There's some misunderstanding. We should give him a chance to explain."

"*We?*" Hector sneered. "*I* don't need to do anything other than follow orders and kill him."

Only one person gave Hector orders, *El Jefe*, the mysterious stateside drug lord who ran Team US—Rio Estrada. But why would he care about her bodyguard?

"There's no mistake. But let's hear him out." Hector gestured to his guy, and the thug removed the gag.

"Listen to her," Javier said. "I'm not a traitor."

"Maybe. Maybe not," Hector said. "But I have one question. Did you know she was an FBI snitch, or do you just really suck at your job?"

A tightness knotted in her chest, squeezing the air from her lungs. She slipped her left hand into her coat pocket and clutched her automatic knife, thumb on the push button.

"Christina." Trembling, Javier stared at her, stark fear etched across his face. "Tell him it isn't true. You're not an informant. Can't be."

Leveling her Beretta at Javier, Hector looked at her. "Confess and I'll spare him."

Javier wasn't guilty of betraying the cartel, but he also wasn't innocent. He was a low-level hit man, tasked to protect her, yes, but mostly to watch her. Be the eyes and ears of the Reaper, who'd assigned him.

This was a game for Hector. He had no intention of sparing anyone.

Saving Javier wasn't possible. She might not even be able to save herself.

"I have nothing to confess." A solid pause to project faux confidence. "Hector—" She stopped herself from saying *please*. The word would only provoke him. He was a sadist, and she refused to incite further cruelty. "Don't do this. You'll regret it."

Flashing a grin, Hector put his finger on the trigger and squeezed.

Bang! Bang! He shot Javier in the chest and his body hit the ground.

Pivoting, Hector turned her own gun on her.

Terror spiraled inside Christina, making her dizzy. Instead of raising her hands in mock surrender, she steadied one on her purse while tightening her grip on the blade in her pocket.

"You've got this all wrong." The need to run burned inside every vein. It took all her willpower to stay still, hold his gaze and keep her wits about her. "I'm not an informant."

"Get the other one," Hector ordered.

His guy marched back to the van.

Other one?

Moments later, the thug shoved a second man, also gagged and restrained, into the light.

Kirk Kehoe.

A spike of panic punched through her.

This wasn't a fishing expedition. Without a doubt, the cartel knew she was an informant. Only one way they could've found out. Kirk's suspicion that a cartel spy had infiltrated his joint task force for Operation Big Sky Guardian was correct. But he'd sworn to keep her identity a secret and her assignment off the books. To ensure her safety.

"What were you saying, I've got it all wrong?" Hector's grin spread into a vile smile full of evil. "Don't worry, I won't be the one to kill you. Someone special is flying in to deal with you personally. *La Parca.*"

Christina's legs turned to water and her knees nearly buckled.

"*He's* taking care of business in Wyoming but lands in—" Hector glanced at his watch "—thirty-two hours."

Not even Hector wanted to say the monster's name.

Things kept getting worse.

Hector redirected the Beretta at Kirk. "Admit she's been an informant from the beginning, and I'll make it quick. Otherwise, I'll give you a lot to regret as you die slowly."

The thug yanked Kirk's gag down.

Hector took out his phone, tapped the record icon and held it up. "Go on."

Kirk stretched his jaw and spit on the ground. "I'm already filled with regrets. For starters, wish I could go home to *the Garden City* and fish for *little bull trout*."

The words struck a chord of recognition in her head.

Was it a message? Was Kirk trying to tell her something?

"Your fishing days are done, old man," Hector said. "What's it going to be? Quick and painless? Or do I get to have some fun?"

"Not a hard choice to make." Heaving a ragged breath, Kirk shook his head. "Who wants to suffer in the end, huh?"

Christina's gut clenched. The cartel already knew, but she'd never thought Kirk would give her up to spare himself pain, much less give a recorded admission.

"Can I get a smoke first?" Kirk asked.

Hector nodded.

His thug moved around, facing the special agent, put a cigarette in his mouth and lit it.

"Although I'm disappointed," Hector said, "I won't get to have any fun, you've made the right choice. *La Parca* wants to hear about her duplicity straight from you. Start talking."

If anyone knew how deadly the Reaper was and what he'd do to her, it was Kirk Kehoe.

It was all surreal. She'd really fallen down the rabbit hole and was lost in the darkness.

Kirk blew out smoke. "Well," he said, speaking around the cigarette in between his lips, "guess I never should've broken Alice's first commandment."

The number-one rule.

Trust no one.

It was a coded message. For her.

"Still." Kirk drew another drag on the cigarette and exhaled the smoke. "Sometimes you've got to turn to someone. No other choice."

"What are you blabbering about?" Hector snapped.

Kirk shrugged. "Then there's the tenth commandment."

Always be ready to run. Fight your way out if necessary.

Christina slowly slipped her right hand into her purse, unzipped the hidden inner pocket and grasped a long, slender piece of cold, solid steel. With a tight grip on the expandable baton in one hand and the automatic knife in the other, she was ready to strike.

Every man in the cartel underestimated her. Because she was a woman. Because she had a pretty face. It was the reason Hector didn't bother to search her, and even now, he didn't have the gun pointed at her; it was trained on Kirk. Hector expected her to roll over and submit.

She was going to disappoint him.

Kirk lifted his head and looked right at her. "As long as Big Sky Guardian succeeds, I don't mind dying. Or suffering. But I won't be the one screaming." Spitting out the cigarette, Kirk threw his head forward, slamming his skull into the face of the guy who was standing way too close.

Bone crunched. The guy howled in pain as he cupped his bleeding nose. Kirk stomped on his foot, kicked him in the knee and threw his shoulder into the guy, taking them both down to the ground.

At the same time, Christina drew the switchblade from her pocket, pressing the button and ejecting the blade with a crisp *snick*. Pulling the expandable baton from her purse, she flicked it out to its full length of twenty-six inches. But she wasn't fast enough.

Hector pulled the trigger, shooting Kirk three times, also putting a bullet in his own guy, and then whirled in her direction.

Ready like a tightly coiled spring, she whipped the baton down across his wrist. Once. Twice. The second blow jarred the Beretta loose and the gun fell from his hand. Another quick strike to his head and she heard teeth crack as Hector stumbled backward. She lunged, thrusting her knife into his thigh, twisted the blade and yanked it back out.

An agonizing shriek ripped from Hector's mouth.

No time to revel in it. She bolted to the driver's side of the van. The door was unlocked, key in the ignition. She threw the gear into Reverse and slammed her foot on the accelerator, speeding back through the tunnel.

The other guy climbed out from under Kirk's body and got to his feet, holding his side like he'd been shot in the abdomen. Took aim and fired at her. The windshield shattered, spraying glass into the van.

Ducking behind the steering wheel, she didn't ease off the gas pedal until she cleared the tunnel, making it outside. She killed the engine and snapped the key off in the ignition.

Christina jumped out and ran. Reaching Hector's vehicle first, she stabbed two of his tires before hopping in her Ford Bronco. In the tunnel, Kirk had told her where to go, and she could only think of one person she hoped might be in the Garden City. Jackson Powell.

After Kirk first recruited her, he grilled her about her past associations. Friends. Enemies. Lovers—she'd only had one at the time, in high school. Jackson.

Then last week, Kirk had urged her to collect as much solid intel as she could ASAP, as though the clock was ticking, and not on their side. He'd promised to get her out, but she hadn't believed him. Kirk had told her Jackson was a US marshal on his task force and would be a part of the extraction team. She didn't know if it was true, but dangling that carrot had gotten her to fall in line.

Christina started her SUV, gunned the engine and sped off.

How would she find Jackson? It wasn't as if she had his address or phone number.

Details she'd have to worry about later.

Now, she needed to get cash and disappear.

Missoula, Montana
Friday, April 13, 6:45 a.m.

SUPERVISORY SPECIAL AGENT KIRK KEHOE—his joint task force leader, his mentor, his friend—was dead.

It was still hard for Jackson Powell to believe, even after seeing the body and walking the crime scene. But what threw him for a loop was that Christina Ortiz was the killer.

Chrissy.

His Chrissy.

The sixteen-year-old girl he used to know never would've shot two men in cold blood. But there was concrete evidence of her guilt.

Jackson shoved aside old feelings. The past was irrelevant. That girl he'd once loved was gone.

Only one thing mattered: Taking Christina Ortiz into custody and seeing justice served.

A tip had led him and his team to where the fugitive was hiding. A classic 1950s-style motel. One story with just ten rooms. They parked their two SUVs, blocking entry to the lot of the City Drift Motel.

Jackson was the only deputy US marshal assigned to Operation Big Sky Guardian. With Kirk gone, there were five other agents left on the task force: Vazquez, from the FBI. Nichols, an IRS criminal investigator. Two from DEA, Tillman and Mirabal, and one from DHS, Walken.

None of whom Jackson trusted.

For weeks, Kirk had suspected there was a leak. The entire team had been polygraphed, under the guise of a routine operational security check. Everyone passed, but even so, any one of them could be the mole. A polygraph wasn't easy to beat, but it could be done. Especially if a double agent had been trained to do so. Which meant Jackson couldn't count on them to cover his back or bring in the suspect safely. There was also no way to tell how many people were in the cartel's pocket. Possibly even other deputies from his office.

To play it safe, he reached out to the US Marshals Special Operations Group in Camp Beauregard, Louisiana. Made an emergency request for assistance. Two had deployed within hours and arrived last night.

Fortunately, they'd sent deputy marshals he'd known for years and had the utmost faith in: Aiden Yazzie and Luis Flores. Jackson would bet his life that neither could ever be compromised by the cartel.

They all got out of their vehicles wearing their tactical gear and quickly huddled. At this time of morning, the street was quiet. Everything was still. No passersby to worry about if gunfire popped off and things turned dicey.

"I can't believe our perp had the guts to get a room at a motel two blocks from the US marshals' building," Tillman said, shaking his head. "Gutsy."

Jackson had no idea what Christina was doing or thinking. None of it made any sense. "That's one word for it."

Yazzie joined them, carrying the battering ram from one of the vehicles. "Ready."

"Okay," Jackson said. "She's in room five." He pointed it out. The other motel rooms on either side were unoccupied, according to the owner, who had tipped them off. "Alpha, you're with me. Bravo, cover the back."

A round of curt nods and everyone dispersed.

Quietly, Jackson led Team Alpha—Yazzie, Flores and

Vazquez—up to room five, sidearms drawn. They were careful not to cross in front of the window, even though the curtains were drawn, and gathered on either side of the door.

Waiting to give the signal, Jackson sucked in a calming breath.

Chrissy. Killed Kehoe and another man.

With a quick roll of his shoulders, he refocused. Got in the zone. She was just another fugitive. Armed and dangerous. He'd treat her as such.

"In position," Tillman said over comms.

Jackson raised three fingers and began the silent countdown. On one, Yazzie thrust the ram into the door, smashing it open. Glock up, Jackson swept inside the room first.

Christina jackknifed up from the bed and was on her feet, fully dressed, with shoes on. She eyed a subcompact handgun on the nightstand.

"Don't do it!" he warned.

"Jackson?" Christina stared at him wide-eyed and raised her palms.

"Hands behind your head!" Flores came up alongside him. "Down on your knees!"

Kneeling slowly, Christina placed her palms on the back of her head.

Yazzie and Vazquez closed in around them.

Flores shoved the fugitive to the floor and handcuffed her.

"I didn't do it," Christina said. "I didn't murder anyone."

Flores hauled her up to her feet. "We don't care."

US marshals were the best of the best when it came to apprehending criminals with warrants out for their arrest. Whether someone was innocent or guilty wasn't their concern. That was a matter for a court of law.

Christina's panicked gaze found Jackson's. "You have to help me. I'm innocent."

Grabbing hold of her other arm, Jackson kept his gun pointed at her. The mere sight of her made his skin tingle and touching her brought a fresh wave of memories to the forefront of his mind, but he shut it all down. He had a job to do and nothing was going to stop him from getting it done. "Christina Ortiz, you're under arrest."

Chapter Two

Missoula
Friday, April 13, 9:07 a.m.

"I'm Special Agent Vazquez." A petite brunette with a sleek bun took a seat across from Christina in an interrogation room. "This is DEA Agent Mirabal."

Another woman sat. Blonde and curvy. Long hair in a ponytail.

After they hauled her in, they'd made her wait in the room for nearly two hours. Wasting precious time. A classic technique—let the perp's anxiety build, in the hopes they'd slip up during questioning.

With her hands in her lap, Christina fiddled with the silver ring on her finger. They'd searched her for weapons and confiscated her phone. She still had her jewelry since they hadn't formally booked her yet, which meant they intended to do it at another location.

Christina looked over the shoulders of the agents at the one-way mirror, where she presumed Jackson was on the other side watching.

She shifted her attention to the women in front of her. FBI and DEA. Probably part of Kirk's task force. Like Jackson. Had Kirk briefed his team about her?

He'd given her the impression her identity would be withheld until the very last minute. With her cover blown and Kirk murdered, something had obviously gone wrong.

But why wasn't Jackson sitting across from her, handling her interrogation?

Vazquez slapped a folder onto the table. "Want to save us time and give a confession?"

"Can't," Christina said. "I didn't do it."

"Sure you didn't." Vazquez scrutinized her. "But that raises two issues. First, your prints, only yours, were on the murder weapon and bullet casings. You came right up in the database."

Part of the process when joining the state bar required her to consent to a fingerprint-based background check. Maybe that's why Hector had used her gun. To frame her. Tarnish her reputation and mess up any case Kirk had built before they killed her.

"It was my gun," Christina said, "but I didn't kill anyone. Hector Ibarra, a lieutenant for the Estrada cartel, did."

"How did Ibarra get your gun?" Mirabal asked.

Taking a deep breath, Christina gathered her thoughts. "Are these really necessary?" She lifted her shackled wrists.

Mirabal uncuffed her.

Christina rubbed her sore skin. "May I have coffee?"

The blonde raised her hand, motioning to someone watching.

Good cop.

Vazquez folded her arms. "Want a pastry, too?"

Bad cop.

"No, thanks. Sugar is deadly."

"Think this is a joke?" Vazquez snapped.

"No," Christina said flatly.

The door opened. A man entered, wearing a Department

of Homeland Security badge. One of the agents who'd been at the motel. He set the coffee on the table and stood in the corner, glaring at her.

"Ibarra," Mirabal said. "Your gun. Talk."

"Hector demanded my gun," Christina said. "I gave it to him."

"So you claim, but that brings us to the second issue." Vazquez put her forearms on the table. "An eyewitness saw you shoot SAC Kehoe."

Shock ricocheted through Christina. "I don't understand. Hector Ibarra gave you a statement?" Certainly, it wasn't his street thug.

"No." Mirabal tipped her head to the side. "The eyewitness was a sheriff's deputy."

Nausea clawed through Christina. "That's not possible."

"The deputy was on patrol," Vazquez said. "Spotted a suspicious silver Ford Bronco parked by the abandoned tunnel." She rattled off Christina's plate number. "The deputy entered through the opposite side. Heard you yelling about money. Then gunfire. He saw you with your cartel muscle and Kehoe. Another man was already dead on the ground. You shot Kehoe. The officer identified himself. You ran while your cartel goon opened fire on the deputy, who shot back, killing the other man. With your plate number, we identified you quickly."

Christina had wondered how her name and image hit the news, a warrant issued for her arrest for a double homicide, within less than six hours. Thanks to her Black and Afro–Puerto Rican heritage, she had almond-brown skin and distinctive features. In Montana, even wearing a baseball cap, she stood out, had a face people remembered.

The person who'd checked her in at the motel had probably reported her whereabouts.

"Talk to us." Mirabal's tone was gentle, almost friendly. "I don't think you waived your right to an attorney because you're a lawyer capable of representing yourself. I think you want to tell us your side of things. We want to hear it."

Christina reached for the steaming cup of coffee, but her hand shook so uncontrollably she reconsidered handling the hot liquid. "The deputy didn't mention Ibarra?"

Mirabal shook her head.

"Your eyewitness is a liar," Christina said. "He's a dirty cop. Check his financials. Dig into his background."

"Let's dig into yours." Vazquez opened the folder. "Grew up in Laramie, Wyoming. Your father was a member of the outlaw motorcycle gang the Iron Warriors. Shot dead in a drive-by four years ago."

It wasn't a drive-by. But it was her fault.

"They're not an outlaw gang," Christina said. Not anymore. Not since it was cleaned up by the former club president, Ripton Lockwood. Former Special Forces, he was like a big brother to her.

"Graduated high school at sixteen." Vazquez continued reading the file. "Went to Southeastern Wyoming University. Accelerated programs. Got your bachelor's and juris doctor in five and a half years. Speak four languages. Impressive. Who paid for your tuition?"

If they were asking, they knew the answer.

Jackson must've told them. Not even Kirk had been aware.

In high school, Jackson had been her best friend long before he became her first...*everything*. She'd told him her secrets. Fears. Dreams. She'd foolishly imagined a future with him. Until she'd realized he didn't love her. He was ashamed of her and believed what his rich family called her. Biker trash.

"The Iron Warriors covered the cost." They'd allowed her to graduate debt-free, from a financial perspective, provided she represented them whenever necessary. They were legitimate, making it an offer she couldn't refuse. "They're my family. They love me and I love them. The money was clean. No crime against family paying for a college education."

"Want to know what I think?" Vazquez asked. "Your outlaw biker family decided to buy themselves a lawyer with blood money. Someone who'd be loyal, no matter what. Through their drug ties, you became associated with the Estrada cartel. Just connect the dots to how you ended up in a tunnel, killing a federal law enforcement officer."

"The Iron Warriors never had dealings with the Estrada cartel. But they did with Kehoe. It was through them—Bobby Quill, actually—that Kirk found and recruited me to be an asset," Christina said, and the two seated at the table exchanged surprised looks. Even the DHS agent appeared taken aback. "Kirk was my handler for six years. I didn't kill him. Hector Ibarra did."

Vazquez narrowed her eyes. "No way Kehoe could've hidden an asset, off the books, for *six years*. But let's say he went rogue, past the point of no return, risked his job cultivating a civilian asset to infiltrate the cartel. That means you've been in deep with the Estrada syndicate since you were, what, twenty-two years old? Quite young. Impressionable age. Easy to get corrupted by all that power."

"Interesting fact," Mirabal said. "The frontal lobe controls judgment, self-control, decision-making. It doesn't fully develop until you're twenty-five."

Wetting her lips, Christina wished she'd asked for water. Kirk had told them nothing about her. Not even that he'd had an asset inside the cartel. "Maybe Kehoe figured if eighteen is old enough to join the military, die for one's country, at twenty-two, I could handle it."

Vazquez flashed a wry grin. "We know seasoned, highly trained agents who've gone that deep for less time and lost their way. Did dirty things they regretted. Committed crimes. Killed people they shouldn't have." The grin faded. "What happened in the tunnel? Did Kehoe discover your dirty deeds, something to do with money? Is that why you murdered him in cold blood?"

They didn't want the truth. To them, she was guilty. They wanted to understand, to get closure. This was personal for the entire task force. Except the mole—a snake hidden in the grass that could strike at any time.

"I'm done talking to you." Christina braced for things to turn nasty. "I'll only answer questions from US Marshal Jackson Powell."

Vazquez slammed a fist on the table, spilling the coffee. "You gunned down Kehoe like an animal! Shot him in the back three times while he was restrained. Why?"

"I'll only answer questions from US Marshal Jackson Powell."

Mirabal's expression hardened. "Murdering an FBI agent is a federal crime. The state attorney general is going to strip the bark right off you. Then they're going to put you in a four-by-six cell for the rest of your life."

Guess the good cop, bad cop routine was done.

"It'll never happen," Christina said easily. The cartel would kill her first. She glanced at the clock on the wall. A chill slithered down her spine. *He* had already landed. She looked past the agents and at the one-way window. "Jackson, verify what I said with Bobby Quill. Then I'll answer any of your questions. You need to hurry."

But would Jackson believe her?

Missoula
Friday, April 13, 11:45 a.m.

GROANING IN FRUSTRATION, Jackson hung up the phone in the office. He wasn't quite sure what he'd been hoping for or expected when he reached out to the Iron Warriors back home in Laramie, but it sure wasn't what he'd discovered.

Part of him wanted third-party verification of the things Christina had told Vazquez and Mirabal. Even if it came from an Iron Warrior. Maybe he just didn't want to accept the grisly alternative: that she was a murderer.

The woman he had once thought he couldn't live without. They had been teenagers in love, planning a future together. Until it ended.

Long-buried shame surfaced. For not doing more to help her with her abusive dad. For giving in to the pressure of his parents' opinions about the Iron Warriors, about her and how they were from two different worlds and didn't belong together.

It was the one regret he carried that sometimes kept him up at night.

Yazzie strode over, eating an apple, and sat on the edge of his desk. "Well, did her story check out with Bobby Quill?"

Others from the team, who were nearby in the large, open room where they occupied desks, stopped what they were doing and looked at him.

Leaning back in his chair, Jackson scrubbed a hand over his face. "Bobby Quill is dead. Along with most of the Iron Warriors. Someone took them out last night."

Around the room, eyebrows raised, a few faces paled, more than one uttered surprise. Vazquez was on the phone, but that even caught her attention.

"Was it a rival gang, some kind of turf war?" Flores asked.

Jackson shrugged. "All I know is it sounded like a targeted hit. Their clubhouse was shot up, taking out bikers and their old ladies. Someone also tracked down their leadership and got them at home, too. The president survived. Barely. A guy named JD. According to him, they did have dealings with Kehoe."

"Okay," Mirabal said, "so Ortiz told us one truthful thing. The best lies are half-truths. Doesn't mean her story isn't hogwash."

"True." Tillman sipped his coffee. "What did this JD say?"

"Many of the Iron Warriors work, or rather worked, for Ironside Protection Services, including Ortiz, who has been out of pocket, handling an assignment for Bobby Quill. It's a legit business. Last year, they even hired a former detective to oversee the IPS office in Wyoming. The owner is a former club president. Ripton Lockwood." A Special Forces hotshot who treated Christina like a kid sister. "The guy cleared out the riffraff and stopped illicit activity. Lockwood opened the first office in Laramie to bring in clean money for the club, but he has offices all over these days. Including in Bitterroot Falls." The town was a ninety-minute drive away. Jackson was close friends with the IPS team there, most of whom were veterans, including Takoda Yazzie, Aiden's cousin. But Jackson had never had a reason to be interested in IPS's history until now.

Flores opened a bottle of water. "Did the club president corroborate that Ortiz was recruited by Kehoe?"

"He doesn't know. Neither does the former detective. If she was, only Bobby Quill was privy to the arrangement. JD is going to contact the IPS owner, Lockwood. See if he was read in."

"Doesn't matter if that part of her story was true," Walken

said. "Vazquez and Mirabal were right. Solid agents have gone deep undercover for too long and gone to the dark side. Even if Kehoe recruited her, and I'm not saying he did, it doesn't mean she didn't kill him."

Tension threaded in Jackson's shoulders. "Yeah, I know."

Vazquez hung up the phone. "If you're going to question her, Jackson, you better do it now. Our respective bosses have made a decision," she said, referring to their superiors at the DEA, FBI, DHS, IRS and US marshals, "and the FBI won. Christina Ortiz is ours. We've been ordered to transport her to the field office in Salt Lake City. They'll book her there."

The FBI only had satellite offices in Montana. The larger, more secure regional office based in Salt Lake City had operational control over Utah, Idaho and Montana.

"US marshals will take the lead on transport," Flores said.

Yazzie and Flores had flown in on a USMS plane and landed at Missoula Montana Airport, fifteen minutes away.

"I'll be on the flight with you," Jackson said.

Vazquez rose from her chair. "Me, too."

With a nod, Yazzie threw away the apple core. "I'll update the pilot. Make sure we're refueled and ready to take off when we arrive." Sighing, he turned to Jackson. "Sucks. We apprehended Ortiz so quickly I thought I'd be able to have lunch with Takoda."

"He'll be disappointed not to see you." Jackson stood. "Once things quiet down, you should come back for a visit with your wife." She was also a marshal with SOG. A tough woman Jackson liked. "I better get to it."

"Are you sure talking to her is a good idea?" Tillman asked, and everyone stared at Jackson. "Considering..."

Considering his history with the fugitive. No one wanted

him to be part of the initial interrogation. Conflict of interest.

Once Jackson had learned his high school sweetheart was suspected of Kehoe's murder, he'd disclosed their prior association and freely provided any clarity on her background file.

"I'm sure," Jackson said. "You guys took a crack at her. My turn." He looked at their IRS CI. "Hey, Nichols, check out the sheriff's deputy, Phillips. See if there's anything suspicious in his financials."

"Sure." Nichols pushed his glasses higher on the bridge of his nose. "I'll get right on it."

"Are you kidding me?" Vazquez rolled her eyes. "Don't tell me you believe her story."

Jackson debated how much to share, but he needed to tell them. Better to do it now while they were all together instead of in Salt Lake City. "Kehoe did have an off-the-books asset, deep cover for six years."

The room fell so silent you could hear a pin drop.

Mirabal hopped out of her chair and marched up to him with such intensity her ponytail swung like a pendulum. "Why are we just now hearing about this?"

"I only found out myself. A few weeks ago. Kehoe didn't give me a name. I only know it's a civilian woman. Someone he needed to push for as much information as quickly as possible and find a way to extract her safely. He described her as a triple threat. A weapon the cartel would never see coming."

"Triple threat, huh?" Walken rubbed his jaw. "Ortiz has got beauty and brains. Can she handle herself, too?"

Jackson nodded. "The motorcycle club taught her." Lockwood had trained her himself in case her dad didn't accept the message that beating her wouldn't be tolerated under his watch.

Vazquez eyed him with blatant skepticism. "Convenient how you tell us this *after* your ex-girlfriend spun her wild tale. A story we can't corroborate with Kehoe because he's *dead*."

Anger sparked inside Jackson, but he tamped it down. "I admitted to having had a teenage dalliance with the suspect. I wouldn't lie for her."

"I guess we're just supposed to take your word for it," Vazquez said.

"Hey." Tillman put a hand on his shoulder. "You want backup in there?"

"No. I've got it." Turning, Jackson strode down the hall to the interrogation room. He grabbed the knob, took a beat. Reminded himself sometimes a person you'd known for years was only wearing a mask, pretending to be a friend, hiding their true face underneath.

That of a foe.

Four years he'd worked on the task force. They were tight, celebrated and commiserated together. But one of them was a traitor. Who had fooled him and most likely gotten Kehoe killed. Jackson refused to play the fool with Christina, regardless of their ancient history.

The others started down the hall, headed to the observation room, where they'd scrutinize everything.

Jackson went inside the interrogation room and sat at the table. He stared into the sultry brown eyes he'd never been able to forget, no matter how he'd tried. The beautiful, wild girl she'd been had become a stunning woman.

A possible murderer.

She flattened her hands on the table. "Thank you for talking to me."

"I'm only here to do my job."

Her brow crinkled. She lowered her head. "Did you talk to Bobby?"

"Bobby is dead," he said gently, and she looked up at him. "Many of the Iron Warriors were killed last night. Attacked at their clubhouse and homes. Possible turf war."

Christina slumped back in her chair as though the words hit her like a physical blow. Tears welled in her eyes. Her hand began to tremble.

A ribbon of unwelcome emotion slowly unspooled through him. It took everything in him not to reach out and comfort her. "I'm sorry. I know what they meant to you."

Tears spilled, running down her cheeks. "It wasn't a turf war." Her voice dropped to a whisper. "That's why he was in Wyoming."

"He who?"

Shaking her head, she whisked away her tears. Glanced at the clock. "You're going to move me. Probably soon. When that happens, you should stay here."

One second, she was grieving. The next, she was telling him what to do.

He was controlling this interrogation. Not the other way around. "I'm willing to entertain the possibility you were Kehoe's asset. But we have a credible eyewitness account. A murder weapon with your prints. Give me something to prove you didn't kill Kehoe."

"There's no body-cam footage, right?"

"Correct. Phillips's camera was disabled at the time."

"Of course it was." Shuttering her eyes, she wrung her hands. "Where did your *eyewitness* say Kehoe was when I allegedly shot him? Standing? On his knees?"

"Standing. Kehoe was running away from you when you shot him in the back."

Christina met his gaze, her eyes glassy and hard. "Kirk tackled one of Ibarra's thugs. He was giving me a chance to get away. They both fell to the ground. That's when Hector shot him, also hitting his own guy in the abdomen. Have the bodies moved to a different county. Use a medical examiner you trust. It'll check out."

He wanted to believe her, but he couldn't forget how easily she could turn a blind eye to illicit activity. Long before the Iron Warriors became legit, she hadn't cared that they were dirty.

"You claim Kirk tried to help you in the tunnel," he said. "But he was restrained."

"My cover was blown. Somehow, the cartel found out he was my handler. Kirk gave me a coded message to come here."

Here? "What was the message?"

"He said he wanted to go home to the Garden City and fish for little bull trout. But Kirk was from New York City, the Big Apple, and he hated—"

"Fishing," Jackson said, finishing her sentence. "The Garden City. Place of the Little Bull Trout. Nicknames for Missoula."

"Exactly." Her face brightened. "A week ago, he told me you were a US marshal on his task force and would help with my extraction. I assumed his message meant you were here in Missoula. Why on earth would I, a wanted fugitive, pick a motel two blocks from the US marshals' building instead of crossing the border into Canada if I were guilty? I planned to wait in the café across the street, see if you showed up. Talk to you."

Made more sense than any alternative. Still wasn't enough. "What information did you give Kehoe over the years?" Proof she was indeed the asset.

"Everything his task force worked on for Operation Big Sky Guardian."

"You know about that?" Jackson asked, wondering why Kehoe had shared such sensitive information with her.

"Where do you think all your actionable intel came from? I *am* Operation Big Sky Guardian. It's all built around the information I gave Kirk. It took me two years to get into a position where I was able to get anything substantial—that's when I told him about a medical imaging company washing money for the cartel."

"The sting was our first big success." The imaging firm with offices throughout the state had submitted more than two hundred million dollars in fraudulent claims to the Montana Workers' Compensation system cleaning money for the cartel.

"The last significant piece of information I gave him was on a money-laundering scheme the cartel set up with the Cutthroat Creek Mining Company."

They'd hit pay dirt with that tip. After Kehoe flipped two employees inside the company to testify and revealed their identities to the task force, the cartel had found out about them. That's when they'd suspected they had a leak.

Christina's answers supported her claim that she was an asset for Kehoe. Jackson was tempted to dismiss any lingering doubts, but he couldn't let their history or emotion cloud his judgment.

Not on this. The stakes were too high.

He also couldn't ignore the questions racing through his mind. "Did Kehoe know about *us*? That we had a relationship?"

Christina glanced at the one-way mirror and hesitated. "Yes. He asked for private details about everyone in my past when he recruited me."

But why hadn't Kehoe told Jackson that he'd made her an asset?

What had really happened in that tunnel? Since no one had known Christina was undercover, not even Jackson, how did Kehoe end up there in the first place with her cover blown?

And had she accomplished their top priority?

Jackson studied her face. "Were you ever able to get any intel on Rio Estrada, the guy who controls the cartel's stateside unit?" They called themselves Team US. The name always made Jackson's gut burn.

Dante Estrada ran the main operation in Mexico. They had pictures of him and monitored his movements. But the younger brother, Rio, proved far more elusive.

Christina shook her head. "I never met him. Only a select few have. That's one of the reasons he's been so successful. You can't track him if you don't know what he looks like and can't find him. And if you apprehend one of his lieutenants, they can't give him up in exchange for a lesser sentence."

"You've been in deep with the cartel, getting high-level intel, and never had a face-to-face meeting where Rio Estrada was present? Do you really expect us to believe that?"

"It's the truth." She held his gaze. "I've spoken to him on the phone a handful of times, but he always initiated the call through someone else's cell. Like he was paranoid about being traced. Otherwise, I communicated to *El Jefe* through Hector Ibarra and…" Her voice trailed off, as though she was reluctant to say more.

"Who else did you communicate through?"

"It doesn't matter." She looked away from him. "One of the *sicarios*. The point is I never met him."

Christina was holding back. Possibly lying. Not a good sign. There was no getting around the fact that six years undercover was a very long time. Lines blurred after a while. Anyone could get fuzzy about which side they were fighting on.

"We are moving you," Jackson said. "To the FBI regional facility in Salt Lake City. Nothing I can do about it. But this is helpful. Something I can work with." He'd ensure the bodies were transferred to an ME he trusted. Nichols was already looking into the sheriff's deputy. Christina had given them plenty to verify she was an asset, but it didn't eliminate her as a murder suspect. Not yet.

He stood to leave.

"Wait." Christina grabbed his hand. "Don't be on the crew that transports me. Stay here."

With the whole team watching, Jackson fought the impulse to curl his fingers around hers and instead pulled his hand free. "Why?"

"It's not safe. Anyone who goes—anyone close to me—might not survive."

Chapter Three

Missoula
Friday, April 13, 1:30 p.m.

As Christina walked handcuffed through the office on the second floor of the US marshals' building, Jackson held on to one of her arms and Vazquez the other. They had allowed her to put on her jacket before shackling her wrists in preparation for transport.

"This is a mistake," Christina said. "You should listen to me."

"Shut. Up." Vazquez tightened her grip, digging her nails through the lightweight material of her jacket, to the point Christina winced in pain. "You can't scare us. Nothing is going to stop us from transporting you to a more secure facility."

Christina looked at Jackson. "At least wear helmets."

They were in tactical gear, with Kevlar vests, but it wasn't enough protection.

Jackson stopped and glanced at a guy with a ruddy complexion and a mustache, DEA badge hanging around his neck. "Tillman, grab some helmets."

"Really?" the DEA agent asked.

Nodding, Jackson said, "Can't hurt."

"I don't need one." Mirabal sat behind a desk. "I'll hang back and get started on the paperwork. All our bosses are going to want to see this report ASAP."

Tillman hurried off, disappearing down the hall.

"You've got the two extra SOG marshals," a Black guy wearing glasses and an IRS badge said. "I was going to continue the deep dive into the deputy. Unless you need me to ride along to the airport."

Jackson slid a furtive glance at Christina.

"If you want him to live, he should stay," she said. "You should stay, too. Help Mirabal with the paperwork."

Vazquez jerked her arm. "Enough out of you."

"I agree," the DHS agent said. Earlier someone had called him Walker or Walken. "Zip it, lady. You're getting on that plane."

Want to bet?

She glanced at the clock.

He was here in Montana. Not in Utah. The odds were high that their task force had proudly announced her apprehension on the news, showing the US marshals' building in the background.

And the mole had every reason to inform him about her pending transfer.

They'd given the Reaper plenty of time to figure out how to get to her. Too much time.

"You keep looking at the clock," Jackson said, drawing her gaze back to him.

To those sky-blue eyes that she used to lose herself in while wrapped in his arms. He'd grown a good inch or two since high school, towering beside her at six-one. Gone was his long hair that straddled the edge between brown and blond, with loose curls around his face. Now it was cropped short in a tidy style typical of a G-man. No more lanky basketball body. Muscles so defined she could almost see them through the white dress shirt that clung to his taut shoulders.

Jackson continued studying her face. "Got an appointment I should know about?"

"A date with death," Christina said dryly, using all her strength not to let her voice shake. "And he always keeps his appointments."

Jackson furrowed his brow and opened his mouth to say something, but Tillman came back, passing out helmets.

"You don't get one," Vazquez said, smirking as she put on hers.

"I'm not the one who needs it." There would be no bullet to the head for Christina. The Reaper wasn't going to grant her the mercy of a quick death.

"Should I come along?" Glasses asked, comfortably planted behind his desk.

Jackson shook his head. "Finish the deep dive on Deputy Phillips. And Nichols, as soon as you find anything, send it out to the group."

Nichols nodded.

A Native American with an athletic build entered the room. He was already wearing a helmet and a different color Kevlar vest with *USMS SOG* stamped on the front.

Special Operations Group. An elite tactical unit trained on the same level as US military Special Forces.

He might stand a chance. Maybe.

"Flores is downstairs, at the secure exit," the SOG guy said. "We're ready to rock and roll." He strode up to Jackson. "Load her in the back of my vehicle. The first SUV."

"No." Jackson strapped on his helmet and grabbed his winter jacket, but he didn't put it on. "She'll ride with me in the second vehicle."

The other marshal put his hands on his hips. "What's up?"

"Nothing, Yazzie." Jackson touched his arm. "I just don't want her in the lead car. That's all."

They must be friends. Close.

"A police cruiser will be in the lead," Yazzie said.

"Just listen to me," Jackson said, "okay?"

Yazzie folded his arms. "Then I'll have Flores drive the second SUV."

"You two should ride together," Jackson said, eliciting a glare from Vazquez.

"Are you buying into her scare campaign?" Yazzie gestured at Christina.

Jackson didn't respond.

"Ortiz is riding with either me or Flores. You choose. This is what we train for, man." Yazzie smiled. "We've got this."

Hubris would be their undoing.

The Reaper trained harder, strategized every possible outcome and was a crack shot. Absolutely nothing rattled him.

Know thy enemy was his creed. He studied law enforcement methods and tactics so he was ready to outmaneuver them. Backup wasn't necessary for him. He was a one-man army.

Getting her was not only a professional obligation, but this was also personal.

"You're not prepared for what's coming," Christina said.

"Head games don't work on me." Yazzie cut his gaze from her and looked at Jackson. "You brought us here to watch your back. Let us."

"What is he talking about?" Vazquez asked. "Watch your back? From what? I thought you requested SOG because we were dealing with the high-threat apprehension of someone who killed one of our own. But he's made several remarks like that. Only this time to our faces. Right, Walken?"

Walken nodded. "It's true."

"I noticed it, too. We all have." Tillman frowned. "The little huddles off to the side with you, Yazzie and Flores, where the rest of us can't hear what you're discussing."

"They helped us catch her," Jackson said. "Mission accomplished. Drop it."

"No, I won't drop it." Vazquez stepped in front of him. "What's going on? There's something else you're not telling us. I can feel it."

Jackson sighed. His jaw clenched. "There's a mole. One of you on the task force is a traitor."

Walken's eyes flared wide. Nichols choked on the coffee he was drinking. Tillman swore. Blondie—Mirabal—shook her head slowly as if in a daze.

Based on Yazzie's expression, he'd already been briefed.

All the blood drained from Vazquez's face. "No way. Impossible," she said, her bluster deflating.

"Someone in this room leaked the names of the Cutthroat Creek Mining Company employees who were prepared to give up information about the money-laundering scheme with the cartel. That's why Kehoe became tight-lipped about everything and had us polygraphed."

"But…" Nichols hesitated. "But we all passed."

"Congratulations to whoever it is for being able to beat a poly," Jackson said. "Until we root out the devil among us, I can't trust any of you. Satisfied, Vazquez?"

The FBI agent stood speechless.

"Let's go," Yazzie said and headed down the stairs.

Moving out, they followed Yazzie. They left the building through a side exit, leading into a small, secure garage that was only big enough for four vehicles. Brick walls. No windows. Steel roller doors on either end.

Two police cruisers with uniformed officers inside sat waiting.

Yazzie gestured to the officers and spoke to Flores before climbing into the first black SUV. Jackson hopped into the back of the second SUV, helping Christina get in beside him. Flores joined them, sitting behind the wheel.

Vazquez unshackled Christina's left wrist and locked the cuff to the grab handle above the right door before closing it. Earlier when they'd transported Christina from the motel to the marshals' building, she'd been sandwiched between agents.

"We should ride in the other vehicle," Vazquez said to Walken and Tillman, not bothering to lower her voice. She flicked a glance at Jackson. "So far, he's the only one I don't trust. The only one who has been keeping secrets from us. About a supposed leak. About Kehoe's unsanctioned asset—his ex-girlfriend, who's been living three hours away in Bozeman. What if she isn't his *ex*? What if they got back together? Maybe he's lying to protect her because he's the leak. We don't know. What else isn't he telling us?" Without waiting for a response, the FBI agent stormed off and got into the back seat of the first SUV.

The other two men stepped away from the vehicles and exchanged words.

Jackson hung his head.

Secrets came with the territory in this business, but it was tearing apart Kehoe's task force. Divide and conquer was the smartest game for the mole to play.

Christina reached over with her free hand and put her palm on Jackson's leg. He looked down at his thigh, where she touched him.

"I wish I had known you were in Missoula," she said. "I wish Kehoe had told me sooner."

"Why?" Jackson's voice was a whisper.

Because I missed you.

Even though he'd turned his back on her and broken her heart, she still thought of him. And every time she did, she ached.

Kehoe had asked her about her first boyfriend, how intimate they'd been, and she'd called Jackson the love of her life. Told him they'd shared everything, had been everything to each other—or so she had thought.

But he never saw the real her. She'd been a plaything to him, someone convenient. The club had warned her. *He won't bring you home to meet his mama. You'll see.*

Christina should've spared herself the grief he eventually brought her and listened to the Iron Warriors.

Looking at her, Jackson covered her hand with his. "Why?" he asked again.

"None of it makes any difference now."

"Sometimes the why behind something can change everything."

It wouldn't bring Kehoe back or get her out of handcuffs or resolve her current predicament.

She turned her head from him, and her gaze met Flores's in the rearview mirror. Pulling her hand back into her lap, she recalled Alice's sixth commandment.

Stay frosty, stay alive.

Christina reined in her emotions, hardening her heart. "Jackson, if things go sideways, don't be a hero."

Tillman got in the passenger's seat in front of Christina.

Walken slid into the SUV in front of them, sitting next to the driver, Yazzie.

The steel garage door lifted, and they all pulled out.

A police escort led the way, lights flashing, siren muted.

The other cruiser followed, bringing up the rear of the motorcade.

"Hey, Flores, did you or Yazzie tell anyone on the team which route we're taking to the airport?" Tillman asked. "Since we have a mole, if you did, maybe we should change the plan."

"Only two routes," Flores said. "Take West Broadway Street all the way for six miles or I-90 then Broadway for the last mile. We discussed it in private, just the two of us. Yazzie chose and I agreed. But we did factor in the warning that we might not be safe." He looked up in the rearview mirror again, and she stared at him.

"That means we're taking I-90," Christina said, holding his gaze. "Fewer chances for someone to intercept us." It still left the last mile on Broadway. The strip of road both routes had in common. "I suggest you don't take the Broadway exit. Pass it. Go farther down. Then get off and double back to the airport."

"If you think we're listening to you, you're delusional. We checked the route," Flores said as they got onto the interstate. "Ran it. Cleared it. There's no place for a sniper to set up on the last mile of Broadway. We've got this."

It only meant the Reaper wouldn't use a sniper rifle. They were out of their league on this one. But nobody was listening to her.

"Suit yourself." She looked out the window.

The ride on I-90 was short. Or maybe time moved faster when you knew you were about to face death.

Everyone in the car was vigilant. Tillman and Jackson had their sidearms drawn. Flores stayed close to Yazzie's SUV, and the police cruiser behind them practically rode their bumper.

They took the off-ramp from the interstate and made a

left onto Airway Boulevard. After three short blocks, they turned right, taking Broadway.

Maybe the Reaper had found the USMS plane at the airport. She assumed it would be marked. Separated from commercial traffic. Perhaps he was waiting to ambush them in the hangar, where there would be less collateral damage. Or even on the plane. Pick them off in an isolated, contained area. A kill zone he could control.

Her heart raced, beating wild against her sternum. Sweat trickled down her spine. She ran her thumb over the smart ring on her index finger. It monitored her heart rate, blood oxygen, breathing regularity, activity, temperature and sleep. If she could see the app on her phone linked to the ring right now, her stats would be off the charts.

Christina clutched the grab handle she was cuffed to and braced for the unexpected. Her stomach roiled, and she hoped she wouldn't be sick.

They passed a sign that stated the airport was half a mile up ahead. Traffic was light, with one green light after another. The motorcade breezed down the road. As they approached a sign with a white arrow indicating the airport on the left, their convoy moved into the turn lane.

No need to slow down with another green light.

The police cruiser made the turn, and the first SUV started to follow.

"See," Flores said, "what did I tell—"

A truck sped through the traffic light and plowed into the side of the first SUV at the intersection. It was a massive airport de-icing truck, with a crane and basket attached. The jarring impact of the collision sent the SUV careening across two lanes, crushing both driver's-side doors.

Flores slammed on the brakes, tires screeching.

Stunned, no one moved; no one uttered anything for a

second, maybe two. Time crawled by in her mind, everything happening in slow motion.

In a blink, the passenger door of the truck flew open and the Reaper jumped to the ground. He held a weapon. A submachine gun, possibly an Uzi.

The sheer ferocity of his expression knocked the air from her lungs. He was just as she remembered. Tall and powerfully built, but not big like a bodybuilder. His hallmark tattoos were barely visible from this distance.

Her entire focus lasered in on him, the world around her expanding and contracting like a snapped rubber band.

Missoula
Friday, April 13, 2:20 p.m.

SHOCK REVERBERATED THROUGH JACKSON. All he could think about was the way that truck came out nowhere at high speed and slammed into the vehicle in front of them. Whether Yazzie had survived. Vazquez. Walken.

Jackson stared at the driver, who'd gotten out of the truck. His heart skipped a beat as he recognized him.

Alvaro Aguilar.

He was no low-level street thug, working for the cartel. No simple *sicario*. No sense of moral decency. No lines he wouldn't cross. A hit man who didn't abide by any rules.

Armed, Aguilar moved quick as lightning. He opened fire on the first police car, shattering the windshield, and then aimed at their SUV, forcing them to duck as bullets pelted the hood. While they were momentarily pinned in the vehicle, Aguilar grabbed a hose hanging loose from the crane attached to the top of the truck, pointed the nozzle at a civilian car two lanes to the right that had stopped near the truck and sprayed liquid over the sedan.

Tillman and Flores both hopped out, using their doors as

shields. In almost the same breath, the cops did the same. But Aguilar had them in his crosshairs and unleashed the full firepower of the submachine gun.

A devastating spray of bullets took out the officers from the lead cruiser.

He had a H&K MP5. SWAT and Special Forces weapon of choice. The lethal piece of machinery had a rate of fire of eight hundred rounds per minute, but he was using three-round bursts.

Aguilar swung the muzzle of the MP5 in their direction. A car window burst, and a bullet struck Flores. Blood spurted from his neck. Flores clamped a palm over his wound just before he dropped.

Jackson opened the door, but Christina grabbed his arm, stopping him from getting out.

"We have to leave," she said. "It's the only way to save them."

Locked to the grab handle, unable to duck, she was exposed. Easy pickings for Aguilar.

Tillman ducked behind the door as bullets tore through the officers behind them. None of the cops wore vests or helmets. They were only simple escorts.

Jackson dug in his pocket, fished out the handcuff keys and freed her wrist. "Take cover and stay down."

Aguilar held a flare in his other hand, struck the base against the pavement—all while firing a barrage of bullets at their vehicle. Tillman took cover. Aguilar tossed the sparking flare at the sedan.

The de-icing liquid ignited, catching fire. Flames engulfed the car. Inside, the panicked driver yelled for help.

Shooting stopped. Aguilar took a knee, using the flaming sedan as partial cover. After a rapid reload, he was up again, a weapon in both hands, the submachine gun in one and a nine-millimeter in the other. The blaze emitted plumes of white smoke, cloaking Aguilar.

Tillman opened fire.

Jerking his arm free from Christina, Jackson hopped out. He got down on his knees and checked Flores for a pulse, but he was dead.

What about Yazzie, Vazquez and Walken? Were they alive? Badly injured?

"Get down!" he called to Christina when she lifted her head, looking out a window.

By the time Jackson stood back up, Tillman was shooting, making his way across the lane to the civilian trapped in the sedan. But he was exposed.

Two bullets hit Tillman, knocking him backward to the ground.

That's why Aguilar had set the civilian car on fire. To distract them. Relying on their instincts to help an innocent person in danger.

Jackson took aim through the shattered driver's-side window of the open door and returned fire.

Aguilar tucked the nine-millimeter in his waistband and gripped the submachine gun with both hands for better control. He just kept coming. Steady. Focused. Like a terminator. Each controlled burst of gunfire was precise.

Christina crawled to the other side of the back seat, closer to him, and remained low.

Incoming shots forced Jackson to take cover behind the door. Bullets punched through the metal, clipping his vest. Jackson swore.

The guy was using hard-core bullets—armor-piercing rounds. Illegal but not impossible to procure.

The level-four body armor they wore had a one-inch-thick ceramic plate only designed to stop one round of AP ammunition. They didn't stand a chance if Aguilar got off enough targeted shots.

"Jackson!" Christina called out. "We have to leave! Please!"

He risked popping up for a look.

The civilian scrambled out of his sedan through the trunk. At the same time, Jackson spotted Walken through the smoke. The DHS agent had made it out of the other SUV. Staggering forward, he opened fire, using the rear of the vehicle for cover.

"He won't stop!" Christina said. "Not until you're all dead! I still need to give you the critical intel Kehoe asked me to collect."

As soon as Aguilar shifted his focus to Walken, Jackson aimed and squeezed the trigger.

Prepared, Aguilar grabbed the nine-millimeter from his waistband, pointing it Walken's direction, and kept the MP5 aimed at Jackson, shooting at them both simultaneously.

Another burst of automatic gunfire riddled the hood and penetrated Jackson's door. Way too close for comfort. Pressed to take cover again, he ducked back down.

Adrenaline flooded his system. It sounded like a war zone. The noise was deafening. Ambushed and attacked. Cops mowed down. Agents under siege. All by a single man in mere minutes. Not long enough for backup to arrive, but once more law enforcement got to the scene, it would only mean more dead bodies.

Kevlar offered no protection against armor-piercing rounds. They were losing this battle.

"This is personal for him!" she said. "We have to go now if you want any of them to live."

His heart pounded like a jackhammer. Jackson had dragged his SOG buddies into this mess, thinking they'd watch his back and safeguard the mission. But he'd only endangered them. Put them in Aguilar's line of fire. Now, Flores was dead. Three more were out of commission—Tillman, Yazzie, Vazquez—status unknown. He or Walken could be next.

How many people were going to die today?

Jackson had to decide.

More armor-piercing rounds punctured the metal, whizzing by his head. The car door was being turned into Swiss cheese.

"If we leave, he'll follow," Christina said. "He won't stop coming for m—" Gunfire cut her off as she screamed. "Please, Jackson! We have to go. It's the only way."

Split-second decision made, Jackson hopped into the driver's seat. Throwing the gear in Reverse, Jackson jerked the wheel and slammed on the gas, jumping the concrete median into the opposite side of traffic on his left.

Forty yards away, the wind cleared the smoke. Aguilar looked calm, his face expressionless except for the intensity in his eyes. The man reached into his jacket pocket, pulled out another magazine and reloaded with the quickness of a military expert.

Walken continued to fire, drawing Aguilar's attention.

Yanking the wheel hard, Jackson did a 180, spinning the SUV around. Any cars that had been sitting idle in the lane, waiting for a light to change, had cleared out of there as soon as the gunfire started.

In the rearview mirror, Jackson watched as a bullet struck Walken, the impact making his body spin ninety degrees before he fell.

Jackson didn't slow down. With that side of the road open, he floored the gas pedal.

The SUV's back windshield shattered, and Christina screamed.

Aguilar bolted across the intersection, grabbing something from his pocket. In the next heartbeat the back of the de-icing truck exploded. Flames and metal shot up into the sky.

He must've had an explosive device rigged to blow.

Most of the truck cabin was still intact. Maybe Yazzie and Vazquez were all right.

Aguilar stopped at a car positioned close to the intersection, about to turn at the light, leaving the airport. Gun up, he opened the door. Threw the driver from the car. Jumped into the vehicle and sped off after them.

Jackson jammed his foot on the accelerator, weaving through traffic, trying to put as much distance as he could between them and the relentless killing machine in hot pursuit.

Chapter Four

Missoula
Friday, April 13, 2:28 p.m.

Police cruisers, a blinding kaleidoscope of flashing lights and earsplitting sirens, roared past them on the opposite side of Broadway Street. Every first responder in the city would be headed straight for the site of the explosion, where officers and agents were down.

It had all happened in a horrifying instant. She could still smell the acrid scent of smoke, the gunpowder permeating the air, the odor of burning metal. The Reaper had been better prepared than even she had expected. Not that she had ever seen him at work in that manner, on that scale. Only the aftermath in pictures. The hellish scene had unfolded with shocking speed, the world erupting into a nightmare of bullets and chaos. Then the bodies started dropping, the number of fatalities rising with each minute that passed.

If they hadn't fled when they did... A chill raked through her.

Christina had no idea how long it would take law enforcement to shift their focus to finding the assailant responsible for the havoc wrought or to resume a manhunt for her.

But she was certain the Reaper already had a solid estimate.

Only someone so calculated and decisive—so utterly cold-blooded—could've planned and executed such devastation without even breaking a sweat. No regard for the lives lost or the families that would be left broken by his carnage.

Christina stared out of the shattered rear windshield, keeping *him* in sight, several car lengths behind them, until Jackson made a hard right turn. Then a sharp left and another right. "What's the plan?"

"I don't know," he said, maintaining a zigzag pattern of driving.

They needed to come up with something. "He's not far behind us." She couldn't see him, but she didn't doubt for a second that he was close on their tail.

"I'm aware," Jackson snapped, his voice strained. He took another hard turn.

"We can't just drive around in circles."

"I'm thinking."

The man pursuing them wasn't thinking. He was planning. Might have already determined what he would do next. They couldn't afford to let him get two steps ahead of them. If they did, they would die.

"Jackson, the guy chasing us isn't a regular hit man. Not a simple assassin for hire. He's something else." Something worse.

Something straight out of a nightmare.

"Yeah. I gathered." Yanking the wheel, Jackson made a right turn, tires squealing. "Alvaro Aguilar. I crossed paths with him a few months ago."

"And you lived to tell the tale? I'm impressed."

"Don't be. He was surveilling a friend of mine in the hopes she would lead him to her father, who the cartel wanted dead. Aguilar was scoping out my friends. An IPS team in Bitterroot Falls. The encounter, if you could describe it as such, was a close call in a restaurant. Completely on his terms. No one got hurt or died that day because it wasn't what Aguilar wanted."

On his terms.

Sounded like *La Parca*, the Grim Reaper deciding who would live and who would die.

"Right now," she said, "he's anticipating our next move. Calculating his options. Mapping out checkmate." That was his talent. His true gift. Not his ability to kill, but how he strategized and orchestrated those kills. "We can't play his game. We won't win." Or rather, survive. "He won't give up." No matter the odds, he wasn't letting go of this vendetta. "There's no stopping him."

"He's not invincible. Every threat can be neutralized."

"That's it," she mumbled to herself. They had to outsmart him. It was the only way. What would a marshal do? Whatever it was, they had to do the opposite. Something the Reaper would least expect. "You can't take me to a police station, or back to the US marshals' building. He's probably counting on that, and if you do—"

"I'll only the endanger the lives of more officers. I know. He's using armor-piercing rounds, rigged that truck to blow, and who knows what else he has up his sleeve." Jackson flicked a glance in the rearview mirror. "I think we lost him."

She hoped so as well, but she knew better. With all his training and experience, he could easily track them.

"We shouldn't count on it," she said. "Underestimating him is the worst thing we can do. We need to ditch this vehicle." With the busted windows and bullet holes, it was going to draw a ton of unwanted attention. "Find another set of wheels."

They had to get out of the city, go off the grid and regroup. She had time-sensitive information about the cartel and was only willing to trust Jackson with it. But he would have to act on it quickly before it became useless. How he was going to accomplish that now, she had no idea.

The only thing that mattered right now was evading the Reaper and getting through this alive.

"I think I might have a better idea." Jackson took the next corner so fast the rear end fishtailed. Picking up more speed, he raced down Reserve Street.

"Care to share it?" She'd examined a map of Missoula while holed up in the motel room, to get her bearings of the city. Sketch out egress routes. Identify places to hide. But she didn't have the layout memorized and had no idea where they might be headed.

Jackson's silence did nothing to steady her nerves. She wasn't used to putting her life into the hands of others with no say in the matter. All it did was make her pulse ratchet higher.

They were approaching a bridge. Glancing over her shoulder, Christina searched for any sign of the car the Reaper had stolen. A little red crossover utility vehicle.

Nothing.

She wondered if he would've taken the time to switch cars and risk losing them.

Doubtful.

As soon as they made it across to the other side of the bridge, Jackson whipped the car down a narrow side street. The entrance had come up quickly and was tucked back behind trees. Easy to miss. He must've driven this way before, she assumed.

The side street opened to the bank of the river. About a

mile down the road, they came to a boat rental shop, and he parked the beat-up SUV.

Taking off his helmet, he grabbed his jacket and slipped it on. "Unhook the cuffs and give them to me along with the key," he said, tucking his gun in his holster.

She did as he asked, handing them to him. "Do you intend to use those on me again?"

"I hope you won't give me a reason to." He slipped the cuffs and key into the zipper pocket of his sport utility pants. "But I'll keep my options open. Come on. Let's go."

Hurrying out of the back seat, she turned toward the water. The Clark Fork River was the largest in Montana. Long and wide and deep. And today, wild. "This is your plan?"

Jackson zipped up his jacket, covering his vest. "Yeah." He took hold of her arm, his grip tight, as though he feared she might flee. Hauling her toward the shop, he looked at her. "Have you got a better one?"

She hated the idea. Would put it in the top three of the worst ones could think of, but it wasn't as if they had a lot of choices. "We could wrench up a manhole cover and take our chances in the sewers."

He threw her a perplexed sideways glance. "Really? That's your idea?"

"Okay, no. I don't have a better one. But I still don't like this one." She looked back over her shoulder at the side street. It was clear all the way to the main road. "We need to be quick."

Jackson nodded as they entered the shop.

An older man with puffy white hair looked up from a magazine he was reading. "Hey, there, Jackson. I just opened for the season last week and you're the first person to set foot in here." The guy looked at Christina. His gaze fell to Jackson's hand on her arm. "I sure didn't expect to see you, especially not today."

"Last-minute idea, Francis," Jackson said as he let her go.

The older man tensed, something unspoken passing between them. "You want to take a boat out?"

"Yeah."

"With all the rain recently, the river is really rough today," Francis said. "So choppy I don't think you'll have much luck catching any fish. I'd advise against it."

"See." Christina gave Jackson a hard look. "I told you. This is a bad idea."

Jackson narrowed his eyes and then cut his gaze back to Francis. "We're not fishing, but we need a boat. We want something fast." He pulled a credit card from his wallet and handed it to the guy.

Too bad they didn't have cash.

Leaving a digital trail when you were on the run wasn't smart.

"Okay. How about the Stingray?" Francis asked. "Gets up to sixty knots."

Jackson shook his head. "Too big. We need something smaller."

"Smaller means slower," Francis said. "You're going to have choose between size and speed."

"Unfortunately, I guess so. We can't take the Stingray. It's too wide."

Wider and bigger were better in her opinion. "Too wide for what?" she asked.

"I'll explain on the boat," Jackson said through clenched teeth. "Since we're in a hurry."

Francis frowned. "I guess take number two." The older man swiped the credit card and gave it back to Jackson along with a key. "The Hamble Dory."

Christina went to the entrance of the shop and looked around outside.

"Don't go anywhere," Jackson said to her.

She raised her palms in mock surrender. "Where am I going to go? Down into the sewer?"

A hint of a smile tugged at his mouth and then his lips flattened again. "Thanks, Francis." Jackson signed the receipt. "You need to close the shop for a bit. Go on a break and grab the keys to the other boats. Take them with you. Have a long lunch somewhere on me."

Everything was calm and quiet outside the shop. No traffic or passersby. She strode back to the counter.

Francis looked at the receipt and raised his eyebrows. "Wow. That's a generous tip."

"The tip is for you to close up," Jackson said, his voice firm. "Right now. Got it?"

Giving a wary nod, Francis locked the register. "Unwelcome company on the way?"

"Possibly." Jackson's tone was grim. "It's safer for you if you're not here."

Francis stuffed the rest of the boat keys in his pocket, but that wouldn't stop the Reaper from hot-wiring one.

Nothing would stop him.

The older man grabbed his coat on the way to the door. "Make sure you get a couple of life jackets."

Jackson snatched two orange life vests and ushered her out the door.

As they made their way down to the dock, Francis turned the sign from Open to Closed and locked up. He even pulled down the steel shutter he probably used during the off-season.

The older man made a beeline to the only other car in the small lot, but he stopped and stared at the bullet-riddled vehicle they had arrived in. Then he looked back at them with a horrified expression. Francis didn't take out his cell phone to call the authorities. He simply hurried to his car.

Jackson stepped into the boat that could only seat four comfortably. To call it small would've been an understatement. It looked like a life-size kid's toy.

She stared at the choppy waves, jostling the little Hamble Dory and the other boats. "Why can't we take a larger one? It'll be safer." Not to mention faster.

"It won't fit where we're going. There's a stream that branches off from the river that we need to take, and those others are too wide." He dropped the life jackets in the boat and took her hand to help her climb in.

She watched Francis speed off down the road. "Do you fish a lot?" Growing up, he hadn't been interested in it.

"Rarely, but when I do, it's only in the summer."

Christina sat on the cushioned bench at the back of the boat near the motor. "You and Francis seemed to know each other pretty well." So well, in fact, the older man hadn't questioned Jackson, aside from safety factors of taking a boat today.

Jackson untied the skiff and pushed away from the dock. "Francis is someone who was relocated here through WITSEC. I was assigned to him. Got him settled. I check in on him and all the others I've helped from time to time. Discreetly."

"Like under the guise of fishing?"

He sat at the wheel. "Exactly."

Jackson wasn't treating her like she was the enemy. Shared confidential information about Francis—probably a slip from the pressure cooker they were in. She'd never been under fire and suspected Jackson had experienced nothing as intense as the mayhem back at the airport. It was definitely enough to cause a lapse in protocol. Case in point, he got her onto this tiny boat instead of hauling her into a police station. Still, none of it meant he trusted her or that she could have faith in him to listen to her entire story and believe her. To understand what she'd endured. What Kirk Kehoe had put her through.

Jackson had let her down before, and she didn't see any reason why he wouldn't again.

People didn't change. Not deep down at their core.

Jackson sat at the wheel. "Did you ever learn to swim?"

"A little. The basics." Enough not to drown if pushed into a pool. So many of her decisions and actions centered around one thing—survival. The rough water rocked the boat. Holding on to the side, she reached for a life jacket. A pool was one thing. This river was something else entirely. "I'm not a strong swimmer."

Jackson checked some things on the boat and started the engine. "We're only going a few miles downstream. It's the quickest way to get to the place I'm taking you. Hang on."

Bracing herself, she held on to the side. "And where's that?"

He pulled off. "Someplace safe to hole up, so I can figure out what to do next."

Christina finished putting on the life vest, clicking the safety buckles in place. Clinging to the side of the boat, she shifted her weight on the bench and stared at the road. Francis had parked his car at an angle, near the entrance, blocking the way for any other vehicles.

That was loyalty to a fault. It would've been smarter for the older man to drive off rather than leave on foot and risk running into danger.

Still no sign of the Reaper. She half expected to see him bolting down the road at a full sprint at any second.

Maybe they had lost him.

The small launch chugged down the rushing river, taking them away from shore. Her shoulders relaxed, but she was far from at ease. They were in little more than a motorized dinghy and the water looked treacherous.

Keeping an eye on their six, she tore her gaze away from the road and glanced at the bridge.

A red car suddenly stopped in the middle of the bridge. Everything inside her clenched. The Reaper appeared at the railing. Her heart sank as her hope for a clean getaway tanked.

He lifted the submachine gun and aimed through the sights. She was right in his crosshairs.

What was the range on that weapon?

She guessed much farther than a handgun's. Close enough for him to make the shot if he bothered to take aim. Even if he was within range, killing her here wouldn't satisfy him. Would it?

But what if he wasn't targeting her?

Jackson.

Christina leaped up and put her back to Jackson, shielding him with her body.

"What's wrong?" Jackson asked.

She swayed on her feet and held her arms out slightly to maintain her balance in the unsteady boat. "It's him. He's on the bridge."

"You need to take cover."

As much as she wanted to do just that, she had to protect Jackson. "No."

It was a risky bet that the Reaper would wait to kill her, the way he wanted, on his terms. If she was wrong, then she was only making herself an even bigger target, easier to hit and kill.

The Reaper lowered the weapon and stared at her. She couldn't be certain since he was too far away, but she could've sworn...he smiled.

All the anxiety pinging inside her over the last thirty-six hours coalesced. A new kind of fear, like a cold sludge, welled in her stomach, pushing on her diaphragm, creeping up around her lungs. "Go faster, Jackson."

In the next breath, the monster raised the submachine gun and took aim again. He held so still, appeared so focused. She wondered if he was debating, if she had miscalculated, if he even drew a breath.

A shot cracked the air, the sound softened by distance, and there was a delay—nanoseconds—before it ripped through her flesh.

Chapter Five

Missoula
Friday, April 13, 2:52 p.m.

The sound of the single shot nearly made Jackson's heart stop.

Christina screamed as she stumbled backward against him, but she stayed on her feet. The boat swerved and he fought to keep it steady in the rough water.

She was hit. But how badly?

"Don't stop!" she called out over the roar of the river. Her voice was shrill with pain. "He won't kill me. Not yet. Not here."

"You can't know that."

"I do!" She groaned. "If that's what he wanted, I'd already be dead. Keep going!"

"Where are you hit?" Jackson pushed the boat's engine as hard as he could. The max on the Dory was twenty-six knots. "How bad is it?" Was it fatal?

Maybe Aguilar wanted her to hemorrhage slowly. There were stories about the cartel not granting their worst enemies a quick death.

Jackson had no idea what they would do to someone they had trusted, who had been embedded in their ranks, spying on them and sabotaging their efforts for years.

He was sure they wouldn't want to make it quick. Or painless.

"Get down!" Jackson ordered.

"No," she said, still stubborn as a mule.

He was desperate to force her to listen and reluctant to let go of the steering wheel.

Getting out of range of that weapon was the only solution, and crashing during the process would only compound their problems.

"Please. Take cover," he begged.

"He'll kill you if I do."

For some reason, she was confident Alvaro Aguilar wouldn't kill her, but he could still severely wound her.

Another gunshot, and a guttural cry tore from her. She staggered, grabbing onto him.

Every instinct to protect her thrummed alive beneath his skin.

With no other choice, he released the steering wheel, leaving the throttle at full speed—hoping they wouldn't crash—and wrapped an arm around Christina, taking her down to the deck.

In the small space, she shifted her legs and hips with a groan, rolling on top of him and covering him once again, like a human shield, when he should've been the one protecting her.

Rapid gunfire split the air. A hail of bullets riddled the boat, knocking out the motor and piercing the hull. But not a single round struck them.

The river still carried them along, but icy liquid seeped into his clothes. They were taking on water.

She raised her head and looked around. "He's gone from the railing. I think he's getting back into the car."

Jackson got up and sat her down. Grimacing, she let out a hiss of pain. He examined her.

Her coat sleeve was torn. She was hit in the arm and the leg.

"I'm okay," she said with a wince.

He inspected her leg closer to see if he needed to tie off the wound. After twelve years apart, she'd stumbled back into his life, wanted for murder, and he'd fled the scene of a massacre with her. No way was he letting her bleed out in his custody, leaving him with more questions than answers.

The last time they'd parted, it was unexpected and terrible. History couldn't repeat itself. He couldn't bear it. There was so much unresolved and unspoken between them.

It was a clean shot. Just a graze. Enough to draw blood and cause pain, but nothing serious.

"You got lucky," he said, almost in disbelief. "Take off your coat. Let me see your arm."

"No time for that." She pointed at the water filling up the boat.

Christina was right.

"We're going to capsize," he said, trying to prepare her. He took off his coat. Shed the forty-five-pound Kevlar vest that would weigh him down. Strapped on a life jacket. "We have to jump."

Eyes wide, she shook her head. "I'll drown."

A rocky wave tossed the boat hard, as if to confirm her fears.

"I won't let you." Jackson took her hand. "Trust me."

"I don't trust Mother Nature. You can't control the river, Jackson."

"We're going in the water whether we like it or not. But I'm right here with you. We'll do it together." Nodding, he got her to stand.

She winced as she put weight on her leg.

"Can you tread water?" he asked.

"Yeah, I think so. It just hurts."

"Ready?"

She hesitated, but after a moment nodded.

Holding hands, they jumped into the fast-moving river. A gasp escaped as the numbing cold jolted him, the shock sending a surge of adrenaline through his bloodstream. The current swept them away as the boat sank.

For several minutes, all they could do was struggle to stay afloat and tread water while the winding river carried them downstream. The current was strong, the choppy water whipping them around, making it difficult for them to maintain their grip. He held on to her tightly, his arms aching, determined not to let go.

The river was going to fork. When the split happened, they needed to be on the right side. The bifurcation held no significance in terms of the route he'd planned, but it would present their only opportunity to escape the relentless current and reach safety.

One chance. They couldn't miss it.

"See the fork?" he shouted, over the sound of the rushing river.

"Yes."

"Stay to the right!" They had to work together, using their legs and arms in tandem to steer themselves in the direction they needed.

"Okay!"

They were rapidly approaching the split. Kicking as hard as he could and paddling with his free arm to guide them, he navigated through the current. Their waterlogged weight dragged against them with each stroke. He could barely keep his face above the surface and Christina wasn't faring any better, but they reached the right branch of the river.

Scanning the shoreline, he searched for the spot where

rocks protruded into the water. He wasn't sure how far down it was, but on calmer days when he'd gone this way, he'd noticed it. A place where they had a chance to make it out of the water.

Where was it?

The wild current grew stronger, throttling them. They hit a choppy wave. His grip on her slipped.

"Jackson!" She took a mouthful of water.

He kicked with everything he had, struggling not to let fatigue get the best of him, not to let the cold or water win—not to lose her in the rapids. She splashed around near him, fighting against the raging river, but she was still out of his reach.

Where were the rocks?

The river curved once more, taking them around another bend. Then he spotted it. Maybe a quarter mile down. "Head for those rocks."

"I can't!" Christina sputtered. "The current." She flailed, and he could tell it was getting harder for her to tread water and steer herself. "It's too strong!"

They had to make it. Failure meant being swept farther downriver, into potentially more dangerous territory. He'd been counting on the boat's engine to peel away from the river and take the stream that branched out in a different direction.

That outcrop of rocks was the one spot where they'd have the slim prospect of making it out of the river. They couldn't miss their only chance of survival. But in order to do it, he had to reach her first.

Jackson kicked, swimming toward her, battling the heavy, churning force of the river. Every muscle strained, every breath a desperate gasp. His legs and arms burned, like wildfire running through his veins, while the icy water chilled him to the bone. With each stroke, he inched closer and closer to her. Pulling even with Christina, he caught the collar of her coat. He dragged her with him, making his way to the river's edge and the fast-approaching rocks.

Doing her best to help him, she fluttered her legs, but most importantly, she didn't panic. On her own and wounded, she wouldn't have made it. He was a strong swimmer, and it was a constant battle for him. For better or worse, they were in this together.

One more stroke. One more kick. He'd keep going until he couldn't do it anymore.

They only had one shot. His focus narrowed to navigating the treacherous waters and reaching that tenuous lifeline.

They were so close to the shore. He had to gamble that the water wasn't too deep there. Unbuckling his vest, he slipped one arm out.

"Here it comes!" No time to second-guess the decision. *Now or never.*

He hauled in a deep breath, dropped under the water, allowing himself to sink until his feet touched the rocky river bottom. Grabbing Christina around the hips, he pushed up to the surface, using every bit of strength he had left, propelling her toward the rocks. At the last minute, he barely snatched hold of a large branch hanging over the river from a fallen tree.

But the current caught his legs, threatening to haul him downstream. Jackson held on for dear life, the river frothing and snarling around him. The branch was slick with mud from the embankment where the tree had toppled but formed a slippery bridge to the shore. Grinding his teeth, he managed to hook his other arm around the heavy tree limb. Straining, he wrestled one leg from the relentless suction of the water and threw it over the branch. Hauling his other leg free of the river took less effort.

Cautiously he stretched his body along the limb, his

breath coming in ragged gasps. He was keenly aware of his precarious position. One wrong move could send him slipping back into the water. He slowly crept across the branch, the tree trunk shuddering as if the roots might be torn free from its anchor any second. Finally, he made it to the rocks.

He spotted Christina. A relieved breath punched from his mouth. She was safe and had collapsed, gagging and spewing water. Slowly, she got up on her hands and knees, crawling up the rocks farther onto the embankment. Away from the water, she sat, her chest heaving, her head hanging like she was wiped out. The feeling was mutual. They'd made it, both alive, though exhausted and drenched. But it wasn't over.

They still had to make the trek the rest of the way to their destination.

Carefully, he scrambled across the rocks, trying not to leave any trace that they had gotten out of the water there. Jackson didn't see Aguilar, but he was certain the killer was still hot on their trail. No way to tell if the killer had taken the time to hot-wire a boat. If he had, more than likely he would've taken a larger, faster one, but it would've been perilous for him to go through the right branch of the river since it was narrower and the rocky outcrop could easily damage the hull of a bigger boat.

"Are you okay?" Jackson panted, coming up beside her.

Coughing up water and shivering from the cold, Christina nodded. She raised her head, her long, dark brown hair plastered around her face. Her full lips were pink and trembling. When her gaze met his, her eyes were weary, but there was still a spark in them. A fire burned.

One he was familiar with—pure determination. None of her self-confidence had faltered over the years.

Even as a teenager, she'd been stubborn and tenacious.

And he had loved her for it.

"I'm...okay," she said, shakily pushing to her feet.

"Take a minute. Catch your breath." He stood up beside her and peered into her face. Maybe it was the adrenaline, or the rush of surviving two close calls, but as he looked at her—shivering and soaked and not a stitch of makeup on—he was struck by how beautiful she was.

"We don't have a minute," she said, coughing again. "To spare." She unclipped the life vest and tossed it in the water. The jacket washed away downstream. "We need to go."

As soon as Christina started climbing up the rocky embankment, she gasped in pain.

"Can you make it?" he asked.

"Yeah. I'm sore and wiped," she said, panting. "But I can do it."

"You sure?"

She scrambled up the rocks. "I'm fine."

Once they reached the ridge, he led the way through the trees, getting them out of sight from anyone on the river. "Let me check your other wound."

She clutched her arm. "It's not bad. It just hurts, but really, I'm okay."

"I'll be the judge of that." He went to unzip her coat, and she moved away.

"It can wait." She glanced around. "Until we get somewhere safe. Any idea where we're going?"

"The plan is the same." He knew people he could turn to all over the state. Looking at the position of the sun and the mountains, he pointed in the direction they needed to go. "But we've got to hoof it."

"How far?" Shivering, she clutched her arms. "I don't know how long we'll last out here in the cold, soaking wet."

The river had carried them most of the way. Cutting across the land rather taking the stream would save them time. "Rough estimate, a mile. Maybe a bit more. If we keep a steady pace, we should be able to make it in twenty minutes."

Her teeth chattered. Nodding, she clamped her lips closed, as though to control the sound, but he could see the pain and weariness in her eyes, the worry bleeding through her expression.

"My face is about to be all over the news. Again. Soon. If not already. Are you confident where we're going will be safe?"

They were going to another person in witness protection. Some people in the program were criminals who had turned traitor. Others were innocent, trapped in a bad situation, resolved to do some good. Those were the ones he'd gotten to know, befriended and checked on beyond what was required. In turn, they treated him like family, since he was one of the only people who knew their true identity, the circumstances they had fled, the loved ones they'd had to leave behind. They owed him nothing, but in a pinch, they'd help him without question.

"It's safe."

"Okay," she said, her breath crystallizing in the air, picking up her step and passing him.

Jackson stared after her. The past adrenaline-charged hour had his head spinning. All the things that had transpired, a whirlwind of violence and chaos, and the things she'd said were settling in his mind. He struggled to reconcile the girl she'd been, wild and passionate, with the woman she'd become. A wily spy.

A lifetime ago, he'd thought Christina was the woman he would one day marry. Of course, they'd only been naïve kids at the time. Sixteen and seventeen. With no real concept of how hard, how ugly the world could be.

Then again, she knew. The beatings she'd endured every time her father got drunk, trying to escape the grief of losing his wife to cancer, and took his anger out on her with his fists.

Jackson had had no clue how to protect her back then. From her father or the club. He'd been the one who was sheltered. Not her. He'd never fully understood what she went through growing up with the Iron Warriors. Maybe he hadn't wanted to see it. The gritty side of her life that his parents had warned him existed. The parts that had forced her to thrive and bloom, like a daisy in the desert, despite the harsh conditions.

She was smart. Shrewd. A survivor. That was what Kehoe saw in her and what had told him she could pull off being an asset inside one of the world's most dangerous crime syndicates.

It was those same qualities Jackson had to keep at the forefront of his mind every step of the way with her. Especially when he questioned her again.

The best assets were master manipulators. Operating in the moral gray zone. The trick was their handlers had to ensure the asset didn't stray too far toward the dark side, getting lost. Without Kehoe to guide him, Jackson had to figure this out and assess her on his own.

His past relationship with Christina, as well as his feelings for her—which might have lessened but never died—his instinct to protect her, were as much an advantage as they were a liability.

Once they reached shelter, warmed up, and she let down her guard, he intended to squeeze every bit of intel that she had been holding back out of her.

For Christina's sake, it had better be vitally important—and she had better tell him the truth.

Chapter Six

Near Greenbriar, Montana
Friday, April 13, 3:27 p.m.

Earn his trust first. Then Christina could tell Jackson the dirty details of her time deep undercover with the cartel.

Otherwise, he'd think the worst of her. There were times she looked back on her actions and questioned her decisions. Hated the compromises she made and the position Kehoe had put her in.

The one person she would never want to debrief her about her time in the cartel was going to push for all her secrets.

When she was a teenager, head over heels in love with him, his parents' judgment of her and his silent agreement with them that she wasn't good enough had been like a knife in her chest. As pathetic as it was, the prospect of him judging her now, condemning her choices, was a fist around her heart.

His opinion shouldn't matter anymore. But it did.

Already, without even deliberately thinking, she was deciding what to share, what to withhold, how to balance the scale between trust and concealment.

She had played the game for so long she didn't know how to stop. After all, that was Alice's fourth commandment: *Anticipate and strategize two moves ahead.*

Not that she had any intention of manipulating Jackson as she'd done for years with the enemy. Jackson was on her side, or at least they were both fighting for the same thing: to bring down the cartel. To cripple their drug-trafficking operation and hamper their money-laundering schemes.

To get an image of Rio Estrada so that they could run it through facial recognition, find him and monitor his every move until the task force was ready to arrest him.

All those lofty goals, which she had been so close to achieving, now seemed like distant fragments of a dream.

None of it mattered if the elements killed them. Or the Reaper.

She stumbled over a rock, pitching forward, headed face-first toward the hard ground. Strong arms caught her around the waist.

Jackson held her close, moving his arms higher to wrap around her, his hands clasped on her biceps. "I've got you." His words punctured the icy haze that had taken hold of her.

Warmth spread, and she found herself leaning into him. "Thanks."

As she pressed against his body for balance, her heart thudded wildly at the base of her throat. He tightened his arms around her, and she realized how badly she was shivering.

Her toes and fingers were numb. They'd hiked through the woods for what felt like forever. Teeth chattering, wounds throbbing, muscles aching, she didn't know how much farther she could go.

"I—I need to t-t-tell you," Christina said. "The intel I had for K-K-Kirk." If she lost consciousness out there, she had no idea where they would end up. Perhaps separated, with her behind bars.

"You will." He kept a tight hold on her. "Soon."

"D-depots. Three. S-s-stockpiles. Weapons. Drugs.

Money." The mother lode of intel she had been compiling. Too critical and sensitive to simply hand over to Kirk until he was ready to extract her. If the task force acted on the information prematurely, seizing everything, it would be the decisive blow that would neutralize the cartel. It also would've exposed her as the leak.

She'd held on to it, waiting for the right time, hoping she could accomplish the prime directive: Nail Rio Estrada.

"You, you have exact locations?" he asked, trembling beside her.

"Yeah." The depots were the central nervous system of Estrada's Team US, and if they seized the contents as soon as possible, before everything was moved, and got their hands on Rio, the task force could crush the cartel's stateside operation. "They're f-full. Now."

"Then we have to hit them."

All she could do was nod. Each breath burned. Her lungs were on fire, even though it was a side effect of the cold.

She looked down at his hands locked on her arm. Big, capable hands. Hands that never fumbled the football in high school. Hands that had once caressed every inch of her body.

There was so much she needed to tell him. About the depots. And other stuff. Years ago, when they'd gone their separate ways, it had been in a fit of anger. She'd said horrible things. After loving him for years, defending him against the club's criticism, she regretted how they had ended things. On such an ugly, bitter note.

"If—if we don't make it," she said, huffing, straining for breath.

"We'll make it." His voice was firm. Confident.

He was always so optimistic. As though he could change reality with the sheer force of his will. It was one of the things she'd admired about him.

To his credit, she hadn't drowned, thanks to him.

She burrowed deeper against him, letting herself remember how he used to hold her. Look at her. How it made her feel.

So safe and wanted. Hopeful. That they could overcome any obstacle. There were never any walls with Jackson, not when they were alone. Their relationship was a beacon of light, illuminating the path to a future with him that she'd wanted more than anything.

She wasn't supposed to reminisce about *before*, because there was no going back. Not one of Alice's commandments—it was just something she couldn't let herself indulge in. It made her feel weak. Too vulnerable. But while she was hiding at the City Drift Motel, she'd thought a lot about the past and him.

What might have been if…so many things had been different.

"Jackson…" She panted, forcing herself to put one foot in front of the other. "There's more. I need to say…"

He pushed branches of a spruce out of the way. "We're here," he said, pointing to a farmhouse.

Relief yawned through her. If she could've teleported over to the house, she would've, but they still had several hundred feet to go.

Smoke rose from the chimney and a sedan sat parked in front of the house.

Clinging to each other, they trudged the rest of the way up to the steps of the covered porch. Jackson released her, knocked on the door and wrapped his arms around himself as they waited.

Footsteps approached inside. The door swung open.

A woman in her early fifties or late forties stood in the doorway. Her red hair was in a French braid draped over her shoulder. She had kind eyes that flared wide, and a look of surprise swept across her wholesome face. "Oh my God. Jackson. What are you doing here?"

"I'm in a bind, Imogene. We are," he said, gesturing to Christina with his head.

"You're on the news. Both of you. They keep showing images of the airport. Aerial footage from a helicopter. What happened?"

"It's complicated. But I could use some help."

"Of course." Imogene looked them over, finally taking in the state they were in. "You're both wet and look like you're about to shatter into pieces. You must be frozen. Your lips are blue." She ushered them inside, closing the door behind them, and Christina welcomed the immediate wave of warmth that hit her. Imogene fidgeted and licked her lips. "Patrick can't know you're here. He went into town. Should be gone for a couple of hours, but there's always the chance he could come back early."

Worry radiated off the woman.

Christina noticed she wasn't wearing a wedding band. A quick scan of the living room and she spotted several framed photos. Most were of Imogene with a young man who resembled her. Same complexion and hair color. Only two of Imogene with a man around her age. Patrick was a boyfriend, but the relationship wasn't casual. They were probably living together.

"We don't want to cause any trouble for you," Christina said.

Jackson nodded. "If I could borrow a phone and maybe your old truck, we'll get out here."

"Give me a minute." Imogene hurried off, disappearing deeper inside the house.

Christina glanced at the fire on the other side of the living room. She wanted to run over and curl up in front of it, but she didn't dare to track footprints through the house.

Imogene returned, carrying blankets and a black duffel. "This is my go-bag," she said, handing it to Jackson.

"You still keep one?"

"Old habits." Imogene shrugged and wrapped a blanket around each of them. "There's a burner phone inside the bag, a portable fast charger, some cash, clothes and shoes. All women's. You look a little smaller than my size, honey. Something should work for you, though it might be a bit baggy. There's also a loaded gun. The serial number has been removed. I know it's illegal, but—"

"It's fine," Jackson said. "Considering."

Imogene fished out keys from a bowl on a side table. She gave one to Jackson. "It's for the truck in the garage."

"What if Patrick asks about it?" Christina wondered.

Rule number five for her, always have a story ready. Some plausible explanation.

"I'll tell him that I loaned it to a friend, but I doubt he'll even notice." Imogene steered them out the door and headed toward the detached garage.

To Christina's surprise, the woman led them around to the back, where there was a staircase.

"You can freshen up in my son's place and get warm." Imogene hustled up the stairs.

Climbing the seventeen steps to the top felt like climbing a mountain. Every time Christina bent her hurt leg, a stinging sensation traveled through the wound.

"Zach will be at the university the rest of the day in classes." Imogene unlocked the door. "Then he has work and will probably spend the night at his girlfriend's. He usually does on the weekends."

They stepped inside.

The studio apartment over the garage was chilly, but warmer than outside.

"There's food in the pantry. Not sure what you'll find in the fridge, though." Imogene adjusted the temperature on the thermostat and flicked a switch, starting a gas fireplace. "Jackson, there's a washer and dryer behind that door," she said, pointing it out, "but feel free to take whatever you need from Zach's closet. After everything you've done for the two of us, he won't mind."

The two of them. Christina's assumption that Imogene had met Patrick here, in her new life, was correct.

"Are you sure?" Jackson said.

"Oh, please." Imogene waved a dismissive hand. "Get out of those wet clothes. Take a warm shower and stay under the water until you feel better."

"We'll do our best to hurry," Jackson said.

"Don't worry. If Pat gets back early, I'll think of something. Maybe send him out again for a nice bottle of wine that I'll insist on having with dinner. Or I'll get a sudden craving for ice cream."

If Christina's face wasn't so stiff from the cold, she would've smiled. She and Imogene would've gotten along, provided they had a chance to get to know each other.

"Thank you," Christina said, still shivering despite the blanket wrapped around her shoulders. "For sticking your neck out like this. I can only imagine what you've heard about me on the news." *Murder suspect wanted in connection to the shooting of an FBI agent and two other men.*

"I've learned not to judge," Imogene said. "Besides, you're with Jackson, so as far as I'm concerned, I'm happy to help. Both of you. Now, go get warm before you catch pneumonia." She set the truck key on the kitchen counter and left them alone.

Jackson strode across the small apartment to the bathroom. Inside, he started the shower. A moment later, he called out, "The water is warm."

Christina plodded into the bathroom and stared at the steaming shower.

"Let me see your arm," Jackson said.

Her arms felt like lead, but she unzipped the coat and shrugged it off.

Tugging on the tear in the sleeve of her sweater, he ripped it wide-open and examined her arm. "Another superficial wound."

"See. Nothing to worry about."

He studied her face. Cold shivers gone, he stood with his shoulders squared and his spine stiff. His eyes were hard and suspicious. His face deadpan while hinting that he knew more than he was willing to say. Whatever he was thinking, it wasn't good.

But the fact that she had no idea what was on his mind bugged the heck out of her.

Grabbing the hem of her sweater, she pulled the ruined piece of cashmere off over her head and dropped it on the floor, leaving her bra on. She bent over and unlaced her boots.

"I'll see what's in the pantry," he said. "Hopefully, there's some soup I can heat up while you're in the shower."

Christina caught hold of his wrist. "We're both freezing and we're short on time," she said, toeing off her boots. "It's silly to waste any of it by taking turns." She unzipped her jeans and peeled them off her legs, swallowing a groan. "I think we can handle it. We're adults who have already seen each other naked."

Even though that was true, she stepped into the shower wearing her underwear. The spray of warm water stung her flesh, but she relished the heat. She stood there and pretended like it was no big deal, being half-undressed in front of an old lover, but it wasn't just any old lover.

It was Jackson, and a stark sense of vulnerability left her unnerved.

Without a glance at her, he left the bathroom.

A shiver raked through her, but not from the cold. Her legs shook. She drew the shower curtain. Flattened her palms against the cool tile, steadying herself. She was exhausted. Every muscle ached.

She rinsed her wounds, both on the left side of her body. Blood washed from her skin, stinging her injuries. Pressing her forehead to the porcelain wall, she sighed.

The only reason the Reaper had shot her was to make her move and expose Jackson. Well, not the only reason, but definitely the main one. Otherwise, he would've done more damage.

He could've killed her. Once he had a chance to do it in the manner he saw fit, he would certainly try, and she would make it difficult.

She was on borrowed time.

A dead woman walking.

Jackson yanked the curtain back, startling her. The only thing he had on was his underwear. Boxer briefs. A nice upgrade from the tighty-whities he used to wear as a teenager.

She took in his muscular physique that still had the smooth athleticism that made him a star quarterback in high school. He stepped into the shower behind her.

"I put my stuff in the dryer." He closed the curtain. "You were right. It's silly to wait. I'm freezing."

Something stirred in her. Something foreign, yet familiar. Something dangerous.

Without overthinking it, she turned around, facing him, and wrapped her arms around his waist. She tugged him fully under the stream of water with her until their bodies were pressed close. Their eyes locked and heat flooded her. "Skin to skin is the fastest way for us to warm up."

Chapter Seven

Greenbriar
Friday, April 13, 3:50 p.m.

Jackson stiffened, unprepared for the shock of her touching him. For the feel of her hands on his waist, her thighs brushing his, her breasts pressed against his chest. Something in him snapped to life. Awareness. Heat.

Thinking about how good the hot water felt wasn't even possible. Not when it was eclipsed by the feel of her soft warmth molding perfectly to him. Just like it had all those years ago. She'd had a tempting figure, even as a sixteen-year-old girl, developing quickly with lush curves. But now she had the svelte, toned body of a woman and was just flat-out gorgeous.

He was tired and sore and reeling from how things had fallen apart, the utter catastrophe at the airport. But at that moment, standing there with her touching him, he felt a quiet joy seeping through him, and it was a total blindside.

His hands slid down her spine as though they had a mind of their own. That immediate pull to her was still there, the same as it had been whenever he entered her orbit, gravity sucking him in. And he didn't resist it.

Jackson stared at that heart-shaped face and those intelligent eyes that had haunted him for years. An overwhelming urge to take her mouth and stake a claim rushed over him.

Before he could act on it, Christina rose on the balls of her feet and crushed her lips to his.

Every cell in his body caught fire at the contact, and the sweep of her tongue across his poured gasoline on the flames.

He was supposed to stop this. Put professional responsibility ahead of personal desire. Instead, he did the absolute worst thing. He kissed her back, like a man possessed. His fingers slipped into her wet hair, his palms cupping her face, and he couldn't get enough of her mouth. Her taste. Her tongue.

A needy groan escaped him. It'd been so long. So very long since he'd been with a woman. Nearly three years. But it was more than a primal reaction. This wasn't just any woman. It was Chrissy. Kissing her was like coming home.

Pent-up need surged through him, exploding into something he couldn't rein in, and his thoughts scattered like shrapnel.

He clung tighter to her and cursed between kisses—at her, at himself, at this awful situation. But having her back in his arms gave him a rush that was stronger than adrenaline in his blood.

She kissed him with such a heady mix of honey and heat that he wanted to lose himself in her. Breathe her into his lungs. Relish the sweetness of this moment—that had finally come after what felt like an eternity of wanting. She curled an arm around his neck, and he pinned her body against the wall. Muscle memory had his hand dipping low to catch her leg under the knee. She moaned in his mouth. Sighed his name.

And the past clawed through him. Every conversation. Every cuddle. Every caress.

Once they'd taken their friendship to the next level as teens, there wasn't a moment when he hadn't wanted her. Stealing kisses between classes, knowing exactly how many minutes they had before the bell rang. Taking her fast in the back seat of his truck. Or slow in his bedroom, where they could savor every second that they were connected, stripped bare and joined as one.

What he wouldn't give for one more day with her. One more hour when she was his again.

Jackson deepened the kiss, craving more, unable to hide it, and drew her closer. In return, she tortured him, rubbing her curves against him, pressing her hips to his, her hands roaming over him, making every part of him turn rock-hard. He slid his hand across her thigh, brushing her wound.

Flinching, she gasped in pain.

The sharp sound brought him back to reality. Terrified by the track his thoughts had taken, how the automatic response of his body to her had overridden everything else, he set her away from him. The sudden loss of her heat and softness was a jolt, kick-starting his brain.

She looked dazed and unsteady at first. "It's okay." A sexy smile danced on her lips. Her eyes gleamed with desire. "You didn't hurt me." She put her palm on his chest. "I want you, Jackson."

Words he'd longed to hear for twelve years twisted his heart into a knot. Why did it feel like a punch to the solar plexus?

His gaze fell over her dainty lace bra—see-through from the water—and then he looked at her injuries. Gashes that didn't even require stitches.

Something about it was off, niggling at the back of his brain. One gunshot resulting in a surface wound might be lucky.

But not two. No way, no how.

He backed up until her hand dropped from his chest and his spine hit the shower wall. "Explain this to me," he said, gesturing to her arm.

"What?" She stared at him, her brow wrinkled in confusion, her lips swollen from kissing. "What are we talking about?"

"Why didn't Aguilar kill you? That man murdered several law enforcement officers without blinking, but he didn't kill you when he could've. *Twice.* Explain it to me."

She recoiled. "On the boat, I told you he wouldn't."

"You did. But tell me why he wouldn't kill you." Presumably, that was the reason Aguilar had been sent.

"Would you have preferred it if he had?"

"Don't." He shook his head. "Don't do that. Tell me why."

She hesitated. "He'll torture me first. To find out everything I told you, to gauge the exposure for the cartel."

A good answer.

The best lies were half-truths. Kehoe had taught Jackson that. Surely he'd taught Christina the same.

Part of him wanted to accept her response. Leave well enough alone. Simply go back to kissing her. Make love to her.

But he couldn't. "Let's say I buy what you're trying to sell. Aguilar still could have incapacitated you. Seriously injured you. Instead, he took two precise, nearly impossible shots, only nicking you. Do you have any idea what kind of skill, what kind of *care* that takes? Explain it."

"I can't." She folded her arms over her chest. "I don't know what he was thinking. I'm not a mind reader."

"I want to believe you, but…" He shook his head.

"What is there to doubt? I gave you proof I'm Kirk's asset."

On the surface it looked like proof. "You told me about cases we've worked on. Things the mole already knows. That isn't concrete confirmation." Maybe he'd been too hasty to believe her and should've doubted every word out of her mouth sooner.

"You think I was never an asset, that the mole told me what to say? Or that I was working for Kirk and, what, turned at some point while on the inside?"

Either way, it would make him a sucker and her the enemy. "I'm not sure what to think. But Kirk Kehoe was more than my supervisor. He was my mentor and my friend. I'm going to get to the bottom of what happened to him. Then I'm going to make the cartel and those responsible for his death pay. Anyone who gets in my way is going to regret it. *Anyone*."

"The depots are the cartel's main hub. It's a huge vulnerability for them. I didn't have to say anything about them."

All unverified. "Supposedly filled with cash, drugs and weapons. All of which could be moved and vanish before we seize them." She hadn't given him anything to act on regarding the depots. No addresses. No intel on the type of security at the sites.

Not that she'd had a chance. If she had disclosed details when they had her in custody, the mole on the task force could've warned the cartel, provided she was on the right side of this.

He was putting everything on the line and wanted to believe her, but he couldn't operate on blind faith.

A crestfallen expression flashed across her face. Her eyes turned glassy. A needle of guilt pricked him, but he had to reel in the automatic response to comfort her.

"I warned you at the US marshals' building," she said. "Told you that you weren't prepared. That anyone near me would be in danger. I tried to convince you to stay behind. But you still doubt me? You think I'm lying?"

She'd been an Iron Warrior, as much as any biker wearing the club cut, long before she was inside the cartel. During her formative years, the club, *her family* was an outlaw gang, doing dirty deeds. She was a woman comfortable in a world rife with deceit and treachery. How else could she have survived for so long inside the cartel?

"I don't know, Chrissy." Shrugging, he glanced at the wounds on her arm and leg. One traitor had gotten close and deceived him. He couldn't pretend that he wasn't vulnerable to it happening again with her. So much had happened so quickly. He needed to sort through it, piece by piece, until it made sense. "It's just—everything doesn't add up."

"No one calls me Chrissy." Something about her hardened, retreated, and suddenly she was like a stranger. "Not anymore."

He'd thought he knew her twelve years ago, but he didn't know her now.

What if she was a double agent?

What would be the end game?

Only one thing came to mind: protect the mole on the task force by drawing suspicion away from them to someone else. Was she setting him up to be the fall guy?

If she was, he was playing right into her hand. An asset found every angle and knew which ones to exploit. "Why did you kiss me?"

Straightening, she jutted her chin up in the air. "Why did you kiss me back?"

I lost my mind. Temporarily. He fled with her and protected her. Then she hooked him even deeper with the lure of more intel, promises of depots that might not even exist. Now she was kissing him and he was kissing her back. He was already compromised. If he slept with her, there might not be any way to salvage his career. "It was a mistake. I allowed myself to succumb to an old temptation."

"An old temptation? That's what you think of me." Hurt slashed across her features, and an equivalent pain he despised feeling ripped through his gut. "Did you ever love me? Or were you just having fun with me back then? Because I was convenient. What was I to you?"

His head registered the redirection on her part, but his heart welled with so much resurrected emotion he wished it would simply stay buried. "You broke up with me. Not the other way around. Remember? Even though you knew what you were to me. What our relationship meant." She had been his whole world. He couldn't imagine a future without her. But none of it had stopped her from cutting him off.

"Yeah, I knew." She glared at him. "You were sowing your wild oats with biker trash."

The familiar words stole his breath, dragging him back to that night. The last one they'd shared together. In his room. Christina had sneaked out the window as the sun came up, and she was supposed to climb down the trellis and wait for him so he could drive her home.

As he finished dressing and looked for his keys, his dad had barged into his room. Chewed him out because he knew she'd slept over. By the time Jackson had climbed down the trellis, Christina was gone. "You heard my father? Everything he said?"

"Every. Single. Word." She looked ready to spit nails at him. "And that's what you thought of me, too, that you could discard me like used Kleenex when you were done."

"No. That's not true. I loved you."

"When your father called me trash, told you to have your

fun with me but not to get serious, or attached, what was your response?"

Shame licked at Jackson's insides, and he lowered his head.

"Nothing," she said, stepping toward him. "That was your response. But your silence spoke volumes. You didn't defend me, didn't fight for our relationship, and it told me all I needed to know. Everything the club said about you, about the almighty Powell family, was true. More importantly, your silence told me a future with you wasn't possible."

He replayed the breakup in his head. When he'd found her, she was so distant. So quiet. He'd tried to kiss her, but she pulled away from him. Gave him an ultimatum. "That's why you demanded I introduce you to my parents. Invite you over for Sunday supper. Why you wanted us to talk to them together and tell them about our plans."

It had felt like a test, only he hadn't realized what the consequences would be if he failed.

That her decision would be final.

"I thought we had time for that," he said. "No need to rush." Get his parents to warm up to the idea first.

If only he'd known the wrong choice meant the end of them.

"But it didn't feel like rushing when you slept with me?" She tilted her head, eyes narrowing. "Wasn't rushing when you snuck me into your house. Up a trellis and through a window, never bringing me in through the front door. To your bedroom, where you could sow your wild oats with me, again and again."

"It wasn't like that," he said. She made it sound dirty. Being with her, not just sleeping with her, but talking to her, holding her hand, listening to her laugh, loving her, had been the highlight of his life. To this day. "We were in a relationship."

"Were we? Your parents didn't seem to know it, and any time we were outside of school in front of grown-ups in town, you wouldn't touch me." Her eyes blazed with fire, but her voice was cold as ice. "You wanted to have your cake and eat it, too. Sleeping with me when it was convenient while appeasing your parents. For a rock-bottom price. All it cost was my dignity. You have the nerve to stand there and say you *loved* me. I think you're the one who's lying."

Chapter Eight

Between Bitterroot Falls and Cutthroat Creek, Montana
Friday, April 13, 6:32 p.m.

It was a mistake. It was a mistake. It was a mistake.

His words blasted through Christina's head over and over again. Touching Jackson was a mistake. Kissing him was a mistake.

Wanting him so desperately after all this time?

The biggest mistake.

But it cut her to the bone that he felt that way about her. Still.

And she'd thrown herself at him. Set herself up for the rejection. To him, she was worse than biker trash now. She was a murder suspect, wanted for shooting three men. One of whom had been his boss and friend.

When he looked at her, he probably saw someone who had spent six years lying and manipulating.

Even if it was all in the name of good.

What had she been thinking? To kiss him. To tell him she wanted him. To think about giving herself over to him, again, after so many years. Only for him to doubt her in every way possible.

Mortifying.

She didn't think. That was the problem. He got in the shower, and she saw him. No scars. No flab. Just masculine beauty. A sexier, grown-up version of her Jackson. She simply acted on autopilot around him.

Now, she was humiliated. Wounded in a way no one could see. Because she'd also gotten quite good at hiding her pain.

"Are you finished?" he asked, behind the wheel of the old pickup truck Imogene loaned him. Driving them goodness knew where. He glanced at her, his eyes cold, his lips curled in distaste.

She clenched her fingers around the pen in her hand and bit the inside of her cheek to keep from crying.

Stay frosty, stay alive.

"Almost." Looking at her notes, she went back to writing down everything she knew about the depots and anything else she could think of that might be useful to the task force. Including methods the cartel used to transport drugs across the border. Smuggling tactics constantly changed, but she knew they'd started shoving drugs inside the side rails and metal framing of livestock trailers. "Is your plan to turn me in to the authorities once I'm finished?"

"If it is, does it mean you won't give me the intel I need?"

She wanted to scream, *yes!* Just to mess with him.

Taking a deep breath, she swallowed her anger and ignored her bruised feelings. "I dedicated six years of my life to this mission. Kirk's last words to me were that he didn't mind dying as long as Operation Big Sky Guardian succeeded." A person's commitment couldn't be any stronger. "I'll tell you everything. Write it all down for you. But you have to promise me that you'll find a way to finish what we started without letting the mole sabotage it."

"You don't care if you go to jail?" he asked.

"Jail?" she scoffed. "Jackson, I didn't kill anyone. Forensics will verify what I said about the way Kehoe died in the tunnel. If for some reason I'm not cleared, there won't be a trial. The Reaper will make sure of it."

"You sound confident."

"Because I am."

"They'll be able to protect you in Salt Lake City. The FBI facility there is secure."

"The facility isn't the problem." There were always weak people who could be compromised. The cartel had a knack for finding and exploiting them. The Reaper would use them to get to her. "There's no stopping him. No place is safe."

Jackson glanced at her, his expression softening. "How did you end up in the abandoned tunnel?"

"Hector Ibarra came to my place in Bozeman. Ordered me to follow him without any explanation. He took me there."

"Write down your address, the route you drove, along with the make and model of Ibarra's car."

"Why?"

"There are a good number of CCTV cameras in Bozeman. Maybe there's footage of you following him to corroborate your story."

"I have cameras at my place, too. Assuming they didn't wipe the security feed, he'll be on it." She had everything backed up to two different clouds, but there was a lot of data stored on there. A safety net she wasn't ready to disclose. She wrote down the other pieces of information, even Hector's license plate number. "Where are we going?" They headed away from Missoula, due west, into the mountains. Not toward Utah either. She had seen signs for Bitterroot Falls, but he passed the exit for the town, and they were taking a road through the woods.

"Safe haven to spend the night, since we couldn't stay with Imogene."

The sun was setting, but she could make out a wooden perimeter fence down the road.

A man stepped out of the tree line, holding a rifle. He wore woodland camo from head to toe. Boonie hat. Neck gaiter that covered the lower half of his face.

Jackson slowed the truck to a stop.

Another man emerged from the woods on the driver's side, dressed the same as the first guy. As he approached them, Jackson lowered his window.

"You need to turn around," the guy said. "That's private property ahead and we don't tolerate trespassers."

"I'm US Marshal Jackson Powell, and I'm here to speak to Joe. Tell him it's not official business. I need a favor."

Eyeing them, the guy nodded. He backed up, pulling out a handheld radio, and keyed it. "Hey, we've got two visitors out front. One is a marshal. Jackson Powell. He's here with a woman. Says he needs a favor from Joe. Not official business."

A squawk sounded. "Hang tight," someone said on the other end.

Christina looked at Jackson. "They're pretty serious about security," she said.

"They patrol the perimeter of the entire camp. Survivalists."

Explained a lot. In her experience, survivalists and preppers tended to be insular and paranoid. "How is it they owe you a favor?"

"Long story. Let's just say they ran into some trouble last year, protecting one of their own, and I was in a position to help them. So I did."

"Why?"

"They made bad a choice for the right reasons." He gave a one-shouldered shrug. "It felt like the right thing."

Sounded like the Jackson she remembered. A goodhearted person who always tried to do the right thing. In school, he came across as a bad boy, but she'd seen through his facade.

The radio squawked again. "Let them in."

"Thank you," Jackson said, and the other man nodded.

They drove down the road and stopped in front of a big black gate. Once it opened, Jackson pulled into a camp and parked off to the side.

She climbed out of the rickety truck and looked around.

A dirt path ran straight through the camp and deeper into the woods. On either side were tents of various sizes, woodsheds and small cabins. A pavilion made of logs and stones with tables and benches was close to the front of the camp. All the structures were covered with camouflage netting. If anyone searched for this place by helicopter, it would be hard to spot from the sky.

"Jackson," a bald man called out.

As he drew closer, Christina guessed he was in his seventies. Tall and sinewy, the man had a weathered face and wary eyes that studied her.

"Hey, Joe." Jackson shook his hand. "I appreciate you letting us in. This is Christina."

Joe looked her over from head to toe.

Christina adjusted the ill-fitting clothes that hung off her slim frame. Jeans and a knit sweater. She was grateful they were clean and warm. Imogene even had a flannel jacket in the bag.

"What's the favor?" Joe asked.

"We need to spend the night. You should know that she's wanted and at this point, the authorities most likely think

I'm aiding and abetting her, but the truth is far more complicated."

Swallowing a groan, Christina shook her head slightly in disbelief. Jackson was too forthcoming and trusting. Her first instinct was to spin a story, weave some tale. Eliminate the possibility of someone calling the cops. Then again, it was Jackson, his honest nature and quick thinking, that had gotten her this far.

Maybe she'd been in the game too long and it had made her jaded.

The corner of Joe's mouth quirked up in a grin. "This wouldn't be the first time we've harbored someone wanted by the law."

"That was your son," Jackson said. "This is different. You should also know besides the authorities there's a cartel hitman after her. We lost him, but your guards on patrol should be aware and keep an eye out. If you're not comfortable with us staying, I understand."

"You helped us when you didn't have to. We owe you and we always pay our debts." Joe turned to someone and whistled. "Hey, set up a tent for these two."

"They can use the one in the northeast corner," the man said. "We got the cabin for the newlyweds finished and they cleared out of the tent."

Joe nodded. "Come on. I'll show you where you two can bunk."

"Thanks," Jackson said, grabbing the bag from the truck. "It's only for the night. We'll leave in the morning."

As they walked through the camp, lit firepits scattered throughout illuminated their surroundings. Christina noticed that it was mostly men, but women and children, too. Families. Hard to tell how many people with darkness falling fast, but she estimated more than fifty and fewer than a hundred. It was a robust, thriving community. They even had farm animals and a chicken coop.

Along the way, Joe grabbed a couple of sleeping bags and lanterns from one of the woodsheds. They passed some cabins that had been built with plenty of space between them.

"Here we are." Joe unzipped the front of a tent that was set back among the trees away from the others. He turned on the lanterns and hung them up on hooks. The tent was more of a small camping yurt, large enough to fit four people comfortably. "No one will bother you. We've got some outhouses on the south side." He indicated the direction. "If you're hungry, go to the first cabin closest to the pavilion. Rabbit stew is for dinner. Breakfast is at sunrise. And I'll be sure to let my guys know to stay alert."

She ran her palm over the fabric of the yurt. Sturdy and thick. Felt waterproof. Did a surprising job of blocking out the wind and cold.

"Appreciate it, Joe." Jackson shook his hand, and the guy left. He dropped the bag in the corner.

They each rolled out a sleeping bag.

Christina sat cross-legged on hers. "I've been thinking about the depots. If you can pull it off, the seizures of everything, the drugs, weapons and money, at all three sites, it will tighten the proverbial noose around the neck of Team US. It'll be hard for the cartel to recover stateside. But you'll have to do it simultaneously. Once one is hit, the others will be alerted. I think you have twenty-fours before they move everything. Forty-eight at the most," she said. "Do you have a plan?"

"I need to bring you in to the FBI regional office in Salt Lake City. I'll need to answer questions myself and explain the actions I've taken." Sitting opposite her, he sighed as though the weight of the world was on his shoulders. "But first, the depots. They're time-sensitive targets. Kirk died to make this happen. But I don't know who I can trust."

His doubt in her went unspoken this time, but it was clear on his face, making something in her chest pinch.

She leaned forward and put her palm on his knee. "You can trust me." Deep down, she knew saying it wasn't enough. She'd have to prove it to him. "I finished." Moving her hand from his leg, she took out the pages of notes and gave them to him.

He looked it over. "The locations are spread far apart. Different towns. Thousands of kilos of cocaine, smuggled across the Canadian border, and fentanyl from China, received through the mail. Millions in cash. Stockpiles of weapons. This adds up to a major operation. It'll take days to coordinate it. The agencies will fight over who's the lead and who will get the ultimate credit. *If* I can get them to listen to me."

"You can't go through the agencies. You have to cut out the bureaucratic red tape," she said, and he narrowed his eyes in suspicion. "Kirk didn't tell you *I* was the asset, did he?"

"Hell, no. If he had…" Jackson clenched his hand, released the fist. Clenched it again. "I would've had him pull you."

"Then that's the reason he didn't tell you it was me." Christina didn't dare think his opposition was because he still cared about her. She doubted he'd once loved her, but not his affection for her. "But why would you have been against it? Because I'm a woman?"

"Yes." He stared at her, his gaze unflinching. "And no. I'm not sexist. You were so young and not a trained agent." He shook his head. His jaw hardened. "Despite what you think, I did love you. I might've been a foolish teenager who didn't want to cause unnecessary waves with my parents, who were only looking out for me, but you're wrong to think I wouldn't have walked away from them and turned my back on their money in a heartbeat for you. I ended up doing that anyway. Can't even remember the last time I went back to Laramie."

She'd heard. Right after graduation, he'd joined the army. Four years later, he became a US marshal. "I notice you didn't refer to it as home."

"It's not." He looked like he wanted to say more but lowered his gaze. Cleared his throat. "You were never biker trash to me. Never disposable." He grimaced. "Everything I said to you back then, I meant. I'm sorry you doubted me." His tone turned angry.

Almost accusatory.

Was he blaming her? "Don't you mean you're sorry for not defending me? For not having the backbone to stand up to your parents?"

He blew out a harsh breath. "You keep doing this."

"Doing what?"

"Changing the subject. Our relationship, what happened between us as teenagers, is ancient history. There are more pressing issues at hand. I already know there's a traitor in the task force, but I need to know if I can trust you—and this intel."

Her cheeks burned, and she wished she didn't care about him. Or their past. "Fair enough. I didn't mean to get us sidetracked. But for the record, you brought up our *ancient history* this time. Not me." She packed away all the messy emotions centered around him and gathered her thoughts. "Do you think there's the slightest chance Kirk put his faith in someone else on the task force? Told them my identity?"

"No." Jackson shook his head. "After he realized we had

a leak, the only person on the task force he trusted at all was me."

"Well, he told someone else about me. In the tunnel, Kirk said he broke Alice's first commandment, which is, *trust no one*."

"Alice's commandment?"

"A list of rules to help me survive. We came up with ten. He called them Alice in the Underworld's commandments. The point is he trusted the wrong person. If it wasn't you and you're positive it wasn't someone else on the task force, then it can only mean one thing."

"He talked to someone outside the task force," Jackson said slowly, like he was thinking aloud. "There are two moles."

She nodded. "Knowing Kirk, I think he would've gone to someone higher up in the food chain."

"Someone he thought it would be safe to turn to. Someone with enough power to facilitate your extraction and authorize a new life for you."

Her chest tightened. "If he risked telling someone about me, it was to coordinate an extraction. It must've been for some other reason."

"An extraction of a high-value asset would've taken more than Kirk Kehoe or the power he had to keep you safe."

"After a while, whenever Kirk talked about getting me out, I stopped believing him." She didn't think he'd ever cared about her. But in the tunnel, he'd given her a chance to escape. It was the least he owed her. "There was never going to be a clean extraction for me, Jackson. By the time I realized that, I was already in too deep. The consequences set in stone."

"What do you mean?"

"Kirk wanted someone who couldn't be traced back to

any agency. The perfect inside person needed to be a civilian. With verifiable ties to the criminal world. The Iron Warriors had a reputation as an outlaw gang, which made my background appear shady by association. I fit, but that meant the real me. Not an alias. If I was extracted and disappeared, if the cartel found out I was a traitor, then my family would pay the price." A wave of grief washed over, and she lowered her head. "And they did. Dearly."

"The hit last night. That was the cartel getting revenge."

She nodded. "He killed them. The Reaper. The same man from earlier." All those lives snuffed out in one night. Because of her.

"Alvaro Aguilar murdered them. I'm so sorry." He reached over and caressed her cheek, drawing her gaze back to him.

Silence ballooned between them, growing heavy and dense.

Sorrow pressed in on her. "I've sacrificed everything for this," she said, her voice a fragile whisper. Tears welled in her eyes, but she refused to let them fall. "You *can* trust me. And the intel."

His mouth flattened in a grim line.

Still, he doubted her. What would it take for her to convince him?

"Why did Kirk choose you?" he asked. "Why not one of the Iron Warriors?"

She hesitated, and his eyes narrowed.

"I need complete honesty, Christina."

"Kirk wanted a woman."

Jackson tensed, his shoulders bunching. "Why?" A bewildered expression crossed his face. "How did he insert you in the cartel?"

"I don't think he came up with the idea until after he met me."

His hands clenched, his eyes glittering in the dim light from the lanterns. "What idea?"

Her stomach churned, heart thudding in her throat. There was no easy way to say it. Simply was best. "Kirk had me get close to someone in the cartel. One night, he sent me to a restaurant. Told me to sit at the bar and be myself. But he wanted me to order a steak and an absurdly priced bottle of wine." Château Pétrus. "In the hopes I would catch the eye of the right person. It worked. Kirk had studied the mark. Knew he had a type. And I was it." She took a breath. "The guy struck up a conversation at the bar. Asked me out. Next thing I knew, we were seeing each other."

"Who was the right person?" Jackson dragged his gaze away from her, looking down at his fists. "Who was the mark?"

She licked her lips, but her mouth had gone bone-dry. "I didn't know anything about him. Kirk told me that he was a fixer for the cartel. But he didn't explain exactly what that meant. Instead, he let my imagination fill in the blanks with things far less dangerous than the truth."

"Who?" Jackson ground out the word, his head lifting, and pinned her with a stare. "Hector Ibarra?"

"Hector?" She squirmed. The man was a cane toad. Highly toxic. Sickening to look at. She never would've let him touch her. "Not him."

She could practically hear it when the wheels inside Jackson's head slowed, the gears clicking into place.

Then understanding dawned on his face. Horror twisted his features. "No, no, no." He shook his head like he wanted to erase the answer from his mind. "*Alvaro Aguilar.* Is that why this is personal for him?"

Her throat closed in on itself.

She nodded.

Jackson surged to his feet. Paced around the tent. Raked his hands through his hair. "Do you know *what* he is?"

"I didn't at the time. Not for two years," she said, the words leaving her breathless. "But I do now." Better than most.

"Two years!" He stopped. Didn't move an inch. His gaze fastened to hers, as though her eyes were a window deep into her soul, and the look he gave her made her wither on the inside.

Growing up around the Iron Warriors, she'd thought she could tell a bad guy from a good one by looking at him. By the way he treated others. Sure, Alvaro had tattoos and was hardened, guarded. Plenty of good guys in the club were the same, even the one who was like a big brother to her.

In those first two years, Alvaro had showed her kindness. Respect for others. Didn't tolerate bullies. Wined and dined her. It was different. Exciting.

But not romantic. He took care of her, protected her. Treated her as though she were a precious toy. A prized possession.

Kirk Kehoe had watched it all happen. Encouraged the entanglement. Allowed her to get seduced by the devil.

"You were with that animal for two years?" Jackson asked, digging in, not letting it go.

"He traveled a lot for the cartel," she said. "I didn't see him every day." Sometimes she went weeks, even months without seeing him. Even though he saw her. She later learned he'd spent a lot of time surveilling her when he thought her guard would be down. "It wasn't a typical relationship."

Jackson made a sound of disgust in the back of his throat. "You know what I mean."

"There are two sides to Alvaro. He can slide between them like flicking a switch," she said. "He only showed me the one I wanted to see. It took time to get in." Much longer than she'd anticipated. "To earn his trust. But I did. Slowly. He started sharing things with me, introduced me to his aunt, stopped testing me in little ways. Eventually, I convinced him to let me work for the cartel, using my skills as a lawyer for them."

"Did the cartel tell you about Aguilar?" Strong muscles in his neck flexed and released. "That he was a murderer with no conscience."

"I quickly noticed the cartel feared him, but, no, that's not how I found out." The ruse of a relationship worked too well, and Kirk started to worry she was developing feelings for Alvaro. Then the Machiavellian FBI agent had decided it was time she learned the truth. "As soon as I told Kirk that I was going to start working for the cartel, he gave me Alvaro's file, filled with pictures of his handiwork. I discovered he fixed problems with a gun or a knife or a garrote or a bomb." Gruesome images sprang to mind, the myriad ways he had hurt and killed others, but she blocked them out. "So many people he murdered. Men. Women." She shuddered. "At that point, Kehoe also told something he'd withheld. That every woman Alvaro had 'dated' eventually ended up dead. I realized if I ever became a problem, he would kill me, too."

"How could you stay with him for so long?" His tone once again turning accusatory. "How could you not see what he was?"

Sighing, she shook her head, weary of the battle.

She'd asked herself the same questions, many times. But how dare Jackson?

"I signed up to stop the cartel. To put an end to their

drug trafficking and save lives." Christina stood up and faced him. "Your beloved mentor and cherished friend, Kirk Kehoe, threw me to Alvaro Aguilar like chum in the water to a shark. Knowing full well what he was—an apex predator. Kirk also knew there would be no turning back for me. No way out, Jackson! You and your task force wonder why I was in for six years. Because I couldn't leave. I was trapped. As Kirk's informant. What kind of man does that to a twenty-two-year-old girl? So, before you judge me, take a hard look at the choices of the one person who set all this in motion."

Chapter Nine

Cutthroat Creek, Montana
Friday, April 13, 8:13 p.m.

Rage engulfed Jackson, burning through him, hot and corrosive, like acid. He spun on his heel and stormed out of the tent.

Marching through the camp, he needed to put distance between himself and Christina. Wrap his head around the things she threw at him. One wicked curveball after another.

Kirk Kehoe wasn't a perfect man. Far from being a saint. Jackson had witnessed him do questionable things, operating in gray zones for years, justifying it for the sake of the mission.

The conversation they'd had two weeks ago came back to him.

"Would you sacrifice one life, ruin one person's future, if it meant putting an end to the Estrada cartel?" Kehoe asked.

"No," Jackson said. "If you're willing to do that to one person, you'd do it to others. The line would keep moving. Where does it end if you keep justifying the means?"

"You need to grow up and stop being so naïve. We don't live in a black-and-white world, and that fact forces us to operate in the gray. You need to accept that. Compromises

have to be made. Sometimes in ways that'll make you not sleep so well. I've had plenty of restless nights. We have to be willing to sacrifice, perhaps even play by their rules, in order to stop the cartel."

Jackson couldn't believe what he was hearing. "Is it really worth it if it means becoming dirty?"

"Those people who would call me dirty, because I've got the guts to stick my hands in the mud and do what's necessary, are the same ones who enjoy the freedoms I help safeguard. And you know what, it makes me really angry. It's time for you to get on board with the program, Jackson. Got it?"

"Some compromises shouldn't be made. So don't hold your breath waiting on me to see things the same way you do."

Kehoe had crossed the line. Recruited a civilian with half-truths. Used her as bait to hook a shark. Trapped her in the cartel. Forced her to live a lie with no safe way out. And endangered her family.

Kirk did that to Christina.

What recourse did she have? It wasn't as if she could've gone to someone in the FBI and reported Kehoe, explained her situation.

To think she was stuck and in danger, living only a three-hour drive away from him. Yet Jackson had been clueless, powerless to help her.

In Kehoe's desperation to fight monsters, had he become one?

Coming to a campfire, Jackson stopped and crouched low, warming his hands. The anger coursing through him ran bone deep. He was so furious with Kehoe for using Christina that if the man was still alive, Jackson would've killed him.

The worst part was that Jackson was furious with himself. For blaming Christina when none of it was her fault.

For hating Alvaro Aguilar.

Not because the hit man was a ruthless, cold-blooded murderer who had ambushed and attacked his team. He hated him because Aguilar had spent two years with his Chrissy, taking her on real dates, sleeping with her, holding her in his arms. Waking up to her face, seeing her smile, hearing her laugh, having her body pressed to his any time he wanted. Hated Aguilar for having the gorgeous, glorious woman she'd become when Jackson had only stolen moments with the girl she used to be.

Jackson had moved forward with his life, left home, joining the army and later the US marshals, but he'd had no luck in moving on from her. He never clicked with anyone else. Hadn't felt that same wild attraction. Never looked at another woman and thought, *I want to spend forever with her.*

Only Chrissy.

Picking up a rock, he tossed it, wanting to kick himself. He'd blamed her all those years ago for ending things with no real explanation. But even after she cut him off, he should've apologized for failing her test. Promised to make it right. Followed through and brought her to his house. In through the front door instead of up the trellis. Sat beside her at the table for Sunday supper the way she'd wanted. With her dignity intact.

All she'd wanted from him was what she deserved. What her self-respect demanded. Instead of giving it to her, he'd tucked tail and let her walk away.

Now, he was doubting her.

His pulse pounded, temples throbbing, and he cursed himself for it.

Separating his personal feelings from his professional obligation, if that was possible, Jackson did believe her about how she became an asset. He didn't want to think Kehoe would sink so low, but Jackson knew what the agent was capable of.

But how much of her story should she share once he brought her in to the FBI, which he'd have to do sooner or later?

The details would open her to scrutiny. It gave her a motive for murder. Theoretically, Kehoe could've coerced her to continue as an informant by threatening to expose her if she didn't. That's how it would be twisted.

They needed evidence that Hector Ibarra was at the crime scene. Forensics to confirm her version of how things played out. Proof the sheriff's deputy was a liar.

If everything she had written about the depots was accurate, seizing the contents would cripple the cartel. It would be a huge win. The biggest yet.

They needed a lot of things to fall into place. Or they were both going to go down as the bad guys.

First, he had to call his friends in Bitterroot Falls. See if they could help him raid those depots. See if they were willing to get embroiled in his mess.

Until he figured out who Kehoe had confided in, sharing Christina's identity as an asset, no one in any of the agencies supporting the task force could be trusted.

His friends were his only solid option on short notice.

Standing, Jackson checked his pockets. No cell phone. His phone was lost in the river, and he must've left Imogene's burner in the duffel.

And the bag was back in the tent. The last place he wanted to go right now.

He groaned. Tipping his head back, he stared up at the night sky. The moon was full and bright. Way out here, in the woods, he could see every star in the sky.

Cutthroat Creek
Friday, April 13, 8:29 p.m.

CHRISTINA COULDN'T TELL if Jackson was merely disgusted with her or jealous.

But jealousy would require him to care about her. Based on the way he'd kissed her in the shower, he was clearly still attracted to her.

An old temptation.

Gritting her teeth, she wasn't ridiculous enough to presume he had any feelings for her after all this time.

He doubted her. Questioned everything she told him.

Frustration simmered inside her. She fiddled with her smart ring, uneasy about the way she'd left things with Jackson.

How could she blame him? He had a traitor in his inner circle. She hadn't spoken to him in twelve years. Kehoe had hidden the truth about her as an asset from him. During the chaos at the airport, she had convinced him to break the protocol that was second nature to him and flee with a wanted fugitive.

Frankly, the best thing for him to do was trust no one. Not even her.

That's what she needed to do.

If only his doubt in her and criticism didn't hurt. His opinion of her mattered. Always had. She wanted to find a way to erase his suspicion.

When she told him about being with Alvaro, he'd seemed more than appalled. Enraged. Like he did still care about her on some level. But there was absolutely no reason for him to be angry with her for trusting Kirk Kehoe. The FBI agent was supposed to be the good guy. She'd had no idea who Alvaro really was when Kirk pushed her in his direction. If she had, she never would've been able to go through with it. Kirk must've known that, too.

The entire time she was with Alvaro, she'd been terrified of being discovered. It was never a real relationship, for either of them. There had been steel gates between them. Parts of herself that she kept secret. Parts that he kept hidden in the dark, locked away. Their liaison was devoid of true affection. Or intimacy.

When she met him, she'd expected to despise him immediately. Instead, he was bold and intense, with a disarming laugh. And that fearlessness had grabbed her by the throat and wanted to pull her right in. His ruthless edge kept her wary, but he wasn't mean. Not to her.

Not at first.

Then she joined the ranks of the cartel and learned just how cruel he could be. How depraved.

Not wanting to think about him, she shoved her hands through her hair, which was no longer straight thanks to the river. A riot of curls that were only manageable due to the surprising hair products she'd found in Zach's bathroom. They must have belonged to his girlfriend. She finger-combed her curls and plaited her hair into a single braid, wishing she had something to tie it off.

Christina got up and went to the duffel. She riffled through the bag, moving the gun out of her way, plucked a rubber band from a wad of cash and fastened it around the end of the braid.

Something glinted in the light from the lantern. The screen of the burner phone.

Her first instinct was to call Ripton Lockwood. For an instant, she wondered whether she should've done it instead of going to the City Drift Motel. Whether she should've asked him to smuggle her across the border, set her up with a new identity so she could start over. Which would essentially flush the last six years of her life down the toilet. All her efforts, all her sacrifices, would've been for nothing.

Shaking off the idea, Christina clutched the phone. She wasn't a criminal and shouldn't be running. The only way out of this was to take down the stateside unit of the Estrada cartel and clear her name—and Jackson's. But she needed to work with him to make it happen.

First, he needed to trust her, as difficult as it might be. They wouldn't succeed if they doubted each other at every turn.

She ran her thumb over the smart ring. Kirk had given it to her last year to keep tabs on her. He claimed it was in case the cartel tried to get rid of her, but she thought he was worried she might disappear. Not at the hands of the cartel. That she would reach her breaking point and simply vanish. The thought had crossed her mind more than once.

The ring was a next-gen prototype with a robust GPS tracker. Kirk had pulled strings and gotten it linked to a common smart ring app in case anyone checked her phone. It would look like any other. Only better. She took advantage of the ring's other features, for fitness, stress management and wellness.

Whether it was still functional after her plunge in the river she didn't know. It was supposed to be waterproof.

She powered on the cell. Thankfully it wasn't a rudimentary flip phone sans web browser or unbridled app store, but a smart device. Now she crossed her fingers for a signal out here in the boonies.

Bars popped up.

They weren't in the middle of nowhere after all, and she was in business. She found the app she needed, downloaded it, logged in. Then she waited to see if it synced with the ring.

The screen read, Searching, as wavy dots flashed.

If it worked, would it be enough to convince Jackson that she wanted the same thing as him? Running, leaving him to deal with the fallout of fleeing with her, wasn't an option. She was going to see this through to the end.

But this was a baby step.

He might need a giant leap, like proof that the depots were legit. Then what?

His plan was to haul her into the FBI facility in Salt Lake City, where she'd have to fend for herself. Where the Reaper would get her.

The app beeped. Pairing with the smart ring was complete.

She closed the app and stared at the phone icon on the screen. Maybe calling Ripton wasn't a bad idea. He was smart and had resources and was family. Her brother, though not by blood. He'd taught her how to protect herself, made her dad stop beating her and dug into the problem. Got her father counseling. Got him sober. Changed him and her life for the better.

Only for her to get her father killed.

And most of the Iron Warriors.

Could she deliberately endanger another person she cared about to save herself?

Cutthroat Creek
Friday, April 13, 8:38 p.m.

THE LONGER JACKSON stood staring at the sky, the more tired he became. He was running on fumes, but he had work to do.

He strode back through the camp. At the tent, he noticed she had zipped the front flap. He considered knocking. Not that there was a door. He pulled the zipper up and stepped inside.

Standing by one of the lanterns, Christina looked at him and stilled. Her face was a blank mask. The burner phone was in her hand.

He flicked a glance at the duffel bag next to her sleeping bag. It was open. Then he stared at her. And at the phone. "Who did you call?"

"No one," she said, her voice a fragile whisper.

The sinking sensation of doubt crept back in. He snatched the cell phone from her hand. "Who did you text?"

"No one. Just let me explain."

"You mean give you a chance to redirect me. You're really good at that." He tapped the phone icon. No calls. "Tell me who you contacted before I find out on my own."

"It doesn't matter what I say, you won't trust me. Will you?"

"You keep giving me reasons not to." It was two steps forward with her and then three steps backward.

"Alice's seventh commandment. There's a thin line between paranoia and vigilance. If you can't tell the difference, then you'll either alienate allies or end up dead in a ditch."

Ignoring her efforts to sidetrack him yet again, he checked the texts. No messages sent either. But both could've been deleted. A common tactic spies used.

"Put yourself in my position," he said. "I'm risking my career. I fled with you. I'm aiding and abetting here. Because your boyfriend, a relentless assassin, is hell-bent on getting you back and I don't want any more good officers to needlessly die by getting in his way."

"You make it sound so romantic." Rolling her eyes, she

huffed. "One thing I can say about Alvaro, at least he never treated me like I was a dirty secret. Not the way you did."

The words were a slap to his face and the blow stung. "When you were cozied up with Aguilar, did he love you?" Regardless of her accusations, Jackson had cherished her. Done his best to show her how special she was to him. Though he was guilty of only doing it when they had been in private. "Did your hit man boyfriend make you feel loved? Huh? Did he? I want to know."

In a flash, all emotion drained from Christina's face, replaced by a stony mask. "He, um." She swallowed, making an audible noise. "He doesn't know how to love."

"What separates us from beasts isn't our intelligence. It's our capacity to love. A man who can't, who only kills, isn't really a man. He's an animal. If that's what you want, he's welcome to have you. *After* I've figured out how to raid those depots and you help me get as close as possible to Rio Estrada. I need to finish this mission."

She took a step toward him and stopped. "When Rio Estrada offered me a position, it came with a condition," she said, and he braced for her to try and divert his thoughts. "If I worked for the cartel, I had to end things with Alvaro. Our relationship, the potential of an alliance, presented a potential threat. I was so relieved. I thought, what luck. I could achieve my goal, get the intel and be free of the devil in one fell swoop. But I was worried about angering him. Even though Rio promised I would be protected. Safe. That Alvaro wouldn't lay a finger on me. Still, I had to come up with some excuse since I still had to see him and deal with him. So I used Alice's eighth commandment. *Half-truths are the best lies.*"

Kehoe's words. What had Kirk done to her? Who did he force her to become in order to survive?

"I told Alvaro I chose the cartel and my career over him because he was never going to marry or have children. He wasn't interested in having those liabilities. Do you want to know what he did?"

Jackson stiffened, his spine contracting one vertebra at a time. *No.* He didn't want to know what pain that animal had caused her. But Jackson didn't want her to hold anything back either. "Tell me."

"Alvaro embraced me and whispered one word in my ear. *Cuidado.*" Careful. "Let me go and nodded like he was almost proud of me. Told me he'd assign a bodyguard to protect me. Smiled. And left my place."

Relief crept through Jackson that she hadn't been hurt. "He didn't yell or make a scene? He didn't hit you?"

She shook her head. "Nope. He's very controlled. Calculated. Doesn't let emotion get the best of him. But after he left, he got on a plane and flew straight to Wyoming. To Laramie, and killed my father. Recorded him dying, slowly, and when he got back, he made me watch the video."

Oh my God. "That's monstrous. I...had no idea."

"How could you know?" She folded her arms. "Instead of me putting myself in your position, put yourself in mine. I've risked my life and I'm *still* risking it, for your mission."

"Christina."

"Get out."

"What?"

"Get out of this tent." Her voice turned soft as cotton. An unearthly composure fell over her. "I don't care where you sleep tonight as long as it's not in here."

"I need to watch you. You're wanted and still in my custody."

"Bet we're both wanted by now."

Was that her goal? "I can't have you running off in the middle of the night."

"Not my problem. I would promise to stay put, but you wouldn't believe me if I did."

Jackson refused to be a fool and let her play him. He unzipped the side pocket on his pants, took out the handcuffs and slapped them on her wrists in the front instead of behind her back. "Consider this vigilance. If you try to run, I'm not going to make it easy." He turned to leave but hesitated.

This was a dangerous game they were both caught in. There was no telling what she'd had to do to survive or what she might still do. Honestly, after the things Kehoe had done, roping her into this and playing matchmaker to a heartless murderer, Jackson didn't blame her.

But he couldn't let his friends be collateral damage.

"Is this a setup?" Glancing over his shoulder, he looked at her. "The depots. If I bring in people I care about, people who are like family to me, to raid the depots, will they be walking into a trap?" Jackson wasn't even worried about himself or whether he was being framed to take the fall for the mole on the task force. He just wanted to stop the cartel without endangering anyone else he cared about. "Is it a setup?"

A thousand emotions flashed across her face, condensing to one that ripped a hole in his gut. "There was a time when I loved you more than anything." Tears gleamed in her eyes. "I would never hurt you. Or set you up. But it doesn't matter what I say. Or what I do." She shook her head. "You have to decide for yourself whether or not to believe me. To have faith in me. Now, get out. I'm tired and I'm done talking to you tonight."

He grabbed one of the lanterns, shoved through the flap of the tent and zipped it closed.

Cutthroat Creek
Friday, April 13, 8:45 p.m.

HOT TEARS ROLLED down Christina's cheeks. She was such a fool.

It was the same old Jackson, who was eventually going to let her down.

She had checked into the City Drift Motel, two blocks from the US marshals' building, to see him, instead of leaving the country like a guilty person. She'd warned him that the transport team would be in danger. She'd protected him on the boat, getting shot twice, but all he saw was that she wasn't severely injured or dead. Told him about the depots and he thought she was setting him up.

No matter what she did, he would never trust her.

Staring at the handcuffs on her wrists, she wanted to scream. But it would solve nothing. She should've called Ripton.

Not that he needed to be dragged into this. She'd done the right thing by not involving him. Better to protect him.

She grabbed the second sleeping bag, unzipped the tent and tossed it outside. Jackson was not going to stay in there beside her. Not caring where he went, she yanked the zipper down, blocking out the cold wind.

Christina switched off the lantern, slid into her sleeping bag and wiped her tears. She was so tired of fighting, of being afraid. Of balancing on a knife's edge between exposure and survival.

Exhaling a shaky breath, she just wanted to stop. Let the tears fall. Finally get some rest.

So, she did.

Chapter Ten

Cutthroat Creek
Friday, April 13, 8:47 p.m.

Following the path, Jackson went to the covered pavilion in the camp and sat near one of the firepits. No one else was around. He laid out Christina's notes on one of the tables, snapped pictures of the pages and sent them in a text message to Chance Reyes. He was a lawyer who ran the IPS office in Bitterroot Falls and was also from Laramie. Their two families were tight. They'd practically grown up together, though Chance was several years older.

After giving it a minute, Jackson called him.

Chance picked up on the second ring. "Who is this?"

"Jackson. Did you get the text I sent?"

"Yeah, but I don't open strange attachments from unknown numbers. You're all over the news. They're saying you fled the scene with a murder suspect and you're both wanted."

"I did." Jackson nodded, and even though his buddy couldn't see him, his shoulders sagged, the weight of his choices heavy on him.

"They're also saying she's a former lover of yours," Chance said.

Another nod his friend couldn't see. By the time he and Christina were in a relationship, Chance had been away at college. "It's true."

"I know. I spoke to Logan," Chance said, referring to Jackson's brother, who also lived in Bitterroot Falls. "He confirmed it. Mentioned a nasty breakup when you two were in high school. This all looks bad, what's being reported. There's even a special tip hotline for people to call if they have information regarding your whereabouts. If you don't mind my asking, why are you running?"

"Short answer is that there's a cartel hit man after her, which is really an understatement. He's the best of the best and it's personal for him." Jackson swallowed the bile rising in his throat. "That one man is responsible for the havoc at the Missoula airport and the officers down."

"Jeez. One guy did that?"

"Christina was an asset embedded in the Estrada cartel, working off the books for my task force. I didn't know. My boss, FBI Agent Kirk Kehoe, was her handler and hid her assignment from everyone to protect her. But her cover was blown. There's a mole in the task force working for the cartel. I don't know who it is. Kehoe didn't trust any of them. So, we figure, Christina and I, that Kehoe must've told someone else. Higher up in one of the agencies. Which means there might be two traitors to worry about. I know this looks bad. I do. There's an alleged eyewitness claiming he saw Christina shoot three men. One being Kehoe."

"Who's the witness?"

"A sheriff's deputy. Brent Phillips. We suspect he might be dirty, but we need evidence. Speaking of which, in the notes that I texted you, Christina wrote down her address and the route she took to the location where Kehoe was murdered. A cartel lieutenant by the name of Hector Ibarra led the way in his car. She wrote down the details. There has to be CCTV footage of them on the road. And she had security cameras at her house. But we don't know if the cartel wiped it. I also need confirmation from someone in IPS that Christina was indeed an asset for Kehoe."

Jackson believed that Kehoe had recruited her. No more doubts there, but he still had to prove it to several agencies that would have to be involved in the raid on the depots.

"Finally, something easy," Chance said. "Consider the last one done. As soon as this shootout at the airport in Missoula hit the news, Lockwood called me. Only he and Bobby Quill knew she was working for Agent Kehoe, but he notified someone in your office. An FBI agent named Mirabal. Lockwood thinks of Ortiz as a little sister and wants IPS to do whatever we can to help her. As the owner, he's throwing the full weight of *all* Ironside resources at this and that's considerable. The guy is talking about flying in. I've asked him to stand down for now. His wife is on bed rest with their second set of twins, ready to pop any day now. But I can't predict what Lockwood will do."

One thing in their favor, third-party corroboration. Lockwood would have a paper trail, and he was willing to commit IPS resources to this. "Do you know if anyone survived at the airport?"

"A lot of dead bodies. Three members of your security team were taken to the hospital. The names weren't released."

Jackson let out a relieved breath that there were survivors. "One of them might be Aiden Yazzie. Takoda needs to know." Jackson was certain Tak would want to go to the hospital and see him.

"Tak is either on the way to Missoula or already at the hospital. What else do you need from me?" Chance asked. "There has to be more we can do to help."

"Actually, there is. But it's asking a lot."

"Hit me with it."

"Most of what I sent you in the attachments is information about three depots holding significant cartel assets. We need to raid them and seize weapons, drugs, blood money before the cartel moves everything."

"How long do you think we have?"

"Twenty-four to thirty-six hours," Jackson said. If they were lucky, they might get more time, but he didn't want to count on it. "This is the part that gets tricky."

"Oh, I thought we already covered the tricky bits," Chance said. "It gets worse?"

"I'm afraid it does, and personal for you."

"That means you're either going to ask me to risk disbarment or involve Winter," Chance said, referring to his girlfriend, who lived with him.

Chance was right.

"I'd prefer to have some kind of official coverage on this," Jackson said. "To make the seizure legal." Worst-case scenario, they could torch the cash, dump the drugs so they would be unusable, and Chance could make the guns disappear. But Christina deserved credit if everything panned out as she described.

The line between vigilance and paranoia was blurry where she was concerned. He wanted to raid the depots and needed hard-core proof that his gut instinct about her wasn't wrong.

After learning someone on the task force, a friend, was likely a traitor, it made him question everything, including himself. And his instincts. He wasn't blind to the fact that when it came to Christina, he couldn't be objective.

"What exactly are you asking?"

"I can't go to the FBI, DEA or DHS. But there are two

DCI agents I trust with my life," Jackson said. He was talking about Winter Stratton and Declan Hart. They were both respected in the ranks of the Montana Department of Justice's Division of Criminal Investigation and could obtain quick search warrants from local judges they knew well.

"Listen, Christina is IPS—she's one of us," Chance said, "and I have the resources to help. But getting Winter and Declan involved is different."

Jackson sighed. That was his Hail Mary to wrap this thing up in a tidy bow. "I get it if you don't want Winter anywhere near this."

"Where are you?" Chance asked. "Why don't you two come to my place?"

"For now, we're safe. On the outskirts of town." They were a thirty-minute drive from Chance's ranch. "I didn't want to come until you knew everything. Fully understood what our presence means and knew how much you were willing to help."

"I'll gather the team and fill Winter in on everything," Chance said. "She'll decide if she's in or out, and I have to abide by her choice. But no matter what, we'll come up with a solution and I'll let you know. Is this a good number?"

"Yeah. It's a burner phone."

"You're welcome to come now, if you want," Chance offered.

"I don't want our presence to influence any decisions." They were both wanted. His friends should be afforded the opportunity to discuss it freely and decide without worrying about letting him down in person. This was a big ask that would put everyone in jeopardy.

"Fine, but I want you both here first thing in the morning."

"Okay." They were already settled for the night. No reason to rush off. "We'll stay put for now, but we'll be there in time for breakfast."

"I'll call you back as soon as we have a plan. Or more questions."

There would probably be lots of questions. Heck, he still had so many for Christina.

"Chance," Jackson said. "Thanks. I appreciate this. I mean, I know she's one of you, but thanks."

"No problem. You're one of us, too," Chance said. "Hey, I've got to ask. What are the odds that your ex-girlfriend is an undercover asset for a task force that you're assigned on?"

"Slim to none," Jackson said. "I think Kehoe recruited me for the task force because he knew about my prior relationship with Christina."

"Wow, that's calculated—and, I hate to speak ill of the dead, deceitful."

That was putting it mildly. "Yeah, it was."

"I've got to go. We'll talk soon." Chance hung up.

What were the odds?

Jackson recalled how aggressive Kehoe had been in recruiting him.

The seasoned FBI agent had requested Jackson by name and had him transferred from Colorado. The only person handpicked for the task force. Jackson only had three years under his belt as a US marshal, had never worked a high-profile case and didn't understand why Kehoe was so gung-ho to have him on the team.

But Jackson hadn't questioned it. The task force was a promotion. Once Jackson joined the team, Kehoe took him out for drinks one night, alone, and got him talking after the third round. Asked him if he'd ever been in love. Not knowing Kehoe had an agenda, Jackson had been honest.

"Once," Jackson said. "Madly in love with my high school sweetheart. When we were together, it was magic."

"What was her name?" Kehoe asked.

"Christina. She was incredible. No one else like her." No one came close. "I thought—" Jackson hesitated, taking a swig of his beer "—I thought I'd marry her."

"You probably saved yourself from a divorce. But this comes from a guy with four ex-wives. So, tell me, what happened between you two?" Kehoe nudged him with his arm. "What went wrong?"

An old wellspring of pain and regret opened inside Jackson. "I messed it up. She wanted my folks to know how serious our relationship was and I didn't. Not yet."

"Why not?"

"They didn't approve."

"If she was so incredible, what was there for them to disapprove of?"

"She was an Iron Warrior. Her family was an outlaw motorcycle gang. My parents had justified cause for concern. I figured, why throw our relationship in their faces when they still had the power to take away my phone and car keys and keep me away from her? I guess I thought once we were in college, we could do whatever we wanted. Get married and be together. Then my parents would have no choice but to accept it." To accept her. "They could gain a daughter-in-law or lose a son. But I miscalculated. Christina's perspective on everything was much different."

"If you ever saw her again," Kehoe said, staring at him, hard, "what would you do?"

"Anything." The word left Jackson's mouth without thinking. "To have another chance with her."

"Interesting. Anything, huh?" Kehoe sipped his whiskey. His jaw clenched. "Strong word."

Strong feeling. "The truth is, I never stopped loving her. And when you know, you know. So, yeah. Absolutely anything."

Never-ending entanglements and new conflicts collided in Jackson's head, knocking against his sense of duty and plain ole common sense. He'd fallen for Christina once, so hard it nearly broke him, and that had proved to be one time too many.

Jackson stared at the cell phone and wondered what she'd been doing with the burner when he walked into the tent. He couldn't push things and ask her again. Not after how he'd treated her. She didn't even want him to sleep in the tent. But she'd had the burner phone for a reason.

Christina Ortiz.

Twelve years of her as a ghost in his head, haunting his memories, plaguing his thoughts, making him regret every mistake that had cost him her love.

And now she was back in his life.

Not as a ghost, but an off-the books asset for Kehoe. A wanted woman.

Who'd kissed him. Claimed she wanted him, even if it had only been in the heat of the moment, or for some other reason that he'd rather not think about too hard.

He could talk himself into accepting anything she said, dismissing caution. Do *anything* in his power—just to have her back, even if what they shared now was a lie.

But this was so much bigger than him. So many lives on the line. The chance to do good and finally crush the Estrada cartel was at stake.

Oddly enough, Christina was right. Jackson had to decide.

Trust the woman he still loved. Or alienate her.

But which choice would get him killed?

Chapter Eleven

Cutthroat Creek
Friday, April 13, 9:50 p.m.

Cold air brushed Christina's face, rousing her. A sliver of moonlight slashed through the darkness inside the tent.

She rolled from her back onto her side, the chain of the cuffs on her wrists jingling. "Get out, Jackson," she muttered. "I don't want you in here."

The soft hiss of a zipper and then no more draft.

Good, he left without another fight.

A rough hand grabbed her shoulder, thrusting her onto her back. Terror pressed down on her as the muscular body of a man settled on top of her. His hand clamped over her mouth.

The Reaper.

Her insides turned to water.

He found me.

A white-hot blast of panic exploded in her brain. She tried to cry out, but his gloved hand was tight over her lips. Her screams muffled by his palm, she kicked at the air through the sleeping bag, trying to fight, but he was sitting on her abdomen, his knees pressed to her shoulders, his legs locking her arms to her sides.

Muscles, solid as steel, had her trapped. She sagged against the floor, flailing uselessly.

"Don't fight me, Christina," he whispered. "If you do, I'll make it hurt, and I'll still get what I came for in the end. You."

She swallowed hard and stopped moving. Her heart hammered against her sternum, air stuck in her throat, her lungs constricting.

Her eyes adjusted to the darkness. He was dressed in all black but wore a camo boonie hat and a gaiter over the lower half of his face like the patrol guards.

"You have a choice." His voice was low and full of menace. "You can get up and follow me into the woods. Leave here with me of your own free will. Or—" Pulling the scarf down below his chin, he leaned forward, bringing his face closer to hers, so she could see his eyes. The single word, *or*, hung in the space between them, like a guillotine over her throat. "I can carry you. I already killed four men to get in here, but I can kill many more on the way out."

That's what he did, strode through the world and death followed, churning in his wake.

"As I scoped out the camp," he said, "I noticed toys. There are kids here. It would be a shame if they got hurt because you made the wrong choice. You've been doing that a lot lately. Making poor choices. Like running from me. And protecting the US marshal on the boat. Jackson Powell." He stared at her, his gun with an attached sound suppressor resting on his thigh. "I'm going to remove my hand from your mouth. Are you going to scream?"

She shook her head.

Slowly, he lifted his palm. "What's it going to be?" he asked, as though she really had a choice.

He already knew how she'd respond after he'd threatened to kill innocent people. To hurt children.

Giving her the illusion of a choice was just part of the game to him.

Squeezing her eyes shut for a second, Christina knew how this would look to Jackson. What he would think of her. But she couldn't let anyone else be killed because of her. Especially not Jackson. Too many lives had already been lost.

She opened her eyes and stared at him. Alvaro Aguilar. "I'll go with you."

A smile curled his lips, but it was cold, radiating smug satisfaction. He bent over, bringing his mouth a hairbreadth from hers. Shuddering, she turned her head away from him and stared at the duffel bag that was beside her.

The black go-bag was open, and the gun was inside.

Was the safety on? Was a bullet already chambered?

"Good girl," Alvaro said in her ear, his breath fanning her cheek. He got off her in a fluid motion, took a knee beside her and yanked back the sleeping bag. His gaze fell to the handcuffs on her wrists. "Someone doesn't trust you."

"He thinks everything I say is a lie."

Alvaro cocked his head to the side. "So, he knows you well."

Her throat tightened, pulse pounding loudly in her ears. Jackson's team was aware they had been in a relationship as teenagers. Everything the mole knew, Alvaro knew.

"He's paranoid," she said. "Thinks I'm a double agent."

Alvaro studied her face for a gut-wrenching moment, and her stomach curdled. With his free hand, he reached into his pocket, retrieving something. He dangled a small key in front of her face, his intense gaze boring into hers.

Always prepared.

He unlocked the handcuffs, removing them, and tossed them to the side.

But why release her? If he had handcuff keys, then he'd probably also brought cuffs. Was he testing her?

"Get up," he ordered.

She had one chance to grab the gun. If she managed to get it, maybe she could take out the biggest threat to her and Jackson. But if she failed and didn't make it, Alvaro would hurt her for trying. The punishment might be worse than pain.

On the other hand, simply leaving with him would be the same as signing her own death certificate.

"Let's go," he said.

At the last second, she decided.

Rolling onto her hands and knees, she surged forward for the bag. She gripped the sturdy canvas. The cold steel of the gun was almost within reach, right there, near the top.

A brutal hand snatched the back of her collar and hurled her to the side. The contents of the bag spilled across the floor of the tent. He shoved her onto her belly, down to the ground, her cheek pressing into the musty sleeping bag. In a swift motion, he seized one of her wrists, jerking her arm behind her. He twisted, forcing her arm upward toward her neck, in a hammerlock, and she winced.

He applied pressure, his grip was tight as a vise, his fingers squeezing hard. She ground her teeth together against the sharp pain radiating from her shoulder joint down her arm.

"I would've been disappointed if you didn't at least try," he said, his tone light, sounding almost amused. "I always liked that about you. Your fire. Your spirit. Your drive." Leaning on her, he intensified the pressure on her arm, the joint in her shoulder pinching. "But now you've got to say it."

Christina clamped her mouth shut, not wanting to give him the satisfaction of groveling.

His weight bore down, crushing the air from her lungs. Alvaro wrenched her arm until she cried out. Tears leaked from her eyes.

"Say it," he growled in her ear. "Or I'll snap your arm like a twig and rip it from the socket."

Alvaro twisted harder, his grip on her tightening so hard it left her breathless, the pain excruciating. He was going to do it.

"Please," she said. "Please."

Keeping her locked in agony, Alvaro hunched over and licked her tears, making her squirm. Then he put his cheek to hers. "As much as I like to hear you beg, that's not what I'm looking for." His lips grazed her mouth. "Try again."

"I'm sorry. Please." She wasn't exactly sure what he wanted to hear, but hoped the combination would suffice. "I'm sorry."

Gradually, he eased off, reducing the pressure on her arm, but he kept his cheek smushed to her face. "Why do you make me hurt you?"

She closed her eyes. Didn't dare move. Barely took a breath.

"This time you're going to get up slowly and you're going to behave. If you don't, the first person I'll kill on my way out is your ex. The US marshal."

Getting off her, he stood and watched her climb to her feet. His gun was down at his side rather than pointed at her.

For a reckless heartbeat she considered tackling him, throwing an elbow to his head and a knee to his groin, but then thought better of it. He was armed and she was outmatched. She'd trained for a moment such as this—had the best teacher, too, former Special Forces. While she had gotten into her fair share of scrapes, she'd never fought a man like Alvaro, highly skilled, who was twice her size and three times as strong. If she had to go mano a mano with him, there would be no contest. He'd overpower her, even unarmed and blindfolded, with one hand tied behind his back.

Trembling, she lowered her gaze, not wanting the hatred in her eyes to make things worse.

"If only you'd been loyal, it wouldn't have to be this way." Alvaro propped his gloved knuckle under her chin and forced her to look at him. "So many Iron Warriors cut down in the prime of their lives," he said, and heartache punched through her chest. "But you still have a chance."

She swallowed around the lump of grief in her throat. "A chance for what?"

"A quick death."

A lie. It had to be. He could've already put a bullet in her head if he wanted it to be quick.

"I don't understand," she said.

"Not yet, you don't." He stroked her cheek with his knuckles, and she cringed. "But you will." His tone was soft, reassuring, but she wasn't fooled by it. "We're going to leave. Once we're out of the tent, I want you to head south. Don't run." He stared at her. "Are you going to behave?"

She nodded.

He studied her face. "I guess we'll see."

This was all a game for him. One he was certain he'd win.

She unzipped the tent and stepped outside. Jackson's sleeping bag was still on the ground.

Slipping out behind her, Alvaro said, "Walk. Due south."

Turning to her left, she stared at the dark pathway as

though it were a portal to hell. She stepped away from the tent and headed south, her legs shaky and weak.

The hiss of the zipper filled the air as it lowered behind her. Christina did as he instructed, going into the darkness, weaving steadily between the trees at a moderate pace. She remembered Alice's ninth commandment.

It was the only rule Kirk had given her that she hadn't understood. Not until this very moment.

If you find yourself in hell, the key is to keep going.

For some reason she couldn't fathom, much less explain, a momentary calmness slipped over her. She would get through this. No other choice. She just had to keep going.

Then that fragile, scraped-together bubble of calmness popped when she heard Jackson's voice.

"Christina," Jackson called softly.

She whirled in his direction. Through the trees she saw him standing in front of the tent, holding a bowl. She glanced around but didn't see Alvaro.

Nonetheless, the Reaper was there. Close by. Watching her. Perhaps taking aim at Jackson.

"I brought you some stew," Jackson said. "It's hot and tasty. Figured you need to eat. We both need to keep up our strength. But not to fight each other. How about a truce?"

Just when she thought he'd lost his golden-boy charm, he proved her wrong.

Clenching her hands, she stood rooted to the spot, even though she had to leave. She wanted to give Jackson a sign. To let him know she was there. But she couldn't risk it.

Leaves crunched as Alvaro swooped up behind her, his hand covering her mouth and nose with a cloth in his palm. His arm wrapped around her, pinning her against him.

She smelled something sickeningly sweet and cloying. Gagging on the scent, she didn't fight him. If she drew attention to their position, Jackson would charge toward them and Alvaro would kill him.

"I'm sorry. For the way I spoke to you." Jackson rolled his shoulders and stretched his neck. "I know you don't want to talk to me, and I don't blame you, but can I come in? I'll do all the talking. You just have to listen."

Her head lolled back onto Alvaro's chest. Fear coiled through her, threading in every fiber of her body. The world spun, branches and stars and sky blending. She tried to focus on the sound of Jackson's voice in the distance, but it was fading. Her vision blurred as her legs buckled.

Alvaro swept her up into his arms and looked down on her face.

The devil smiled.

Darkness clawed at the edges of her vision, dragging her under, and Christina felt it in her bones—she was doomed.

Bitterroot Falls
Friday, April 13, 11:15 p.m.

JACKSON PACED BACK and forth in Chance's kitchen. Pinching the bridge of his nose with his thumb and forefinger, he tried and failed to control the panic pulsing through him.

Chance had already called in the IPS team for a huddle and assembled them when Jackson arrived. He looked around at all the people who had gathered to help—Bo Lennox, Eli Easton and Autumn Stratton, Winter's older sister. Both DCI agents sat at the counter as well.

"Are you sure that she didn't take off and kill the four patrol men on her way out of the camp?" Winter asked.

Sandbags of guilt settled on Jackson's shoulders for going to the camp in the first place. Thinking that it would be safe for one night. Exposing Joe's people to such danger.

Four men dead and they'd only been there for a matter of hours.

There's no stopping him. No place is safe. Christina had warned Jackson, and he'd lowered his guard for a few minutes, and now she was gone.

"She *is* wanted for murder," Declan said, "of three other people."

Jackson stopped pacing and pressed his palms to the cool marble countertop. "Christina isn't a murderer, okay? She's many things." A liar. A master manipulator. A survivor. "But a murderer isn't one of them."

"You're sure?" Bo asked with a raised eyebrow. "You two have history. Maybe it's clouding your judgment."

"If it had been any other suspect in your custody," Chance chimed in, "would you have broken protocol and fled the scene with that person?"

Jackson had asked himself the same things. Questioned and doubted Christina every step of the way. His decision to cautiously trust her wasn't made lightly.

Eli sat in front of an open laptop, clacking away on the keyboard. "I tried to access the CCTV footage at the scene so we could see what happened at the airport for ourselves, but all the cameras went down right before the incident."

Aguilar must have disabled them. To add confusion for the authorities. Mirabal, Nichols and the higher-ups in the agencies wouldn't have a clear picture of how things unfolded. For all they knew, Jackson could've turned traitor and helped attack his own team. They would be left to fill in essential blanks on their own, and he had yet to give them his version of the situation.

"You absconded with a former lover," Winter said. "That's what happened. Now you're wanted, too, and want to make us complicit. I agreed to help raid the depots and

I have a judge who is willing to get out of bed and sign a warrant. But now Ortiz has disappeared. And Jackson, your story leaves me with a lot of troubling questions that you haven't answered. I need to understand it."

"Honey." Chance put a hand on Winter's arm, and she pursed her lips. "You and Declan are free to walk away from this. We can handle it without you both if it's too messy. But I think I speak for every IPS member when I say that we don't abandon our own. We're in. Whether Jackson's story adds up or not. Lockwood confirmed Christina Ortiz was an FBI asset. He wants us to find her and keep her safe. It doesn't matter if she ran off or was taken. That's our mission."

"I'm just supposed to sit back and let my sister and you," Winter said, pressing a palm to Chance's cheek, "get involved. Incriminating yourselves. While I pretend this conversation never happened?"

"That's the deal, honey. You make your choices, and I make my mine, and at the end of the day, we respect it."

"We're getting off track." Autumn refilled her mug with coffee. "Jackson, you said you caught Christina on the burner phone at the camp. Was that about an hour or so before you discovered she was gone? Maybe she didn't kill anyone. Maybe she contacted this hit man. If she did, we need to know. What's his name again?"

"Alvaro Aguilar," Bo said, looking down at notes he'd taken.

The group scrutinized every word out of Jackson's mouth. Not that he could blame them. He was asking them to risk a lot, professionally and personally, to help him. Still, being grilled by six of them amounted to a tough interrogation.

"Look, I'm not a hundred percent certain that she didn't leave the camp on her own. All right?" Jackson's voice was louder and sharper than he intended. "I'm sorry. I know everyone is only trying to help." He sucked in a deep breath. "I caught Christina holding the phone. Not using it, per se. There were no calls made or texts sent from what I could see. That doesn't mean she didn't delete anything."

"There's nothing I'd like more than to get to the bottom of this," Eli said. "But we can't mistake suspicion for certainty." Eli held out his hand. "Give me the phone. I'll comb through the metadata and we'll see."

Jackson pulled the burner from his back pocket and passed it to him.

Eli connected the cell phone to the laptop with a USB cable. "One more thing. You wanted us to check to see if there was any CCTV footage of Ortiz leaving her apartment and following Hector Ibarra. There was. Footage of them together in the parking lot of her building, as well as on the road, headed in the direction of the old railroad tunnel where Kehoe was murdered. But eventually they turned off into an area that doesn't have any cameras. I can't prove he was at the scene."

Frustration bubbled higher, along with Jackson's anger and fear.

"Take a seat, Jackson," Autumn said.

"No. I don't want to sit. I need to do something." Anything. Even if it was limited to standing and pacing. Sitting felt like surrender. "That's why I came straight here as soon as I realized she was missing."

"Please. Indulge me." Autumn motioned to one of the stools near her.

Jackson took a seat at the massive kitchen island and tried to keep an open mind, considering Autumn wasn't just an investigator with IPS. She was a forensic psychologist and former FBI profiler who had been instrumental in solving several cases. Biting back any more complaints, he did as she asked.

"You told us your motorcade was attacked as you were en route to the airport to have Ortiz transferred," Autumn said. "I want you to take us back to that moment, right before you left the scene with her. Tell us what happened."

"Why?" Jackson huffed. "What's the point?"

"We need a clear picture. Please."

"Everything fell apart so quickly. A truck came out of nowhere and hit the SUV in front of mine. Aguilar, a high-level hit man for the cartel, jumped out of the truck. He killed all the police escorts so fast. Then Flores was hit. Aguilar sprayed a civilian vehicle with de-icing fluid and lit it on fire. Tillman went to help the driver and was hit. I released Christina from her cuffs so that she could take cover. As I returned fire, I realized that Aguilar was using armor-piercing rounds. Christina was screaming that we needed to leave. That Aguilar wasn't going to stop until everyone was dead so that he could take her, because it was personal for him. She told me she still had vital intel to give me."

"And you believed her?" Autumn said.

"Yes."

Autumn's grip on his shoulder tightened just a fraction. "Why?"

"She warned us at the US marshals' building that there might be trouble. Told me that death was coming for her. We should've listened."

"After she mentioned the intel," Autumn said, "you decided to leave."

"Yes. No. Walken emerged from the other SUV and began shooting. I didn't want anyone else to die. We were losing. We were being slaughtered."

"Okay. So, you left with Ortiz," Autumn said. "But why

didn't you go back to the US marshals' building? Or a police station?"

Jackson opened his eyes. "I underestimated him. His reach. His determination. His capacity for murder and mayhem. He was ten steps ahead of us. And he has at least one mole inside the task force helping him. We think he might have another one even higher up. If we went to the US marshals' building or a police station, he would've expected it. Been prepared for it. The man is a cold-blooded killing machine." Jackson raked his hands through his hair. "I had to do what he would've least expected. So, I took Christina to the river to get on a boat. And I thought we'd lost him, too, once we made it to the camp. Until I realized Christina was gone."

The team was quiet, their faces grave. It was better than them rushing to pick apart and question everything.

"You told us that you and Christina argued at the camp," Autumn said.

Jackson nodded. "Yeah, about the way Kehoe recruited her. The compromises and sacrifices she had to make. I didn't like it." The idea that she had been in a relationship with Aguilar still burned him to the core. "And I needed to be sure I could trust her. That I was looking at this whole thing from every angle." He understood Winter's concerns.

Autumn nodded, her expression compassionate and patient. "Then why do you think she was taken from the camp if the handcuffs were on the ground? If Aguilar took her by force, wouldn't he have left them on her?"

Jackson had believed Christina when she told him that she would never hurt him or set him up. But voicing that conviction based on sentimentality wouldn't pass muster with this group.

"The go-bag that Imogene gave me was still in the tent.

Along with the gun and the cash. If she was going to run, she would've needed to take both. Also, the contents of the bag were strewn across the floor, like there was a scuffle. I think Aguilar deliberately left the cuffs to make me believe she just took off."

Jackson propped his elbows on the counter and dropped his head into his hands. "I was supposed to protect her. Help her finish what Kehoe started. What she and I both signed up to do. Bring down the cartel. Now, that animal Aguilar has her and I don't know how long he'll torture her, asking her questions, making her pay for her betrayal, before he kills her. What I do know is that Christina saved my life on the boat when she didn't have to. She made tough sacrifices and didn't lose her way in the darkness. She's in danger. I know it. I've got to find her before it's too late."

If only he had believed in her sooner.

Chapter Twelve

Deer Valley, Montana
Friday, April 13, 11:51 p.m.

Her head throbbed as the drowsy haze dissipated. Dryness coated her throat like she'd swallowed sawdust.

Christina opened her eyes. Stared at a dark hardwood ceiling. Her palm glided over plush fabric. Soft amber light from a lamp illuminated the room. She was on a bed.

Sitting up, she put her feet on the floor. A familiar room whirled, slowly settling in place. Alvaro came into sight.

He sat in a leather midcentury lounge chair, his ankle resting on his thigh, his hands folded in his lap. A glass of wine and a bottle of Château Pétrus were on a small table beside him.

Taking in the spacious bedroom she hadn't been in for four years, she reoriented herself. Noted the open door to the hallway, windows and French doors to a balcony. If memory served her correctly, there was a rocky drop. The mountainside house had floor-to-ceiling glass spanning the rear of the home with sweeping views of the valley below. The back side, where Alvaro's bedroom was located on the second floor, was cantilevered over the steep slope. In the daylight, it offered immersion into the surrounding treetops and a holistic connection to the valley with direct views of the shoreline below. It also meant the only way out of the room was through the door that led to the rest of the house.

Alvaro had several pieds-à-terre all over, but he'd chosen to bring her here, to his house. It was the most secure. But it was also where they'd spent many nights together if they weren't at her place.

Her gaze fell on a water bottle on the nightstand. Picking it up, she wondered how effective the lamp would be as a weapon. She opened the bottle and chugged some water. If he wanted to drug her again, she couldn't stop him. She estimated the odds were in her favor that the water was safe.

"Tell me something," Alvaro said. "Whose clothes are you wearing?"

A laugh bubbled up in her throat, and she choked on the water. "That's what you want to know?"

He was unarmed. At least, she didn't see his gun. Was it to lure her into a false sense of security?

"Among other things," he said, "but let's start there."

"They belong to someone who was kind enough to loan them to me after I made it out of the river."

"Don't you mean after you and Jackson Powell made it out of the river?" he asked, staring at her, gauging her response.

She put the water bottle up to her lips and sipped slowly.

"I set out fresh clothes for you." He gestured behind her.

Glancing over her shoulder, she looked at the light blue sweater and jeans that were neatly folded on the other side of the bed. The tags were still on. "You bought me clothes?"

"I figured if you survived the river you'd need them."

It would've been easy to see the action as thoughtful, but she recognized it for what it was. Strategic. He'd probably bought the clothes before he tried to get her out of police custody.

"I'm eager to know if I remembered your size," he said. "Try them on."

She glanced at the tags. "The size is right. You have an excellent memory."

He poured more wine in his glass, drawing her gaze to the tattoos across his fingers and the ink scrolled on the back of his head that was only visible when his dark hair was shorn close, like it was now, accentuating his attractive Latin features. "You'll be more comfortable if you get out of those rags. Change."

Squirming on the inside, she didn't so much as blink. "I'm fine. Really."

"It wasn't a suggestion."

She felt like she was swimming for her life in shark-infested waters. Waiting to be attacked and ripped to shreds.

"Okay." She picked up the clothes, plucked the tags off and started toward the attached bathroom. Each step she took, she expected him to stop her and force her to change inside the bedroom. In front of him. But he didn't.

For some reason, he allowed her the small courtesy of going to the en suite. Any dignity she was afforded was given by his grace. It was all about power.

She grabbed the knob to shut the door.

"Leave it open," he called out.

Staring at him, she removed her hand from the doorknob.

A chime resounded through the house, a sensor letting him know someone was coming down his driveway. The house was tricked out with security features.

Alvaro pulled out his cell phone and checked the screen. "Hector is here. He's dying to see you."

"Great. He's not my biggest fan since our last encounter."

"Never has been. The only thing that ever stood between you and Hector was me."

That statement couldn't be more accurate.

Was she supposed to thank him? Part of her felt as though she should. But how did one thank the devil for his protection and all the strings that came attached?

Alvaro glanced at the screen. "He's parking. Should be up in a couple of minutes." He set his phone down. "Unless you want him to watch you undress, I suggest you get to it."

Her anger spiked. Anger hid the fear, so she clung to it.

The front door opened with a beep. "Where are you?" Hector yelled.

"Upstairs," Alvaro said. "My bedroom."

The door slammed shut. "You better not be having fun with her." Hector's tone was furious as he cursed her, calling her foul names. "This is serious business."

"Serious business can be fun." Alvaro sipped his wine, not taking his eyes off her. "All a matter of perspective. It's important to enjoy one's work." He tapped his watch, indicating time was running out for her before the toad was in the room.

Footfalls started up the steps.

Quickly, she ducked out of sight, going deeper into the bathroom, removed her shoes and stripped off the ill-fitting clothes. Gathering her thoughts and trying to formulate a plan, she shoved her legs into the jeans, the luxurious denim hugging her thighs, and fastened them. Threw the cashmere sweater on. Then she pulled her boots back on without bothering to tie the laces and looked around for a weapon. She opened the linen closet. Bypassing the towels and sheets, she grabbed the small storage bin where he kept extra razors. It was empty.

There was nothing in the closet that she could use and if

she tried to rummage through the cabinets under the sink, Alvaro would see her.

Hot bile burned the back of her throat.

"I suggest you hurry up," Alvaro called out.

She shut the closet gently and hurried back into the bedroom.

Hector reached the top landing. His gaze met hers, and he glared at her.

Christina widened her stance and curled her fingers into fists. She couldn't take on Alvaro. Hector was a different matter. She was going to give it to him as good as he gave it to her.

Hector limped down the hall and into the room.

"Don't touch her," Alvaro said, his voice calm, borderline indifferent.

"How's the leg?" she asked Hector. "Sorry I hobbled you. I was aiming for a femoral artery and was hoping you would do the world a favor and just bleed out."

Alvaro chuckled, the sound of that disarming laugh reminding her of their early days.

"Did you check her for weapons?" Hector asked Alvaro as he eyed her with caution. "She's always armed."

A hard lesson Hector had learned one night, years ago, when he'd cornered her outside at a party and she'd dared to pull a microcompact gun from a thigh holster under her dress and pushed the muzzle against his groin. She'd drawn a gun on Hector Ibarra—an Estrada lieutenant. An offense that would've gotten her killed if not for someone far worse intervening.

No one crossed the Reaper. Not even lieutenants.

Christina wished she had her Springfield Hellcat, fully loaded, on her now. But she would've settled for her solid steel baton.

"I'm pretty sure she's clean," Alvaro said, staying seated.

He didn't sound certain, which meant he hadn't searched her for weapons when she was knocked out cold.

"Pretty sure?" Hector muttered. "What does that mean?"

"I don't need a weapon to handle you," she said. Her fists and feet would do just fine.

Shuffling toward her, Hector called her another dirty name. "You cracked a tooth and I'm going to have this limp for the rest of my life." Anger engraved every line in his craggy face. "You're going to pay for that."

She flicked a glance at Alvaro. His hand clenched and his eyes narrowed as Hector closed in on her.

Reevaluating the situation, she braced for the incoming blow that she could've easily dodged.

Hector struck her across the face. The force sent her stumbling backward, but she let momentum take her down to the floor. The coppery taste of blood filled her mouth.

In a blink, Alvaro was on his feet and in motion, crossing the room. Lean and powerfully built, he moved with the smooth, lithe grace of a predator as he grabbed Hector by the throat, shoving him away from her. Then Alvaro seized Hector's right hand, the one the lieutenant had used to hit her.

The sound of bones snapping echoed in the room.

Hector howled in pain. "You broke my hand!"

"A bit of an overstatement," Alvaro said. "Only a few fingers. I did warn you. Don't touch what belongs to me. Only I get to damage or break my property." He pushed Hector out of the bedroom. "Go wait downstairs." He slammed the door and turned to her. "See. Serious business can be fun."

"You knew he would do that," she said, standing up. "Hit me even after you told him not to."

A grin pulled at the corner of his mouth. "And you knew that if you didn't strike first, I would take care of him."

"I didn't know." But she'd suspected. Hoped. "Why the game? Why did you want to hurt Hector?"

"Do I need a reason?"

"No, but you have one."

The half grin spread into a smirk. "You and Hector have always had such a contentious relationship. He rubbed me the wrong way one too many times when it came to you. Consider it my last gift to you," he said. "Sit." He gestured to the king-size bed in an easy-breezy manner, but it was a command.

As she sat on the bed near the nightstand, he picked up the chair and brought it over near the bed. His cool composure and calm demeanor that returned were disquieting.

Alvaro set the chair across from her and dropped into the seat, sitting so close their knees touched. Resting his forearms on his thighs, he stared at her. "My compassion for you is inconvenient."

"Said the spider to the fly caught in his web."

"You're not giving either of us enough credit. I'm far more severe and brutal than any spider, and you were never a harmless fly, were you." Alvaro reached for her face, and she recoiled. Rising from the chair with lightning speed, he grabbed her braid, wrapped it in his fist and tugged her head back until she was staring at the ceiling. With his thumb, he wiped the corner of her mouth. Looked at the blood on his finger and licked it off. Then he let her go and sat back down. "But you were the one weaving the web. Like any good spy. So good I never suspected. Too good."

Her nerves tightened. She clutched the edge of the bed. "How did you find me at the camp?"

"There's honor that must be respected. A code that shouldn't be broken. And if someone makes the mistake of betraying that, there's nowhere to run. Nowhere to hide." Alvaro covered her hand with his, and she tensed.

"Why do you cringe when I touch you?" he asked. "I've never hit you. Never laid a finger on you in anger. Not until today."

"Just because you never hit me, you think you've never hurt me? You murdered my father because I chose the cartel over you. Then you made me watch the video of you doing it."

"Actually, you chose Kirk Kehoe and to serve the FBI over the cartel. And over me. But you think I killed your father to hurt you?" he asked, his dark brows shooting together. "The man who beat you as a child. Who once put you in the hospital as a teenager."

"I don't understand. If it wasn't payback for me leaving you, then why did you do it?"

"I was impressed with you for choosing the cartel instead of our relationship. It was a gutsy move. I wanted to show you how deep my feelings ran for you. I killed your father as a gesture of my affection," he said, and her gut clenched.

Rather than sending flowers or buying her jewelry, he committed murder.

Sick and twisted.

"I never wanted that. My father made mistakes when I was younger. But he needed help back then. He was grieving and had mental health issues. After he went to therapy, started taking medication and got sober, he became his old self again."

Alvaro shrugged. "Well, now I know why you didn't show the gratitude I had expected."

Christina let out a sigh of disgust. "You've never felt affection for me. Or compassion. Only possession of me. That's why you hurt Hector. For touching what you think belongs to you. And that's why you gave my bodyguard orders that I wasn't to be with another man."

"Affection. Compassion. *Possession.* They're not mutually exclusive." Leaning closer, he wet his lips and rubbed his chiseled jaw. "There's something I haven't been able to figure out. When we were together, I watched you for two years. Shadowing you, monitoring your every move and all your communications. How did you meet your handler without me knowing?"

"Kirk wanted to meet in diners and coffee shops. Or at his office. I refused. I used dead drops."

He waved a finger in front of her face. "You mostly used dead drops, but not all the time. I know you met in person, too."

Alvaro knew a lot. Who was his source?

"I told Kirk to arrange meetings around fake appointments. At the dentist's or doctor's offices." In lieu of a checkup, root canal or sick visit, she met Kirk in secret.

Alvaro nodded. "You always were smart."

"Since we're sharing, how did you find me at the camp?" she repeated.

He rubbed her smart ring with his finger. "After the leak about the cartel using the Cutthroat Creek Mining Company for money laundering, I cloned the phones of the lieutenants. And yours. To see who the snitch was. Everyone looked clean. The app for your ring came up on the cloned phone and I found I enjoyed monitoring your vital statistics as well as your GPS location. That's how I was able to track you to the camp."

"Why didn't you just kill me?" she asked, aware she was on borrowed time and the clock was ticking.

"I don't like the ingratitude in your tone," he snapped. "You draw breath because I will it."

She lowered her gaze. Her gut told her to talk less and listen more. She was still alive for a reason.

His will had nothing to do with it.

"It's come to my attention that over the years, you've recorded things. Taken videos at parties and of meetings."

To capture an image of Rio Estrada in case he ever showed up. But the feed was never live for Kirk to see in real time. She passed along a few for reference, but most of the footage he'd never seen. Two weeks ago, he'd insisted on a meeting. Told her he wanted all the surveillance recordings. That he had gotten special permission to use a new classified facial recognition program called Odin's Eye that a gray-hat hacker designed. He thought it was possible Rio Estrada was in fact in the footage and that no one ever told her he was present or singled him out, since his identity was supposed to be kept a secret. Kirk believed they might be able to pinpoint Rio using the program.

"How do you know that?"

"Where's the footage?" he asked, ignoring her question.

She hesitated.

"This is how you earn a quick death," Alvaro said. "By telling me."

Christina had assumed he would interrogate her about what information she had shared, but he was more interested in the video footage. That's why she was alive.

"Kirk Kehoe didn't have it," he said. "Not all of it, anyway. But you do."

She weighed her options, but it was difficult to strategize with him sitting so close, assessing everything about her. "It's on a hard drive."

"Where?"

"Hidden at my place," she said, and he narrowed his eyes in annoyance. She didn't want to test his patience. "In the floor in my closet. There's a safe. The code is 1107."

He considered her words. "November seventh. The day we met."

The day her life changed forever. But if he wanted to read some sentimentality into it that pertained to him, she wasn't going to stop him.

Christina simply nodded.

"Speaking of that night." He glanced at the bottle of Château Pétrus on the other side of the room. "Was it a setup from the very beginning?" He looked back at her. "Or did Kehoe approach you after I started seeing you?"

She had to assume he already knew the answer. He enjoyed a lot of fine wine, but he'd chosen that specific bottle. It wasn't for the sake of nostalgia, and it wasn't a coincidence. "Kirk sent me to the restaurant and told me what to order. He also told me to be myself when I met you. But you weren't what I expected."

Alvaro put his hand on her throat, gently, and pressed his thumb to her carotid artery. "What did you expect?"

In that moment, she needed to be honest. He would sense a lie.

"I thought you would be mean-spirited and small-minded. But you were cultured and charismatic. Interesting." Seductive. "You made it easy."

His grip on her throat tightened. "Easy for you to fool me?"

Christina shook her head and forced herself not to clutch his wrist defensively. Holding his gaze, she leaned into his grasp. In his eyes, she saw the danger lurking there. The edge to him was razor-sharp. "You made it easy to be around you. To be attracted to you." And to her shame, she had been before she knew the truth. What did that say about her? "It wasn't all an act, not in the beginning."

"It wasn't all real either."

"I was always afraid."

His eyebrows drew together. "Of me?"

"Of being discovered. Exposed. Of what you would do to me if—*when* you found out."

"Legitimate fears." His thumb pressed harder to her artery. "What about your backup to the hard drive?"

"Backup? There's just the hard drive." The lie flew from her lips without thinking.

"The only problem with that answer is I know you're not a fool." He let her go and opened the drawer of the nightstand, took out a tablet and offered it to her. "Log in to your cloud storage system, where I'm sure you have it backed up."

"But I don't." Although the data was indeed backed up, on two different clouds, if she gave one up too easily, he'd would be able to tell she was hiding something else.

Alvaro moved his free hand to her knee. Slid his palm up her thigh to the spot where he shot her and tapped the wound lightly.

In the silence, her nerves ratcheted up with each passing moment.

"Log in," he finally said, his voice low but hard as steel, "and the US marshal you're so eager to protect gets to live. I'll leave him alone. Continue to pretend that it's not backed up and I'll torture him first. How long do you think that Boy Scout will last before I break him and he begs for mercy?"

She took the tablet, brought up the website and logged in.

He snatched it back, reviewed the files and initiated a transfer of everything from the cloud to his tablet. "Once the transfer is complete, I've got to go to your place to get the hard drive. It had better be there, exactly where you told me."

"It is," she said. "I promise."

"Your promises mean nothing. Unlike mine. I always

keep them. I'm leaving Hector to babysit. I'll make sure he stays downstairs. But if the hard drive isn't where you say, I'm going to give him ten minutes with you."

Ten minutes for her to break more of the toad's bones. "Would that be to punish me or Hector?"

Alvaro smiled.

She tried to flash one back in return, but she couldn't quite get her mouth to obey. "Are you going to shoot me here when you get back? Or are we going to take a drive to another abandoned tunnel?"

How much time did she have?

"Not here," he said, lightly, amusement still curving his lips. "Rio will decide the time and place. I imagine it'll be somewhere in Missoula. *El Jefe* wants to speak with you, face-to-face, and then watch me kill you. But I never said anything about shooting you."

"You said a quick death. I imagined mercy for giving up years of surveillance footage."

"Then you imagined wrong. I'm not a merciful man, and *quick* is a relative term. A person's death can be drawn out for days. Even weeks."

Horrible scenarios whirled in her mind, the dread of what was to come making her nauseous. "Then how will you do it?"

There were terrible ways to go. Drowning. Being buried alive.

"After everything you've done, what do you think you deserve?" His smile faded, his eyes growing dark and somber.

The question was rhetorical. But he just stared at her as if waiting for a response.

"I don't know," she said, knowing any answer she gave wouldn't be good enough.

"*I* brought you into the cartel. I vouched for you with Rio.

Protected you. Championed you every step of the way. And what did you do?" His tone turned scathing. "You stabbed me in the back." His jaw tightened along with the muscles in his neck, sending a chill through her. "I gave you a rare gift, but you didn't want it."

He stroked her cheek with his knuckles, and she strained not to flinch. "So, when I kill you, it has to be up close. It has to be the most personal, most *intimate* kind of death. Not with a bullet. Not with a blade. Not with a garrote. Nothing between us. I'm going to use my bare hands and squeeze the life out of you." He trailed a finger down her throat. "Slowly. While I look into your eyes, and my face will be the last thing you ever see."

Chapter Thirteen

Bitterroot Falls
Saturday, April 14, 12:20 a.m.

Jackson poured another cup of hot coffee and sipped it while watching Chance and Winter as they spoke privately in the dining room.

They didn't appear to be arguing, but she wasn't onboard either. Jackson was aware the situation was complicated for Winter. The Stratton sisters were practically family to him. The youngest one, Summer, was engaged to his brother Logan. They all hung out together, with the rest of the IPS team as a part of their clan. Sunday funday brunches, drinks, game night get-togethers when he was able to drive up from Missoula and crash at someone's house.

Summer and Logan's engagement party had reunited him with his parents, who Jackson hadn't seen since his oldest brother got married. With his siblings getting engaged and hitched, Jackson had finally started to thaw, warming to the idea of seeing his folks. He'd stayed away from home for so long—since he was eighteen—Logan had told him the family joked that Jackson was the forgotten son. No one ever talked about him since he was a sensitive topic.

His brother hadn't intended it to be mean, but it had been

a telling reminder that in icing out his parents, he'd inadvertently done the same with his brothers.

Distanced himself to punish his parents as much as himself.

All because of Christina.

"Hey," Autumn said, coming up alongside him. "Are you worried my sister is going to turn you in?"

"The thought had crossed my mind."

"Don't worry, she won't. It would make things too awkward at Summer and Logan's wedding." She flashed a smile.

He appreciated her attempt to distract him with humor, even though he knew Winter well enough to understand she didn't mind making others uncomfortable, especially if she was doing something she believed in. The DCI agent would feel zero remorse about turning him in if she thought it was the right thing to do. "Winter only wants to protect you and Chance."

"It's not her job to protect us." Autumn put a hand on his arm and rubbed. "Besides, if Winter interferes with Chance's work, it'll sow the seeds of distrust between them and open the door to Chance doing the same to her. She doesn't want that. You're in no danger of her handing you over to the authorities."

Bo joined them. "You're safe with us."

"What about him?" Jackson gestured to Declan Hart, who was helping Eli connect his laptop to the television in the living room.

Autumn smiled. "Declan is a team player."

"But which team takes priority?" Jackson wondered. "IPS? DCI? Or just having Winter's back?"

"If it comes down to him choosing, I think IPS will win," Bo said, sliding a side glance at Autumn.

Maybe Bo was picking up on the same things as Jackson. That Declan was Team Autumn all the way. The DCI agent was always sneaking glances at her and seeking to be helpful wherever she was concerned.

Jackson was counting on the ties that bonded them.

"Walking us all through the details of what happened helped," Autumn said. "Declan and Winter needed to hear it. They needed to be convinced as cops, not as friends or family."

"Is that why you had me go through that exercise? For their benefit?"

Autumn tipped her head from side to side. "We all needed a clear picture, but it was mostly for them. We'll be better off having their assistance on this every step of the way."

"Hey, can everyone come into the living room?" Declan said. "Eli found something."

All sidebar conversations stopped, and they gathered in the other room.

"I finished going through the metadata on the phone," Eli said, bringing up the phone screen on the television. "Christina didn't contact anyone."

"You're sure?" Winter asked.

"Yep. A hundred percent." Eli nodded. "No calls. No texts. But seventeen minutes before Jackson contacted Chance, someone downloaded an app for a smart ring onto the phone." Eli typed some command on the laptop and brought up the open app from the phone onto the television screen for everyone to see. "The ring has a GPS tracker."

They'd confiscated Christina's weapons and cell phone, but they hadn't removed her jewelry. "We didn't book her in Missoula," Jackson said. "Christina was still wearing a ring. She must've downloaded the app as a way for me to keep tabs on her. To prove to me that I could trust her." The misery he'd caused her with his suspicion. She'd tried to tell him that they were in this together, allies, and he'd treated her like the enemy. "This means I can find her." And get her away from Aguilar.

"Looks like she's about an hour's drive from here," Eli said, bringing up a map and pointing to the spot. "The GPS location looks fairly accurate. Pinpointed down to a house in a remote area."

Jackson set his coffee down. "Then that's where I'm headed."

"Hang on," Winter said. "You're not going anywhere."

"Like hell I'm not. I came here for help. Not to be hindered."

"Let me finish." Winter crossed the room over to him. "You're not going anywhere alone. If Autumn and Chance are in this thing, I am, too."

"So am I." Declan put a hand on Jackson's back. "But we need a plan."

"You're right." Jackson took a beat and gathered his bearings. "If we go up against Aguilar half-cocked with no plan, we're all as good as dead."

Deer Valley
Saturday, April 14, 1:40 a.m.

TRAPPED.

No way out.

Christina got up from the floor, the handcuff on her left wrist jingling, put the lid down on the toilet seat and sat. She wondered exactly when Aguilar had decided he was going to hold her hostage at his house.

He had installed a twenty-four-inch ADA grab bar on the wall in his bathroom and handcuffed her to it. She hadn't noticed it earlier when she changed clothes.

At least he'd left her with water and access to the facilities. It could've been worse, considering. A lot worse.

My compassion for you is inconvenient.

Sometimes he said and did things that proved to her he was complicated. It tempted her to believe he wasn't really a big, bad beast.

That was what truly made him dangerous.

The boogeyman was obvious. Alvaro was more subtle. More insidious.

A well-disguised monster, with two sides to him. One that showed her glimpses of humanity.

Then there was the other side. The Grim Reaper, doing what he did best. That side had murdered her father and slaughtered most of the Iron Warriors and the convoy to the airport in cold blood, along with countless others. And when the time and place were right, he wouldn't hesitate to kill her, too. Part of her thought he'd relish it, find satisfaction in taking her life.

Putting her feet on the wall, Christina pulled on the eighteen-gauge stainless steel bar. It didn't budge in the slightest, and all she got for her efforts was a sore wrist.

She shifted on the seat, turning as much as she could, and checked the drawers of the vanity beside it. Tipping her head back, she groaned in frustration.

Empty. Alvaro had cleared out the drawers.

The only other things within her reach were a ceramic soap dispenser, a hand towel and the sink. There was no built-in medicine cabinet behind the mirror. If only she had a bobby pin or a paper clip, she could use it to unlock the handcuffs.

The bedroom door opened. Leaning forward, she peered around the vanity into the adjoining room.

Hector limped into the primary bedroom, still wearing his leather jacket.

Sitting back out of his line of sight, she yanked on the cuffs again and again. To no avail. She looked around for anything she could use as a weapon, but Alvaro had made sure to leave her with nothing.

"*Abejita.*" Hector stopped in the doorway to the bathroom, resting his forearm on the frame. Three of his fingers were bandaged together. "You're so quiet now. What happened to all your buzzing?"

"Aren't you supposed to be downstairs? Where it's safe for you?"

"Don't you mean safe for you? Alvaro is almost in Bozeman. Too far away to protect you now."

"Protect me from what?" She grinned at him. "The likes of you?"

Hector shoved his hand into his jacket pocket and pulled out a Taser. "What do you have to say now?"

Her grin faded as the knot of fear in her gut tightened. "You should be afraid of not listening to Alvaro, but if you were smart, you'd also be afraid of what I'll do to you if you get close enough."

"You're a dirty snitch, but you won't tell him. I can't see you whining to him about me giving you the beating I owe you. Not with the position you're in, traitor. And I won't leave any bruises on your face to tip him off." Hector hit a button on the Taser, and the stun gun crackled with electricity.

Standing, Christina grabbed the soap dispenser and smashed the mirror. Using the towel, she picked up a large, jagged shard. "Come on, toad. Take your chances. Let's see how it goes for you." No matter what, she wasn't going to let Hector get out of this unscathed.

The toad shuffled inside the bathroom, and Christina prepared herself.

"*Cuidado*, Hector." Alvaro's voice came over a speaker.

"If she doesn't kill you, I'll do far worse to you than break more fingers. You're going to have to drink all your meals through a straw for the next month."

Hector looked around, checking the ceiling and corners.

Christina knew some of the security features included cameras throughout the house. Fortunately, she had discovered them and their locations before trying to bug his place the way Kehoe had wanted.

She hadn't thought Alvaro would've been monitoring things while he was gone and busy driving to Bozeman.

Then again, why wouldn't he?

Backing out of the bathroom, Hector shoved the stun gun in his pocket. "Hey, can you hear me?"

"Yes," Alvaro said. "I can."

"I took something for the pain." Hector limped through the bedroom, headed for the hall. "It made me loopy. I wasn't thinking straight."

"You have one job. It's simple. Babysit. Don't mess it up and don't tick me off."

Raising a palm, Hector nodded. "Yeah, yeah." He shuffled down the stairs and out of sight.

Christina looked at the camera hidden in the vent. "Have you been watching me try to get out of these handcuffs this whole time?"

"Yes," he said, and she could hear the smile in his voice. "I'm almost to your place. For your sake, I really do hope that hard drive is in your safe. Because I always keep my promises, Christina, and Hector is just itching to have a go at you."

Deer Valley
Saturday, April 14, 2:05 a.m.

"STOP HERE," JACKSON SAID, right before Chance turned the Chevy Suburban down the road that led to the house where

Christina was being held. "We should go on foot the rest of the way."

"Why?" Bo asked. "We might need to make a speedy exit."

"The house is registered to an LLC," Jackson. "We have to assume it's his. If so, we should expect robust security measures."

After this turn, there was only one house down that road. It afforded a lot of opportunities to use creative safeguards.

"He makes a good point." Eli looked out the window. "We all have sensors leading up to our houses," he said, referring to the IPS crew. "We should expect the same if not more from this guy."

"But don't you guys also have sensors in the trees, too?" Autumn asked. "To detect people walking around your property." As the newest member of IPS, her home security was less comprehensive than that of the others.

"Yeah." Bo nodded. "May as well drive. He'll know we're coming either way."

"Taking the vehicle is faster and gives him less time to prepare," Declan added.

Jackson shook his head. The group had no idea who they were going up against. They'd taken the time to swing by the IPS office and load up with gear they thought they might need, but they needed to think outside the box when it came to Aguilar. "How do we know the road leading up to the house isn't booby-trapped? There could be a spike strip ready to pop up and puncture our tires. Who knows? I underestimated this guy once. I lost friends and officers because of it. We have to expect the unexpected. I say we leave the vehicle."

"Agreed. We go on foot," Winter said. "The house is less than a quarter mile down."

Chance cut the engine.

They all got out of the Suburban, wearing body armor, but none of the vests were rated level four—capable of stopping one AP round. But it was the best they had on such short notice.

Eli and Bo each grabbed one of the handles of the battering ram they'd decided to throw into the vehicle at the last moment. There was no telling how difficult it might be to breach the house or what they would be up against once inside.

Cutting into the woods, they started their trek toward the isolated house that sat on a steep slope. His brain kept supplying awful possibilities of what was happening to Christina, each one more terrible than the last. He tightened his grip on his drawn gun, keeping his head on a swivel.

Chance whistled, drawing their attention, and pointed to a sensor mounted on a tree.

They'd just lost the element of surprise. Aguilar knew they were coming.

Deer Valley
Saturday, April 14, 2:14 a.m.

A HIGH-PITCHED beeping sounded in the house. It was an alarm of some sort, but Christina had never heard it before and didn't know exactly what it meant.

For a moment, she wondered if Jackson had found the app she'd downloaded on the cell phone. If she hadn't been so stubborn, letting her anger get the better of her earlier, she would've told him about it. Then she'd know for certain that help would be on the way.

The beeping stopped.

"Hector, listen to me," Alvaro said through a speaker on the lower level of the house.

She was thankful the toad had left the doors open so she could hear what was going on.

"People are on their way up to the house," Alvaro said. "They're going to try to breach, but they won't get in."

"You don't know that!" Panic raised Hector's voice.

"I do," Alvaro said, calmly. "There are steel doors on the exterior of the house, fire-rated at six hours, impervious to battering rams. Hinge-area breaching charges won't work."

"What about the back side of the house?" Hector asked. "The whole thing is made of glass. I've got to get out of here."

"The windows are made of a bullet-resistant polycarbonate material."

"It'll stop a bullet, but what if they're able to break through it?"

Alvaro sighed over the speaker. "The polycarbonate resin can withstand repeated assaults. It has ballistic and forced-entry protection. I have exterior measures on the front and rear of the house that I can deploy to eliminate the targets once they're in position there. All you have to do is sit tight."

Christina's heart pounded against her breastbone. *Jackson and his friends.* She couldn't let anything happen to them.

Yanking at the handcuff, Christina had to get free. Had to do something to warn them.

If Jackson died trying to rescue her, she'd never be able to forgive herself.

"Sit tight? Is that a joke?" Hector did nothing to hide the alarm in his voice. "It'll take you hours to get back here. By then, this place will be crawling with SWAT."

"Stop walking toward the door." Alvaro's voice hardened. "Listen to me. They can't get in. Not unless you let them in. I can take care of most of them from here."

"Most isn't cutting it. I'm getting out of here." Footsteps hurried down a hall, the gait unbalanced.

"If you leave, I'll bury you beside her," Alvaro said, the edge in his voice chilling. "I swear it."

"First you'll have to get your hands on both of us."

"Hector!" Alvaro roared through the speakers and cursed. "Christina, if you're not shackled in that bathroom right where I left you when I get back, I'll make the Boy Scout and those helping him pay. I can see them on the cameras. I know what they look like. It won't be hard to find out their names and where they live. And I won't stop with them. I know about the Shooting Star–Longhorn Ranch, where Jackson Powell grew up with a silver spoon in his mouth," Alvaro said, sending a chill down her spine. "About his brother, Logan, who lives in Bitterroot Falls with his pretty fiancée. Be a good girl and stay put."

She swallowed around the lump forming in her throat as her chest tightened.

"Do you understand me?" Alvaro's voice was razor-sharp.

The lights suddenly went out, cutting off the speaker, and leaving her in darkness. The power must have been cut.

A trickle of relief ebbed through her at not having to listen to one more menacing word from the Reaper.

Not hollow threats. Promises he would keep.

The house was quiet, and for a moment she wondered if something had happened to Jackson and the others.

Gunfire erupted outside.

Beads of sweat rolled down her spine. Clenching her hands, she hoped Jackson and his friends would be all right. Too many good guys had fallen in this war against the cartel.

Alvaro's threat echoed in her head, rattling her to the core. What if Jackson did get inside? Could she leave with him? *Should* she, even though she knew it would only endanger them?

Footsteps pounded through the house. Four people. Maybe more.

"Christina!"

Jackson.

At the sound of his voice, fear evaporated as a little flare of hope spiked.

"I'm here! Upstairs," she said. "The main bedroom on the right!"

The lights popped on. A backup power source?

Of course, Alvaro would have a generator, but how long until the security cameras reset?

Footsteps hurried up the stairs.

Then she spotted Jackson hitting the top landing, His gaze found hers, and he bolted to her. Wrapping his arms around her, he let out a sigh of relief, one that washed over her.

"How did you get into the house?" she asked.

"Ibarra left the door open as he made a break for it through a side exit."

"Is everyone okay?"

"Yeah." Nodding, he took out a handcuff key and released her. "Where's Aguilar?"

"Bozeman. We need to get out of here right now, but we have to be careful. He has exterior security measures on the front and rear of the house. I got the impression they were deadly."

"They are. We discovered a trip wire connected to a Claymore mine as we approached the house through the woods. We'll leave the same the way we came in—through the side door."

He took her hand, and they ran to the staircase. With their fingers interlaced, they hurried down the steps, where others were converging.

"It's clear," said a big guy.

Jackson gave a curt nod. "Aguilar isn't here."

A car started out front. From the wall of windows, they spotted a Mercedes speeding down the driveway.

Hector. That toad was getting away.

A woman made a beeline toward the front door. She had the look of law enforcement to her.

"Wait!" Christina said, stopping her. "There are security measures outside. Maybe hidden guns or something. I'm sure they'll be near the front door."

An explosion rocked the night, and the Mercedes burst into flames as it bounced into the air. The fireball clattered to the ground with pieces of metal falling around it.

"I guess you were right about possible booby traps on the road," a different man said. "He had an IED out there."

If you leave, I'll bury you beside her.

Alvaro had warned Hector Ibarra. Then he warned Christina, too.

"Jackson, maybe it would be better if you left me behind."

"What are you talking about?" Jackson asked, staring at her in confusion.

"Alvaro saw everyone on the security cameras. He told me that if I left with you, he would find your friends and make them pay."

"He's just trying to scare you."

"It's more than that. He knows about your family's ranch in Wyoming. He mentioned it. The Shooting Star–Longhorn. And Logan, who lives in Bitterroot Falls with a fiancée."

The two women in the group exchanged concerned glances. They resembled each other, with the same kind eyes, similar features, smooth brown complexions.

"He knows about Summer," one woman said to the other.

"Jackson." Christina clutched his arm. "I can't endanger your family or your friends. In the past couple of years, as Kehoe pushed harder for more information, I came to terms with the idea that my days were numbered. If you walk away without me, just go now, Alvaro will leave you all alone."

"He's a monster," Jackson said. "Nothing he says can be trusted."

"You can trust that he will come for me," Christina said, "and then he'll come for the rest of you." She looked around at the group. Letting go of Jackson's hand, she backed away from him. "All of you should go. I'm not worth it. Just forget about me."

Jackson cupped her face with both of his hands and stared into her eyes. "You're worth it. Do you hear me? You're worth everything to me. I'm not leaving here without you."

His words wrapped around her like a warm blanket, sheltering her from the storm of fear and violence and uncertainty.

"Neither are we," another man said, patting Jackson's shoulder. "You're one of us. Your *big brother* told me to find you and keep you safe. We're going to do just that. All of us. Now, we should get going."

Looking at her, Jackson held out his hand. "We're going to finish this together."

Christina tugged the smart ring from her finger and threw it on the ground. She took his hand, wrapping her fingers around Jackson's, as reckless as the action might have been. *Together.* "Let's go."

Chapter Fourteen

Bitterroot Falls
Saturday, April 14, 3:58 a.m.

His family was safe and so was Christina. Jackson took comfort in that, even though there was no way to know how long that certainty would last.

Aguilar's threat was real. That cold-blooded killer posed a clear and present danger that couldn't be ignored.

On the hour-long drive back to Bitterroot Falls, Jackson had contacted Logan and explained while Winter made the same phone call to Summer. Time was of the essence since Aguilar was in Bozeman and could be in Bitterroot Falls within hours. His brother took the news that he and Summer needed to lie low for a few days well. Far better than his parents did.

It had been impossible for Jackson to keep Christina's name out of the discussion with his parents, since the manhunt for them had made the national news. Both *wanted*. Jackson had made it clear the onus for this mess was on the FBI. On his task force. On him. His mother, who was a pillar of strength, cried on the phone while his father grumbled, but to their credit, neither uttered a negative word about Christina.

Probably fearful Jackson would subject them to another decade of permafrost. No calls. No visits. No connection.

After twelve years, this thing with Christina was coming full circle, but he still had no idea where they would end up.

In the guest bedroom, he glanced out a window that afforded him a sweeping view of the Lady Luck Ranch, which was more of a compound. Chance had his ranch hands running patrols of the property. They were all armed, working in teams, with dogs at their sides. The ranch was on lockdown until it was time to leave for the raid on the depots.

The faucet in the en suite bathroom stopped and the door opened. Christina came out of the bathroom, her face clean, her curls loose around her shoulders, and sat beside him on the bed. Chance's house was massive, with plenty of bedrooms, but the entire team was here, with more people coming. Lockwood was sending additional personnel to help with the raid and neutralize the threat of Alvaro Aguilar. It was going to be a full house.

"What time do we leave to raid the depots?" she asked.

"Waylon Wright, a former detective who is in charge of the IPS Laramie office, should be here with more personnel within the hour. We'll brief everyone and head out. Should hit the depots right before sunrise." His gaze fell to the cut on her lip. Someone had hit her. "Did Aguilar do that to you?"

She shook her head. "Hector Ibarra. But I let him."

He didn't hide the alarm or confusion from his face.

"Don't ask why." She put a hand on his thigh. "Please."

He took a deep breath, letting that question go. Running his hand down her arm, he noticed she was wearing a different outfit. Expensive. Better suited for her, fitting her like a glove. "You changed your clothes."

Shuttering her gaze, she bit her lower lip. "Alvaro made me."

Pure rage burned in his belly. "Did he—"

"No, he didn't." She pulled her hand away from him and rubbed her palms over her thighs. "He's never..." Pursing her lips, she kept looking down at her lap. "Alvaro is sick and twisted. Cruel. But he wields his power in a different way."

Jackson clutched her shoulder, wondering what she had endured over the last several hours. That monster, Aguilar, had had her within his grasp. He might not have hit her or forced himself on her, but something had happened. Jackson was sure of it.

"You're not all right," he said. "You can tell me what happened. Whatever it is, I'm on your side. Okay."

She nodded. "I'm fine. Really. Thanks to you and everyone else." Scooting closer to him until their legs touched, she gave him a small smile, but concern wrinkled her brow and fatigue clouded her eyes. "Aguilar didn't hurt me. He just talked to me." She shivered as she pressed her hand to the base of her throat.

"After I saw the chaos in the tent, I imagined the worst."

"We had a little tussle at the camp. But it was just sport for him. He was having fun. I was in the woods with him when you showed up at the tent with a bowl of stew. I heard you apologize."

"You were still there?" he asked. "That close?"

"Yeah, I was. I wanted to call out to you, but he would've killed you."

"If only I had been two minutes earlier—"

"Then you'd be dead, and I would still be handcuffed to the rail in his bathroom." Lowering her head, she clutched her knees. "That would have been more than I could bear, if he'd gotten to you."

"I'm just glad he didn't torture you." He put a hand on her back. "I thought he would've put you through the wringer to get information."

"He was only interested in one thing—video footage I've recorded over the years of meetings and parties. Kehoe gave me a couple of devices hidden in necklaces. In case I ever met Rio Estrada, or he popped up unannounced. Everything was stored on a hard drive and backed up in the cloud. He didn't have to torture me to get it. His threat to hurt you was enough to get me to cooperate."

Jackson took her hand in his. "Aguilar didn't say anything about the depots?"

"No." Christina shook her head. "Maybe he's not aware that I know what they're being used to store."

"How do you know about them?"

"I took care of a lot of legal business for the cartel. Like buying guns wholesale directly from weapons manufacturers rather than the piecemeal way they were going about before. Or setting up a charity for them, which was legitimate and stayed that way for a while. But now they're using the tax-exempt organization to launder money. There was no way for me to tell Kirk about it without it leading back to me as the leak. As for the depots, I found the properties. When I pushed Hector to give me an idea of how they'd be used so I could pick the right ones, he let too much information slip. Any time I followed up with him about how they were working out, he'd tell me more. Later I started getting updates from his guys, discreetly. Then Kehoe was worried about a mole in the task force and started talking about pulling me. Soon. So, I found out when the depots are usually full. There's always stuff flowing in and out, but for some reason, once a quarter, all three have full stockpiles worth millions. The time is right now, but I don't know how long before they begin distribution."

"But Aguilar was more concerned about the video footage?"

"That was his main focus," she said in a way that told him it wasn't Aguilar's only focus, making Jackson worry again if she was okay.

"Did that have something to do with why he was going to Bozeman?"

"To collect the hard drive from my place. He also erased it from my cloud."

Jackson swore, wishing they could catch a bigger break. "If that was Aguilar's priority, then it's a good bet that Rio Estrada is on that footage somewhere. I wish he didn't have the hard drive and hadn't wiped what was stored in your cloud."

"But I have a backup to the backup. A second cloud. We still have it."

How he wanted to kiss her. "Good thinking." Beautiful. Brilliant. Full of boundless bravery.

She was his greatest temptation.

His only love.

Years ago, he'd been naïve, thinking he could have his cake and eat it, too. Christina's words had really hit him hard. Now he realized sacrifices had had to be made. For the right reasons. In the right ways. This time, he wanted Christina enough to give her his all.

"Jackson," she said. "There's something I haven't had a chance to tell you. Kirk never looked at most of the footage, since we're talking about hundreds of hours, and the goal was to capture Rio Estrada on video. Right before my cover was blown, Kirk got permission to use Odin's Eye."

"The facial recognition program?" he asked.

"Yeah. Kirk had the idea of running all the footage through Odin's Eye and thought we might be able to pinpoint Rio that way. Maybe he was there at one of those meetings or parties and I wasn't aware of it, since only a few people know who he is and what he looks like."

"To access a high-level program like Odin's Eye, Kehoe would've needed permission from someone above his pay grade. And he would've needed a very good reason to justify it. Like having an undercover asset with hundreds of hours of video footage that needed to be screened and filtered."

"Maybe whoever gave him access, or at least pretended that they would, is the person who blew my cover."

If the request had been made through official channels, there would be a log of it. Not that he could get into any systems as a wanted fugitive. And knowing Kehoe, the request had probably been made unofficially.

Once the raids were completed, and hopefully successful, he would reach out to the task force and speak to whoever was in charge. Take it one step at a time from there.

"I'm sorry that I gave you such a hard time about being undercover. The compromises you had to make to survive. To do Kehoe's bidding." He sighed. "The lies you had to keep track of and the stories you must've needed to create on the fly. How did you do it?" He hoped he didn't sound judgmental.

Jackson only wanted to understand what she'd gone through and sympathize.

"I WINGED IT," Christina said with a shrug, "made stuff up and pretended a lot." She got up from the bed and moved to the window. "When you're undercover for so long like I was, the truth becomes a matter of circumstance. It wasn't all things, to all people, all the time. Neither was I."

He rose and strode over to her. "That sounds like a tough way to live."

"It was a good way not to die, though."

"It's kind of hard to trust someone when you don't know who that someone really is."

Her chin jerked up and her body locked. "Yeah." Was the cloud of distrust still hanging over their heads? "Do you not know who I am? Do you still have doubts about me?"

"I didn't mean that about you." Jackson put his hand on her shoulder and squeezed lightly. "I was talking in general about being undercover. About the need to make the truth a matter of circumstance. Not truly being able to get close to anyone. How hard that must have been. How much strength that must've taken, the guts you needed to persevere."

He wrapped an arm around her. Turning into him, she pressed her forehead to his chest. Once again, the utter peace, the quiet security of his presence, washed over her the way it had when he was extracting her from Aguilar's house. Part of her wanted to soak it in until the grime of the past six years disappeared from her skin, her mind, her heart.

"I'm sorry I've been such a jerk," he said. "After everything Kehoe put you through, you didn't deserve it."

"You were playing it safe. I don't blame you." Not anymore.

"Still."

"I owe you," she said. "For coming to my rescue."

"You don't. It's okay." He caressed her cheek, drawing her gaze to his. "This is all Kehoe's fault. He never should have recruited you and trapped you in that position. If I had known, I would've forced him to pull you. Even if I had to report him to the FBI to do it." Jackson took a breath. "I guess you're right, and that's the reason he didn't tell me."

"Earlier tonight, if it was the other way around, and it was down to me to save your life, would you trust me to do it? Be honest."

"I trust you. With my life." Caressing her face, he held her gaze. "And I'm always honest."

"When you were at the tent while I was in the woods, I heard you talk about us having a truce. Does that make us allies now? Friends?"

"Yeah." He stroked her bottom lip with his thumb, and she shivered with desire. "Of course."

"Is that all you want us to be?" She slid her hands up his chest. "Just friends?"

Waiting for his answer scared her spitless. She'd never stopped wanting Jackson. Never stopped loving him.

Then he grinned, and it had a boyish, earnest quality to it she found so sexy. Aguilar had meant it as an insult when he called Jackson a Boy Scout. But it was the best way to describe him.

Honorable. Resourceful. Good.

"I want so much more," he said. "When it comes to you, I want everything. Always have. Still do." He lowered his mouth to hers and kissed her.

Something inside her sighed with release, her tired body stirring to life. She hadn't realized how much she needed this since the last kiss they'd shared in the shower.

He tasted like a mix of coffee and mint, and the smell of him was still so delicious. It hadn't changed. Not one nuance to it. He didn't wear cologne or aftershave. His scent was pure male and all his. And she recalled lying in his bed, clutching his pillow to her body, face shoved into the sheets, taking in the smell of him before she had to sneak out the window.

Responding to the warmth of his body and the scent of his skin, she opened herself to him. Jackson deepened the kiss, upping the ferocity, stoking all the longing that bubbled inside her. She could always count on him for that. It was as if they were always starving for each other.

Her body responded instantly, heating at his touch. She leaned into him in search of more. More friction. More pressure. But what she really wanted was him.

"Jackson," she breathed.

"Do you know what hearing my name on your lips still does to me?"

"No. Show me."

"Are you sure this is what you want?"

She bit his bottom lip in answer. "I'm sure I want you."

Those blue eyes flashed, all heat and promise. Warmth and concern. "Say it again," he rasped.

Her Jackson was back.

"I want you."

"Never stopped wanting you."

Picking her up, he carried her to bed and laid her down. His body was hard and muscular over hers.

Her heart thundered in anticipation. "I missed you." It was a whisper, barely audible, each word weighed down by heartache and history and unfulfilled hunger.

He kissed her and groaned, the sound tearing through him, tearing through her. His hand slid up to curve around the base of her head where it met her neck; he held tight, took her mouth and kissed her deep and hard and long.

It hurt. The pain of that desire was almost unbearable, but also, utterly beautiful.

She melted against him like hot wax, meeting the heat and intensity of his kiss. Wrapping her arms around his neck, she pushed her fingers through his hair and sighed at the delicious sensations he made blossom inside her. The past forty-eight hours had been a stark reminder of how quickly everything could unravel and end. And here she was with Jackson, and he was making her *feel*.

At her lowest points, when she was alone and abandoned and afraid, she'd learned to do things to remind herself that she was still alive, still breathing and still had something to fight for. But no one and nothing made her feel more alive and aware than Jackson.

Peeling off her clothes, he took possession of her mouth, kissing her like he couldn't get enough, and it was the same for her. That thread of desperation coiled inside her, threatening to snap.

Maybe it was like this because they knew this thing between them had an expiration date. Only the date kept moving, changing.

Her heart ached, on the verge of shattering for this beautiful man who still had such a hold on her. No matter how much time they had together, she was going to make the most of every single second with him.

Chapter Fifteen

Bitterroot Falls
Saturday, April 14, 5:31 a.m.

Having Christina back in his arms, no matter how briefly, was perfection. They'd both grown and changed. Being with her still blew his mind, but in a different way. Better. What they had to share was so much deeper. He only hoped they'd have a chance to truly reconnect, to discover who they both were now and see if they might finally have a future together.

But there was so much that needed to be done before that was possible.

The last thing Jackson wanted to do was disentangle their limbs, pull away from her and get out of bed. But he did it. Had no choice.

At first light, they would raid the depots.

Waylon Wright and five others from another IPS office had just arrived, flying in on helicopters that had touched down on Chance's property. Three helicopters since they had three objectives to accomplish in three separate locations simultaneously.

When Lockwood stated he was willing to put all his resources behind this, he'd meant it.

Just as they were about to get started with the briefing, a familiar face walked into the living room.

"Takoda." Jackson went over to his buddy and gave him a hug. "How's Aiden?"

"Angry. Bruised. He's got a broken arm and several fractured ribs. But he's going to make a full recovery. His wife flew in, too. She's livid and ready to get the guy responsible."

Charlie Killian-Yazzie was a force to be reckoned with.

"How about the rest of my team? Who else survived?"

"Lucky there were any survivors. Some of the rounds used by the assailant were armor-piercing. They're estimating maybe every third or fourth bullet was an AP round. All the police officers were killed. Along with Flores and Walken."

"The last time I saw Walken, he was on his feet and returning fire."

"An AP round got him in the chest. But Tillman made it. Regular bullets put him down temporarily, knocking the wind out of him, and leaving his sternum bruised. Vazquez made it through without a scratch on her. Just a concussion and whiplash. The other two from your task force were at the hospital. Mirabal and Nichols."

"Any idea who's in charge of the task force?" Jackson wondered.

"Bigwigs from several agencies are in Missoula, duking it out for control." Takoda handed him three business cards.

Oscar Baccarin—FBI. Dawn Quinones—DHS. Gabriel Garcia—DEA.

"I've met them all," Jackson said. "But I can't say I know any of them well enough to say who should win."

"For now, the three of them are overseeing the manhunt for Ortiz and you, as well as the apprehension of the assailant. They don't have a name or an image of the guy. All the CCTV cameras were down."

"The guy responsible is Alvaro Aguilar. He's a serious problem." Jackson didn't want to get into the nitty-gritty specifics at the moment. They needed to focus their attention on the raid. "I'm surprised you're here and didn't stay in Missoula until Aiden is released from the hospital."

"My cousin insisted I get out of there and make myself useful. He's been telling the head honchos that if you fled with Ortiz, it was only to save both your lives. They were willing to consider it for a while, but the longer you go without checking in, the worse it looks."

Jackson nodded. "Yeah, I'm aware. But the situation is complicated. After the raids, I can check in. I can't risk being located or anyone getting wind of the seizure of the cartel's depots until it's done."

Takoda patted his shoulder. "Well, I'm here to help. Just let me know what you need me to do."

They were moving out in a little less than thirty minutes from now. Sunrise was around seven and they needed to kick this off while it was still dark. If all went as planned, they would land a major blow to the cartel. One that would help justify his reason for being on the run with Christina.

"Eli." Chance's voice brought Jackson's attention to the front of the living room. "Pull up the images and the blueprint."

Jackson cut through the crowd, making his way closer to the front next to Christina.

Aerial images of the three sites they were about to hit came up on the screen. They were old farming properties. Alongside the photos, Eli brought up a digitized blueprint of one of the barns that Christina had downloaded from her secondary cloud storage.

"Christina," Chance said, "you're the only one who's been to the sites. Do the honors, would you?"

She nodded stiffly and rose from the sofa where she was seated. Something seemed to shift in her. The moment she was standing at the screen, she looked comfortable, poised, filled with purpose. In control.

"The security teams at the sites rotate on shifts. They sleep on-site in the farmhouses. The goods that we're looking for will be stored in the barns. They're half the size of a football field. Fifty yards long, half as wide. Inside the barns, they've constructed another building."

Winter passed her a laser pointer, and Christina used it to indicate the location of the building inside the barn.

"To keep it simple, I'll refer to the interior buildings as the Vault. They are situated inside the west corner of the barns. The Vaults are designed as a stronghold in the event there was a security threat."

"So," Christina added, assessing the bleak faces around the room, "consider the Vaults to be safe rooms on steroids. If we don't take advantage of the element of surprise, anyone inside could theoretically seal themselves up tight and hold off our raid until reinforcements arrive."

Chance stepped forward. "Each helicopter will land less than half a mile from the sites, where we will be met by more backup, waiting to transport us the rest of the way in vehicles. Based on the information provided by our confidential informant," he said, gesturing to Christina, "DCI was able to get us warrants. One of the grounds included in the basis for the warrant was the use of farming land and livestock trailers to smuggle drugs. This tidbit enabled me to reach out to friends I trust in the Montana Livestock Association. Their agents are sworn law enforcement officers. Several of them will meet us at each landing site and will assist with seizures and arrests. The Estrada cartel was not mentioned when I made these arrangements. That piece of information is on a need-to-know basis only. For now, they don't need to know." Chance turned to the biggest guy in the room. "Waylon, anything to add?"

"The fellas I brought with me will divide up among the three groups," Waylon said in a booming voice. The former detective was built like an Abrams tank, standing at six-five, weighing a good 230 pounds. "I go where Christina goes. Lockwood made it clear my number-one priority is her safety. Everything else is secondary for me. Got it?"

Heads nodded.

Sounded good to Jackson. With Aguilar out there on the prowl, it was going to take a team to keep her out of that man's reach.

Jackson was determined to put an end to the Estrada cartel's stateside unit, but he would sacrifice doing that and more—if it would keep Christina safe, he'd walk through fire.

Somewhere in Glacier County, Montana
Saturday, April 14, 6:26 a.m.

EACH HELICOPTER TRANSPORTED a five-member team. Christina sat in the chopper, scanning the faces of the rest of her team as they headed to their designated site—the one that held millions in cash.

They were as ready as they could be with such a short lead time. Nonetheless, her thoughts were scattered and her heart was in turmoil. So many people were risking their lives for the sake of this mission, to help her clear her name and keep her alive. Alvaro already had Jackson in his sights, but soon *La Parca* would learn the names of the others who'd dared rescue her: Chance, Winter, Eli, Autumn and Bo.

A single question played on repeat in her head: *Is one person worth jeopardizing six others?* And now, there were even more here to protect her.

Jackson reached over, took her hand in his and squeezed as though he could read her mind. She glanced at him. He sat next to her. Silent. Tense. Steadfast.

The entire team wore tactical-level body armor and gear that Waylon had brought with him. Though Christina would've preferred one of her personal handguns, Waylon had given her a sound-suppressed Smith & Wesson M&P like the rest of the team. She wore the pistol in a drop holster on her right hip. The sling of an M4 hung over her shoulder.

She gathered that the forensic psychologist hadn't seen much action in the field. One of Winter's conditions for Autumn going along on the raids was that she was not to be involved in direct combat. When Autumn had tried to shut Winter down, Declan stepped in, agreeing that the psychologist shouldn't be subjected to line-of-fire casualties since they had a robust team for the raids.

Christina was curious how it would work out, since Autumn was on the team with Chance and Winter, while Declan was in the helicopter with Christina, sandwiched between Waylon and one of the Iron Warriors who had survived. He was a new member, only having joined in the last three years, and she didn't know him, but she appreciated the fact that he had volunteered for this messy situation after the club had been hit.

Before they had loaded up in the helicopters, Chance's final words to everyone had been straight and to the point: "Each team is to breach the farmhouse and the barn at the same time. MLA agents will hit the farmhouse while IPS and DCI will take the Vaults. Disable alarms. Immobilize hostiles. Hit the Vault fast and hard, taking out the guards inside. Secure the cash, weapons and drugs. Radio in. Mission accomplished."

Sounded solid in theory. Now they were going to test it.

"ETA sixty seconds," Waylon said. "Final comms check commencing now."

They all wore Bluetooth communication earpieces under their sound-deadening hearing protection and voice-activated throat mikes pressed against their necks.

Waylon called out everyone's name one at a time and waited for a return *check*, indicating they were good.

As the helicopter set down at the landing site, they spotted their MLA backup waiting in two black SUVs. The five of them hopped out of the chopper. Waylon and Declan made quick introductions, explained the plan and gave them several stun grenades to immobilize the guards at the farmhouse. IPS took one vehicle while the MLA agents were loaded in the other. They waited until the others touched down at their respective sites and then rolled out.

It took them a few short minutes to arrive at the location. The two vehicles peeled away, each headed toward their target.

A calm came over Christina as she closed her eyes and touched her gear, making sure she could locate any part of it without looking. She made sure her helmet was securely fastened.

They stopped short of the barn and left their doors open as they got out, not wanting to give away their position. Waylon grabbed breaching charges they might need to blow the Vault doors. Her big brother knew how to prepare for a battle and had ensured they'd have everything for a worst-case scenario.

Declan wanted to be the first one through the door. Everyone followed him and stacked up along the barn wall. Christina hung tight between Waylon and Jackson.

They were all aware that once Declan opened that barn door, there was no turning back. They had to run almost forty yards to reach the Vault, take out the two guards—provided the intel she had was still good—and then set and blow the breaching charges to get inside.

At the same time, the livestock agents would cut the electricity to the farmhouse and storm inside and use the stun grenades on the foot soldiers, who were hopefully sleeping.

About a hundred things could go wrong, including finding the Vault empty, and there was only one way that this would go right. This rushed operation had been thrown together in bad conditions and without proper recon and surveillance. Still, they needed everything to go exactly according to plan at all three sites.

Jackson grabbed her hand and gave it a gentle squeeze. The gesture eased her nerves.

"If things go sideways, don't be a hero," he said, using the words she'd spoken to him on her.

All she could do was smile. Things could go to hell in a handbasket and heroics wouldn't be a factor. It would simply come down to having each other's backs, and this time, they completely trusted one another.

This was it.

Declan pulled the pins on the stun grenades and tossed them inside the barn. A couple of thunderous bangs echoed along with bright flashes of light.

"Go," Declan said, sweeping into the barn in time with the livestock agents breaching the house.

She followed the team in, with Jackson bringing up the rear.

Two guards were still on their feet, but the flashes of light had temporarily blinded them and the concussive bangs had left them disorientated. It didn't stop them from shooting, aiming wildly.

They dived behind an old tractor that was inside the barn, taking cover.

But the two guards were exposed. Easy targets.

"On one, two, three," Declan said in their comms, and the five of them laid down fire in the direction of the enemy, putting down the guards without taking any casualties.

An alarm went off at the farmhouse, the screeching sound grating on her already-raw nerves like sandpaper. The house must've had a backup generator.

Not wasting time, they hurried down to the other end of the barn. The Vault was locked.

The former detective, Waylon, set the charges, and they all ducked behind the rear of the vault. "Breaching in three, two, one," Waylon said, giving the countdown, followed by the huge roar of an explosion.

The Vault door blew down with a bone-rattling *boom* and fell in a cloud of smoke.

They were in.

The team moved to the entrance of the Vault. Once the smoke cleared, they stared at high stacks of bundled cash neatly laid out on a metal table. She'd never seen so much money.

There had to be at least twenty million here. Possibly more.

Score one for the good guys.

Chapter Sixteen

Bitterroot Falls
Saturday, April 14, 10:40 a.m.

"It's time," Jackson said, back at the Lady Luck Ranch, looking around the kitchen at most of the team. They had successfully pulled off three rushed raids, coordinated simultaneously, seizing cartel assets. Winter, Declan and Chance were at DCI headquarters, where everything had been turned in and logged as evidence. No fatalities, though a couple of livestock agents and four Iron Warriors had been injured. Now Jackson had to contact the task force. "Are you all set up?" he asked Eli.

Their resident techie was going to mask the location of his cell phone. If anyone tried to trace the call, they would get fake GPS coordinates that would bounce to a new location every sixty seconds.

"Almost ready," Eli said. "Just give me a few more minutes."

"Who are you going to speak with?" Christina asked. "Anyone left on the task force could be the mole. You still can't trust any of them."

"Department chiefs from DEA, FBI and DHS have flown in," Jackson said, setting the business cards Takoda had given him on the marble countertop. "They've got boots on the ground here and are in charge of the task force. I guess I'll speak to one or maybe all of them. If they're available."

"Wait a minute." Christina folded her arms, her brow furrowing. "Three department heads are all in Missoula?"

"Yeah." Takoda nodded. "I met them at the hospital when they arrived and came in to check on the survivors." He picked up his mug and sipped his coffee.

Jackson moved closer to her. "What's up?"

"I don't know." Christina shrugged. "Maybe it's nothing. But Alvaro was waiting to kill me. He said Rio wanted to talk to me face-to-face and watch Alvaro…" Her voice trailed off as she clutched her throat. "Watch him eliminate me. He told me that it would probably happen in Missoula. I mean, that can't be a coincidence. Right?"

Jackson considered what she was saying. "We suspected that Kehoe told someone higher up about you being his asset. If it was to gain access to the Odin's Eye facial recognition program, then it would explain why he'd risk sharing that. He'd go to someone he was close to, someone familiar with the task force."

"You think the second mole is one of those three chiefs," Bo said, "and Rio is meeting with them?"

"What if it's bigger than that?" Christina looked around at everyone. "What if it's worse?"

Autumn took a seat on one of the stools. "Worse how?"

"This whole time," Christina said, "Kirk and I thought that Rio Estrada's identity was such a closely guarded secret so that he couldn't be found and tracked. To make it harder for a foot soldier or someone lower in the food chain to give him up in exchange for immunity if they were ever caught."

Takoda set his mug down. "You think it's more than that?"

"Possibly a lot more," Christina said with a nod. "What if

Rio Estrada's identity is so well safeguarded because *he is* the second mole, with a contact at a higher pay grade than Kehoe in the federal law enforcement hierarchy?"

Like a bad smell, the words hung in the air. Those in the kitchen shifted uncomfortably, their expressions varying from disbelief to denial.

"Whoa." Autumn reeled back. "Do you realize the magnitude of what you're suggesting?"

"Yes." Christina sighed. "I do."

Autumn shook her head. "Someone from the cartel can't just walk in off the streets and join one of the three-letter agencies. There are background checks, in addition to a robust protocol, put in place to prevent exactly what you just proposed from ever happening."

"Hear me out." Christina grabbed a stool and wearily sank down on it. "Before Pedro Estrada was killed and his son Dante took over the cartel, Pedro sent his younger son, Rio, to live in the United States. Where the kid just dropped off the grid. What if he assumed the identity of an American citizen? What if the ultimate goal was to embed a top cartel member inside one of the three-letter agencies?"

Autumn's jaw went slack.

"That's why Kehoe was murdered," Jackson said. He had wondered why the cartel would risk killing an FBI agent. "If an asset is discovered inside the cartel, they eliminate the traitor. But not the handler. Too much heat. They wouldn't dare to do it. Not unless that agent posed an equal or greater threat than the asset. Like Kehoe. Because he had footage of Rio and wanted to run it through Odin's Eye. It's also why Alvaro Aguilar was more concerned about getting all the surveillance footage you've accumulated over the years instead of worrying about depots or anything else you might know."

"Okay, let's say your theory is right." Waylon grabbed a bagel from one of the platters of food that had been laid out on the counter and slathered cream cheese on it. "What do you do with that? How do you test or prove it?" He bit into his bagel.

"You spoke to Rio on the phone, right?" Jackson asked, and Christina nodded. "I'm about to call these guys now. I can request a conference call with all of them. You might be able to recognize his voice."

"Did he ever use a digitizer or modulator over the phone?" Takoda asked.

"No," Christina said. "His voice never sounded altered."

"Well, we're ready to go." Eli handed Jackson the burner phone that was connected to the laptop with a USB. "Who are you going to try?"

Jackson looked between the cards and chose Dawn Quinones. Levelheaded woman. Ambitious but not cutthroat. She might, *might* hear him out. "I'll start with DHS."

He dialed the number, and the phone rang and rang. Jackson hit the speaker icon so the group could hear everything.

"Quinones," the deputy chief intelligence officer said, finally answering.

"This is US Marshal Jackson Powell."

"Jackson? Where are you? We've been looking for you and Christina Ortiz. Is she alive? Is she with you?"

"She is."

"You have to bring her in," Quinones said. "After that unmitigated disaster at the airport, we have a lot of questions for you."

"I understand, but I want a conference call with SAC Baccarin and SAC Garcia. Please patch them in."

"How about you come in with Ortiz and talk to all of us? We're here in Missoula, at the US marshals' building. It's essential we get the suspect back in custody and this situation under control as quickly as possible."

"Ortiz is innocent of the charges, ma'am," Jackson said. "She didn't murder anyone."

"Forensics came back. It did corroborate Ortiz's version of events. Kehoe was on the ground when he was shot from above. Not while he was running away. Also, there were bullets from two different weapons found in one of the victims, as Ortiz stated. I understand Nichols was assigned to investigate the sheriff's deputy, Brent Phillips, who was the alleged eyewitness. We have found that the deputy has used large sums of cash to pay for his current lifestyle, including vehicles and jewelry. Amounts that can't be explained by his salary. It's also a red flag that his body camera was disabled at the time. We're digging into this."

Sliding a glance at Christina, Jackson watched relief fall across her face. He gave her a reassuring nod. "I appreciate the update, ma'am. I also have evidence that Hector Ibarra was indeed at Ortiz's apartment the night of the murder and that she followed him to the tunnel where Kehoe was killed. We should be able to match some of the tire tracks at the scene to those on Ibarra's vehicle."

"That's excellent work," Quinones said. "But we still need you and Ortiz to come in."

"First, I need to speak with Baccarin and Garcia. You have sixty seconds to get them both on the line or I hang up," Jackson said and waited.

Ten seconds later. "Okay," Quinones said. "Let me see what I can do. Hold on."

He glanced at Christina and mouthed, *You can do this.* She nodded.

"Jackson, are you still there?" Quinones asked right before time was up.

"Yes, ma'am, I'm here."

"Okay, good," Quinones said. "I've got Baccarin and Garcia on the line with me."

"Gentlemen, can you both hear me?" Jackson asked.

"This is Baccarin. I've got you loud and clear."

"Garcia here. Jackson, why don't you tell us why you're on the run with a murder suspect?"

"We've heard a lot of troubling things from your team," Baccarin said. "But we want to hear your side of things. In person."

They'd have to settle for over the phone. "On our way to the airport," Jackson said, "my convoy was attacked by a high-level hit man for the Estrada cartel by the name of Alvaro Aguilar. I fled the scene with Ortiz to prevent Aguilar from murdering the suspect, who is in fact an asset for the FBI, recruited by Kirk Kehoe. She has been working undercover inside the cartel. All the valuable intelligence for Operation Big Sky Guardian came from Ms. Ortiz," Jackson said.

"We did receive a copy of paperwork from Mr. Lockwood, the owner of Ironside Protection Services," Quinones said, "and have verified Special Agent Kehoe's signature."

"However," Baccarin said, emphasizing the word, "we don't have anything official on our end here at the FBI. As it stands now, it appears that Kehoe went rogue by recruiting Ortiz as an unsanctioned asset."

"Is there anything else to substantiate the claim that she is or was an asset inside the cartel?" Garcia asked. "Besides information that the task force is already aware of. It has been suggested that you might be perpetuating that claim because you were once lovers with Ortiz. Some have even questioned whether you are currently involved with her."

Jackson didn't look at Christina. If he did, the entire

room would see the truth on his face—that they had once again become intimate. Even though he was surrounded by friends, loyal people who had his back no matter what, or in the case of Waylon, intended to do whatever was necessary to protect Christina, it wasn't something he wanted to advertise.

"As a matter of fact, yes, there's more to prove she was an asset," Jackson said. "Since I've been protecting Ortiz, keeping her safe, she has cooperated and shared more critical intel that the Montana DCI acted on earlier this morning. They raided three of the cartel's key depots. Large seizures were made. Thirty *thousand* pounds of pure cocaine and over a thousand pounds of fentanyl, estimated to be worth over half a billion dollars, plus thirty million in cash and weapons."

Resounding silence followed for several seconds.

"If that's true," Baccarin stammered, "then we'll—"

"It's true and it can be verified with the Montana DCI headquarters. I believe Director Isaacson is expecting a call from one of you." Winter and Declan's boss was thrilled with the results of the operation.

"Jackson, this is a major blow to the cartel," Quinones said, "to their financial operations and their efforts to distribute drugs throughout our country. A raid of this scope and magnitude is what's needed to stop these criminal enterprises in their tracks. That's impressive work."

"Yes," Garcia said. "Excellent work. I wish you would've looped us in on it. This seems like the perfect time to come in with Ortiz."

Jackson glanced at Christina and mouthed, *Do you recognize one of the voices?*

She shook her head, and the theory that Rio Estrada might be one of the agents on this phone call fizzled right in front of him.

"I'm afraid I can't do that just yet," Jackson said, responding to Garcia. "Ortiz's life is still in grave danger. There's a mole in our task force and a second traitor somewhere higher up inside one of the agencies. I believe this is why Kehoe was assassinated. He told this higher authority about Ortiz being an asset. She only survived as long as she did because she was off the books. Kehoe also requested access to Odin's Eye from that person, to run hundreds of hours of surveillance footage through it in the hopes of identifying and tracking Rio Estrada."

"Those are serious claims," Baccarin said.

"That program," Quinones said, "is highly classified. Any access to it is documented."

"Do you still have this surveillance footage?" Garcia asked.

Christina grabbed Jackson's arm and shook her head. Then she snatched paper and a pen and quickly scribbled something down.

Nodding, Jackson understood the message. "I haven't seen the footage, but Ortiz still has it. She has saved it somewhere safe. A cloud storage that no one knows about. But she's reluctant to share it until certain promises are made. Once she's been cleared of murder charges and there's documentation guaranteeing she'll be given a new identity in WITSEC, only then will I bring her in and she'll turn over the footage."

"Jackson," Baccarin said, "that's not acceptable. You're not calling the shots here."

"Sir, I'm afraid those are the conditions. I'll make contact again once she's been cleared of the charges." Jackson disconnected the call.

"That was an aggressive play," Autumn said. "It might

perpetuate the speculation that you and Christina are involved."

Jackson shrugged. "There's no way around it. I have to be assured that Christina will be protected."

Waylon grabbed another bagel. "Do you think they'll go for it?"

"I don't know. But that surveillance footage got Kehoe killed, which makes it valuable." Jackson turned to Christina. "Why did you want me to say that you were holding back the recordings?"

"The cartel will want to eliminate anyone who has access to it or has seen it," Christina said. "Better to let everyone think it's being contained."

"You didn't recognize Rio's voice," Takoda said. "I guess he's not our second mole."

"What now?" Bo asked. "How do we find Rio?"

"There's only one way," Christina said, full of conviction.

A shiver of trepidation raced down Jackson's spine. "No. Whatever you're thinking, there's some other way."

Tilting her head to the side, Christina stared at him. "I don't think there is."

"Please fill me in on what I'm missing," Waylon said around the food in his mouth.

"We have to flush him out." Christina straightened her shoulders. "Rio wants to see me, to speak to me in person."

"And then watch Aguilar kill you," Jackson added, which was an essential factor she seemed to be forgetting.

"We use me as bait." Christina tossed the words out so casually. "First, to hook Alvaro, and then Rio."

"No way." Jackson shook his head and waved his hands to emphasize his point. "That's not happening."

"I second that." Waylon took another bite of his bagel.

"I'm inclined to agree with them," Autumn said. "It's too dangerous. There has to be another way."

"Such as?" Takoda asked. "I'm not eager to use someone as bait either, but it sounds like it could work. It also might be the only way to find out who the higher-level mole is."

"Takoda is right," Christina said. "I could get Rio talking. His guard will be down, and he might give us everything we need if he thinks Aguilar is going to kill me anyway."

"It's too risky." Jackson stared at Christina, trying to make her see sense. "I can't take the chance of losing you." He just got her back. "Give us some time to come up with a better plan."

"I know you're worried about what *might* happen to me if I do this. But we all need to consider what *will* happen to everyone else if I don't." Christina got off the stool and went to him. "Aguilar saw their faces. Chance, Winter, Autumn, Declan, Bo, Eli. He's in the process of getting their names and addresses right now. By tonight, he'll know about this ranch. Is everyone supposed to go into hiding along with your parents, Logan and Summer?" She shook her head. "There is no time. We only have one solid option. We need to get to Rio before Aguilar gets to any of your friends. You can get them both. Rio and Aguilar. Kill two birds with one stone. But that means using me as bait."

Conflicting emotion welled inside Jackson, flooding him to the point he thought something inside him might burst. "I love you." The words just slipped from his lips, and she stared at him, wide-eyed. In all their time together, he'd never said it in front of others. When they were in public, he had worked hard to hide how he felt. To keep their relationship under his parents' radar. "I never stopped." He took her into his arms and lowered his face to hers. "I can't do this because I don't know how to keep you safe."

Could he protect her from Aguilar?

His doubt overwhelmed him.

How could she expect him to gamble with her safety? To allow her to be taken or harmed?

"You love all of them, too," Christina said, the gravity of her tone getting to him. "So we have to take the chance."

"Lockwood won't like it." Waylon folded his arms. "I don't like it."

"Then you two need to provide input to make it work," Christina said to the former cop. "I'm going to finish what I started, and I am going to do everything in my power to keep Alvaro away from you all."

"You're the one who told me that he's no regular hit man, no simple assassin for hire, and that underestimating him is the worst thing that we could do. I believe all that now." Jackson tightened his arms around her. "How do we beat him without losing you?"

He'd let her down twelve years ago. To do so again could cost her life.

"When Aguilar took me from the camp and talked to me at his house," Christina said, her voice low, "I realized something. I did what I didn't think was possible—I hurt him. My betrayal cut deep. Who would've guessed, but the monster has a heart." Christina slid her palms up his chest and pressed her forehead to his. "I'm his blind spot. His judgment is cloudy where I'm concerned. Somehow, we have to find a way to exploit that and use it against him. To beat him. To win."

Chapter Seventeen

Bitterroot Falls
Saturday, April 14, 6:10 p.m.

Glancing around behind her, making sure her face was visible to the security cameras, Christina finished her transaction at the self-service kiosk. She'd used cash to pay for her ticket on the eight o'clock Greyhound bus from Bitterroot Falls to Whitefish, which was only sixty miles from the Canada–USA border. Grabbing the ticket and putting it in the same jacket pocket as the gun, she spun around and headed for the door.

She tugged the hood of the insulated jacket down over her hair and lowered her head as she went two doors down to the café.

Inside, Waylon was seated at a table and Charlie Killian-Yazzie was at the counter. Killian-Yazzie wanted in on the action if it meant taking down the man who had injured her husband. Jackson trusted her with their rogue plan, and no one could deny that having a SOG member on the team was a good thing. Waylon and Killian-Yazzie were the only two Alvaro wouldn't recognize. They had ordered and were eating.

Christina slipped into a booth near the back, close to the

restrooms. She sat next to the window and scanned outside. Winter, Chance and Declan were still hung up at DCI. The rest of the team was divided between two vehicles. Jackson, Eli and Autumn in one. In the other were Bo and Takoda.

They had eyes on her, but she couldn't see any of them. Which was the point. Since they didn't want Aguilar to spot them, the team was vigilant, staying out of view of all cameras: traffic, CCTV, ATMs, and any store surveillance.

A waitress came over and set down a menu. "What can I get you?"

"Cheeseburger and fries," Christina said.

"Anything to drink or just water?"

The idea that this might be her last meal occurred to her. "Can I get a chocolate milkshake?"

"Sure thing." The waitress picked up the menu. "It'll be out in a few minutes."

Christina shoved her hood back. "No rush. I'm going to be here a while."

"Is someone joining you?"

That was the plan. "I'm waiting on the eight o'clock bus to Whitefish."

"Oh." The waitress nodded. "You're welcome to hang out here as long as you like. People do it all the time."

"Thanks," Christina said, and the woman went to put her order in.

Someone from the team had already called the special tip hotline set up for the manhunt and reported seeing her at the Greyhound bus station. Between that and the high likelihood Alvaro was using a facial recognition program to locate her and others from the team, she anticipated that he would reach her before any cops did. He had an uncanny way of tracking people down. No doubt he would have found her eventually, even if she hadn't been wearing the smart ring yesterday.

The waitress brought her milkshake and food.

Looking around the café every so often, she didn't let her gaze linger on either Killian-Yazzie or Waylon. The former was chatting up the waitress while picking at her food. The latter ordered a piece of pie and got a refill on his coffee.

Christina nibbled on her food, biding her time, but inhaled half her milkshake.

There were only a handful of other patrons. No one was in a hurry, and that made it easy to linger without standing out.

Her fries had grown cold, and the waitress had poured her a cup of coffee, removing the empty milkshake glass. She started to wonder if she'd have to actually get on the bus to Whitefish that would be leaving in an hour and wait to be intercepted on the route.

A strong hand curled on her shoulder. She turned to see Alvaro standing beside her booth, wearing a black cowboy hat and leather gloves. He must've sneaked in through a rear entrance and come up behind her.

"Get up and hug me," he said, and when that deep, coarse voice hit Christina, her body froze, her gaze glued to his. "Now."

She blinked up at him, shaking off the momentary paralysis. Slowly, she scooted out of the booth and stood on shaky legs. Wrapping her arms around him in an embrace, she faced the restaurant and could see the others. Killian-Yazzie glanced at her once, but Waylon pretended not to look in her direction at all.

The plan was for Jackson, Eli and Autumn to be in the first car to follow them.

Waylon, Takoda, Killian-Yazzie and Bo would be in a

second vehicle that would tag team with Jackson's, taking turns, so that one car wouldn't be spotted tailing her.

Alvaro's arms closed around Christina, but not in a hug. His hands slid over her body, checking her. He took the gun from her jacket pocket and shoved it into his.

The team had expected him to find the gun since the bulge was obvious. But she still had two more weapons on her. A knife and a Kubotan—a pointed, pocket-sized rod with spikes.

He fished out money and dropped cash on the table, more than enough to cover her bill plus a generous tip.

The waitress spotted them and came over. "Hey, are you leaving so soon? I thought you were waiting for the bus to Whitefish."

Smiling, Alvaro curled an arm around Christina's waist, bringing her close to him.

"Not anymore." She forced herself to grin. "I've got a ride."

"I couldn't let my girl take Greyhound," Alvaro said, letting that charismatic side shine through. "Besides, we have some unresolved things to sort out before I can say goodbye. Got to make sure I give you the send-off you deserve." He kissed her temple. "I did promise, and I am a man of my word. Right, darling?"

Christina swallowed around the cold lump in her throat. "You always keep your promises."

"Ah, isn't that sweet," the waitress said. "Getting a lift from your fella is better than taking the bus. You're lucky."

"Yep." Christina nodded. "Lucky me."

Keeping his arm around her, Alvaro led her to the door and shoved through it outside. He hauled her to the passenger's side of his SUV. "Take off the jacket."

"What? Why?"

"Take it off or I do it for you."

A sour taste filled her mouth. She shrugged out of the jacket like he told her to do.

He snatched it from her hand and threw it to the ground.

She stared at the jacket that had the Kubotan hidden inside the lining. Now she only had one weapon left.

Alvaro forced her into the passenger seat. Locked the door. Hurried around the front, his head on a swivel checking the area. Climbed in and cranked the engine.

Opening the center console, he took out a pair of handcuffs. He slapped one cuff on her left wrist and the other to his right, locking her to him. "Anywhere you go, I go," he growled. "These cuffs aren't coming off until you're dead. Got it?"

There would be no running from him. No chance for her to escape.

Taking a deep breath, she focused on the silver lining. Her right hand was free, the one she needed to reach her last weapon.

"You did a bad thing this morning." Alvaro zoomed out of the parking lot. "Do you have any idea how much trouble you've caused?"

"I have some idea."

"Really." He turned the steering wheel, making a hard right, and tugging on her arm that was shackled to his. "Well, take what you think you know and multiply it tenfold." A muscle ticked in his jaw. "Clever of you to have a backup to the backup of the surveillance footage."

The higher-level mole had told him about it. She restrained any reaction, didn't even glance at him.

"After I'm done with you, I'm going after your friends. I won't stop there either. I'm going to kill them and their families," he said, and she steeled herself against his scorched-earth tone. "If Rio hadn't already decided that you die today in Missoula, I'd save you for last. Make you watch what I'm going to do them and then deal with you. But I want you to know that I'm going to hurt your Boy Scout the worst. Do you understand?"

Alvaro was precariously close to the edge. So close to losing his temper completely, an event that rarely happened and always left bloody bodies in his wake.

"Answer me!" he snapped, his eyes gleaming with rage.

She took a deep breath as he got on US Highway 93, headed south to Missoula.

"I ran from them to keep them safe," she said, her voice almost a whisper. "I didn't show anyone the footage. There's no need—"

He banged his left fist on the steering wheel. "As if I can believe one word out of your lying mouth."

Christina closed her eyes and saw Jackson's face, recalled the scent of him, the warmth of his body pressed against her, the way it had felt to make love to him one last time.

Her one regret was not telling him she still loved him.

How do we beat him without losing you?

Resisting the concern in his eyes, she had told Jackson what he needed to hear, and the team had come up with a solid plan.

They couldn't take the chance of her having two-way comms but had inserted a tiny, wireless device that was a two-in-one GPS tracker and surveillance microphone—the size of a paper clip—inside the lining of her bra. It only had a battery life of sixteen hours, and she hoped it would be long enough.

Christina was terrified of this. Coming face-to-face with Alvaro once more. He was going to do everything in his power not to let her slip through his grasp again. But Jackson didn't need the weight of her issues and fears dumped on top of his own.

To be honest, she wasn't sure if what Jackson wanted was possible—to stop Alvaro *and* save her.

Maybe the only way to beat him was for her to sacrifice herself.

Outskirts of Missoula
Saturday, April 14, 9:15 p.m.

"OKAY, I'M PULLING BACK," Bo said over comms. He was several cars ahead with Waylon and Tak. "They're one mile from the Missoula exit."

"Roger," Jackson said, behind the wheel of a Suburban. They each drove a different make and model of vehicle, so as not to alert Aguilar that he was being tailed. Jackson pressed down on the accelerator. "Taking the lead."

Passing the Jeep Bo was driving, Jackson spotted the dark Tahoe that Christina was in. He hung back, not needing to get too close to follow them since Eli, sitting beside him in the passenger seat, was monitoring her GPS tracker on his laptop. Autumn was in the back seat. She had agreed to come along in a support role and would steer clear of any danger since they were all operating on little sleep and she had the least amount of tactical experience.

Aguilar took the exit for Missoula.

Staying several cars back, Jackson followed them through the city.

"It looks like they're heading toward a warehouse district not far from the river," Eli said. "Traffic is about to get sparse, and it'll be easier for Aguilar to spot us. We need to hang back. For now, stay on this road and I'll guide you from the GPS tracker."

Jackson nodded. "Okay."

"Can I ask you something?" Christina said, her voice transmitting from the microphone she wore through the laptop. "If this is the last conversation I'm ever going to have, there are some things I'd like to know."

"What?"

"Kehoe told me that you killed all the women you've dated," she said.

"Not all."

"I'm not talking about one-night stands. I mean women you saw regularly. Why?"

"Some got pushy or disrespectful." Alvaro's voice was hard and steely. "Others were too curious, sticking their nose where it didn't belong."

"I was curious," Christina said. "How did I last two years?"

Silence.

"Make a right at that traffic light." Eli pointed. "Then straight for a mile and another right."

"You...you pleased me," Alvaro said. "I didn't get tired of you. Somehow you kept me intrigued. On my toes. It was smart of you to become my lawyer, so that we had attorney-client privilege, making me feel like I could talk to you. Tell you things under the sanctity of that umbrella. I didn't even realize I was being played. Then you wanted to join the cartel, and I didn't have to hide anything anymore. I could let you see the real me."

Anxiety pulsed through Jackson. This tête-à-tête between Christina and Alvaro only made it worse. She was trapped in a vehicle with Aguilar. Handcuffed to that animal who had every intention of killing her.

"Did you know that Rio would make me choose, ask me to end things between us?"

"No," Alvaro said. "But I understood the reason. No alliances that could threaten *El Jefe*."

"Why did you continue to protect me from Hector and the other lieutenants?" she asked.

"You were still mine. My girl. My pick. The horse I was backing in this race."

"What race?"

"Eventually, *El Jefe* would have to name a successor. At least before today. I wanted to see how high you could climb with me at your side. I never knew what idea you would come up with, that was outside the box, like starting the charity, or what you'd do next. I just never thought it would be this. To betray me."

"Is Rio on the surveillance footage I have? Is that why it's so important?"

"Yes," Alvaro growled. "You have no idea what you've done. But Rio will explain it to you."

They drove for another five minutes.

"The topography changes up ahead," Eli said, "and is going to leave us exposed. If we don't want Aguilar to see us coming, we're going to have to kill the lights in a few minutes. In fact, it might be better for us to take one vehicle from here."

After relaying the slight change in plan to the others, Jackson pulled over. Once Bo caught up to them, the others packed into the Suburban.

A mile from the position where the GPS tracker stopped, Jackson switched off his lights and slowed down. They reached the top of a hill. Down below there was a dilapidated warehouse on the edge of the river. No traffic or any activity or other structures in the vicinity, like the warehouse hadn't been used in quite some time. The SUV Christina and Aguilar had driven in was parked near the warehouse. But a large bay door was open where trucks would've once driven in and out for loading and unloading.

Why didn't they park inside?

They couldn't take the road that led straight down to the warehouse. The open bay door offered Aguilar a clear line of sight to any approaching vehicles. That wasn't the only problem. Large windows lined the sides of the warehouse, and the land around it was flat with no trees. They wouldn't be able to get anywhere close to the structure by car.

Following the ridgeline, taking the long way around, Jackson had to drive off-road to make sure the team stayed out of sight. With no lampposts or headlights on, the moon covered in gray clouds, obscuring any light, he drove blind—the tires jarring over rocks and ruts.

The Suburban hit a muddy patch, slowing to a standstill as its tires spun uselessly. Tapping down on the accelerator in hopes momentum could get them out, the vehicle shuddered, going nowhere.

Jackson swore. "We're going to have to push and see if we can get it out of the mud."

While everyone hopped out and Autumn moved up front behind the wheel, Eli patched the feed from Christina's microphone into their earpieces, so that they could keep tabs on what was happening inside the warehouse.

Takoda checked the surrounding area with a dual-screen infrared binocular and night-vision device to make sure no hostiles were in sniper positions or posted as lookouts. "All clear."

They got on either side of the vehicle and pushed. Autumn gave it some gas. The wheels spun, spitting out mud but not carrying the SUV forward.

"We need traction," Jackson said, wishing they had a couple of sturdy planks of wood.

"What's inside the bag?" Christina said, her voice in Jackson's earpiece splitting his attention.

"You'll see," Alvaro said.

Seconds ticked by, bleeding into minutes as they gave it another go, trying to shove the Suburban loose from the mud. Fatigue magnified Jackson's frustration.

"We've got a flat over here," Killian-Yazzie called out.

Jackson growled and slammed a fist on the side of the vehicle. How long would it take to change the tire while the Suburban was stuck in an awkward angle and mired in muck? Five minutes? Ten?

Time they didn't have.

"Alvaro." Christina's voice broke. "Why are you planting explosives throughout the warehouse?"

"This is what it's come to," Alvaro said, "because of all the damage you've done."

Explosives.

Once again, Alvaro was several steps ahead of them. Jackson's chest tightened at the thought of Christina being inside the warehouse that was rigged to blow.

"A vehicle is headed down the road, toward the warehouse," Autumn said, redirecting the team's attention to the sedan closing in on Christina's location.

They needed to infiltrate the site on foot.

"Let's leave the Suburban," Jackson said. "We need to get down there." He looked at Autumn. "Monitor the laptop. If she leaves the warehouse or you see anything that we can't, give us a heads-up."

Autumn nodded. "Sure thing."

Once the team members secured their weapons and loaded up with extra ammunition, they moved out.

Their position on the ridgeline was too far from the warehouse for Jackson's liking. They had to trek over a mile across rough terrain. It would take them precious minutes to reach Christina. But they had no other choice.

"How long until Rio gets here?" Christina asked, her voice soft and shaky in Jackson's ear, making him quicken his pace.

"Not long now," Alvaro said. "*El Jefe* is inbound and will be here in a few minutes. Your time is almost up."

Jackson moved even faster. They were so close to reaching their goal, to get their hands on not only Aguilar, but also Rio Estrada, who had eluded his task force and every law enforcement agency for years.

Wearing gear, hauling weapons, and fatigue weighing them down, they stepped up their pace across the land. Christina was once again risking everything. Not only for the mission but to safeguard the entire IPS team and their family and friends.

The sedan drove inside the warehouse that seemed so far away.

Jackson controlled his breathing, though his heart raced. Going as fast as he could, he tore across the land, trying to get to Christina, feeling as though he was moving in slow motion.

Now that Aguilar and Rio were in that warehouse, where explosives were set, things could go sideways at any moment, and only one thing was certain.

Christina was in grave danger.

Chapter Eighteen

Missoula
Saturday, April 14, 9:35 p.m.

The sedan finally drove inside the open bay doors of the warehouse that hadn't been in use for years.

"Rio's here. Come on." Alvaro opened his door and got out of the vehicle, waiting for her to climb over the center console to his side.

Still handcuffed to him, Christina had no choice but to follow him.

They headed inside the warehouse to where the sedan had stopped. The trunk popped open. As they drew closer to the vehicle, she saw what was inside. A corpse in a black body bag.

Alvaro picked up the body, jerking her arm as though it were attached to a doll. Her hand inadvertently brushed the bag. It was cold. Alvaro set the body on the ground.

The driver's door opened. But the trunk blocked Christina from seeing who got out of the car. Footfalls drew closer as someone came around the vehicle.

Rio Estrada stepped into sight.

Confusion washed over Christina as familiar brown eyes locked with hers.

"Hello, Christina. While I wish I could say it's wonderful to see you again, the opposite is true."

The face and voice snapped together in her mind like an errant jigsaw puzzle. Rio Estrada was a woman—not a man. *El Jefe* was the same person Alvaro had introduced to Christina as his aunt.

But the voice she recognized as that of Dawn Quinones.

"I don't understand," Christina said. Nothing added up. Quinones over the phone didn't sound anything like Alvaro's aunt in person. But the woman standing in front of Christina now was the same one she'd had dinner with four years ago. The same wise, elegant lady who had embraced her, taught her how to make a traditional mole sauce and encouraged her ambition as an independent working woman.

"Is this better?" the woman asked, using a heavy Mexican accent with the timbre of her voice lowering a bit. "Sound more familiar?"

"Yes." A chill ran over Christina. "But the Rio Estrada I spoke with on the phone..."

"Simple enough to produce with a top-of-the-line AI voice generator. For the right price, instead of it sounding digitized or fake or somewhat off, it comes across as human. Natural. Doesn't it?"

"You had me fooled," Christina said.

"That was the point."

Now Christina understood why they needed to get the surveillance footage. She had been wearing a necklace with a camera the night she had dinner with Alvaro's aunt. Kirk hadn't been interested in watching the video of her learning how to make mole sauce with a sweet lady. The FBI agent had only been thrilled that she was making such headway with Alvaro.

"What should I call you?" Christina asked. "*Tia* Aguilar? Rio? Dawn?"

She shrugged. "Whatever you prefer, but *El Jefe* has a lovely ring to it. Doesn't it?"

"How long have you been living in the States?" Christina reined in her composure, needing to keep the conversation going until Jackson reached her.

"Since I was five. I took the place of an American child, who was close to my age when they died. Dawn Quinones. I assumed her identity."

Christina thought about the grieving family who had lost a child. "And they just went along with it?"

"Not at first. But once they realized who my father was, a powerful cartel boss who could have them killed with a snap of his fingers if they didn't cooperate, they agreed. I also think I filled a hole for them, gave them another child to love and care for, even though they were constantly reminded that I was an Estrada and would never truly be theirs. My father paid the Quinones family quite well for their silence. After he passed away, my older brother continued to fund my life here and ensured I had protection. Sent dear Alvaro, my cousin, not nephew, to be my right hand."

That's why all the lieutenants listened to and feared Alvaro, and the reason a hit man was able to wield so much power. He was the right hand of *El Jefe*.

"The other mole," Christina said, "who is it?"

"I have many. But the one on the task force?"

Christina nodded. "Vazquez? Mirabal?"

"Tillman."

"But he was shot in the chest twice." Christina had witnessed it.

Alvaro drew her gaze. "I shot Tillman twice in the armored vest. With regular bullets. Only every third round in the submachine gun was armor-piercing."

All that skill and precision and drive used for evil instead of good. Such a waste.

"Whose idea was it for you to infiltrate the federal government and become an insider for the cartel?" Christina asked. "Your father? Your brother, Dante?"

El Jefe laughed. "Of course not. Neither my father nor brother thought a woman could cut it in the cartel. I had to prove myself as I went up, along every rung of the ladder. It was my idea to infiltrate federal law enforcement and become the Estrada cartel's most powerful asset. I was a visionary, thinking outside the box. When Alvaro told me about you, I thought we might be kindred spirits. After I met you, I saw so much of myself in you. So much raw potential. My greatest prospect." Her smile faded, her expression turning downright sinister. "But you turned out to be Kirk Kehoe's asset, and my greatest disappointment."

Christina flicked a glance at the corpse on the ground.

Rio, Dawn, *El Jefe* sashayed over to the cadaver and unzipped the body bag. "I should've killed you and Kehoe sooner. Because of you and Jackson Powell, this is what I'm reduced to," she said, gesturing to the dead woman, who somewhat resembled her, and then Alvaro handed *El Jefe* the detonator. "With today's massive seizures of our product, cash and weapons, totaling close to half a billion dollars, and my identity soon to be exposed on your surveillance footage through Odin's Eye, I'll be recalled home. To Mexico. But I intend to stay here, controlling what I built, Team US. Running my network of traitors that I've created and cultivated. Tillman is only one of many. And the only way I can do that is if no one is looking for me. That's why I switched my dental records for hers. In the rubble of the explosion, they'll find two corpses. Mine." She eyed the dead body and then looked back up at Christina. "And yours."

Alvaro whirled on Christina and seized her throat with both his hands.

Instinctively, she clutched his wrists, trying to pry his grip loose. But it was no use. She fought for air as her windpipe was constricted.

Christina stomped on Alvaro's foot. Tried to kick his knee with her boot heel, a move that would bring the biggest assailant down, but he was too close for it to be effective. She threw a hard knee into his groin.

Growling in pain, he lifted her from the ground. Kicking, she clawed at his fingers, her feet dangling in the air. In a swift motion, Alvaro slammed her down onto the concrete floor.

Agonizing pain blasted through her skull. The sudden impact stunned her, and her hands slipped from his wrists.

Bearing down on her, Alvaro tightened his hands on her throat in a steel grip.

Her weapon. If she could reach it, she might have a chance. Christina bent her right leg, dragging her heel as close to her butt as she could. She jerked the cuff of her pants up to her shin, exposing the knife. Snatched it from the holster strapped to her calf. Jammed the blade low into Alvaro's back.

"No!" Rio screamed.

Pain registered across his face. His grip loosened on her neck. A hiss seeped from his lips.

Christina pulled the knife out and stabbed him again. This time straight into his side, aiming for his belly.

Clenching his jaw, Alvaro clutched her throat once more and squeezed harder. "We'll go together," he growled, blood coating his teeth.

"Alvaro!" Rio cried. "I need you!"

Christina fought with everything she had, but her strength was draining, diminished by her struggling lungs and still no match for his brute force. Gasping for air, she kicked. She clawed. She drove the blade into his flesh again. The backs of her eyes stung with unshed tears. Her lungs burned, starved for oxygen.

On her back, on the cold concrete floor, the fight seeping out of Christina, her world ending, she stared into Alvaro's face, cursing the injustice that he would be the last thing she would ever see.

Heavy footsteps pounded into the warehouse.

Two sound-suppressed shots whispered through the air. Alvaro froze. His eyes went blank as the intensity in him deflated and his grip on her throat slackened.

Jackson kicked Alvaro's body to the side before he collapsed on her.

Christina hauled in a huge, desperate breath. Coughing, she dropped the bloody knife and clutched her throat.

The rest of the team surrounded Rio Estrada, with their weapons pointed at her. They took turns screaming at her to stand down and drop the detonator.

Jackson unlocked the handcuff, releasing her from Alvaro.

She was free. From the cartel. From the Grim Reaper. *Finally free.*

Another shot was fired.

The detonator clattered to the floor, and Rio grabbed her wounded wrist. Then the team swept in closer to Rio, wresting her arms behind her back, driving her down to her knees and handcuffing her.

Kneeling beside Christina, Jackson gathered her into his arms. "Tell me you're okay." He pressed her head to his chest and stroked her hair. "My heart stopped when I saw him on you and something inside me shattered." He shifted her away to arm's length, his gaze raking over her. "Talk to me, Chrissy."

She clutched him, determined never to let him go. "Say that again," she rasped, her throat sore and achy.

"What? Talk to me?"

Shaking her head, she smiled and cried, tears rolling down her cheeks. "The other part."

"Chrissy," he said, and there was so much warmth and adoration in the way he called her name.

She nodded. "I love you, Jackson." A part of her had never stopped and would always love him.

He bracketed her face between his palms and stared into her eyes. "You mean the world to me. I don't know what I would've done if I lost you for a second time."

Christina was grateful he didn't have to find out. They were both alive and together.

Holding her, Jackson helped her up to her feet. Christina stared down at Alvaro.

The monster was dead. Her nightmare was over.

She pressed her palm to Jackson's cheek. "We did it. We beat them." Despite the odds. "We won."

Jackson lowered his mouth to hers and kissed her, softly, tenderly. "And now it's our time."

"For what?"

He caressed her face. "For us to have the chance we deserve."

Missoula
Sunday, April 15, 6:23 p.m.

"SON, I'M SO glad that everything got sorted out so quickly," Jackson's dad said over the phone.

The three-day ordeal didn't feel short to him or Christina.

But thanks to Autumn's quick thinking, things had been resolved smoothly. The former FBI profiler called SACs Baccarin and Garcia and patched them into the feed from Christina's microphone. They heard everything Dawn Quinones, aka Rio Estrada, had to say firsthand.

The elusive Rio was now behind bars, cutting a deal for a reduced sentence in exchange for disclosing the names of every mole she recruited in one of the federal agencies. Valuable information that was powerful leverage. Rio might not serve a life sentence, but with a long list of charges, including espionage, obstruction of justice, and drug trafficking, she would stay locked up for a long time. Right along with every traitor who agreed to work for her, starting with Tillman.

"My main concern was getting to the bottom of everything," Jackson said, "and clearing Christina's name."

"She's a hero for what she did. All those lives saved by that huge drug seizure. I can't imagine what it must've taken to be undercover for so long."

His father would never truly know. Most of what he referred to was from what he'd seen on the news. "A lot of sacrifices and compromises on her part. She's lost years that she can't ever get back as well as loved ones. But it would be nice, and go a long way with me, if you could say all those things to her when we come back to Laramie for the funerals of the Iron Warriors."

"I will. Both your mother and I will make things right." His father sighed. "We've made a lot of mistakes with you boys. Meddling in your love lives. Trying to maneuver you all like pawns on a chessboard. We meant well. Truly. But we realize that we should've done things differently and taken a more hands-off approach. I'm sorry that my words and actions drove you away from us for so long."

As the youngest, Jackson should've been better prepared for his parents after watching the disasters they'd caused for his brothers. "I appreciate it, Dad. But I'm not the one who needs to hear it."

"Christina will hear that and more from us. You've got my word. And we'll be at the funerals, paying our respects. Every Powell in town. Your brothers and their wives want to make sure Christina feels like family."

That was the most Jackson could ask for, and he was certain Chrissy would be touched by it. Not only would every Powell in Laramie be at the funeral, but his brother, Logan, and his fiancée Summer, along with the rest of the team, were all going to attend. Jackson appreciated this chosen family, who had his and Chrissy's backs no matter what, more than he could ever express in words.

Christina crossed the threshold of his bedroom and leaned against the door jamb. Wearing a cashmere turtleneck dress that covered her bruised throat and sexy boots, she batted her lashes and rubbed her tummy, letting him know in no uncertain terms that she was starving.

But she looked good enough to eat.

"Hey, Dad, I've got to go. Chrissy and I are heading out to dinner."

"Put her on the phone for a quick minute. I want to say hi."

His father's quick minute would turn into twenty. "We have a reservation, and I don't want to be late."

"All right," his dad said, sounding genuinely disappointed.

"We'll see you on Wednesday. Give Mom my love. 'Bye." Jackson disconnected the call, grabbed his black Skyline Stetson from the dresser and put it on. He strode over to

Chrissy and pulled her into his arms. "You ready for our first date?"

Putting her finger to her chin, she twitched her lips like she was thinking about it. "I guess technically this is our first real date."

He'd taken her to do plenty of things when they were younger. To the movies. Out for picnics. Horseback riding. Swimming in the lake. But this was different. Somehow this meant more. Sort of like telling her that he loved her in front of the whole team. Years ago, he'd said it often, but only in private, making her feel like their relationship was a dirty secret. Now, he wanted to shout about his feelings for her from a mountaintop to the entire world. And one day, when he asked her to marry him, he would do it in front of his family and the Iron Warriors. How he'd pull that off, he wasn't so sure, yet, but he'd figure it out. She deserved nothing less.

"I can't wait to have plenty more firsts with you," he said.

Curling her arms around his neck, she grinned. "Such as?"

"First bubble bath together. Vacation. Somewhere warm so you can wear a bikini. Massage. I'll do the rubbing while you do the enjoying." He winked at her.

Her grin spread into a smile that warmed him down to his soul. "I like the sound of those firsts." She gave him a quick kiss, and he loved the way she tasted. "You know, there might be some rocky ones along the way."

"I want them all. The good. The bad. The rocky. Because that's real. Together, we can survive anything, and I'll never be fool enough to let you go again."

"Anything," she agreed. "And you better not be."

With this incredible woman he loved at his side, as his

partner, he could *do* anything. Overcome anything. Even anger, guilt and shame.

Their life together was just beginning, and he couldn't wait to share everything with her.

* * * * *

*Look for the next thrilling installment
in the new miniseries
Ironside Protection Services
by Juno Rushdan
Coming soon to Mills & Boon Heroes
Wherever Harlequin books and ebooks are sold.*

COMING SOON!

We really hope you enjoyed reading this book. If you're looking for more romance be sure to head to the shops when new books are available on

Thursday 21st May

To see which titles are coming soon, please visit
millsandboon.co.uk/nextmonth

MILLS & BOON

FOUR BRAND NEW BOOKS FROM
MILLS & BOON MODERN

Indulge in desire, drama, and breathtaking romance – where passion knows no bounds!

OUT NOW

Eight Modern stories published every month, find them all at:

millsandboon.co.uk

LET'S TALK
Romance

For exclusive extracts, competitions and special offers, find us online:

- **f** MillsandBoon
- **X** @MillsandBoon
- **◉** @MillsandBoonUK
- **♪** @MillsandBoonUK

Get in touch on 01413 063 232

For all the latest titles coming soon, visit
millsandboon.co.uk/nextmonth